DRIVING THE TIDE

LEE JACKSON

SEVERN RIVER
PUBLISHING

Severn River Publishing
www.SevernRiverPublishing.com

This is a work of fiction based on actual events. Names, characters, places, historical events, and incidents are the product of the author's imagination or have been used fictitiously. Although many locations such as cities, towns, villages, airports, restaurants, roads, islands, etc. used in this work actually exist, they are used fictitiously and might have been relocated, exaggerated, or otherwise modified by creative license for the purpose of this work. Although many characters are based on personalities, physical attributes, skills, or intellect of actual individuals, all of the characters in this work are products of the author's imagination.

ISBN: 978-1-64875-482-1 (Paperback)

ALSO BY LEE JACKSON

The After Dunkirk Series

After Dunkirk

Eagles Over Britain

Turning the Storm

The Giant Awakens

Riding the Tempest

Driving the Tide

Into the Cauldron

The Reluctant Assassin Series

The Reluctant Assassin

Rasputin's Legacy

Vortex: Berlin

Fahrenheit Kuwait

Target: New York

Never miss a new release! Sign up to receive exclusive updates from author Lee Jackson.

severnriverbooks.com

To the Medics and Flight Nurses,
Unsung Heroes and Heroines of WWII.
Because of them,
Many lives of our war fighters were spared,
And many more came home to lead normal lives.
They must always be remembered.

PROLOGUE

January 9, 1944
Isle of Sark, Guernsey Bailiwick, Channel Islands

The Dame of Sark, Marian Littlefield, met the ferry from Guernsey at the dock at Creux Harbor. As passengers disembarked, German guards checked identification papers and certificates granting permission to travel. Having satisfied the hated bureaucratic requirement, the people proceeded on foot through the rock tunnel and up the long Harbor Hill road leading to the plateau eighty feet above sea level. The guards then applied equal diligence as passengers taking the return trip to Guernsey also presented their travel documents.

The pattern was well set in this, the fourth year of Nazi occupation. Sark's residents had become accustomed to the annoyance, along with all the other Nazi-imposed irritants that had made life barely tolerable on their island, which, before the Germans had arrived, they had described as "a little piece of paradise."

Marian searched the crowd for a particular man, but she could not do so overtly or she would certainly draw unwanted attention. For the man, such attention could prove fatal.

His name was Joseph Wakley, and he carried three pieces of paper folded tightly together and concealed in the heel of his shoe. Under normal times, the papers would be considered innocuous, not anything that would bring officialdom to exact the death of the messenger. However, these were not normal times, and Wakley's three sheets of fine paper comprised the latest edition of the *Guernsey Underground News Service*, better known as GUNS among its readers.

The newsletter, for it could hardly be termed a newspaper, was published by Charles Machon on Guernsey. He was a linotype operator of the *Guernsey Star*, and his papers were surreptitiously distributed across Guernsey to select subscribers. They were then carried by secret courier to Sark and Jersey, where they were further dispersed. In the case of Sark, the distributor was Hubert Lanyon, who ran the local bakery and general merchandise shop.

Normally, Lanyon would have gone to the wharf himself to retrieve the courier and the three sheets of compromising paper, but this morning, he had sent his son to ask Marian if she would do the honors. He had taken ill, and did not entrust to just anyone the safe transfer of the newsletter from the courier to his shop. His son, a young boy, had knocked on Marian's door and said, "My father asked if you could do his normal weekly chore."

Marian had immediately sent the lad back with a message that she would be happy to oblige, and thus she now searched the crowd unobtrusively for Wakley. In her mid-fifties, she was the recognized ruler of Sark under the only remaining feudal system in the western world, and she was very thin due to the depravations of German occupation. Her husband, Stephen, was an American by birth and a naturalized British citizen. If he were present, he would be senior co-ruler under the medieval precept of right-of-wife. Instead, he was interned in Ilag VII at Tittmoning Castle, Laufen, Bavaria for having been a commissioned officer in the Royal Air Force during World War I.

Despite her position, Marian had endeared herself to her fellow citizens, and they had, to a person, stayed on the island because she had asked them to do so in the interest of saving their culture when the German blight finally ended. She had not foreseen how bad things would become: insufficient food, children without milk, scarce medical care, teeth falling out of people's mouths for lack of proper vitamins...

A German mandate required all residents to surrender their radios under penalty of death. A few, including Marian herself, still had some hidden away, but electricity had become sporadic, and the possibility loomed that they would have neither lights nor the ability to hear news from the outside world. Hence, the *Guernsey Underground News Service*, the largest and most widely distributed of several such illicit newsletters, had become sought after, hungered for, and the recipients were always mindful of the penalty for being found with a copy.

Having spotted Wakley, Marian approached him indirectly, first making quick eye contact, then moving closer and pretending to be surprised to see him. The guards, knowing her by sight due to her stature on the island and the respect she had demanded and received from their superiors over the long occupation, were careful not to interfere in her conversations. She, however, took every precaution.

"Ah, Mr. Wakley, how nice to see you. What a surprise. Are you here for the day, or will you be staying longer?"

"Just enough time to pop in at Hubert Lanyon's shop to pick up an order."

"Oh, dear. I'm afraid he's taken ill and might not be there. I'm going that way. I came down to see some friends off, and then I'll be happy to walk with you to his shop. We can catch up on things."

Wakley accepted the invitation affably, waited patiently with Marian as she bid farewell to departing passengers, and then walked with her out of the harbor. "I don't understand why Hubert sent you all the way to the wharf," he said when they were well into the shadow of the tunnel.

"Just an overabundance of caution. I didn't mind. I needed the fresh air and the exercise. Where do you carry GUNS?"

"In the heel of my left shoe."

Marian laughed. "Then I suppose we should wait until we're inside Lanyon's bakery. Getting it from you here might raise questions."

Once inside the shop, Wakley removed his shoe, pried off the heel, extracted the three sheets of paper, and handed them to Marian. She scanned them, then remarked with a touch of sarcasm, "And for this, our lives could be forfeit."

1

January 17, 1944
Southwest of Monte Cassino, Italy

Lieutenant Colonel Paul Littlefield plugged his ears with two fingers as a BL 5.5 in. field artillery gun a few yards away launched an ear-splitting projectile over a long, wide field and across the Rapido River. It targeted a German troop position in Castelforte, a village spilling from the foothills of a mountain in the Apennine range onto flatter ground stretching a thousand yards to the river's north bank.

The gun's piercing concussion shook the ground as its barrel spewed fire and lurched upward before it settled in a cloud of dust on its large rubber tires. Paul watched the crew as a soldier yanked open the breech and let the brass casing fall out. Two more men, sweating under the heavy load of the next projectile on a canvas cradle between them, manhandled the round into the tube, while a third man shoved it into the chamber with a long rammer. Yet another tossed in several small packets of propellant, while a fifth set the charge. The first man slammed the breech shut, grabbed the lanyard, and glanced at the battery commander standing a few feet away.

The officer dropped his hand and yelled, "Fire!"

With only seconds having passed since the previous salvo, the gunner pulled the lanyard. Flame belched in concert with a line of identical artillery guns, all aimed toward the tiny village three miles away. The ground trembled, and the air exploded with terrible thunder. The heavy guns bounced into the air from the force of their launches and then settled down amid acrid swirls of gun smoke and dust.

The crews hurried through their actions for the next barrage.

Paul shifted his attention to watch the inevitable eruptions of dirt and debris that would arise from Castelforte. As his eyes swept past the gun, two clucking chickens with wings flapping scurried between him and the gun crews. Then, on a road just feet in front of the upward-slanting barrel of the artillery piece, Paul caught sight of a bent, swarthy man in wrinkled clothing and a worn-out fedora leading a firewood-laden donkey. The two paused momentarily; the man stared vacantly at the gun and crew and then proceeded past them.

Paul shook his head at the incongruity of the scene. The sound of dull thuds followed by the blast of bursting shells reverted his attention to Castelforte. Smoke blanketed the town against the backdrop of the mountains.

A wave of revulsion overtook him as images flashed through his mind of many such villages the Allied armies had entered and left in desolation as they pursued the *Wehrmacht* north. He had tried to imagine how the hamlets had appeared before the Germans and the Allies had clashed on their way through them. Even under winter's gray skies, the beauty of the landscape along the route to the Gustav Line could not be hidden, but it was stained by ruin. Such would also be the lot of Castelforte.

The *Wehrmacht's* high command had obviously mandated a scorched-earth policy as it orchestrated an orderly withdrawal up the Italian boot, destroying anything that could be useful to the pursuing Allied army, which was being aided by an active popular resistance. The slow-moving battle meant the destruction of roads, bridges, railroad tracks, factories, power plants, and even dwellings and shops. Much of what remained was destroyed by the Allied armies fighting their way north to Rome.

A recurring image flashed across Paul's mind, one he struggled to blot out, of entering a blighted, unknown village and finding the shrapnel-pierced body of a little girl. She was alone, her lifeless hands clutching a ragdoll as her home smoldered beneath her. She had lain so still, her face frozen in fear, eyes staring, her cheeks stained from tears crusted by fine dust—the residue of falling bombs. He had picked her up tenderly and carried her to the edge of the village where partisans gathered their dead for burial, and he had stayed with her until her tiny body had been interred. Then he had knelt over her grave, his throat constricted as tears forced their way from his eyes.

Since the amphibious landing at Salerno nearly five months earlier, the infantry battalion he commanded as part of the British 10th Corps attached to US General Clark's Fifth Army had battled its way fifty miles northwest over freezing peaks and valleys burned into wastelands. Trees lining the roads were bereft of leaves and blackened by fire. Crop fields lay desolate. Foot soldiers plodded through thick muck or pushed jeeps along roads that had been churned into knee-deep mud by heavy war machines under constant rain. During rest breaks, the men huddled in the drizzle beneath their helmets and ponchos to enjoy a cigarette, read a letter from home, or try to boil water for tea in their tin canteen cups over tiny fires.

Combat in the mountains had been the worst. To reach the summits, soldiers trudged in a line a third of the way up the rugged slopes alongside long lines of supplies-laden mules. From that point, the terrain was too uneven and jagged for the animals' hooves, so the soldiers lugged the provisions on their backs up the remaining distance to the craggy cliffs, often returning multiple times for more loads.

Paul recalled the first time he had made such a trip. He had trekked up Monte Sammucro with the battalion he commanded, the first of the Queen's Brigade, after the Germans had been dislodged from their positions overlooking the town of San Pietro. He had been exhausted on reaching the summit in the middle of the night, his lungs heaving for more oxygen. Then, as dawn spread across the misty crest, he had been aghast at the sight of wan soldiers hunched into the crevices along the summit. Visibly worn down by freezing temperatures, inadequately protected by their uniforms, shocked by frequent German artillery shelling and raids, underfed and gripping their tin canteen cups for the warmth of tea at every opportunity, they maintained remarkable spirits. They rose to attack when ordered or to defend when the enemy assaulted, and they took turns trudging down the rugged mountainside to meet the mule lines and lug supplies back up to the crest.

The pattern had been set. The Germans initially occupied key high ground and villages. The Allied forces bombed, strafed, shelled, and frontally attacked with infantry and tanks until the enemy retreated to the next village or mountaintop northward on the Italian peninsula toward Rome, leaving desolation in their wake. Such had been the case with the village where Paul had buried the little girl, and such was now unfolding in Castelforte.

The campaign to take Monte Cassino had started six days ago when, before dawn, the French Expeditionary Corp consisting of the 3rd Algerian and 2nd Moroccan Divisions assaulted the *Wehrmacht* 5th Mountain Division on the Allied right flank in a fierce battle to the northeast of the Benedictine monastery on the crest of Monte Cassino. The German positions were annihilated by the Arabs who used great stealth to approach their targets and attacked with knives and swords. However, as the battle developed, the German division was replaced with the 3rd *Panzergrenadiers*, a mechanized enemy unit. It held off the expeditionary force from its major objective at Atina, and then re-concentrated its field artillery on the center of the battlefield.

Paul knew those guns were now aimed toward a bend in the Garigliano River in front of strong German defenses where the US 36th Infantry Division would launch a river crossing simultaneous with his own attack across the Rapido. His face set hard with the knowledge of what was to come in his sector on the Allied left flank to the southwest of Monte Cassino. He turned and strode to the farmhouse twenty-five yards behind the guns that served as the battery's observation post. Ducking his head through the door, he called to an officer in front of a large field map peering out a window through binoculars toward Castelforte.

"I'll be rejoining my battalion now," he said.

The officer lowered the binoculars and nodded at Paul. "Good luck. I'll see you on the other side of the river."

Paul glanced at his watch in the dark. The smaller of the two luminescent hands pointed to nine, the larger to twelve. At that moment, he heard a solitary muffled "poof," a break in the air, barely audible. A small red orb arced across the star-strewn sky. It floated past his position, over the river, and landed in enemy territory, signaling the start of the Allied assault.

The guns by the farmhouse, now far to his rear, thundered. They were joined by five hundred others of many calibers in a line extending east and west. Their projectiles hissed as they flew far above Paul's head and detonated across the river with dull thuds, creating a thick smokescreen. Their fire lit up the southeastern sky.

Paul turned to his signaler and uttered a single word into his radio mic: "Move." Unseen to his left and right, soldiers of three infantry companies, nearly three hundred men, crept through the wet grass and mud toward the Garigliano River. Beyond them to his right, an adjacent battalion of the Queen's Brigade maneuvered toward the river. Behind him, a battalion remained in reserve. Far off to Paul's left, the foot soldiers of the 167 Brigade moved forward on line.

The mass of units swept across the fields to the Garigliano's near bank and entered the frigid, fast-flowing waters while German 88 mm guns rained down heavy fire. On the south bank, a British mortar platoon returned salvo after salvo.

The staccato of machine guns and the crackling of rifles resounded, their bullets kicking up small fountains in the river. Flares cast a ghostly light, revealing horrifying details of soldiers wading into the fast-moving stream in the face of merciless fusillades.

Paul reached the south bank and peered through the orange half-light. Large groups of men had waded partway across the open expanse of water from fifty to a hundred yards wide. Other soldiers launched small rubber boats laden with more soldiers and ammunition, and engineer teams had begun constructing Bailey pontoon bridges for the tanks that would follow.

The unrelenting deluge of lethal fire continued, with thousands of artillery rounds finding their marks. They left large pits in the ground that soldiers clambered through, burdened by their heavy equipment after navigating the river and climbing up its bank. Already, bodies floated in the fast-flowing water amid dark swirls of blood. Desperate cries of the wounded punctuated intermittent interruptions of gunfire.

Fortunately, the climb out of the river had not been difficult in Paul's sector, but his battalion was slowed by gunfire. He anticipated that the enemy would seek only to delay the British advance there, and that his troops would thus meet comparatively light resistance on the expanse of flat ground above Garigliano's north bank. Nevertheless, between the relentless fire of artillery, machine guns, and rifles as the battalion advanced through the muddy terrain and barbed-wire obstacles, the unit took steady casualties. Paul grimaced as he contemplated that his soldiers would encounter even more punishment when they reached the base of the foothills. Then the Germans would open a blistering defense intended to mow down the infantry.

The troops pressed on, and before morning's first light, they had secured San Lorenzo, which lay across the road to Castelforte. Paul established his headquarters on the upstairs floor of a farmhouse midway across the open fields.

The way east out of San Lorenzo skirted the foothills and intersected two parallel roads leading up into Castelforte. Overlooking both villages, Monte Damiano rose into the heavens, providing its German occupiers clear views of the lower approaches and deadly fields of fire against the British attack. German artillery rounds ranged in front of and behind the rambling, two-story farmhouse and then zeroed in on it.

A dispatch rider approached Paul. "I have a message from brigade," he said.

Just then, a loud shriek split the air and deafening explosions shook the house. Dust and smoke swirled, plaster fell from the walls, bits of cement flew through the air, but the sturdy stone walls withstood a direct artillery hit and then another.

"I have orders," the rider gasped amid the clearing dust when the shelling abated. He produced a small map of the area. "Your radio traffic to headquarters is coming in garbled. You're to reposition your units farther northeast along this line." He indicated the position to Paul.

Paul stared, aghast. "That makes no sense. My companies will execute the main attack into Castelforte. To get to that position, we'll have to cross in front of friendly units, expose our left flank, and attack from the worst position."

"Sorry, sir. These are your orders."

Paul set his jaw. "We'll have to confirm."

Just then, another officer coughed his way through the dust. "I say, I'm looking for a runner from division headquarters." Reading Paul's skeptical look, he said, "I'm Lieutenant colonel Greene." He extended his hand to Paul. "I've just taken over command of 167 Brigade. I'm afraid my boss caught a fatal round to the temple on the way in. We're setting up headquarters just downstairs."

Paul whirled on the courier. "Which unit are you carrying orders for?"

Looking chagrinned, the soldier replied, "The 167, sir."

"Wrong unit," Paul growled testily.

Sensing the tension, Greene cut in. "Not his fault," he told Paul. "I had sent a runner to inform division that I would come here to set up my headquarters pending the next advance. That message was for me."

Paul chuckled wryly and rubbed his face wearily. "I did the same thing. My runner should be arriving at my brigade HQ about now."

"We'll have to operate carefully," Greene said with a tinge of frustration. "On the way up here, I passed through another battalion headquarters setting up downstairs."

"The fog of war," Paul muttered. "This misdirected message almost created a major calamity. The silver lining is that you and I can coordinate directly. My battalion will spearhead the attack into Castelforte."

"We'll protect your left flank and move in behind you when you've secured the village." Greene paused and surveyed the ground to the north through a window, and then continued with a note of sarcasm. "Higher headquarters thinks this village is a minor aim. The major objective is the high ground around St. Benedict monastery on top of Monte Cassino. But we cannot bomb or otherwise damage the abbey."

Paul nodded with a sigh. "It's fourteen centuries old. Even the jerries respect its historic value." He glanced out the window. "But they must be using the ground around it for observation, and they're well dug in down here. Tanks, tank destroyers, and masses of infantry are hunkered down nearby, and their artillery is relentless. Minor or not, seizing Castelforte will be a hellacious fight."

2

Claire Littlefield stood in front of her accustomed seat before the desk of Commander Edward Travis in his office at the British intelligence center housed in the sprawling Bletchley Park estate. The main task there was decoding and analyzing enemy wireless messages.

Travis motioned for Claire to sit down while he finished a call. Then he hung up the phone and turned to her. "We didn't get to Rome by Christmas last year as hoped," he said, "but at least the Italians are our 'co-belligerents' now. Not quite the same status as allies, but it'll have to do. At least they're not fighting against us. What are you hearing about them out of Berlin?"

"Italy is a hellish front, as you know, sir. The weather bogged our troops in mud, so we didn't make nearly the progress we had planned for. The Germans won't concede that front easily, as indicated by orders going out from their high command to the field. Recall that Erwin Rommel, among others, urged Hitler to abandon southern Italy and mass troops in the Po Valley in northern Italy in preparation for an all-out defense of Germany against an Allied invasion. But Field Marshal Kesselring advised Hitler to stay and wear down the Allies fighting up Italy's boot. The *führer* took the latter advice."

Claire's once ready smile still flashed frequently, but her countenance was guarded, her brown eyes possessing a practiced, neutral expression. Bletchley Park was among Britain's most secret intelligence assets, a facility able to intercept and decode Germany's highest-classified transmissions almost as fast as they were sent. Claire led one of the decoding and analysis teams whose specific task was to monitor wireless traffic coming out of the German High Command in Berlin.

The oath of secrecy that Claire and everyone working at Bletchley had sworn was onerous, requiring under penalty of death that not even families or close friends could know the work being done there. Claire and her associates accepted the prohibition and abided by it without protest, knowing the potential consequence of the enemy learning of its existence and capabilities.

Among Bletchley's contributions was supplying intelligence that led to locating and sinking the battleship *Bismarck*, which had threatened the British fleet in the Atlantic; and providing communiques between the German High Command and Field Marshal Rommel in North Africa such that British ground commanders knew Rommel's orders almost as soon as he did.

Claire's fluency with the German language and her analytical prowess had brought her abilities to the attention of her superiors. She had distinguished herself in several intelligence coups, including taking the lead in locating the *Bismarck*, and she had thus been promoted to head a team of decoders and analysts.

Travis leaned forward, his eyes narrowing into a studious expression behind large spectacles. "I questioned the wisdom of going into Italy. It's built for defense." He shook his head in serious incredulity. "With the Apennine Mountains forming its spine and all the subsidiary ranges running from them to both sides of the peninsula, it's a veritable fortress. Throw in the rivers and streams that flow from the mountain heights to either the Tyrrhenian or Adriatic seas, and it becomes all but impenetrable." Raising his eyebrows in a jocular fashion, he added, "Perhaps that's why God put the Vatican there."

Claire nodded. "The terrain in the Po is flat. It allows flexibility to move troops quickly eastward toward Venice to defend incursions coming out of the Balkans into southern Austria, or to go west toward Milan and meet an invasion of southern France. The Alps in the north prevent a direct Allied frontal assault through Switzerland. So, if we gained the Po Valley, we would be in position to bomb Austria and southern Germany. But to get to it, we have to go through all those natural barriers you mentioned. Our troops were never equipped for that—nor were the Americans. The saving grace is that neither were the Germans. The fact is that we have two opposing armies fighting in the mountains and valleys of an Italian winter with no cold weather equipment—in some cases, not even gloves."

Travis grunted while he contemplated. "Refresh my memory," he broke in after a moment. "Why didn't the Germans follow Rommel's advice? It would have saved them and us a bloodbath coming up Italy's boot."

Claire took a moment to gather her thoughts. "Kesselring advised that the *Wehrmacht* should defend fiercely at various lines farther south in Italy; engage in attrition there. He convinced Hitler to use the mountains as natural barriers and firing points and to reinforce heavily where needed. He argued that doing so would exhaust Allied soldiers and their morale, kill thousands of them, use up our supplies, wear out our equipment, and buy time to harden their homeland defenses. He also wanted time to complete development of some of their experimental weapons."

"Like the atomic bomb," Travis said gravely.

"Yes, sir, and their rockets and pilotless bombs."

Travis nodded. "The V-1s and V-2s." He sighed. "Our bombing raid over Peenemünde bought us time to deal with those, but not nearly enough. We knocked out production facilities and some of the scientific community that was developing them, but we didn't deliver a death blow. When those weapons are fully developed and in production, our people will suffer more terror from the skies."

Remembering the carnage in London and other British cities during the Battle of Britain and the *blitz*, the two contemplated the horrific thought in silence. Then Travis cleared his throat. "Is your brother Paul still in Italy?"

Claire nodded stoically, managing to stem the emotion that so often rose unbidden for the loss of loved ones and the rubble of homes across the UK caused by countless *Luftwaffe* bombing sweeps. "Yes, sir," she sniffed. "The last I heard, he was as safe as is possible while fighting at the front."

"Is he still commanding an infantry battalion?"

"That's my latest information."

"How are your other brothers, Lance and Jeremy? Do you hear from them?"

Claire nodded. "I'm afraid Lance is stuck in a German POW camp for the duration. Allied orders are going out to our captured men to terminate escape plans."

"I'd heard that. Escaping POWs could interfere with Resistance efforts needed to support invasion operations."

Claire chuckled ruefully. "That'll rankle Lance to no end. He's not one to sit still and wait out anything."

Travis laughed gently with her. "And Jeremy?"

Claire sighed. "Fortunately, he's home at the moment, but he'll be going back to work with the Resistance in France very soon. I don't know when."

"And what about your parents? I trust they're hanging in there?" An embarrassed look crossed Travis' face. "I don't mean to pry. I'm just interested and concerned."

Claire brushed aside his comment. "Thank you for asking," she said numbly. "Ironically, I get more news from my father in the prison camp in Germany than I do from my mother on Sark. They are able to pass information between them. I don't quite understand why that is the case, but mail coming from the camps is less censored than the Red Cross messages that go directly between here and the Channel Islands."

Travis sighed. "One of the vagaries of war. Well, I wish your family all the best." He shifted in his chair. "Tell me about the Gustav Line. What has the German High Command ordered in that regard?"

Claire shook her head and blew out a breath. "I pity our soldiers there now. It's freezing, the mountains are steep, and for the most part, the Germans have the high ground. Both armies are stalled for offensive operations by winter weather, but Kesselring ordered those defensive lines established south of the Gustav, and Hitler ordered that they be defended vigorously. Kesselring's intent is to bleed us there, defend aggressively, and destroy anything useful as he pulls back.

"The line is at the narrowest part of the Italian peninsula, extending from Minturno on the west coast at the Tyrrhenian Sea, across the Apennine Mountains, to Ortona on the Adriatic Sea in the east. The only avenues of attack are along Italy's coasts.

"Two lesser defensive lines, the Barbara and the Termoli, straddle the mountains parallel to and farther southeast of the Gustav. Just southwest of Gustav on the southern end is the Winter Line. It extends to the Rapido River, and of course there is the Hitler Line to the north of Gustav, also in its western sector. It's the last line of defense on the way to Rome.

"All of these defensive positions are hardened with concrete and structural steel, each one formidable in its own right. Taken together, they're almost impenetrable and effectively stall our main thrust in Italy toward the capture of Rome."

"Hmm, yes," Travis responded pensively. "And Highway 6 along the west side of Italy leads through the worst parts of those mountains into the Liri Valley. It skirts below Monte Cassino, just south of the Gustav. A Benedictine monastery sits on the crest of that mountain. And to continue north, our armies will have to cross two fast-flowing rivers, the Garigliano and the Rapido. A hellacious battle is shaping up there now.

"We went in at Salerno because that was the limit of air support based in Sicily. But now, with captured airbases farther north in southern Italy, we're assaulting at Monte Cassino, and we'll soon land an amphibious force up the coast at a village called Anzio. I suppose we're doing that either to catch Kesselring's army in a pincer or for the two elements of the Fifth Army, at Cassino and Anzio, to link up and push into Rome."

"Is there anything in particular I should be listening for, sir?"

Travis frowned. "That monastery above Cassino is a hundred miles south of Rome. There's a position a short way down the slope to the west on another promontory—they call it Hangman's Hill—and there's a castle farther east about three-quarters of the way down that's also an imposing firing position. And behind Monte Cassino, Monte Castellone towers above the monastery.

"The interlocking positions give commanding fields of fire on anyone using the road to get into the Liri Valley and approach Rome from the south." Travis sighed in resignation. "And of course General Clark's Fifth must do just that. Or at least, that's the plan. He'll have to achieve a breakthrough into the Liri because it's the only area where he can deploy enough tanks to support the infantry without sinking in alluvial soil. Then, he'll continue his drive to Rome via Hwy. 6."

Travis took to his feet and examined a map of Italy on the wall behind him. "The monastery itself is fourteen hundred years old, and I'm told it's magnificent," he continued. "The Germans stated publicly that because of its historical value, they will cause no harm to it, but we suspect their soldiers already occupy it for an observation post. We'd like to know for sure, one way or the other.

"From there, they can observe all our movements and call in fire at will. The last thing we want to do is alienate the locals and the wider Catholic population by destroying it if that can be avoided. But we might have no choice. Operations will have its own probes out, but if your team hears anything at all about it being used as a defensive position or gun platform, let me know straight away."

"Yes, sir. Of course."

3

Stony Stratford, England

Claire arrived home that evening to find an inconsolable Chantal Boulier being comforted by her older sister, Amélie. Despite the six years that separated the siblings, they looked enough alike to be twins, with petite figures, honey-colored eyes, and auburn hair. The stresses of war had lined Amélie's face prematurely and aged Chantal beyond her eighteen years.

A little boy, Timmy, stood looking on. He had been orphaned as a toddler by the bombing of a ship off the coast of France and rescued by Claire's youngest brother, Jeremy. Although Jeremy had been appointed his legal guardian, Claire had cared for the child for nearly four years while her brother was at war. Timmy's wide, serious blue eyes under blond hair indicated his understanding that a sad event was unfolding before him. He ran to Claire as she entered and clung to her while continuing to watch Amélie and Chantal.

"What's wrong?" Claire asked anxiously on seeing the downcast faces in the living room. Amélie's arms were wrapped around Chantal in a comforting embrace while her sister choked back sobs.

"It's Horton," Amélie said.

"He's going to fight in Italy," Chantal blurted. "He'll be killed or horribly wounded."

"Oh, dear," Claire said as dismay gripped her. Sergeant Derek Horton had survived being stranded in northern France after the British army's evacuation at Dunkirk. He had escaped overland with Claire's middle brother, Lance, and had served as a covert operator with the French Resistance alongside Jeremy.

A later operation had endangered and exhausted Amélie to the extent that she had been evacuated from France to England and was now staying with Claire. Chantal had accompanied Amélie, and then had spent the past three months in training at MI-9's spy school while Amélie rested and recuperated.

Claire started across the room to further console Chantal. Just then, Horton appeared carrying a glass of water. His stocky frame filled the doorway and his concerned eyes repressed his normally mischievous grin. Looking bewildered and helpless, he stared at the three women. "I'm sorry, mum," he said, glancing at Claire. "I just stopped off to say my goodbyes until I return. I didn't know she'd take it this way."

Chantal detached herself from her sister and threw her arms around Horton's neck. She clung to him wordlessly with her face buried against his shoulder. He stood with his arms spread apart, still holding the glass of water and looking bewildered. Then, he closed his arms around her and patted her back with his free hand.

"There, there," he soothed in French. "I'll be all right."

Chantal continued clinging to him silently, her body shaking with constrained sniffles.

"You're going back to France to fight with the Resistance," Horton told her, oblivious to the irony of his words compared to his comforting tone. "You'll be in far greater danger than I will."

Chantal still clung to him without speaking. Then Horton drew her into an embrace. "I'll be all right," he whispered. "Really, I will. I love you."

Startled, Chantal stood back, staring at him. "What did you say?"

Horton's eyes were big and round as if he had surprised himself. "I'm sorry. I didn't mean to say that. It just slipped out."

Tears brimmed Chantal's eyes, and she nodded. "I know. You were being nice." Her shoulders hunched, she brought her hands to her face and started to turn away.

Horton reached for her arm. "N-no. I haven't thought of anything but you since we kissed last month at Christmas. I have all these feelings..."

Chantal stopped and faced him with questioning eyes.

An awkward silence descended on the room. Behind them, Claire and Amélie watched in sadness-tinged amusement while ushering a wondering Timmy from the room.

Chantal watched them go and then turned back to Horton. "Go on."

"I-I don't know anythin' about love," he stuttered. "I've been a soldier since I was eighteen and fightin' a war. You were fourteen and a little girl when we met—"

"I was nearly fifteen, and you're only three and a half years older than me." She tossed her head. "I'm not a little girl now."

Horton chuckled and drew a deep breath as he appraised her figure. "No, you certainly are not." He twisted around and searched the ceiling, as if he might find the right words there. "Look, I know nothin' about romance. I just know that when I think of you, and when I'm near you, I'm happy. Happier than I've ever—"

Before he could complete his sentence, Chantal rushed over and threw her arms around his neck. "I knew you'd love me, sooner or later." She pressed her lips to his, and when she drew back, breathless, she murmured, "I knew I'd never give up."

Then a pained look crossed her face. "I've suddenly become the happiest and the most miserable girl in the world. You're going back to that awful war."

Horton took her hands in his and kissed them. "And so are you. But I promise you, wherever you are at its end, I'll find you, and you'll never be rid of me."

A knock on the front door interrupted their embrace. "I'll get it," Claire called from the kitchen, and moments later she entered the room with Jeremy. His resemblance to Claire was striking, with the same sandy hair, average height, square jaw, and winning smile. Aside from their masculine and feminine differences, only their eyes varied, hers being brown and his green.

He halted in surprise at seeing the couple still entwined. A broad grin crossed his face as he fixed his gaze on Chantal. "You always said this day would come," he said in French, allowing for Chantal's limited English fluency.

Her cheeks turned flaming red as she cast him an impish smile. "Nature's course," she replied. "It was unstoppable."

"And you." Jeremy shot a mock-accusing look at Horton.

The sergeant smirked sheepishly as he shrugged. "I was helpless."

Jeremy chuckled. He recalled the first time he had met the spunky girl in Dunkirk, when Amélie and their father had rescued Jeremy from nearly certain capture by the Germans. Although initially traumatized by having to flee her family's home, Chantal had since developed into one of the most effective reconnaissance and surveillance field agents in the Resistance around Marseille. There, she had met and fixed her affections on a reluctant Horton while he was a British operator advising the Resistance before returning to England. Only the promise of training at MI-9's spy school and the prospect of seeing Horton in England had convinced Chantal to accompany Amélie to London. The three had reunited at a Christmas celebration at Claire's house for the first time since arriving in Great Britain.

Amélie and Timmy joined the gathering in the living room. Timmy ran to Jeremy and begged to be picked up while yelling delightedly, "Jermy, Jermy."

Jeremy picked up the child and placed an arm around Amélie's shoulders while she embraced Jeremy and kissed him lightly. She glanced at Horton and Chantal. "You've seen the new budding romance?"

"Another one that's being interrupted by this damnable war," Chantal interjected fiercely. Her eyes teared up again, and her voice broke. "Horton's going to Italy. He'll be in that mess at the Gustav Line. The casualties are already high."

Jeremy spun around to stare at Horton. "Is that right? You're going to Italy?"

Horton nodded. "Partially true, sir. I'll be a replacement and probably on the Gustav. But other operations are afoot. I'll go where they send me, and I'll know where that is just before arrival."

Heavy silence bore down on the gathering. As Claire listened to the conversation, her mind flitted back to her discussions with Commander Travis earlier in the afternoon concerning the savagery of the Gustav. She cast a worried glance at Horton. Then, forcing a smile, she called out, "Let's at least enjoy our evening together. Shall we sit?"

As they settled on the divans and overstuffed chairs in the living room, Jeremy's expression turned grim. "I'm afraid I'll throw a wet blanket on the notion of a good evening together," he said. When all eyes had fixed on him, he shifted his gaze to Amélie and Chantal and announced, "We're leaving for France tomorrow. The three of us will fly out together. Madame Fourcade will be here shortly to fill us in."

Claire listened, stunned, suddenly envisioning the room empty, leaving only herself and Timmy. Each of the others gone, perhaps never to return. She closed her eyes, dropped her head into her hands, and rested her elbows on her knees, an uncharacteristically forlorn figure.

Sensing her emotional anguish, Timmy detached himself from Jeremy, crawled up into Claire's arms, and hugged her neck. "Don't cry, Gigi," he said. "Things will work out. You'll see."

Claire squeezed him as she broke into a teary smile.

Chantal stared at Jeremy, then leaned against Horton's chest with an arm over his shoulder and sobbed quietly.

Amélie and Jeremy sat close together watching the others.

At last, Claire said, "Let's get all the bad news out on the table, shall we? Then perhaps we can try to enjoy the rest of our evening. I'll start. Fortunately, I know of no news concerning Mum and Dad worse than what we already knew. So, I suppose that's good news. The same goes for Lance, although with rumors of an Allied invasion into France, POW escape plans will be discouraged. That won't sit well with him. And I don't even like to think about Paul somewhere in Italy." She turned to Jeremy. "Anything on our cousins?"

He shook his head. "Josh is still flying in the Pacific somewhere. He's been downed twice, but he's come through without any disabling injuries. Zack is on the mend from his wounds at San Pietro. My guess is that he'll re-enter combat in Italy sometime soon."

"I met him here at Christmas, right?" Horton broke in. "I'll keep an eye out for him in case we cross paths. Doubtful, though. He'll be with an American unit."

"What about their sister, Sherry?"

"I had lunch with her a few days ago," Claire cut in. "She was on the verge of requesting reassignment after having to treat her own brother aboard an evacuation flight from Italy. It's enough that she takes care of the seriously wounded on their way to safety. I can't imagine her horror on seeing Zack suffering as he was. But she's stiffened her spine, and she's going back to being a flight nurse. My hat's off to her. I should be doing more."

"You do enough here, taking care of Timmy," Jeremy said, reaching across to tousle the boy's hair, "and keeping track of all of us, not to mention staying in contact with Mum, Dad, and Lance. And you must be doing something valuable at that estate where you work. What's the name? Bletchley Park?"

Claire nodded slightly and smiled. "I do what I can, but given what all of you and others have been through, I'm left feeling that I haven't fully done my part."

"You're keeping a home worth coming back to," Horton interjected. "It's what we all fight for, and that's not nothin'."

"Well, thank you for that, Derek. Now, if this is to be our last evening together, let's make it a good occasion." She smiled down at Timmy. "As he says, things will work out. You'll see."

As she spoke, someone knocked on the front door, and when Jeremy opened it, he found Madame Madeleine Fourcade standing there. She was a small woman with sharp features and hair pulled tightly around her head. Highly intelligent and well educated, she had foreseen Nazi intentions even before the war started, and had been instrumental in forming and then leading Alliance, the largest Resistance organization in France.

Her rented villa in Marseille had been her main headquarters early in the war. That was where Jeremy, Horton, Amélie, and Chantal had operated together for the span of months until operational considerations had brought them to England. Gestapo infiltration had almost destroyed Alliance two years earlier. Fourcade had escaped arrest and rebuilt the organization, but it was again betrayed, and she had barely avoided capture via a special Lysander flight sent to rescue her. She had been brought to London for rest, but she continued attempting, with mixed results, to re-build her organization through trusted lieutenants still in France.

Fourcade smiled broadly on seeing Jeremy, and she kissed him on both cheeks as she stepped through the door. As he guided her into the living room, she took note of the long faces greeting her and took a deep breath. "I see Jeremy has already broken the news," she remarked.

As they nodded, Chantal cried out, "And Horton is going to fight in Italy."

Fourcade stood still, momentary alarm showing in her expression before vanishing into professional neutrality. She faced Horton. "Be careful, my friend. We want you back alive and healthy."

Horton nodded. "The bullet to do me in has yet to be made," he replied. Then he threw his arms wide, grinning. "Does that sound brave and trite enough for the occasion?"

Strained laughter ensued.

"How are *you*, Madeleine?" Claire asked, rising from her seat and crossing to embrace Fourcade. "I know things have been trying for you being in England while the war rages in your country. And Jeremy told me that you've been worried about the fate of your most trusted aide, Colonel Léon Faye, I think. Do you have any word on him?"

For a moment, Fourcade blanched. Then she shook her head. "No," she said hoarsely. "His Lysander flight back to France landed badly. The ground was rough and there were too many people at the airfield, most of them unknown. One of our other agents who landed with him told me that he only had time to whisper to Léon to get out of the area immediately. That's the last anyone we know saw him, and we've had no other information."

Her expression hardened into one of stoicism. "We go forward. We have no choice."

Thoughtful quiet descended on the room. "It's so good to see all of you," Fourcade said, deliberately interrupting the silence. She forced a smile. "I've just come from a Christmas party at the home of William Waldorf Astor II, the son of Viscount Astor." She enunciated each word of the title with slight sarcasm. "It was all very posh. My dearest friend from Paris, Nelly de Vogüé, invited me along. She hoped to cheer me up, but the affair was like an evening before the war, as if no combat was happening at all. They had long tables set with fine crystal and silverware. Candles were lit and cast a warm glow. The women wore their jewelry, all with diamonds, and the men had fine tuxedoes and polished shoes. Champagne flowed and everyone chatted and laughed as if nothing at all adverse was going on.

"Rather than being cheered up, I was happy to escape and come where people know and understand the ravages the Nazi machine is waging on common people here and in France, and that we must fight them with everything we've got."

Jeremy faced her and took both of her hands in his own. "You're welcome here, where you're much loved," he soothed. "Let's hope for good news of Léon soon."

Classically handsome, Léon Faye had at first clashed with Fourcade. He had favored an armed coup against Marshal Philippe Pétain, the titular head of the German-controlled Vichy-French government, the part of France not directly governed by the Nazis. She saw Léon's plan as inviting a massacre of their own people.

Despite their differences, romantic tension between the pair grew, and after they had reconciled their operational disparities in favor of Fourcade's view, it blossomed as Léon had not only subordinated himself to her command but also agreed to be her chief of staff. In that capacity, he had recruited former senior military officers to join Alliance.

Together, they had built the organization to be the largest and most effective across France, supplying streams of information to British military intelligence, carrying out acts of sabotage, and aiding escaped POWs to avoid re-capture and navigate through enemy lines to friendly territory.

Fourcade and Léon had been separated by mission imperatives prior to the Gestapo infiltration and near-destruction of Alliance, but they had reunited in London and worked together to re-build from afar. Then, several months ago, Léon had departed for France again. Fourcade had gone to see him off, and as the Lysander lifted into the sky, she was seized by a premonition that she would never see him again.

That same sense now gripped her as she gazed around at the serious faces, all of whom had their eyes glued on her. "Yes, the fight continues," she told Jeremy in response to his remark about Léon's current status.

Then, observing how closely Horton and Chantal sat together, she smiled. "I see that you two have found each other."

Chantal's face broke into a crestfallen smile as she leaned into Horton. He shrugged and pulled Chantal closer while kissing her forehead.

"I'll get drinks," Claire said. She detached herself from Timmy and crossed the room to a cabinet.

Fourcade settled into an overstuffed chair and faced the gathering. "I still have work to do here," she told them. "I'll be returning to France in March. The three of you"—she nodded toward Jeremy, Amélie, and Chantal—"will return to Lyon tomorrow and rejoin Georges Lamarque. The emphasis now is on preparing for the invasion. We'll be conducting sabotage of all sorts and running reconnaissance missions."

Anticipation flashed over Chantal's face, and she sat up. "So it's finally going to happen. Do we know where or when?"

Fourcade shook her head. "No. You'll get full instructions on arrival. That's all I can tell you at the moment."

Claire crossed the room with a tray laden with a bottle of brandy and six snifters. "Enough of business," she announced. "Let's enjoy being together while we can."

4

January 18, 1944
Lyon, France

The journey across the Channel had been as uneventful as any Jeremy had taken, aside from the coincidence that it occurred a year to the date since his last trip into enemy territory. They had flown at night aboard a Lysander, the plane of choice for covert flights into Occupied France because of its short takeoff and landing capability. At once made more pleasant and more worrisome by the presence of his travel companions, the Boulier sisters, the crossing had otherwise been without incident.

They had touched down in the dark in the same field in Thalamy where Jeremy had previously landed, and they were whisked away from the small plane by unknown French partisans. Then they had heard more than watched as the aircraft lifted into the air for its return trip to RAF Tangmere on Britain's southern coast, presumably with passengers they had not seen. After three more days of traveling at night and sleeping in barn lofts during the day, and having scant food, they arrived, quite spent, at the apartment of Madame Marguerite Berne-Churchill, no relation to the British prime minister. She had been a model and was now a practicing physician who also performed as Madame Fourcade's secretary in Alliance.

Marguerite greeted the three warmly, but they noticed the deep stress lines on her exquisite face and how thin she had become. Through Alliance, she and Fourcade had become acquainted, and when Fourcade had needed to escape Marseille ahead of a *Gestapo* dragnet, Marguerite, given the codename Ladybird, had offered her own apartment to be the new headquarters for Alliance.

Because her bedroom was the only area large enough to accommodate sleeping quarters as well as space for office furniture, she had made it Fourcade's quarters, thus allowing for private conferences. She had then occupied another bedroom. Further, she had offered the services of her own teenage children as couriers.

"How good to see you all, healthy and well." She embraced each guest and kissed them on both cheeks. "Come and sit," she said, leading them into her sitting room. "It's still too cold to be outside on the veranda. How is Madeleine? I miss her. I'm sorry I don't have much to offer for refreshments, but—" She shrugged and arched her eyebrows. "You know how things are these days." She shook her head. "And getting worse." Smiling brightly, she added, "But I still have some brandy from the old days."

She retrieved a bottle from a cabinet and four crystal glasses. As she poured, she glanced at Chantal mischievously. "How is young Sergeant Horton doing? Are you still pining after him?"

Seeing Chantal suddenly fighting back tears, she looked quizzically at Amélie while handing her a drink. "Did I say something wrong?"

When Amélie explained, Ladybird covered her mouth with her elegant fingers, her eyes widened with dismay. "Oh, you poor child." She set the brandy on a coffee table and went to encircle Chantal in her arms.

"She's hardly a child anymore," Jeremy observed. "With the missions she's run and the training she's just completed—"

"Of course. I didn't mean otherwise," Ladybird protested, "but being parted is traumatic enough in a romance without a war putting the lives of both parties at risk."

Chantal sat up, a stoic expression on her face. "I'm all right," she said in a professionally neutral voice. "Thank you," she told Ladybird as she disentangled from the embrace. "You are most kind."

She reached for one of the brandies. Then she stopped and glanced questioningly at her sister, once more an adolescent seeking consent.

Amélie laughed lightly. "You don't need my permission. I'd say you've earned a glass of brandy at the very least."

"Hear, hear!" Jeremy said with a big smile. He stood and hoisted a glass in the air. "A toast to the little girl I met four years ago who's all grown up." His expression turned serious. "You've come up a hard way, accomplished some truly remarkable things for the Resistance, and retained your humanity. And now you're a trained agent. We're proud of you."

Amélie and Ladybird also stood and raised their glasses. "To Chantal," they said in unison.

Chantal stared at them, her face turning crimson. Then she grabbed her glass. "You're making me blush," she said, and laughed. "Now I really need this." She downed her drink in one gulp and immediately started coughing.

When she had recovered and all four were once more seated, Ladybird addressed them. "Madeleine told you before your flight that emphasis is now on preparing for the Allied invasion of France, is that correct?" Seeing their affirmative nods, she continued. "We don't know the time or place, but we have to prepare for it to be successful. Georges Lamarque will be here tomorrow and will explain your planned individual contributions."

She looked back and forth between Jeremy and Amélie. "Unfortunately, that means we will cause a separation between you two lovebirds for a time."

The two exchanged anxious glances. "We're prepared for that," Jeremy said.

Amélie breathed in sharply and exhaled, but nodded her agreement.

"I don't know much, so I don't have much to relate," Ladybird went on, "but Amélie, I think that you'll be traveling back to Paris with Georges. Something to do with a person codenamed Amniarix."

Amélie hardly dared breathe. Few in the Resistance knew of Amniarix's existence, and fewer still knew her identity, that being one of Alliance's most closely guarded secrets. Amélie had been her main contact in Paris, and carrying a message from her to Alliance had caused Amélie's arrest. Recalling how close she had come to swallowing two cyanide pills sewn into her sleeve, Amélie shuddered. A Resistance team had rescued her from a cell in the *gendarmerie* in Valence just as she was peeling the lethal tablets from a hem on her jacket.

If Ladybird sensed Amélie's discomfort, she did not let on. She turned to Jeremy. "You're headed for the Vercors Massif in the southeast of France. That's all I know except that the place is breathtakingly beautiful."

She glanced sharply at Amélie with a sudden thought. "Maybe I should be speaking with you individually. You shouldn't know too much about what the other is doing. If any of you three are captured—"

"We know how to protect each other," Jeremy interjected. He held up his right sleeve. "My pills are sewn in here, and they're easily accessible. I can promise that I won't divulge anything I shouldn't, particularly about Amélie and Chantal. They both went through hell in saving me."

"I have mine as well," Amélie said softly. "But I agree that we should know nothing more about each other's missions."

"I have mine too," Chantal chimed in, some of her teenage mischievous spirit reentering her voice. The others stared at her, obviously not having thought about the notion of Chantal also carrying cyanide.

"What did you expect?" she said on seeing their reaction. "I went through the same training both of you did. I know how to shoot, I carry a pistol." She sensed the others staring at her and chuckled. "If a man tries to force his way on me, it's likely to be the last thing he'll ever do, whether I have my gun or not. If I find myself in a tight spot..." She left the sentence unfinished.

Amélie held Chantal in a concerned gaze. Then she sighed and dropped her forehead into her hand. "This damned war."

Jeremy put his arm around Amélie and pulled her to him.

"So tell me, what will I be doing?" Chantal persisted, her eyes wide and bright, breaking the somber mood.

"Don't be so eager, girl," Ladybird chided lightheartedly. "This is serious business." She pushed a strand of hair out of her own face and shrugged. "I only know that you'll be working with an artist, a famous one. At least he's famous in France. I have no idea in what capacity, or where. We were asked to provide someone who is adept at surveillance—"

"And I'm the best there is." As soon as Chantal spoke, a cloud crossed her face. "But working with an artist sounds dull. What am I supposed to do, mix his paints? Clean his brushes?"

"I'm sure there's more to it than that," Ladybird said, laughing. "But don't wish for too much excitement. Haven't you seen enough misery in this war?"

Maturity and thoughtfulness returned to Chantal's countenance. "I have," she said somberly. "I didn't cause any of it, but I've had to deal with it." Nightmare images floated across her mind of the German *SS* officer who had caused her and Amélie to flee their home in Dunkirk along with their father. The two men had fought at the edge of a cliff. Chantal shuddered and drove the memory from her mind.

"I know," Ladybird said. She held Chantal's hand momentarily. "I've heard." She straightened. "Enough talk for now. You must be tired. I'll scrape together what I can for dinner." Looking around the apartment, she remarked, "The sleeping accommodations are as they were when you left: Madeleine's room has a double bed, then there's the—"

"I'll sleep on the couch," Jeremy said brusquely. "There'll be no wedding or the possibility of babies until this war is ended."

Amélie looked up with a bleak smile. "I won't leave orphans or a war widower behind," she said. "We're getting married on Sark when all of this is done," she told Ladybird, "and you're invited."

Georges arrived the next day. A tall, impressive man with classical French looks, he was a well-known professor of mathematics at the Paris Institute of Political Science, a post that allowed him remarkable freedom of movement within Nazi strictures. When war broke out, he organized a Resistance group, the Druids, a subnetwork of Madame Fourcade's Alliance group. It carried out Resistance actions throughout France. After the first major *Gestapo* sweep had reduced Alliance from an organization of thousands to just five members, he had helped rebuild quickly, and as a result, he was one of Fourcade's most trusted lieutenants.

After greetings, he told the group, "I apologize that we don't have more time." He redirected his remarks to Amélie. "We're both needed in Paris. I'll fill you in as we have opportunity along the way, or at worst, at my apartment once we get there."

Noticing Jeremy grimace, he chuckled. "Nothing to fear, my friend. She'll come there to brief me and to be briefed. We don't have time, opportunity, or inclination for anything more." He smiled at Amélie and added, "Despite how lovely she is."

He redirected his attention to Jeremy. "Amélie's heart rests with you, and we all know it. To ease your mind on her security, we'll use the same measures to bring her back to Paris as we used to extract her the last time she was there. When the time is right, we'll bring her out the same way."

Amélie stiffened at the recollection of her train trip out of the "City of Lights," now dimmed under the yoke of German tyranny. Taken into custody by a *Gestapo* officer, she had considered her life to be near its end once more. She had been saved only by the fast action of a Resistance group that had shadowed her for the entire trip.

"Right now," Georges said, providing a welcome break to her thoughts, "I need to spend a few minutes with Chantal." He turned to Ladybird. "May we use the 'office?'"

"But of course. No one's in there now." She waved them toward the bedroom where the sisters had spent the night. The décor was decidedly French Provincial but had been arranged to fit a plain round table and some chairs, with the bed shoved to one side to make room.

"I'm to work with an artist?" Chantal asked somewhat impatiently as she took her seat. "That's not very exciting. I doubt he talks much. He'll be too busy painting, and what am I supposed to do, watch him paint? That might be interesting at first, but—"

"You *are* a bundle of energy, aren't you?" Georges laughed. "Look, Fourcade herself recommended you for this assignment. It's an important one. Now listen to me."

His tone of voice caught Chantal's attention, and she became serious. "Sorry. I'm listening."

"I'm sending you to a man codenamed Dragon. You'll learn more about him when you meet him. To tell you more now is unwise because his family is quite prominent. For the moment, all you need to know is how to contact him, and I'll provide that information.

"He'll introduce you to Robert Douin, a famous artist, at least in France. You might have heard of him. You'll have papers identifying you as Douin's niece, and you'll say that you are going to assist him. His son Rémy will be with him as his apprentice. He's fourteen, and thus would be your cousin. You'll need to know those details and others of their backgrounds and you must be able to regurgitate them without hesitation for ID confirmation while going through checkpoints."

Now Chantal was listening with rapt attention. Her favorite memory was of a mission she and Horton had done together two years earlier. He had been reluctant, but to her the event had been a lark, an escapade. It had been along a beach on the Cotentin Peninsula, and the results had contributed significantly to defeating German air superiority; or so she had been told. But she neither understood nor cared to know how that could be the case.

In order to distract German guards, she had pressed against a hesitant Horton and kissed him passionately. For her, that had been mission accomplished.

That memory floated vividly in her mind with remembered sensations. In the intervening months since that foray, she had asserted her own place in the Resistance, insisting on greater roles despite dangers, and her abilities had been recognized. Therefore, when Amélie had been evacuated to England for a much-needed rest, convincing Jeremy's boss, MI-9 Director Major Crockatt, to allow Chantal to accompany Amélie to England to be trained in covert operations had not been difficult. Chantal's age had been a question mark, but when Jeremy pointed out what she had already done and would continue to do for the Resistance, the rationale prevailed that she could be more effective and probably save her own life if she received proper training.

Chantal forced her attention back to what Georges was saying.

"Here's the background for you to memorize," he went on while Chantal wondered what she had missed while her mind had strayed. He handed her a sheaf of papers. "You'll spend the rest of the day doing just that. You go in tomorrow."

Chantal gulped. Before now, she had always been with people she knew and trusted on her assignments: Maurice in Marseille, Horton at Cotentin, members of the local Resistance on other missions. This time, she would travel alone through hostile territory to an unfamiliar destination to meet with someone she did not know and could identify only through subtle elements of specific clothing at a given time and place, and verified with an exchange of scripted non sequiturs.

"That will be all for now," she heard Georges say through a mental haze. "I must get Jeremy started, and you have studying to do."

"I'm sorry you won't be coming back to Paris with us," Georges began after Chantal had exchanged places with Jeremy and left the room. "Last time around, we knew the danger of letting the secret that Amélie carried fall into enemy hands. We couldn't allow that at any cost. We don't anticipate anything of equal significance this time, so you won't be involved in her security. I've discussed with Fourcade how we should assign you now—"

Jeremy interrupted. "But the danger to Amélie will be just as great, correct?"

Georges gazed at Jeremy, seemingly unsure of how to respond. "Her job will be the same as it was before—to be a visible symbol of support to Amniarix and carry messages between us as necessary. That agent is under tremendous stress, particularly after the bombing of Peenemünde within a few days of bringing out information about the target. I'm sure more than one senior German officer loses sleep at night wondering if their own loose lips brought that about.

"To legitimize her presence in Paris, we've arranged a job for Amélie working behind the counter in a butcher shop. It's located equidistant between my apartment and the area where Amniarix operates, and it caters to high-end restaurants favored by *Wehrmacht* officers. She might pick up information by being alert, but her main task is to provide Amniarix with moral support." He paused. "I've told you more than I should."

Jeremy scowled slightly. "I don't like it."

"Look, my friend," Georges said sharply, "you can like her mission or not at your pleasure, but it's not yours to influence one way or another. She knows the risks. Chantal will be in at least as much danger, maybe more."

"I thought so," Jeremy muttered, chagrinned. "I'm just as concerned for Chantal. She's become a little sister to me, but you tell me how to send either of them into war and feel good about it."

Georges frowned and sighed. "You're sending neither of them anywhere. "They've volunteered. Either of them can back out at any time."

Jeremy massaged his temples. "You know they won't."

Georges nodded. "The sooner we get the three of you on your separate ways where you won't see each other, the better. *You* must concentrate on *your* mission.

"A major operation shaping up needs Alliance support in the southeast of France. We're shorthanded because of the *Gestapo* sweeps. The second one almost put us out of business again." Bitterness edged his tone. "They tortured and killed hundreds of our operatives. I've lost many close friends to the *Gestapo*." He breathed in deeply. "So I understand your fears regarding Amélie and Chantal."

Jeremy nodded in resignation. "Sorry," he said glumly. "I was thoughtless. What do you need?"

"We're sending you to the southeast where the Resistance network, Jockey, built a stronghold at the Vercors Massif. Are you familiar with the area?"

"I can't say that I am."

"Our operative there is Francis Cammaerts, codenamed Roger. He'll identify you by your codename, Labrador.

"The area is an aberration in France, a place where the people have managed a degree of independence while surrounded by German occupation." His voice rose with a touch of enthusiasm. "A massif is a principal mountain mass, and this one is fantastic. Before the war, the northern half was a favorite place for skiing. An incredible gorge divides the area into northern and southern halves. The southern part is on a high plateau with rich farmland. Because the area is so high and difficult to access, the Germans have left it alone for the most part. That's aside from a horrific raid they did last year at a village called Échevis."

"What happened there?"

"It's better for someone there to tell you. I don't have details. As I was saying, we have a man in place who could use your help."

"Who's 'we?'"

"Roger, Alliance, and our Resistance Partners. Jockey is independent of us, but we've cooperated on operations. I've traded written messages with Madame Fourcade via Lysander flights. Your fluency in French and German are very useful, and so is your operational experience, and you do a great impersonation of a *Gestapo* officer. I've seen—"

"That's not my favorite thing to do, I assure you," Jeremy interrupted. "Every second, I'm expecting to be found out." Twice before, he had been compelled to masquerade as a Gestapo officer, once to smuggle his brother Lance out of Switzerland after a successful escape from a POW camp in Germany, and once to rescue Amélie, who was being held for the *Gestapo* in a gendarmerie north of Lyon.

Georges grimaced. "I can imagine. That's just an element that could come in handy, though it's not your primary role by any means. Roger, the SOE agent, is very capable, but he's spread thin and could use your backup. The uncertainty regarding time and place of the invasion confuses planning and mission-specific training." He stood and stretched his arms high overhead while he arched his back. Then he settled back into his chair. "Sorry. Long day."

He studied Jeremy while he mulled. "Last year, after their losses in North Africa and on the eastern front, the Germans pushed Prime Minister Laval to order all French men from age eighteen to fifty into slave labor for war production. Single women too, from ages twenty-one to thirty-five. Tens of thousands of the men and some women went underground. They escaped into the countryside, particularly the mountains. Those individual fighters, *les maquisards*, organized into militias, primarily in the mountainous areas, to fight the Germans. The call themselves the *Maquis*.

"That area, the Vercors, is where huge numbers of them gathered. The people there call it 'The Fortress.' You'll understand better when you've been briefed in situ."

"When do I leave?"

"That's uncertain too. You might be stuck here a while. I'll get a message to Fourcade for final confirmation and coordination. You'll go as soon as we get word to send you. Ladybird will have the contact information and she knows how to arrange travel." He smiled obliquely. "It takes only one phone call."

The night was too short, the hours rushing by as Jeremy and Amélie spent them together on the sofa in the living room. Ladybird and Chantal had retired to their rooms, the former out of courtesy, and the latter with mock petulance. "Don't do anything," Chantal chided facetiously. "I'll be watching." She laughed and then skipped into the bedroom and closed the door.

Georges had departed for other appointments in Lyon. The city crawled with Resistance leaders who had to pretend they did not know each other when crossing paths in its streets. Its labyrinth of highways and railway intersections, warehouses, and cellars made the city an ideal location for a major *Gestapo* headquarters. Those same resources combined with a centuries-old local culture of fierce independence and defiance against government intrusion also attracted many Resistance groups. The result was that Lyon became a hotbed of espionage.

Amélie had watched her sister skip off to the bedroom and then turned to Jeremy. "She's still a little girl at heart. I'm glad that this war—the attempted rape, the way our father was killed—hasn't destroyed her spirit. Still"—Amélie caught herself as her lips trembled—"I'm afraid for her. What are they sending her to do, and where?"

She dropped her head into both hands. "I remember back in Dunkirk, that day I saw you hiding from the Germans on the beach and went out to divert them. Chantal told me that I was so brave, and that she could never do such a thing. Now, she seems fearless, and I'm scared all the time."

Jeremy pulled Amélie to him. "Daring without fear is stupidity," he said. "Acting when you're terrified, that's courage. I'm sure Chantal has her share of fright." He closed his eyes and sighed. "I'm afraid for Chantal and for you."

Amélie took his hands in hers and pressed them to her lips. "I don't know where you're going either, or what you'll be doing, but it's dangerous. That's a given. Know this—" She teared up and found herself momentarily unable to speak.

Jeremy started to embrace her, but she held his hands firmly while she regained composure. "Remember when we were at Madame Fourcade's villa in Marseille. You were getting ready to leave on that submarine back to England. We were alone in the garden, and you took my hands like this." She tightened her grip. "You told me that you were going to leave your heart where it belongs, in my hands."

"I remember," Jeremy said softly. "That seems so long ago. A lifetime, but it's not been even four years." He pulled her hands up to his lips and kissed them.

"I want to tell you," she whispered, "that these warm hands still hold it, and will, for as long as you want them to."

5

January 19, 1944

After a stoic if heart-rending farewell, and bundled in coats against freezing weather, Amélie and Georges left for the railroad station. She remained quiet, forcing emotions away so as to present an acceptably compliant face to German guards while passing through checkpoints. Patriotic forgers of the criminal underworld had provided fresh, up-to-date documents. For travel purposes, she would pose as a newly recruited assistant for the notable mathematics professor. Once in Paris, she would receive another set of papers to cover her employment at the butcher shop.

The journey by train was a depressing event. As opposed to other times when Amélie had ridden it, French citizens seemed to have settled into acquiescence. She sensed that her countrymen had largely recognized and accepted their fate in this new, *Bosch*-ordered world with Nazi swastika-emblazoned blood-red banners festooning every portal and hanging at regular intervals along the roofs over the station platforms. Soldiers armed with submachine guns roamed the terminal with wolfish German Shepherds, but instances of unleashed, growling attacks on travelers were fewer, and people being led away in *Gestapo* and *SS* custody were less frequent. The population at large had learned proper obeisance.

Aside from an unearthly quiet among passengers during which guards routinely patrolled the carriage aisles, suspiciously eyeing those involved in hushed conversation over the clackety-clack of the train, the five-hour trip was uneventful. On arrival at *Gare de* Lyon in Paris, Amélie and Georges took a circuitous route on public conveyance or walked along well-populated streets, stopping into shops and watching their back trail for faces seen too many times, or other evidence of being followed. Only when finally satisfied that such was not the case did they make their way through the checkpoints at *Pont de l'Alma* to cross the Seine, stroll under the bare branches of *Quai d'Orsay's* tall trees, and finally turn onto *Rue* Fabert.

Even then, they walked past the eight-story building cast in French Provincial style that housed Georges' apartment. Instead of going straight in, they sat for a while in a park across the street, ever watchful, before approaching the front door. Only when safely inside did they speak freely.

"Those train rides take the life right out of me," Amélie remarked while taking off her coat and unwrapping a scarf from around her neck. "With all those Nazi guards roaming everywhere with their guns and dogs, it's nerve-racking."

"I'll start a fire if you'll pour us some sherry," Georges said. "That'll warm us up." Once settled in overstuffed chairs with the room warming up, he told her, "You can use the extra room and sleep here tonight. Tomorrow, I'll take you to meet the family you'll be living with. Having you under their roof puts them in great peril. I'll brief you now."

"Every direction we turn, there's danger," Amélie said angrily. Then her face took on a concerned expression. "Before you start, I have a question. It's none of my business—" She paused, and then continued cautiously. "It's about Léon Faye. I know he was supposed to be in London for a while. Have you heard anything about him? Is he all right? You know she and Léon... Well, you know."

Léon had become a favorite among fighter pilots in the French air force before France's capitulation to Germany. When the Nazis took over control of northern France and its western coast, the remainder of the country and the French colonies were left as an ersatz autonomous zone with its capital in the resort town of Vichy. Léon had remained with Vichy French forces in North Africa.

Then, with Major Loustaunau-Lacau, codenamed Navarre, the very man with whom Fourcade had first built Alliance, Léon had proposed the coup against Marshal Pétain. Léon had sought Fourcade's support on Navarre's specific recommendation.

Electricity had sparked between the two. Léon was a tall man with thick dark hair and an aquiline nose. He conducted himself with exquisite courtesy, but his gray-green eyes could not completely disguise his roguish spirit. On first seeing him, Fourcade's cheeks had flushed red, and she found herself almost breathless.

Despite the chemistry, Fourcade had been aghast at the idea of the coup attempt, pointing out emphatically that Léon proposed a military operation requiring large numbers of trained, armed, and equipped men. Her organization would be overrun quickly, she said, resulting in a bloodbath. She told him flatly that Alliance would not participate.

At first taken aback, Léon had departed, but he returned many months later after having been released from arrest for his anti-Vichy-government activities. Fourcade had offered him the job of her chief of staff, pointing out unequivocally that the arrangement would mean that he must follow her orders. He had accepted without reservation, subsequently recruiting many former senior members of the released French military.

Now, contemplating how to reply to Amélie's inquiry about Léon, Georges sighed. His brow furrowed. When he finally spoke, he did so with obvious reluctance. "We don't know where or how he is. We know his plane landed at Thalamy on the night he flew out of Tangmere, but then he disappeared. That was during one of the *Gestapo* purges. Fourcade wrote to me that as she watched his plane take off, she was gripped with an overpowering sense that she would never see him again. So far, that has been the case. We don't know if he was captured or killed."

Amélie listened with growing dismay. "We all love him," she murmured. "He brings such life. Our poor Madame Fourcade. How does she carry on?"

Georges shook his head. "How do you? How do any of us?"

"But she bears the burden more than most because Alliance operates on her orders," Amélie replied. "She's seen friends disappear or die carrying out her instructions. She always says that we have to carry on for those who sacrificed, and for future generations. We have no choice."

They sat in silence, staring into the fire and sipping their sherry. Time passed slowly as the two contemplated the strange world that had supplanted the one they had known while growing up. Those times now appeared surreal, like the old world could never have existed. The present one was the reality that must be dealt with every minute.

Georges re-filled their glasses.

Amélie watched him absently, and then sat up straight. "Brief me. Tell me my mission."

Georges took a deep breath. "It's the same as when you were in Paris before," he said. "No major differences aside from your cover: instead of selling flowers in an open-air market, you'll be helping out behind the counter in a butcher shop. Your main purpose is to stay in contact with Amniarix, that is Jeannie, to let her know that we are here supporting her, and then to be her courier, as needed."

"I'm glad to do that, but I'd have preferred the flower market."

Georges chuckled. "I understand, but at this time of year there are no flowers to sell in an open market. This new arrangement provides some advantages. First, you'll live with the butcher's family. For the curious, you're his niece who wanted out of the countryside. Living by yourself with few social contacts raises more questions.

"Secondly, you'll be closer to the *Wehrmacht's* Paris headquarters. Instead of waiting for you to come around to some pre-arranged rendezvous point, if Jeannie needs to get a message across quickly, she can come to the shop and pass it along. She suggested the arrangement."

"I can see the sense in that. Waiting for me to appear and not being sure when or if that would happen adds stress, especially if her message is urgent. When will I get to see her again?"

"She should be here anytime. I sent a message ahead about when we would be arriving. I know she'll be excited to see you as soon as possible." Georges knew the background of the two women and the shared dangers that had sealed a deep friendship. "The third advantage is that if she needs to disappear quickly, she can enter the shop and never come back out. Her escape route is already fixed."

"That's a relief," Amélie interjected. "I worry about her so much. I got a four-month rest in England, but she's been here on the job the whole time."

"You nearly lost your life getting her documents into Allied hands," Georges replied. "She doesn't begrudge the time you spent in London. Besides, bystanders could have identified you that night on the train. We had to get you out."

"Have it your way. But what Jeannie has done for our side of the war is incalculable."

The two women had met two years earlier when Amélie had been selected to determine if someone sympathetic to Great Britain worked within the *Wehrmacht* headquarters at Dinard, which had been responsible for planning an expected German invasion of the United Kingdom. Unbeknownst to Amélie, the probability that such a person existed, including the name, Jeannie Boulier, had been identified at Bletchley Park. Amélie's mission had been to contact Jeannie to determine if she was willing and able to gather information from inside the German planning office and pass it along to the Resistance. Jeannie agreed, and Amélie became her courier.

Subsequently, when Jeannie fell under *Gestapo* suspicion and was arrested, Amélie and others in the Resistance had mounted a successful mission to rescue her. One of the casualties of the mission had been Amélie's own father.

Jeannie had then moved to Paris and quickly wormed her way into the *Wehrmacht* headquarters there. She was soon passing along invaluable German intelligence, including a treasure trove of documents that had resulted in the entire Royal Air Force mounting a rapid bombing sweep over Peenemünde, an island in northern Germany where V-1 and V-2 rockets were under later-stage development. They were to be launched with lethal payloads at London and Britain's heartland.

Once again, Amélie had been Jeannie's courier.

Amélie shuddered at the memory of having been discovered and arrested by a *Gestapo* officer while carrying the documents. Once again, she had been rescued.

A soft knocking on the front door in a recognized pattern pulled Amélie back to the present. She jumped to her feet and opened the door to find

Jeannie standing there, prim, elegant, with perfectly coiffed light-brown hair, sparkling brown eyes, and an impish grin.

Amélie grabbed Jeannie's hands and pulled her inside, closing the door softly behind them. Then she whirled and threw her arms around her friend. "I've been so scared for you," Amélie whispered.

"I'm fine," Jeannie said, and stepped back. "Let me look at you. You look rested."

"And you look remarkably poised for what you do every day." Amélie left unsaid that Jeannie appeared thinner, her eyes set deeper inside lightly darkened circles and creased with lines at the corners.

"Yes, well, it's a paying job, and we all must eat." Jeannie laughed. "Are you going to invite me in for a drink?"

Georges was standing behind them at the doorway between the foyer and the living room. "Ah, my favorite former student," he said. He stepped forward to embrace her lightly and kiss her on both cheeks.

"My favorite professor," Jeannie returned. He had taught her at the Paris Institute of Political Science, and she had been his star student. A chance meeting on a train with no place to sit had resulted in a long conversation, and Georges had been largely instrumental in securing Jeannie's employment at the *Wehrmacht* headquarters. He had dubbed her with her codename, Amniarix.

"Seeing you again is so good, but that's being selfish," Jeannie told Amélie while Georges took care of refreshments. "I'm sorry you're back in Paris. But having your face to break up the tension of my job will be immensely reassuring."

"I don't know how you keep doing what you do," Amélie muttered.

"How can I do otherwise? France needs for me to keep doing it." For the space of a second, her smile disappeared, her shoulders dropped, and her lips trembled. She brought her palms up over her face. "I'm terrified most of the time," she whispered. "If I'm found out, what they'll do to me is unspeakable."

Almost as quickly, she straightened her shoulders and regained her composure. "But they'll never see the fear." She wiped moisture from her eyes and let out a nervous laugh. "Don't want to spoil my makeup."

Amélie regarded her with awe. Then she leaned forward and took Jeannie's hand. "Right now, my reason for being is to support you."

6

Caen, France

Chantal glanced about Caen's bus station with forced calm. She tried to be self-possessed and not appear furtive. Her stomach clawed with nervous tension that she hoped did not show on her face. Then she remembered that she was supposed to be playing the part of an adolescent, and thus she should not appear too self-contained—except that she was in a country occupied by foreign armed troops. How should she look? The spy school had not covered the topic of a young woman behind enemy lines passing herself off as a school-age girl.

Georges had instructed her on how to identify her contact, known to her only as Dragon. He would be wearing a narrow-brimmed brown hat with a black band, but as she glanced about, she saw many such hats.

A vendor's stand was to be the initial rendezvous point. Dragon would stop and buy a kilo of whatever produce was available, and then mention to the vendor that the sky was unusually gray at this time of year. Chantal was supposed to laugh and say that the fruit was never good until spring anyway.

A further identifier for her was that Dragon would wear a green sweater under his jacket, and when he mentioned the gray sky, he would lift his left arm and look at the time on a gold watch. Then he would leave, walk to a nearby café, and take a seat inside. She would follow at a distance, enter, and take a seat at another table.

When Dragon was satisfied that neither he nor she was being surveilled, he would leave by the back door. She would join him there, and together they would walk until picked up by a car.

Chantal had dyed her hair dark brown, braided it, and wore a yellow scarf around her neck. With a beige coat over a white blouse and a blue skirt, she looked like the schoolgirl she was supposed to be.

"Don't worry about the vegetable vendor," Georges had told her. "He's one of ours, but he won't interact with you unless something happens to interfere with making contact."

She had made her way to the main exit and found the vendor, identified by having a flat-bed cart with giant wheels, the only such wagon painted dark green among several others that formed an informal market. She ambled over and started inspecting the displayed wares, greeting the vendor but otherwise entering into no conversation.

Her angst had diminished somewhat for having completed a nerve-racking train and bus trip and transited through multiple checkpoints. Her ID was now proven. And having arrived in Caen, she was performing a normal chore among people carrying out similar activities. Her anxiety subsided.

Then she heard a man's voice stating that the clouds seemed unusually gray this time of year. He stood at the end of the cart next to the vendor and was reading his gold watch. He turned slightly toward her without looking directly at her, and his jacket opened to reveal a green cardigan.

Chantal forced a laugh, hoping it sounded real. Without looking up, she said, "Yes, well, the fruit is never any good until late spring anyway."

The rest of the plan worked flawlessly, and soon Chantal was walking in an alley next to a man she did not know and preparing to get into an unknown vehicle to go—where? Her heart beat furiously again, and her cheeks flushed hot. *I'm doing the worst thing I was warned not to do as a child, getting into an automobile with strangers.*

The man walked rapidly. Chantal nearly had to run to keep up, but within seconds, a sedan appeared ahead of them and pulled to an abrupt halt. Dragon got into the left rear and motioned her to the right.

"You've done well, *Papillon*," Dragon said as the vehicle pulled away.

Chantal stared at him. Her breath came in short gasps.

He smiled. "Take a moment to calm down. *Hérisson* personally chose you for this mission and gave you that codename."

Chantal relaxed slightly, and then more by degrees. "*Hérisson*" was Fourcade's codename, and her habit was to assign the names of animals, or an insect in this case, to her agents. *Butterfly. A beautiful insect and a sweet codename.*

"I am Jean Sainteny," Dragon said. "You'll be safe at my farm. It's about thirty miles from here along the coast near a town called Saint-Laurent-sur-Mer. You'll be able to rest there, and all will be explained."

Chantal nodded and managed to sputter, "*Merci.*" Then she sat back and viewed the scenery outside as the spire of *Église du Vieux Saint-Sauveur* and stately residences of Caen slipped by and the auto entered the country-side. After a while, she turned to Dragon. "I thought we weren't supposed to know each other's real identities."

He chuckled. "Cloak and dagger," he said. "People are enthralled by it. Most of it is necessary most of the time, but not all the time. I know some of your background. I mean no insult, but you are very young to have done what you've done. It must have been terrifying at times."

Chantal turned to the front as images intruded on her mind of a German soldier forcing himself on top of her and pulling down her under-wear; and then of Amélie beating the thug over the head with a shovel, over and over... She deliberately replaced the horrific memory with the vision of kissing Horton on the beach at Bruneval.

"At times, it's been scary," she murmured.

"My thought is that you'll be more effective if you know who is behind you and supporting you."

Chantal looked up into Dragon's eyes. They were kind, and behind them was a firmness of expression that immediately bolstered her own confidence. He was tall, a thin-faced man, perhaps in his mid-thirties, with dark hair and a high forehead. She extended her hand. "I am pleased to meet you, Monsieur Sainteny."

They stood in front of his farmhouse, a single-story, rambling structure set on a long, barely perceptible downward slope, facing west. The sun shone through intermittent clouds and glimmered off the dark waters of the English Channel. A stiff wind blew, mussing Chantal's hair. She pulled her coat tightly around her.

"We received a request from British intelligence through Madame Fourcade's Alliance for a detailed sketch-map along Normandy's coast," Dragon told Chantal. "It needs to show the ground inland of the beaches from just south of Quinéville to just west of Cabourg.

"We can guess why the drawing is needed. An invasion is coming. We hope for it, and the Nazis expect it." He turned to see Chantal's reaction, but she remained staring out to sea. "I'm sure it will happen, but we don't know where or when. It might be here, or it might be elsewhere."

"This artist will sketch the whole beach?" Chantal cut in suddenly, incredulous. "How long is it?"

"Just in our sector, about eighty miles. Landing here would be a problem because we have high cliffs, the ports are far apart from each other, and the distance between here and the English coast is four times greater than at Calais. There, it's far shorter, about twenty-five miles, but the Germans have that area more heavily fortified. I'm sure the Allied commanders are gathering similar intelligence on every potential landing site. There are no easy choices.

"The artist you'll work with, Robert Douin, has been on this project for four months. His son Rémy helps him, but the project needs to speed up to complete the work on time. Over the years, Douin has helped restore several churches along Normandy's coast, so he knows the local populations, and he has access to the belltowers. From those heights, he can see for miles. Rémy spots details he can't quite see, and when necessary, the boy will get as close as he can for a better view."

"So, what's my role? Monsieur Douin seems to have the project under control."

Dragon heaved out a breath. "It's not as easy as it sounds. From up here, all seems peaceful. We're about a mile off the coast. If you walked closer to the beach, you'd see massive *Wehrmacht* gun emplacements, their barrels aimed out to sea to fire on enemy warships. Walled-in, interconnecting roads run between them. In the sand and surf below the cliffs, miles and miles of barbed wire are stretched thick between five-foot-high posts set in quadrangles. Steel obstacles intended to rip the bottoms out of landing craft are all over the beach and out in the surf."

He stopped and glanced at Chantal. "I assume you know what I'm talking about—"

"Living in France, I'd be stupid not to. I was trained in England, to include recognizing both English and German military vehicles, weapons, and fortifications. I know the Nazi war materiel. Allied too."

Dragon's eyes widened in admiration. "I didn't know the extent of your training. In any case, contact between Douin and me must be limited. We've had indications that the *Gestapo* is becoming suspicious of him. But he must finish his work, and then I'll deliver it to Alliance."

He paused to study her face. Seeing no reaction, he went on. "We need you to augment Rémy in observing and reporting details of what Douin can't see. We're running out of time and he still has between here and Hameau de Fontenay to finish."

Once more, he watched Chantal's face, but it remained inscrutable. "Everyone living in this area is scrutinized by the Germans. A young girl would be the least suspicious." He glanced at her and chuckled. "Far be it from me to call you a child, but I'm told that when necessity arises, you're quite adept at being one."

Chantal's heart thumped as she understood the implications of her mission. She would be collecting detailed information about military emplacements along the Atlantic Wall in Normandy. *Is this the type of information that Amélie carried around in her head? How did she hold up month after month? Will I trip up?* She took deep, controlled breaths to restore equanimity.

Watching her face, Dragon thought he saw tiny twitches of Chantal's jaw, a few blinks of her eyes, fleeting indications of an internal struggle. "Are you all right?"

She glanced up at him and nodded. "I'll be fine. I can do this."

Robert Douin was unlike anyone Chantal had ever met, and he certainly did not fit the image of a covert operator. He would have stood out in a crowd just for his tall stature, but he went to pains to ensure that he was unforgettable, with a bushy mustache and goatee, velour suits, and a wide-brimmed felt hat.

His uproarious sense of humor won him many friends, but he was also known for a slicing wit and opinions that he defended with vigor. Chief among them was his anger that France had allowed Germany to overrun the northern provinces and, more recently, the rest of France. He openly voiced his disgust for Marshal Pétain, not only for capitulating but also for embracing Nazi dogma and policies.

Douin had learned his art, sculpture and painting, from his father, who had been the director of the École des Beaux Arts in Caen. Douin had succeeded to the position in 1930, and his fame had grown, but when the Germans invaded in 1940, his passion became to rid France of any vestige of *les boches*. In November of that year he joined a Resistance group operating near Caen. A year later, recruited by Dragon, he joined Madame Fourcade's Alliance, and soon led a local subsector of roughly forty members. The group included tradesmen, professionals, fishermen, and teachers.

In August of last year, Dragon approached Douin with the request from Britain's MI-6 for sketches of Normandy's coastline. "*Sacré-bleu!* No one besides me can do this job," the big man had exclaimed. His eyes burned with excitement. "I will deliver more than they could ever ask for. It will be the most important work of my life." He had glanced out the corner of his eye at Dragon, jutted his jaw into the air with mock dramatic flair, and declared, "This will be my masterpiece."

By the time Chantal was introduced to the endeavor, Douin and his son Rémy had hiked and bicycled along the Atlantic coast from Cabourg to Saint-Laurent-sur-Mer on their way to the Cotentin Peninsula.

"So we meet, *Papillon*," he said when introduced to Chantal at Dragon's house. He bowed with a flourish, took her hand, and kissed it. "Greetings. You are welcome here. We still have much work to do."

Nonplussed at his flamboyance, Chantal blushed. Unsure how to respond, she just said, "*Merci.*"

Douin looked her over with a critical eye and then motioned for Dragon to join him in a hall outside the living room. There, the two men engaged in whispered conversation. Chantal watched and noticed that Douin glanced at her furtively a few times through the door, and then she heard him say with some exasperation, "She's too small. She won't be able to carry anything of any size, and our loads are not light."

On impulse, she stomped across the room. With curled fists on her hips, she addressed him indignantly. "Monsieur Douin, if you don't want me here, I don't want to be here."

Startled, the two men stopped talking and stared at her.

She stared back, resolve in her eyes. "Dragon said you needed help with reconnaissance. There's no one better than me. I was trained for it in England by British intelligence and recommended by *Hérisson*. You're worried that I'm small?" She glanced away, took a deep breath, and looked directly into Douin's eyes. "I didn't understand that I came to be a pack animal, but for your information, I pushed a man over a cliff."

She warmed to her point. "I'm trained to kill with these." She raised her fists for Douin to see. "And the course I took required that I carry heavy backpacks and weapons over long distances, up and down mountains, following a compass and a map. So if you don't want me here, let me know now. Maybe I can serve France better elsewhere. But I will tell you this, I want our country liberated just as much as you do, and I'll do whatever it takes to make that happen."

Dragon covered a wry smile with his hand.

Douin continued a shocked stare.

Chantal stood red-faced, eyes flashing, exuding defiance.

Suddenly, Douin let out an involuntary laugh. "I believe you." He stepped close to her and took her hands in his, turning them over while examining them. "I'll remember to watch out for these." Shaking with hilarity, he turned to Dragon. "I haven't been so thoroughly scolded since boyhood."

Wrapping a long arm around Chantal's shoulder, he said, "All right, *Papillon*. You'll come with us." He chuckled again and added in a cajoling tone, "But we must have a conversation between ourselves about who is the boss, and it cannot be you."

Chantal looked up and grinned. Then she moved away and curtsied. "I'm at your service, sir."

Douin laughed with genuine humor. "Well come along, child." He turned and started toward the front door, then stopped and turned back to Chantal. "Don't take offense when I call you that. If you're to be my young niece, we need to adopt the part starting now."

"Yes, Uncle," Chantal replied with a toss of her head and an overly sweet smile. "When do I see my cousin Rémy?"

Douin rolled his eyes. "I can see this is going to be interesting."

Aside from the lack of a mustache and goatee, Rémy was the image of his father and tall for his age. In contrast to Douin's grandiosity, his manner when greeting Chantal was serious and polite.

Later, when she was alone, Chantal thought about the difference between Rémy now and herself nearly four years ago. He seemed so self-possessed and purposeful. At fourteen, she had been a scared little girl as the *Wehrmacht* swept into Dunkirk. That seemed a lifetime ago.

Her outburst had surprised her. She had blocked the memory from her mind of having pushed an *SS* major over a cliff at Dinard. That had occurred as the officer was about to arrest her and the Resistance group sent to rescue Jeannie Rousseau.

"How does this work?" she asked Rémy the next day at the base of a church belltower as they began the day. Douin was upstairs, sketching.

"You mean the bells?" Rémy joked, and then added, "I know what you mean. My father leans on his fame in Normandy," he explained. "If he tried to be secretive, he'd be acting suspiciously."

Chantal again noted the boy's maturity.

Rémy continued, "He's known to be eccentric and for his landscape art, among other things. Everyone knows that he's helped restore some of the churches in the province, so his roaming between them isn't unusual.

"We carry a few unfinished sketches with nothing incriminating on them to show anyone who's curious. Sometimes, if we can't see what we need to from the towers, we'll sit out in a field filling in details like access roads to the beach, antitank trenches, or supply storehouses and ammunition dumps behind the battlements. People come by to see what he's doing, including sentries, so we show them the prepared sketches."

"That would be a bit frightening. How am I supposed to help speed things along?"

"For a few days, you'll stay with me when I go out to check details. I'll show you what we're looking for and how to annotate for my father's needs. Then, we'll move double the distance we've been doing between locations. One of us will go over the ground from the limit of the last section we've done, and the other will do the next section after that. We should finish up in half the time."

Chantal considered the scale of the project. "That'll be a massive sketch. How will we put it all together? You can't be carrying the whole thing everywhere you go."

Rémy shook his head. "We don't. When we've finished a section, we leave the sketch in a dead drop. A courier in my father's group retrieves it and takes it to another dead drop near a particular farmhouse. We seal the sketches and rotate couriers. They receive their instructions just prior to execution, and they don't know what they're carrying or who picks up from the dead drops. The farmer and his wife tape the sections together into one continuous roll in their wine cellar and hide them.

"When we've finished the full sector, we'll get the roll to Dragon. He doesn't know where the sketches are taken, and frankly, neither do I. Only my father and the couple at the farm do. Dragon is responsible for security details after he receives the full, completed sketch. We'll deliver it to him, and he'll deliver it to Alliance."

Chantal closed her eyes in contemplation. She took in a deep breath and then, with a thrust of her chin, she indicated two bicycles leaning against the belltower. "Will we be using those today?"

Rémy nodded.

"If we're stopped, what's our story?"

"We're going to the next town to find drawing pencils for my famous father. Oh, and that brings up one other thing. If we're stopped, you'll do most of the talking."

Chantal shot him a skeptical look. "And why is that?"

Rémy sighed. "To divert attention from me. People think I'm older than I am because of my height. I look like I'm approaching military age. The Nazis are grabbing young men for forced labor in their arms factories in Germany."

Chantal's eyes filled with fury. "My father taught my sister and me not to hate," she growled in a low voice. "Right now, I'm finding that lesson very difficult to follow."

"Me too," Rémy replied. "I've had to present my papers many times to prove my age, and even then, I think only being the son of the famous Robert Douin saved me."

Chantal stalked over and grasped one of the bicycles' handlebars. "Lead on."

7

Fifth Army Field Headquarters, Caserta, Italy

Major General Fred Walker, commanding general of the 36th "Texas" Infantry Division, strode through the US Fifth Army headquarters labyrinth at the Royal Palace in Caserta. The contrast between the living and working conditions of the staff in this place compared to those of his soldiers in the field was not lost on him. For opulence, the majestic twelve-acre estate-turned-military-fortress rivaled seventeenth-century French King Louis XIV's Versailles.

Walker paced through the architecturally grand, arched corridors inlaid with gold and hung with tapestries and large paintings. He passed windows overlooking well-groomed gardens, fountains, and waterfalls extending into distant hills, and finally arrived at Lieutenant General Mark Clark's suite. "Is he in?" he demanded of an orderly. Without waiting for a response, he pushed against an intricately carved door.

Sitting at his desk, Clark glanced up, surprised. "Shouldn't you be with your unit?" He spoke sharply while hauling his six-foot six-inch frame from his chair and leaning over his desk. "Your operation launches in a few hours."

"We're ready, General. This meeting is off the record. I came to discuss the plan one more time because I don't believe in it.

"I've briefed before that I can have my division moved upstream and attack Monte Cassino from the north where the river is shallower, slower, German defenses are weaker, and we'll have friendly units on our flanks. I can do that within two days." His eyes bored into Clark's. "I think that's a better idea."

"We've been over all of this, Fred—"

"Hear me out one more time, sir, please."

Clark stood straight and folded his arms, an imposing figure. "Make it quick. Keep in mind that I've got another operation going on in two days that I'm monitoring too."

"Yes, sir. Operation Shingle at Anzio. I'm well aware of that. The Germans—"

"Look," Clark cut in, "we're expecting Field Marshal Kesselring to panic when we put our boys ashore at Anzio. We think he'll pull forces out of the Monte Cassino area and send them north to support against that operation. That will relieve pressure on your units. The British surprise attacks at Minturno and Castelforte southwest of your position worked. When we pull off that landing at Anzio, we'll link up with our forces from the south and push on to Rome within days."

"As I was about to say, sir," Walker said grimly, "the Germans diverted three divisions down there, and they stopped the British advance before it reached its objective at Sant'Ambrogio. My troops now face that increased German strength, including the 15th *Panzergrenadiers*. That's one of the best and most experienced units in the *Wehrmacht*, and unlike the Sant'Ambrogio offensive, we won't have the element of surprise.

"Even when you succeed at Anzio, we'll still have a hostile army in southern Italy capable of fighting its way north. It's already proven that in the way it built the Gustav Line after we invaded Italy in the south." Walker shook his head. "As I recall, the landing at Salerno didn't work out so well."

As soon as he uttered his last sentence, Walker grimaced.

Clark's face turned deep red. "You recall correctly," he said evenly. "You might also remember that surprise was blown there." He put his hands on his hips and glared. "I'll accept the public blame, but I didn't do it." He seethed with anger. "And you might recall that because of an oversight that Winston Churchill ascribes to himself, I was left out of the conference at Carthage where all of this was planned between him and Ike."

Chagrinned, Walker lowered his head slightly. He did remember. He also recalled that just hours before the botched amphibious operation at Salerno, General Dwight Eisenhower himself had broadcast worldwide that Italy had capitulated to the Allies. The *Wehrmacht* had immediately executed Operation *Achse* to capture and neutralize all Italian military garrisons and stores, and had taken over Italy's coastal defensive positions. So, although the Germans had not detected the landing force at Salerno early on, they had their own units emplaced at key locations and were able to move rapidly at a moment's notice. They did so at first sign of the Allied landing. As a result, the fight at Salerno had been more intense, costly, and lengthy than had been anticipated.

"I won't dispute that, sir," Walker said quietly. "I was there. I know what went down." He straightened up and held Clark's gaze steadily. "I see the current situation differently, though. The 46th Division already attacked across the Gari or Rapido, or whatever the river is on the southeast side of Sant'Angelo. The division got caught in the strong current and took incoming from German field artillery for way too long. It was beaten back, and it can no longer protect my left flank. The place we have to cross is at a curve with an even stronger current against reinforced fortifications, and the Germans expect us. How many boys are we willing to sacrifice?"

He let the rhetorical question linger, and then went on. "As I understand, our main ground objective in the south is to seize the high ground on Monte Cassino in order to command the Liri Valley and allow our tanks through to Rome along the Casilina Highway 6."

Clark eyed Walker a moment. "That is correct," he said at last. "But we're bogged down around Cassino, and we're looking for a breakthrough. And when I say 'we,' don't forget that I also take orders from 15th Group Commander, Field Marshal Wilson. Your mission is included in my orders.

"You should know, too, that Winston Churchill enthusiastically supports the move on Anzio, and he personally sold it to Eisenhower. He also communicated directly with Roosevelt about it. He argued that we should use our superior naval and air power to leap past the forces bogging us down in southern Italy and mount an operation to seize the capital. The president had no objection as long as the operation did not interfere with preparations for the cross-Channel invasion of France.

"Anzio was my idea, but it's got a lot of support. An amphibious operation behind enemy lines has never been done before. When it succeeds, we'll outflank the Gustav and cut enemy supply and communication lines. We'll be in Rome within days."

Clark paused and stretched. The war seemed wearing on him as well. "By crossing the Rapido and Garigliano rivers in the south," he continued, "Fifth Army units will be in position to seize the high ground on both sides of the Liri Valley. Then we'll head north to link up with the force at Anzio, and we'll catch Kesselring's 10th Army between us. That should take a week."

Walker looked skeptical. "Kesselring's pretty wily. He was chosen over Field Marshal Rommel to command the *Wehrmacht* in Italy. He built the Gustav and the other fortified defenses across Italy, and he almost shoved us off the beaches at Salerno. He doesn't sound like a guy to panic, and he's bound to bring in forces from other areas."

Clark raised his hands in a calming gesture. "General Montgomery's 8th Army will support in the southeast along the Adriatic coast. It'll cross the Sangro River and capture Pescara. That'll keep Germany from shifting forces from that area to Anzio. And if Kesselring doesn't pull his troops off the Gustav, the elements at Anzio will join with the 8th Army and push him north. If the rest of the plan works as well as our attacks at the Garigliano, we'll march into Rome together by the beginning of February."

"That's a big 'if,' sir," Walker groused, and then muttered, "It looks like another Gallipoli to me," referring to a disastrous amphibious landing that Churchill had devised and led during World War I. The consequences had followed Britain's prime minister throughout his career.

"I wouldn't bring that up again, General," Clark said tersely. "One of the main reasons for doing the Italian campaign at all is to draw German forces out of the Soviet Union so that the Red Army can turn back the *Wehrmacht* up there. The strategy is working. The siege at Leningrad is going badly for Germany. The winter is killing their forces, and we expect that operation to end soon. The *Wehrmacht* is already sending divisions this way."

Clark glanced at his watch. "We're out of time. You have your orders, General. Either follow them or let me know right now that I need to put someone in command who can. Frankly, I believe the plan will succeed."

Walker breathed in deeply and took a moment to ponder. When he spoke again, he chose his words carefully. "Sir, I trained this division and I'll lead it. The die is cast. I won't watch my men go in without me." He looked directly into Clark's eyes. "I'll give it my all. You have my word."

8

South of Sant'Angelo in Theodice, Province of Frosinone, Italy

Staff Sergeant Zack Littlefield looked through the evening twilight across the soldiers of his squad grouped together in the 36th "Texas" Division's assembly area a few miles east of the river marked "Rapido" on their sketch maps. Damp fog hung in the air. The men engaged in various tasks preparatory to battle: checking their gear, filling canteens, cleaning their weapons once more, drawing ammo and rations, writing letters home; or, having completed those actions, they sat hunched against the winter cold as darkness descended while they waited for the order to move to the line of departure. Around them, soldiers from other squads of the platoon occupied themselves in similar fashion, conversing quietly or grabbing a few winks of shut-eye.

Zack had rejoined the division following his convalescence in England for a concussion that had kept him in a coma for a few days following a direct hit on his tank at the battle at San Pietro. When he arrived back in Italy following recovery, the division was reorganizing and replenishing.

Bigger than most men, Zack had dark hair that contrasted against the sandy color of his Littlefield cousins of Sark. Then again, his uncle was their stepfather.

Zack had been an athlete in high school, excelling as his football team's quarterback, and in that capacity, he had developed his natural leadership skills. His plans for college had been interrupted as he had immediately volunteered for the army at the war's outbreak, and he had seen the thick of combat at Kasserine Pass in North Africa, also in Sicily at the first landing, and in Italy at Salerno and San Pietro. His tenacity and judgment had gained him the trust of superiors and subordinates alike, but his battlefield promotions had resulted from casualties that had devastated the ranks and created gaps in leadership, a dismal recognition that he drove from his mind.

Zack strolled through the evening twilight to where his assistant squad leader, Corporal Rick "Tanner" Perez, reviewed pre-planned targets with the squad's Browning M1919 .30 caliber machine gun team. Tanner was a lean man, gaunt under the travails of constant motion and combat. When meeting him for the first time, Zack had thought the soldier must have just barely passed the army's size requirements, for Tanner was small. But he carried his load well, and although mentally and emotionally fatigued like all the veterans who had been among those originally deployed with the 36th Division, his calm, deliberate manner and attention to the men in his charge had gained him respect.

"The old-timers are griping," he told Zack when the two had stepped away a few yards to speak privately. While they talked, far off to their left, booming and explosions from the big German artillery guns kept up an incessant barrage.

"What's their beef?"

Tanner took in a deep breath and let it out. "You've heard it all before, but they're louder this time. They feel like our Texas Division has been sent into the thickest combat an unfair amount of time. We were among the first troops to land at Salerno and went through that bloodbath. Then, that attack through the mountains with tanks to take San Pietro was just plain stupid. That wasn't tank country. The infantry and armor couldn't support each other. We all know it, and we took huge casualties."

He glanced sideways at Zack. "You know nobody at the top ever got on the ground to take a look-see, and you got your bell rung when your tank had no place to go and took a direct hit. Now we're going to cross a deep, fast river at a curve in the dead of winter, at night. We've got no one covering our right flank, the 46th Division was already sent packing on our left for being exposed to artillery fire too long while trying to cross that damnable river. And at least forty percent of our strength are replacements." He tossed his head back and closed his eyes. "Hell, out of our eleven-man squad, seven are fresh out of training. They've never seen combat except in movies and training films."

He looked around through the remaining twilight. "We're too far back from the attack position," he hissed. "The engineers already complained that they had to carry the rubber boats too far across muddy ground. They made a lot of noise, and we're not even sure that they put the boats in the right places."

Zack listened without response, but when Tanner seemed to have wound down, he said, "Is that all?"

"No, it's not," Tanner replied, fury seeping into his voice. "We're making a frontal assault on a heavily fortified position without support. We'll be open targets. The men know that. The ones who have survived the campaign so far wonder why, and why us? It's time for another division to take the lead."

Zack liked Tanner and was surprised by the corporal's sudden and uncharacteristic outburst. He knew a bit about Tanner's background. The small man had been a bull rider and clown in Texas rodeos prior to the war. His father had owned a large dairy farm in Austria until the early twenties, but being Jewish and sensing hostile sentiment growing across Europe, including in France, Germany, and his own country, the elder Perez had sold all his holdings and moved his family to a cattle ranch he purchased near Gonzalez, Texas.

Vowing never again to be driven from his home without a fight, the patriarch had been drawn to the town by the legend of its response to Mexican General Castañeda in 1835 during the Texas War of Independence. The general had demanded that the town turn over a cannon it had been gifted four years earlier to fend off native tribes. The town's reply came in the form of an attack on Castañeda's forces under a flag emblazoned with the words "Come And Take It" below a sketch of the cannon and a Texas star. Less than a year later, Texas was its own independent republic.

The Perez family had reveled in the wide-open skies and the free spirit of the open range. Only eight years old when arriving in Gonzalez, young Perez had embraced all things Texan, including cow-punching, rodeos, and colorful speech with a Texas twang. Early in his teens, he began bull riding and then clowning in the ring to distract raging bulls after their riders had been thrown into the dust. He had been affectionately dubbed "Tanner" by the ranch hands, "'cuz a man's got to have a handle."

Two years ago, in the aftermath of the Japanese attack on Pearl Harbor, Tanner had stood in line with thousands of other young men to volunteer for the 36th Infantry Division. Originated as a Texas National Guard unit that had seen combat in WWI before being retired at that war's end, it was reactivated and returned to federal service in anticipation of an attack on the American homeland a year before the Japanese surprise attack at Pearl Harbor. As a result of its history, when the division departed for North Africa after nearly two years of training, it was composed almost exclusively of Texan soldiers.

When the moment came for Tanner to depart for basic training, his parents had driven him to the train station. While his mother held back tears and sniffed into a handkerchief, his father had bidden him a stoic and proud farewell, telling him, "Go free our homeland."

Almost immediately, the division had been called up for combat duty, a move that had been much anticipated. Shortly after completing training, it shipped out to North Africa, arriving just as the campaign there was won. It then transferred to Sicily, intended to be one of the lead American major commands to land on the beaches there. However, the commanding general of US forces in that campaign, Lieutenant General George Patton, sidelined the division in favor of one that had already been blooded during combat in North Africa.

After the Sicily campaign was won four months earlier, the Texans moved on to Salerno. There, the green troops were transformed into battle-hardened soldiers as they met the enemy in fierce fighting on the beaches. By then, the Italian dictator, Benito Mussolini, had been deposed. The country surrendered to the Allies and then switched sides to fight alongside them against Germany.

Expecting to make a surprise landing at Salerno, the 36th, now part of

General Clark's Fifth Army, stormed ashore to find a fully prepared German force ready and able to meet them in fierce fighting. The ultimate objective, Rome, expected to be achieved within weeks, became seemingly unattainable, stopped by the impenetrable Gustav Line and its subordinate defenses across Italy. The Allied army inched forward over rain-soaked ground, across mountain ridges and peaks in deadly winter.

From Salerno on, the Texas Division had been at the spearhead on Italy's western front and suffered the most casualties. The survivors became the "old-timers," often in their late teens or early twenties. Untested replacements filled in for fallen, battle-hardened veterans. As the latter fell in combat, the pool of old-timers shrank, and combat claimed more raw replacements as well.

Tanner had been in the thick of fighting starting in Salerno. He had been part of the carnage he never expected to see, and he sometimes worried about losing his humanity. He seldom saw the faces of the enemy while they were living, but on the way north up the Italian boot, he had passed by many German corpses and often wondered if his bullets had snuffed out the light in any of the blank, staring eyes. For his own sanity, he shunted aside those concerns, concentrating instead on doing his best job and caring for his squad members, of which only four remained of the original nine, including himself.

Tanner's mind had many times wandered involuntarily to his lost comrades. One had lost a leg to an artillery explosion as the division had pushed north beyond Salerno. The man had been evacuated for immediate treatment and would be sent home when sufficiently strong to survive the trip.

Another had taken a shot to the forehead during a close-in firefight in the villages. He would be buried near yet a third member of the squad who had caught a machine gun volley across his chest. They would be interred in one of the new military cemeteries rapidly filling along the coast.

When such memories intruded, Tanner blocked them and their emotional toll by concentrating even more on his task at hand. On this evening, that meant ensuring the squad was fully supplied with ammo, rations, and water, and that the machine gun crew knew the positions they were intended to occupy, their fields of fire, and pre-planned targets.

Zack had entered combat nearly a year before Tanner, having fought in North Africa as a tanker at Kasserine Pass, then as a tank destroyer gunner at El Guettar, and after that as an infantryman in Sicily. His leadership abilities had been noted, and before the 36th Division landed at Salerno he had been re-assigned as a tank commander along with other combat veterans to provide blooded experience at the front line. When his platoon sergeant was killed, he found himself in the acting platoon sergeant role, and when all soldiers in the platoon senior to him were wiped out in the opening salvos of fighting at San Pietro, he was thrust briefly into platoon leadership. Badly wounded himself a few minutes later, he had been evacuated to England to recover, and was then returned to the 36th, once again as an infantryman in charge of a squad—with Tanner as his assistant squad leader.

Together, they had fought north along the western edge of the Apennine Mountains, crossing its rivers, traversing burned-out fields, orchards, and vineyards as well as the scattered rubble of what had been villages, and witnessing the steady loss of men they had come to care for. Their comrades had been replaced by wide-eyed, scared, inexperienced soldiers, who nonetheless followed orders, moved toward the sound of guns, and often sacrificed their lives before their first day of combat was through.

"We've got a job to do," Zack said in response to Tanner's observation that a division other than the 36th should take the lead. "If I could change things, I would, but that's beyond my pay grade."

"I know," Tanner said somberly. "I'm just letting you know what the men are saying, and I happen to agree with them." He turned to observe the squad wanly. "Their real gripe is not so much that we're taking the lead again, but where we're attacking. They're tired, Zack. Tired to their bones. Word travels about the lay of the land. They know we're going in under too little artillery and air support, with unprotected flanks, at a curve in a fast-flowing river, then uphill to seize Sant'Angelo on top of a forty-foot bluff. That position is reinforced by the 15th *Panzer Grenadiers*, one of the most vaunted fighting units in the *Wehrmacht*, or so we've been briefed."

Zack waited quietly while Tanner paused and then continued. "The men even think they know why we're doing it—to draw German forces away from another Allied amphibious landing somewhere farther north along Italy's coast. We're sacrificial lambs on a suicide mission. That's the way they see things, and I don't think they're wrong." He paused. "I'll tell you frankly, Zack, they're losing confidence in our leadership, all the way to General Clark himself." He took a deep breath. "The rumor floating around is that our CG, Walker, tried to talk Clark into letting us attack northeast of Monte Cassino where the river is shallower with a slower current, and is less defended. Clark refused."

"I know," Zack said, "I've heard the chatter." The sun had set, and Zack could now barely make out Tanner's outline in the remaining light. "That perception is widespread, at least in this unit. We've talked about it at company meetings, and the skinny going around the platoon sergeants is that the men are pissed off big time all across the division.

"But we don't have time for that now. We do what we're told, and our job is to attack across that river, occupy Sant'Angelo, and be ready to push ahead to seize the heights at Monte Cassino."

"We won't make it, Sergeant," Tanner said in a low voice. "I'm smart enough to calculate odds, and we've got none." He took a deep breath and let it out slowly. "We'll do our best, but do me a favor, will ya? If you make it and I don't, make sure they put a Star of David on my tombstone."

Zack smiled wryly and grunted. "I'd bet on you as much as anyone." By way of lightening the mood, he said, "So tell me, is that the Gari or the Rapido we'll be crossing?"

Tanner chuckled. "Your guess is as good as mine. It's marked on the sketch maps as the Rapido, but some of the locals we've questioned say it's the Gari."

"So many rivers to cross," Zack said, almost in a whisper. "I guess we can leave it to the historians to sort out which one that is, so long as we stay on our azimuth, in our lane, and wade across the river in front of us." He glanced down at his luminescent watch. "It's time to pull a combat inspection on the squad."

9

January 21, 1944

At 0200 hours, under a black sky and a new moon, Zack led his squad through the squishy mud across the wide-open fields to the river's edge. Already, the 36th Division artillery guns launched barrage after barrage across the river, with no noticeable damage. The Germans must have dug in deep and hardened their defenses.

Zack thanked the god of darkness and hugged every depression and used every bit of scraggly vegetation for concealment, but it was sparse, and too many other squads were attempting the same stealth far off to his left and right. Doing a quick estimate, he surmised that somewhere around three hundred and twenty squads amounting to roughly thirty-five hundred soldiers on a patch of ground four and a half miles wide must be creeping through the mud toward the meat grinder that would consist of every caliber of German guns waiting for them across the river and up the bluff to Sant'Angelo.

The air was cold and damp, but at least struggling through the muck, made worse by those who had already passed by ahead of them, warmed Zack's body and he was soon perspiring. Despite the men strapping down their equipment to cut down noise, the squish of many boots sinking into mud and then being pulled out could not be muffled, nor could every rattle of a rifle against an ammo bandolier, or the swish of water in canteens. For a force intent on advancing with stealth, every sound his squad made seemed to Zack to echo across the fields to immediately give away individual positions. But he doubted those noises could be heard above artillery or the rapid staccato of machine guns or even just the rush of the river, particularly when factoring in the battlefield clamor that must be occurring among the Germans themselves. Adding to the miserable conditions was an overwhelming stench oozing up through the muck.

Zack thought the caution almost comical given that the 15th *Panzergrenadiers* anticipated the assault, had zeroed in on pre-planned targets along the expected approach, and were already answering the salvoes of the division's artillery with their own. Enemy machine guns had begun to probe, their tracers like arrows of light as they hissed by. The battle had barely begun, and already acrid smoke permeated the air.

Far off to the right, an artillery round exploded and then Zack heard anguished screams that ended abruptly, and then more to his left after another strike. He called a quick halt and took a headcount. All of his men were present, and so far, none had been touched by enemy fire. However, ambient light reflected off the wide-open eyes of the green troops. Those of the old-timers were mere slits.

They started out again, the withering enemy fire becoming more concentrated and the cries of the wounded more frequent as the unit approached the river. Then they were at the water's edge.

A cold gust of wind blew off the surface. It swirled around and touched the sweat-dampened uniforms, immediately chilling Zack and his soldiers. The sound of the river rushing by, heard as a whisper as they approached, now rose in decibels to a low roar, and when the squad stepped into the icy water, they caught their collective breaths.

An enemy flare floated across the sky. Immediately, the soldiers froze in place, each holding a palm over an eye to protect night vision. From across the river, a fusillade of small arms and machine guns opened devastating fire, launching a deluge of molten steel at the attacking force.

Up and down the riverbank, soldiers fell.

During isolated breaks in firing, Zack heard the *thump* of mortars, followed seconds later by their rounds exploding amongst the loose tactical formations. The flare burned out. In its residual light, Zack scanned the river. Out in the middle, boats loaded with soldiers tossed in the current. On some, its passengers struggled with paddles, attempting to steer to the opposite shore. On others, the soldiers were lifeless, the boats deflating and sinking, victims of the murderous firestorm.

Tanner sidled alongside Zack. "We've located our two boats. They were upstream about fifty yards. Follow me."

Zack did, and when he arrived at the site and did a quick headcount, he found he was missing three men. "Which ones are they? Where are they?" he asked.

"Lost," Tanner replied grimly. "Don't know how, or if they're dead, wounded, or just separated. One of them was Jason, the Browning ammo bearer. So now we're short his ammunition, and we need someone to fill in for him."

"Take Jonesy," Zack ordered. "He knows what to do. Take the weapons team on one boat. I'll take the other one with the remaining three privates. Let's go."

No sooner had they cast off than another full-scale barrage fired from across the river. The current caught the two boats and turned their bows downstream. The men paddled furiously, managed to right the direction, and headed to the opposite shore.

All about them, men cried out in pain, calling for medics, but most of those were caught in the river's strong flow and washed downstream. Some managed to wade to the opposite shore in the freezing water and scrunched against its shelter while bullets flew above them.

Zack's two boats arrived at the embankment, but when the men scrambled off, he found that another squad member had been lost—half of his face blown off. With the help of his comrades, and under the limited shelter of the steep shoreline, they pulled the dead soldier from the boat and far enough above the water to be found later.

"We're out of place and we don't know who's on our left and right," Zack told Tanner. "But we do know the objective. Pick a site up this bank, set up the machine gun, and aim at any enemy position firing lots of flares going over our heads. Stop shooting when their tracers stop. No need to give away our location."

"Roger. I'll take the other two and crawl up to the top of the bank to take a look. Maybe we'll see something useful."

A crackling line of muzzle flashes was all that could be seen over the edge of the embankment. As the night wore on and more US soldiers arrived on the northern bank, they found disorganization, with individual soldiers separated from their squads, larger organizations disconnected from their higher headquarters, and all facing the blistering fire from the bluffs of Sant'Angelo.

Some men had seen their squads wiped out with only two or three survivors. Two such fortunate privates scrambled ashore below Zack's position, and on hearing their plight, he pressed them into service in his squad.

The cold night dragged on. The volume of fire diminished on both sides to sporadic shooting as opposing foes conducted reconnaissance by fire, or as identifiable targets became visible. As morning twilight increased visibility, Zack checked with Tanner. The machine gun ammo was running low. Zack sent two soldiers to scour the beach for any that might have been carried to shore by now fallen soldiers.

"Keep your heads down," he admonished them.

They returned an hour later with a full load taken from a Browning team that had succumbed to a mortar round at the crest of the riverbank. He looked into the two men's eyes. Both had just seen their first night in combat, and their fear was palpable.

"There's bodies all over the beach and in the water," one of them said. He shivered in the frigid air and blew into his hands to warm them. Then he fixed his gaze on Zack. "Sarge, are we going to make it out of here alive?"

Zack looked into the young face now lined beyond its years. "We'll give it our best shot. That's all I can promise. Meanwhile, we've got a job to do. Get that ammo up the bank to Corporal Perez. Then get down low, clean your weapons and your gear, and spell each other while keeping watch on that bluff. Get some rest too, dry off, and stay as warm as you can..."

A skeptical look crossed the soldier's face.

Zack raised a placating hand. "I know. We're not outfitted with cold weather gear, we're wet, and the weather isn't helping. But we'll probably assault again tonight, so do the best you can. Chow down on some rations, but conserve. We don't know how long we'll be here. Dig foxholes. While you're watching the bluff, memorize the ground between here and there. Look for depressions that might give us cover. We'll compare notes later. I've already instructed the others."

The two soldiers moved away to fulfill their orders. Zack rolled onto his back, closed his eyes, and heaved a sigh. The operation had gone far worse than even Tanner had anticipated. He clambered to his knees, took his small entrenching tool from his utility belt, and started digging.

Hours passed, and as the sun rose and illuminated the battlefield, heavy fire from Sant'Angelo started up again. Zack's squad was low enough that direct fire rounds whizzed over their heads. He scanned back across the river, and his heart sank.

For as far as he could see, artillery craters marred the landscape. At a narrow place downstream in the river, shot-up rubber boats choked the flow. Bodies of soldiers had hung up on some of them. The water itself was a murky red.

Upstream, a steady line of American soldiers ran across a narrow footbridge. Along the bank on the friendly side, even more waded into the water to attempt to cross.

"They won't make it," Zack muttered to himself. "They're carrying too much heavy equipment and the water's too deep and fast."

German field artillery, fully ranged and confirmed, rained down thousands more rounds, and the cries of the wounded lifted into the air and were swept away by the breeze. The river turned scarlet. Zack gasped at the sight. A sudden burning in his chest caused him to think that he had been shot, but then he realized that bile had suddenly surged into his throat, brought on by the scenes of horror. He took several deep breaths to stem his sense of despair and glanced back the way he had come. Many soldiers on the south bank had turned from the river and retreated to safer ground. Zack watched them grimly, joined by Tanner and other squad members.

"I told the machine gun crew to stop firing," Tanner said. "No use pinpointing our position for the Germans. We need to save our ammo anyway." He gestured across the river with his hand. "We're stuck."

Zack nodded. "Let's make sure the men are well dug in. The Germans will start aiming their mortars on this side of the river to clear out whatever's over here."

No sooner had he spoken than the distinctive pop of mortar rounds propelled from hollow tubes filled the air. "Get under cover," Zack yelled at Tanner. Then he ran to his foxhole and dove in. Seconds later, the ground on both sides of the river erupted in explosions.

10

Zack hunched inside his foxhole as mortar rounds rained down. On the friendly side of the river, the continued assault had been terminated, but on the enemy side, many stranded US soldiers hunched along the shore. On crossing in the frigid waters, the embankment had seemed a formidable obstacle. Now it offered only shallow protection from German direct fire and none from indirect fire.

When the barrage paused, Zack left his position and crawled around to check on his squad. He hardened his senses against the ghastly sight of two more dead bodies, their blood already crusting, and one with a direct mortar hit to his chest. Almost overcome with nausea, Zack turned and crawled to Tanner's machine gun nest just below the crest of the bank. "How are we settin'?"

"We lost another ammo bearer," came the grim reply. "That last batch of mortars got him."

Zack closed his eyes. Weariness numbed him, mind and body. "We lost two more down below," he said. "That brings our current strength to eight, and the Krauts have this position spotted. We need to move."

He glanced upstream. "Early this morning, we saw a company hoof it across a footbridge the engineers had put in. I didn't see them pull back, so they must still be there. We'll head that way and see if we can link up."

Tanner nodded. "I'll get the gun crew ready and take up the rear."

"Keep everyone low. If the bank dips down too much, we wade in the shallows. Better cold feet than cold corpses."

"Roger."

Five minutes later, the squad started northeast along the riverbank. The machine gun team once again had three men, and besides Zack and Tanner, three remaining soldiers made up the rest of the small unit, including the two who had joined them during the night. Despite his best effort not to think of them, the five that Zack had lost occupied his mind such that he was almost thankful for the tactical details he must think through to keep the rest alive and meet his mission.

His mind went to his first combat skirmish in the desert at Kasserine. He had been a gunner on a tank that took a direct hit. He and the loader had jumped off just before it blew up. No one else had escaped the vehicle, and Zack never knew if the loader had survived or not. The soldier had just disappeared in the ensuing dust.

Then, in the mountains overlooking San Pietro, Zack had commanded another tank traveling down a trail poorly suited for armor, where it could not support infantry, nor could infantry support armor. But the company had been ordered down that road, with insistence for the route coming down all the way from Fifth Army headquarters. That meant General Clark.

Once again, Zack's tank took a direct hit, and when he awakened from a coma in a military hospital in England, he learned that, once more, he was the only survivor. Now, he was on another apparently foolhardy mission ordered by General Clark, he had lost five soldiers, and seven others were now in his charge and looking to him to get them through this battle and back to safety.

He turned to observe those coming behind him. At the rear of the column, Tanner caught his glance, nodded, and gave him a thumbs up to signal that all the men were accounted for.

As he turned back around, a sense of foreboding gripped Zack. He and Tanner had become fast friends on the Italian campaign after Zack had rejoined the 36th as an infantryman. So closely had their minds melded in combat that they needed only a few words or hand and arm signals to grasp each other's meaning and execute. They had come to rely on each other for their lives. Suddenly, Zack realized that he had come to regard Tanner as close as his brother and sister, Josh and Sherry.

As the thought crossed his mind, he looked skyward. "Please God, don't let me be the sole survivor again, and in particular, don't let anything bad happen to Tanner."

Thoughts of Zack's siblings brought to mind images of home and his recently deceased mother. They seemed so far away, almost as if they had existed only in his imagination. He shook off the morose feelings. "These men are my family now," he muttered. "We fight for each other. We keep each other alive."

As Zack and the squad followed along the riverbank behind the point man, they passed by other small units, some whole, some reduced to one or two privates. In those latter cases, Zack ordered them to join his squad and follow along, cautioning them to keep a healthy interval. As they finally approached the bridge, the line of bedraggled soldiers had grown to seventeen in possession of three machine guns and ammo.

Meanwhile, sporadic searching fire from Sant'Angelo skimmed the crest of the bank followed by more mortar barrages; and field artillery occasionally hissed by overhead to harass more distant targets among the remaining elements of the 36th that had not yet crossed the river.

As they neared the bridge, a staff sergeant made his way toward them. He spotted Zack, recognized him as the leader, and approached him. "Hi, Sergeant, I'm Tom McCall. I got a wounded man out there and I need help to get him back in. He's been there a couple of hours."

Zack looked around. "Where's your squad?"

McCall's shoulders slumped. "We're all that's left, me an' Smitty." He gestured over the top of the bank. "I led the machine gun crew, and we was covering a company as it crossed the river on that bridge. We took lots of hits. Smitty was the last to go down. Every time I try to get to him, we get a rain of fire. I don't mind dyin' but I'd rather get Smitty back here first."

Zack looked back at the line of exhausted soldiers now crouched along the riverside. "How do you want to do this?"

"I'll go out and get him. I need someone to go with me to help carry him back, and I need your squad to lay down covering fire. I'll show you the targets. There's three machine gun sites."

Zack stared at him. "You know we'll draw fire, and not just from the machine guns. With that much firepower suddenly erupting from here, the mortars and artillery will zero in on us too."

McCall blew out a long breath of air. His eyes beseeched Zack. "We can't leave him out there."

While they had been talking, Tanner moved forward and listened in on the conversation. "I'll go," he said quietly.

Zack regarded him and slowly shook his head. "No, you won't. I'll go. You position the squad."

Tanner started to protest.

"You've got your orders," Zack said. "Set the machine guns where you can get maximum vantage on those three positions. McCall will show you where they are. When we go, open up with everything we've got. Tell the machine guns to shoot short bursts, but keep up a steady fire until we can grab Smitty and pull him back. Then, as soon as we make it back to the bank, scatter!"

Tanner started away, but Zack restrained him with a hand on his shoulder. "We're going to bring unholy hell down on this position," he said. "Tell each man that he can move to a safer place and not participate in this."

Tanner looked him in the eye and grasped his hand. "One of us won't make it out of this alive," he said. "Remember, a Star of David on my tombstone."

Zack held his gaze and his grasp. "Ah, hell," he said, "at the end of all this, I'll watch you clown at the rodeo in Gonzalez."

They shook hands, and Tanner went to set the men in place. Zack noticed that none had moved to a safer distance. Then Zack and McCall crawled to a place where they could see over the top of the bank while staying in shadows. Smitty was sprawled about thirty yards out in a depression that had provided a bit of cover from enemy fire. The machine gun had been set up there. Barbed wire obstacles had been spread across the ground.

"Mortars got us," McCall told Zack. "They hit the gun site and my men on the river while I was crawling between them." His eyes took on a haunted expression. "I shouldn't be alive."

"Let's go get Smitty," Zack said. He looked down the riverbank to where Tanner had taken his position. Between them, the riflemen were prone in a line below the crest, guns aimed forward, their eyes on him.

Tanner raised his hand and dropped it. Immediately, the machine gun spat out bursts sweeping across the designated positions over the flat ground above the river. The riflemen opened up with scorching fire.

At the same time, Zack and McCall raised themselves to a low crouch and ran, leaping over a stretched-out roll of barbed wire, zig-zagging toward the wounded soldier. Before they reached him, enemy tracers whizzed by.

A bullet struck McCall's leg. He stumbled, but continued to run. Seconds later, he and Zack were next to Smitty. The soldier was unconscious, his head lying in a pool of blood.

McCall pulled a field dressing from his jacket pocket, and within thirty seconds, he had wrapped Smitty's head with it, covering the wound. He tied it with the knot on top to apply pressure. Then, he dismounted the Browning and crossed it under his other arm next to his chest. "Grab him under one arm," he called to Zack. "I've got the other one. Get an ammo box too. There's a full one right there." He pointed.

Incredulous at McCall's presence of mind and doubtful that the two of them could handle Smitty, the machine gun, and the ammo, particularly with McCall's wounded leg, Zack complied rather than argue.

A burst of enemy machine gun fire kicked up dust at his feet. Adrenaline spurred. He grabbed the box in one hand and Smitty's shoulder in the other; McCall grabbed the opposite shoulder, and together they pulled Smitty back toward the river.

The exchange of gunfire continued at a high volume and increased in intensity from the friendly side as Zack and McCall struggled with Smitty and their armaments load. The firestorm abated and became erratic to an extent from the German side, but then mortars started falling.

The two sergeants struggling with their loads came to the barbed wire, now presenting a critical obstacle since they could not leap over it with their burdens. "We'll have to lay him across, jump it, and drag him over."

Zack stared, doubtful. "We'll cut him up."

"So will those guns," McCall barked. "It's his only chance."

As gently as possible while under fire, they laid Smitty on his back across the barbed wire. Then McCall threw the machine gun over the barrier and vaulted over it.

Zack followed suit, chugging the heavy box of machine gun links and barely landing it in the dirt on the other side before jumping. Then he reached back across the wire, grabbed one of Smitty's hands, and started pulling, only vaguely aware that the mortars rained down along the river in greater volume.

McCall was already tugging on Smitty's jacket, which had snagged on one of the barbs. He jerked the sleeve, and the material ripped. Blood seeped through where the skin was torn.

Smitty's head lolled lifelessly. The two sergeants supported it as best they could while continuing to pull Smitty over the wicked strands, ripping more clothing and drawing more blood, but then he was free of the wire. With no time to look around, they dragged him over the edge of the river-bank. Only then did they notice that firing from the squad had ceased.

So had the enemy machine guns and the mortars.

The unearthly quiet that followed dawned slowly on Zack. He had collapsed with his back against the riverbank to catch his breath while McCall checked Smitty's vital signs and continued administering first aid. Zack became dimly aware that the only prevalent sound now was that of the river rushing by.

Suddenly alert, he rolled to his right and gazed down the embankment where he had left the squad. He gaped in horror. The shore was pock-marked with craters, body parts, and streaks of blood.

In disbelief, Zack rose to a crouch. Nausea overtook him and he retched. Forcing himself to look again, he started forward. Keeping his head down, he crouched along the full length of the squad line, his heart sinking the farther he went, the stench of death rising into his nostrils. He found no one alive, most with severed limbs, and only a couple with whole bodies.

At the end of the line by the machine gun, he found Tanner. The weapon had been destroyed, and Tanner's body was draped over it and riddled with shrapnel. The soldier who had been the assigned gunner lay sprawled a few feet farther on, his blood still draining away. Zack figured that the gunner had been killed and Tanner had taken his place to meet the same fate.

Carefully, gently, Zack pulled Tanner's still body off the weapon and laid him out farther down the slope. Before leaving him, he wrapped Tanner's head in his arms. "I'm sorry," he whispered as moisture welled in his eyes. He wiped it away, and went to care for the bodies of as many of the others as he could find.

McCall met him halfway back, also attending to the dead.

"How's Smitty?" Zack asked.

"Not good. If we don't get him to an aid station, he won't make it."

Just then, rounds whizzed through the air at close range followed by the staccato of a German machine gun. Both men ducked their heads.

"Those Nazi gun nests have got to go," McCall growled. He crouched low and ran back to where he had left Smitty and the rescued machine gun. From the ammo box, he pulled out several bands of ammunition, draped some over his shoulder, loaded the gun, and started up the bank.

Zack watched him with increasing concern. "What're you doin'?"

"We're in an obvious choke point, and more of our guys'll come this way. Those gun positions have got to be taken out."

"You can't do that all by yourself." Zack fought to keep his voice down.

"Maybe not, but I can do what I can do." McCall gestured toward Smitty. "If I don't get back, make sure he gets to an aid station." With that, he loped up the bank, stopping only long enough to check the machine gun and scan across the field. Then he raced toward the closest German position.

Zack grabbed a rifle, threw himself prone at the crest, and peered after McCall, now in Zack's direct line of fire to the gun nest. Zack grunted in frustration. He could not even provide suppressing fire. He hurried a few yards to his left and tried again, but McCall had closed the distance and once again blocked supporting fire.

Remarkably, the Germans had not opened up on McCall. Then, when he was thirty yards from their position, he stopped. The German machine gun spat at him but missed. McCall held his weapon firmly against his hip and triggered two bursts.

The enemy crew did not respond.

A second machine gun opened fire on McCall. It too missed. He shifted fire to their position, and it too fell silent.

Then, the third nest opened up. McCall whirled and charged, holding the trigger down until the last of that band had been expended. The gun nest fell silent as McCall disappeared into a cloud of gun smoke.

Zack watched in admiration, disbelief, and dread as the entire scenario unfolded. Aside from intermittent shooting in other parts of the battlefield, a hush had fallen.

Zack waited, scanning the area where he had last seen McCall, but the sergeant did not reappear. Zack waited longer, then checked Smitty's pulse. It was weak.

The winter sun hung low in the sky. Soon, not only would darkness prevail, but the 36th Division would no doubt execute its next wave of the assault. Zack and Smitty could get caught in the crossfire.

Zack studied the river's current. As he watched the swirls and eddies, he saw no element that gave an advantage. Nevertheless, he had to make a move soon and without hesitation, or Smitty had no chance at all.

Crouching next to him, Zack pulled the wounded soldier's upper body into a sitting position. "You're going to live," he growled just above a whisper into the limp soldier's ear. "Too many people died to make sure you do."

He lifted Smitty and carried him into the cold, rushing water. With his left arm under Smitty's shoulder and across his chest, Zack shoved off into the current, hoping to swim downstream to the opposite shore.

11

VI Corps Headquarters, Naples, Italy

The phone on Major General John Lucas' desk rang. The call was one he expected and when he picked up the receiver, he merely said, "I'll be right out to meet him."

At fifty-four years of age, lines creased his face, making him appear older than his years, as did his white mustache and thinning hair. In recent months he carried a persistent grim expression bordering on gloomy. Events of the past few weeks had deepened apparent apprehension that he attempted to mask with little success.

His career had been steady since graduating from the University of Michigan. He had seen action in World War I, progressed during the interwar years through assignments of increased responsibility and rank, and had commanded two other army corps. As commanding general of VI Corps, he had led his troops throughout the four-month Italian campaign under General Clark.

He rose from his seat with a mixed sense of anticipation and unease, the former for the joy of seeing an old friend, and the latter for sobering advice the friend would deliver. Before he could reach the door, it burst open, and there stood Lieutenant General George Patton with his famous grin, steely eyes, polished black helmet liner with three silver stars, and his ivory-handled pistol on his belt. He strode across the office to shake Lucas' hand. "Good to see you, John," he said warmly.

A smile broke across Lucas' face as concerns momentarily dissipated. "It's great to see you, George. Sit. Sit." He indicated an upholstered chair and sat in one across from it. "How're you weathering the storm over your infamous incident?"

Called the "slap heard 'round the world," the newspapers had clamored over a story of Patton having smacked two soldiers in a field clinic. The press had called them shell-shocked. Patton had considered them to be malingerers.

He chuckled. "Hell, if I'd known slapping those cowards would cause such a tizzy, I'd've kissed 'em both." He grinned. "So my first piece of advice, my friend: don't slap any soldiers." His tone became somber. "The question is, how are you handling what you've got on your plate. Anzio's not going to be a cakewalk."

Lucas rose and crossed to a cabinet. He returned with two bourbon-filled shot glasses, handed one to Patton, and sat back down in his chair. "Cheers," he said, and they downed the liquor. "I'll tell you honestly, George, I'm pissed. I've been dealt a losing hand."

Patton sucked in his breath. He took two cigars from his jacket and offered one to Lucas, who declined. Patton lit up. "I came to say goodbye, ol' buddy. I don't see how you get through this one alive."

Lucas let out a sardonic laugh. "You never did mince words."

"You're working for a prima donna."

Now Lucas let out a peal of genuine laughter. "It takes one to know one."

Patton laughed with him. "You're right on that score." He continued somberly. "Clark's looking for headlines. He made a mess of things at Salerno, but somehow our boys carried that battle despite the chaos. But look at the lost time and soldiers. Now our boys've got to do it again." He puffed on the cigar. "What are the issues?"

Lucas stood angrily and paced to a window overlooking the harbor. "How about, for starters, that I'm supposed to command Operation Shingle, but I wasn't included in the planning."

Startled, Patton cut in, "Are you serious? Why?"

Lucas shrugged. "I don't know. Two weeks ago, members of my planning staff were flown to Marrakech and met with Winston Churchill himself. Without me. Clark had a second planning meeting three days later, and I was excluded again." His exasperation grew. "Operation Shingle has been on-again, off-again for some time. The Brits still hold to the notion that we should invade Europe through Italy despite the setbacks and casualties, but we're bogged down at Monte Cassino." He explained Clark's concept of leap-frogging around the German flank to go in behind the Gustav Line at Anzio. "He thinks Kesselring will panic and draw troops away from the south to defend the immediate approach to Rome."

Patton stuck his cigar in his mouth, folded his arms, and leaned back in his chair. "On paper the plan sounds good. Counting on Kesselring to panic is a stretch. What are the other problems?"

Lucas rubbed the back of his neck. "This operation has been thrown together. The only unit of size that I have is the 3rd ID—"

"Lucian Truscott? That's good. He's a fighter."

"General Truscott is a terrific commander, but I should have at least one more division and probably two. As I was saying, the operation was thrown together. Higher headquarters has been scraping together materiel from anywhere they can find it in the Mediterranean Theater without taking any from what's needed for the cross-Channel invasion of France."

"That's still months away."

Lucas sighed. "Exactly. We don't have enough landing craft for a larger force, the ones we have are pretty beat-up, and the 3rd ID has never done an amphibious landing." He scoffed. "Hell, yesterday we did a rehearsal along a beach a few miles south of Salerno." His eyes widened in exasperation. "It could not have gone worse."

Patton blew out a series of smoke rings. "Don't you think you might be exaggerating a bit, John?"

"You tell me," Lucas growled. "The navy dropped the landing craft too far out to sea. Not a single unit made it to shore less than ninety minutes late. None made it to the right beach."

Startled, Patton sat up straight. "That bad, huh?"

Lucas nodded dismally. "Lucian went to see Clark and made a personal appeal to do the rehearsal over, and he was refused. Clark said that the date for the operation was fixed and could not be changed. When Lucian told him that he was not asking to delay Shingle, just re-do the rehearsal, Clark said there wasn't time."

Patton's jaw dropped at the last comments. "Lucian didn't go over your head, did he?"

"Nah. He wouldn't do that. He went through me with my blessing. But you haven't heard the worst yet."

Patton stood and stretched. "There's more?" He walked to the window and watched the harbor. "Lots of activity down there."

"Yeah. Getting the equipment we have ready to go. And all the local kids are down there watching and calling, 'Anzio! Anzio!' If Kesselring doesn't know we're coming, he needs to fire his intel chief. But to answer your question, yes, there's more."

He blew out a breath of air. "That rehearsal was so messed up. The LCTs disembarked in the dark and opened their ramps. They dumped two battalions' worth of field artillery and communications equipment into the ocean. That's equipment we can't replace in time."

Patton whirled in shock. "So what are you going in with?"

Lucas shrugged. "Good troops. My gripes are not about them. But it's just the 3rd ID with augmentation from the 6615th Ranger Force and the British 1st Division."

"Hmm. That's a little light for the objective," Patton interjected. "You and I both commanded the 3rd. It's solid, and that Brit division is good. It fought down through France during the Phoney War, evacuated at Dunkirk, and saw action with us in North Africa."

Lucas nodded in agreement. "The trouble is that we don't have the vessels to bring in the rest of the corps, so the 1st Armored Division, the 504th Parachute Infantry Regiment, and the 36th Engineer Combat Regiment won't be there."

Patton's eyebrows arched. "That's a tough row to hoe." He added wryly, "I hope those Rangers do better than the ones at the Chiunzi Pass."

Four months earlier during the invasion of Sicily, the Rangers had landed at a fishing village, Maiori, at the base of the Sorrento Peninsula. The Germans observed them come ashore and allowed them to climb to the top of the Chiunzi Pass between Salerno and Naples, and then attacked from their flanks. Some died; most were captured and then paraded through Rome to demonstrate the inferiority of the elite US fighting force for the world to see.

"Colonel Darby, the founder of the Rangers, will be leading them at Anzio." Lucas shrugged. "I'm sure he learned from what happened at Maiori. But when the odds are overwhelming…"

"Maybe you should talk to Field Marshal Alexander."

Lucas grunted through a small smile and tired eyes. "I did. He told me, quote, 'We have every confidence in you; that's why you were picked.'" Lucas added sardonically, "Nice to have everyone's confidence. I feel like a lamb being led to slaughter. You wanna know the last thing Clark said to me?"

Patton stared expectantly.

Lucas went on. "He told me, 'Don't stick your neck out, Johnny. I did at Salerno and got into trouble. You can forget this goddamn Rome business.' Can you believe it? That sounds to me like an inviolable order not to be too aggressive. I'm a cautious man by nature, but that's crimping even *my* style. And then there's the order itself."

He walked to his desk, picked up a sheet of paper, and handed it to Patton. "This has got to be the worst order ever devised. Previously, my written instructions directed me to land at Anzio and Nettuno, establish a beachhead, and *seize* the Alban Hills.

"The Albans are high ground that command the beach from a few miles inland. Now Clark has changed my orders to read '*advance* on Alban Hills if the opportunity presents itself.'" Lucas spread his hands out to indicate his frustration. "So what am I supposed to do once we get there and set up the beachhead. Hold up and wait for reinforcements? Take the Albans if I get the chance? Under what conditions? Head on over to capture Rome? It'll only be forty miles away." He took the sheet of paper back from Patton and waved it in the air. "These are the vaguest orders I've ever seen."

Patton knocked ashes from his cigar into an ashtray. "You're up against it, brother. I won't lie to you. If you succeed beyond establishing that beachhead, Clark will look brilliant, and if you don't, you'll be the fall guy. What are the enemy dispositions?"

Lucas shrugged. "We'll be landing in force behind XIV Panzer Group opposing Fifth Army units at the Cassino front. That should be considered an emergency demanding all of Germany's available resources in Italy.

"Our intelligence estimates that my VI Corps should expect initial resistance from a division assigned to coast watching, four parachute battalions from Rome, a tank and an antitank battalion, and miscellaneous coastal defense personnel. That would be about fourteen thousand men. By the next day, they could have another division, an *SS* infantry regiment from north of Rome, a regimental combat team from XIV Panzer Group reserve, and maybe elements of the Hermann Goering Panzer Division.

"By the second or third day, we'll have weakened their 8th Army front, and they'll know it. They could bring in the 26th Panzer Division. That would up their headcount to roughly thirty-one thousand men in the sector."

Patton whistled. "That's quite a formidable force."

Lucas nodded in agreement. "If the attacks in Cassino succeed, that should pin down their reserves there. Clark's intel shop doesn't think that the *Wehrmacht* could bring reinforcements quickly from northern Italy. He's relying on our overwhelming air superiority to curb that. He estimates they have no more than two divisions they could bring from north of Florence, and they'd take sixteen days moving them."

He shook his head. "I'm not so sure. Kesselring threw up the Gustav, the Winter, and all those other reinforced defensive lines across the mountains in no time. He's as wily as they come."

"I've seen that. What can I do to help?"

"Nothing, really." Lucas shook his head morosely. "It's too late. Clark won't like you stompin' around in his backyard, so with only two days to go to execution, anything you do would probably make things worse." He smiled wanly. "But thanks for flyin' in to see me. You raised my spirits."

"Glad to oblige, my friend, and I can offer a consolation. Broadway has an adage, 'If the rehearsal is terrible, the opening will be perfect.' Maybe Anzio will go perfectly."

"We can hope."

Patton looked down at his watch. "Let's have another shot of bourbon, and then I'd best get goin'. I wanted to come by to say goodbye." He frowned as he watched Lucas pour the drinks. "John, there's no one in the Army I'd hate to see killed as much as you. I don't see how you'd live through it. Of course, you might be only badly wounded."

The two friends finished their drinks, and Lucas walked Patton out. In the outer office, as they shook hands, Lucas' aide appeared to escort Patton to the entrance.

The legendary general addressed the man. "No one ever blames a wounded general for anything." He pointed toward Lucas. "At Anzio, if things get too bad, shoot that old man in the back end, but don't you dare kill the old bastard."

12

January 22, 1944
Off the Tyrrhenian Coast, Vicinity of Anzio, Italy

Staff Sergeant Derek Horton gazed from his perch by the gunwale of the LCT Mark 3 tank-landing craft. It transported thirteen Universal Bren Gun Carriers and fifty-four men of the 5th Grenadier Guards' Carrier Platoon of the 24th Guards Brigade, British 1st Division. The grenadier platoon had been attached to the division for Operation Shingle, part of the first wave of Allied soldiers to land at Normandy. The carriers were lined up two abreast on the floor of the LCT while the men lounged around and between them. In the darkness, ambient light allowed Horton to see only dim reflections from the vehicles' small armored hulls.

He found remarkable that a vessel such as the LCT could be fashioned to carry so heavy a load with a draft shallow enough that it could be sailed straight in close to shore with its bow over the line where water met sand. It could then drop its flat bow to serve as a ramp and allow vehicles to drive onto a beach. Originally built to carry eleven Sherman tanks, the LCT handled the much smaller and lighter Bren carriers and their crews with room to spare.

Horton had marveled equally over the gun carriers. The tracked vehicles had been designed during World War I to carry food and supplies to troops at the front while protecting its crew with armored sides. Newer models had been developed as fighting vehicles, and Horton had seen several converted originals in combat at Dunkirk, but he had never ridden in one until being assigned to this platoon. Now he led a section of three carriers, each with a crew of four men. Replacements with experience on the carriers being scarce, Horton had been considered the best choice among those available for the position, and he accepted the job without objection despite being one rank higher than the requisite level.

The main armament on each vehicle was a Bren .303 light machine gun, but the #2 vehicle also carried a 2 in. mortar with thirty-six rounds; and the #3 vehicle brought a 3.3 in. man-portable anti-tank weapon, a PIAT, which fired a two-and-a-half-pound projectile out to an effective range of one hundred and fifteen yards. All the carriers had been equipped with a tow hitch, and the #4 vehicle would drag a 57 mm Quick-Firing 6-pounder anti-tank weapon. Those crew members not carrying special weapons were armed with Enfield Infantry rifles, and Horton's #1 carrier was equipped with a No. 38 wireless set manned by a signaler for communicating with his platoon leader.

Now, as the LCT lolled in the undulating sea off of Italy's northern Tyrrhenian shore, Horton tried in vain to pierce the darkness, to see something, anything. All was quiet aside from the low rumble of the vessel's idling engine and the moaning of a stiff breeze that blew across the water, drenching the soldiers hunched down on the craft's deck with salt-laden spray.

Apprehension mounted as the minutes ticked by and the moment approached when the temporary tranquility would be torn asunder by the sudden and ferocious unleashing of rockets and heavy gun projectiles from myriad battleships, destroyers, cruisers—any shipboard platform capable of lobbing massive destructive power across miles of night sky. The projectiles would detonate on a narrow band of beach running from Horton's immediate front where his platoon expected to land, south five miles to Anzio, and then east a mile to Nettuno.

Surprising to him was that neither he nor anyone else had seen any indication that the enemy had detected this invasion force. He had expected to see flashes of fire from the barrels of shore-based guns with attendant whistling and hissing through the air before sharp concussions that, if they did not score hits on targets, would at least churn the water into rough waves.

But nothing.

Horton had participated in the disastrous amphibious landing rehearsal three days earlier south of Salerno, and the experience had raised his concern. His unit had done its part by showing up in the right place at the right time, fully equipped, but the US Navy had dropped the grenadiers off late, in the wrong place, and too far out to sea. Grousing among the troops late that night had revealed that the same had happened across the entire amphibious force. *Could the same thing happen tonight?*

Horton had also heard the stories of the US Rangers at Maiori during the landing on the south coast of Sicily. *Could the* Wehrmacht *be luring this invasion force in as it had then, to be attacked from the flanks and rear?*

He shook off the thoughts. He had been glad to re-join the 24th Guards in 1st Division on his return to England last year after working with the Resistance in France. The unit had a long and storied history originating in 1656 as a security force to protect the exiled King Charles II until restoration of the monarchy in 1660. Over the centuries it had fought in various conflagrations, including the Napoleonic Wars, the Crimean War, the Second Boer War, and in France during the Great War. Members of the Grenadier Guards also performed the ceremonial duty of guarding Buckingham Palace. More recently the 24th Guards had fought in North Africa, Sicily, and Italy.

Horton had been with the 3rd Battalion of the Guards during the Phoney War in 1939. The unit had fought south into Belgium and France ahead of the German *blitzkrieg*, and had been part of the rearguard at Dunkirk to hold the *Wehrmacht* back while the British Expeditionary Force evacuated back to England.

During the last night of that operation, Horton had engaged in a firefight and become separated from his unit. The next morning, he had gazed in disbelief through the grassy berms of the Dunkirk beach at a harbor empty of the ships and private boats and yachts that had been part of the armada that Churchill had conjured up from the British citizenry to rescue his army and bring it back to England.

Horton had hoped to gain passage on one of the boats in the flotilla of vessels and make good his escape from France with the rest of the British army ahead of the Nazi juggernaut. Instead, on the beach that morning, he saw huge stockpiles of British military equipment lined up in the sand. Convoys of trucks, utility vehicles, and staff sedans were parked bumper to bumper all the way to the edge of the surf; ammunition boxes were stacked in rows, their respective weapons sitting next to them with barrels aimed at the sky. Field artillery, armored cars, tanks, and motorcycles stood in silhouette against the background of the sea, their main guns blasted off, disabled, so as to be of little use to the enemy.

As incredulous to Horton was the crowd of civilians on the beach, some standing back as if afraid to approach the equipment, others eagerly going through the abandoned materiel. More puzzling to him was the absence of a German presence. The British defeat had been decisive, and its army gone, leaving behind spoils of war that would cause the *Wehrmacht* to salivate, yet the Germans were not yet on the beach.

Horton took advantage of that absence to retreat north and east of the city, staying out of sight and moving at night until, three days later, he had made his way to the countryside. Alone, starved, thirsty, he found himself pilfering from garbage cans for food and drinking water from puddles.

He started finding other British and French soldiers in the same plight —abandoned by their armies in enemy territory. Small groups formed, but without any specific aim or plan.

Then Horton had met Sergeant Lance Littlefield, a natural leader in the same state of affairs. Lance motivated a group of ten to head south overland through France, trying to stay ahead of the German army and look for a boat leaving for England at one of France's southern ports. His alternative, should that fail, was to hike on to Spain.

Against all odds and being endangered often with near capture by the *Wehrmacht*, the small group had reached Saint-Nazaire. Eight had jumped aboard a trawler headed to England. Subsequently, Horton and Lance had found passage on a British troop ship sent to evacuate more of the many thousands who had been stranded. That ship, the *Lancastria*, had been promptly sunk by a Stuka dive bomber.

Horton and Lance had survived and were rescued from the sea by a member of the French Resistance. Out of options for a quick return to England, they had joined the Resistance and participated in a sabotage operation. It had succeeded, but Lance had been captured.

Thinking about Lance, Horton shook his head. The last word he had received was that the former sergeant, now a British commando lieutenant, was a POW in a high-security camp in Colditz Castle, on the eastern side of Germany. After having made a successful escape, he had been recaptured during an operation in Norway.

Horton had made his way south to Spain, reached Gibraltar, and from there, he was returned to England. During a debrief at MI-9, a new branch of British Military Intelligence established to help POWs escape and return to Britain, Horton had been introduced to Jeremy and Claire Littlefield. They had come to MI-9 seeking information about their brother Lance. A fast friendship had formed that brought Horton into the Littlefield family fold as close as their siblings.

MI-9 then recruited Horton and Jeremy to work for the organization in France with the Resistance. Both spoke French fluently, Jeremy for being a native of Sark where French was a common language, and Horton for being the product of an Irish father and a French mother who insisted that he learn her language.

Jeremy had also been trapped at Dunkirk and fled from there. He had been aided in his escape by the Boulier family. Amélie had spotted him on the beach as the German army descended on it. Putting herself and her father at great risk to help Jeremy, she had been found out. Consequently, she, her father, and Chantal had fled to Madame Fourcade's villa in Marseille, which was then beyond German reach.

Reunited there with Jeremy, a romance between Amélie and Jeremy had blossomed. Horton had been introduced to the sisters there as well, and very soon, what became evident to all except Horton was that Chantal doted on him. She was then fourteen. Although not even four years older than she, he was a combat veteran with a job to do. He had regarded her as a little girl.

Thinking of her now as the landing craft bobbed in the waves offshore at Anzio, he laughed at himself. That had been four years ago. Both sisters had joined in very dangerous Resistance missions. For that matter, Horton and Chantal had together pulled off a crucial reconnaissance mission that had resulted in Britain's obtaining critical information about German radar.

She's matured. He chuckled. *Blimey, how she has matured!*

An image of Chantal's face formed in his mind. An almost over-whelming hollow feeling seized his chest. *I'm here, and she's in France, fighting in the Resistance.*

Fear clutched his chest, the fear of never seeing Chantal again.

Hundreds of screaming rockets arced over the sky, lighting up the heavens and jolting Horton from his reverie. They were followed by the boom, boom, boom from as many gunships lobbing heavy ordnance onto the beach and beyond.

The first volley hit, and a thunderclap of explosives echoed across the waters. Even before they died down, the next volley raced through the air and made its mark, followed by another and another...

Horton covered his ears with his hands and tried to see through the darkness again. Land was visible in flashes of light from the explosions, but he could make out no detail. He glanced around at his comrades. They were scrunched together, also peering out over the gunwales, the round-eyed wonder and fear in the fresh replacements' eyes distinguishing them from the grizzled visages of fierce combat veterans.

On rejoining the 24th Guards, Horton had been assigned to the grenadiers platoon in the 5th Battalion. The 3rd was fighting with the 6th Armored Division in the southern Apennines. Although the 5th was an expansion unit, it had fought in North Africa, Sicily, and up the shin of Italy's boot, distinguishing itself as a highly effective fighting force. But it had suffered many casualties, and thus, large numbers of green troops filled its ranks. Horton was technically a replacement, but his background and experience was known; so despite not yet having reached his twenty-second birthday, he received the deference of a slit-eyed, grizzled combat veteran.

He thought about that as the naval bombardment continued. He had been green at Dunkirk and survived by his wit and the good fortune of having run into Lance Littlefield. He had certainly known his share of sabotage engagements and close calls with the Resistance in France, but he had also enjoyed an element of freedom that was absent from the grenadiers. He understood the necessity for regimentation, but he had to admit that he missed his autonomy. He could think of a thousand places he would rather be right now, and the notion dawned on him that, for the moment, he shared more in common with the newbies than he did with the veterans. *I've never assaulted a beach. How will I do? How long will I last?* He let out an impatient grunt. *When will the bloomin' jerries start shootin' back at us?*

The softening-up barrage went on for twenty minutes, and when the rockets landed, they tore up barbed wire, detonated landmines, and sliced through steel obstacles. Likewise, the big artillery rounds dropped onto buildings, roads, electrical stations, and sundry other targets, hitting them with concussive power that tossed debris high in the air, creating enormous black clouds and leaving pungent smells of spent munitions to be swept out to sea.

Then, all was quiet.

Horton glanced over the gunwale again, expecting to see the shooting flames and hear the booms of field artillery and the staccato of machine gun fire, but he neither saw nor heard anything of the sort. He glanced at a couple of the veterans, barely able to see their faces in the ambient light. They seemed to be as surprised as he was.

The vessel's engine rumbled to a roar, kicked into gear, and sped toward the shore. Horton's heart beat faster, and his palms became sweaty.

Standing next to him, Horton's driver began taking in audible, quick, deep breaths and letting them out. Horton turned to the young soldier whose eyes were wide, their whites glistening in the darkness. The man was shaking.

Horton clapped him on the shoulder and threw an arm around the soldier's neck. "Don't worry," he said. "You'll do fine."

13

Five miles north of Anzio along Italy's west coast, the fleet of infantry and tank landing craft bounced through the waves headed to the left extremity of Peter Beach, the designated attack zone that terminated on the right flank east of Nettuno. Horton's gut churned more violently the closer they came to shore, and he imagined the same must be occurring with the fifteen thousand men of 1st Division, the British contingent of the assault force, as they contemplated what they would face when the ramps dropped.

He peered into darkness across the gunwales toward the beach, expecting the salvos of bullets, artillery shells, and rockets that must come their way at any moment. But so far, no enemy response had been seen or heard.

The boat slowed, ground against sand, and halted abruptly. The men lurched forward a bit, caught their balance, and immediately vaulted into their positions aboard their vehicles.

Horton gripped the carrier's handles. His breath came in short bursts, and despite the cold air, perspiration ringed his neck and dripped from his temples.

His would be the first vehicle out of the LCT.

Driving into what? Still no enemy response.

He watched the LCT's bow. Mechanical noises sounded, and its ramp lowered. Beyond its edge, Horton saw the thin line of white sand. He leaned down and clapped the driver on the shoulder.

The engine revved, the gears meshed, and the carrier lurched forward. It rambled down the ramp, straight into salty water.

The heavy steel ramp now canted to the right as the sand beneath it had given way. The carrier drove to its end and dropped into three feet of surf, but the 85 hp engine revved, the tracks caught traction, and the little vehicle surged forward and up, clearing the water's edge and driving onto dry land.

Horton whirled to see the two other vehicles of his section execute the same maneuver, also arriving safely on the beach. They spread out on either side and behind him and followed as he headed inland toward the platoon's first position across the beach. Reaching it, they doused their engines, and listened.

Astoundingly, they were met with no resistance.

Lieutenant John Michael Hargreaves, the platoon commander, would be in the first vehicle behind Horton's section, followed by the remaining three sections. Hargreaves was a rather plain-looking man with light-colored hair, average in height and build, but with a winning smile and a sense of humor that his platoon members appreciated. He had led the veterans through combat and had gained their confidence.

They reached the position without incident and established a defensive line to their front. Hargreaves gathered his section sergeants around him.

"This is spooky," one of them said. "No sign of the enemy."

Hargreaves motioned for quiet, and everyone listened to the noises around them. All down the beach to the south were the sounds of more landing craft coming ashore and spilling their cargoes of soldiers, tanks, trucks, field artillery, and whatever implements were needed for a successful amphibious invasion.

A few hundred meters inland, local dogs barked wildly and sometimes in chorus, presumably in cottages where local residents hunkered down. No doubt, some people, during the naval bombardment, had anticipated that their homes could fall victim to either side of the conflict and had fled for safer ground.

"Let's keep our guard up," Hargreaves said. "I've been ordered to check with General Penney. He has a mission for us."

Hours later, dawn broke with the sun's fingers stretching behind an overcast sky across the Alban Hills and out over the sea. For as far as Horton could see down the beach, landing craft lined to disgorge their human and materiel loads, while more loitered offshore for a turn at the beach. Others backed away to make the return journey to their mother ships to pick up more rounds of soldiers and cargo. Still more vessels were inbound.

Not a shot had been heard anywhere along the beach, and word had dribbled down that General Lucas was ecstatic that a perfect surprise had been sprung on Field Marshal Kesselring and the vaunted German war machine. Scout aircraft had detected no German forces in the area, and neither had infantry patrols sent out during the night.

"Here's the scoop," Hargreaves told his four section leaders on return from 1st Division headquarters. "The CG wants to know where the enemy is to our front. We're going to reconnoiter the Albano Road. We'll go through Aprilia, which is a village at a major crossroads. Whoever controls it controls the area, so getting good information there is key.

"Depending on what happens between here and there, we'll go on to another village, Campoleone. We'll skirt by Lake Albano and—get this— the pope's summer residence at Castel Gandolfo." He pursed his lips. "We'll go as far up as we can until we make contact with the enemy, and then scoot back here."

Observing the somber looks on the noncoms' faces, Hargreaves chuckled. "I'm not saying this is going to be a walk in the park, but it could be like a Sunday drive. And we're grenadiers, so we should be able to handle it. No one's detected any enemy anywhere—well, let me qualify that. Down near Anzio, they shot a German soldier out for a cigarette along the beach. He must have resisted. And they've taken some Nazi prisoners. Apparently, Anzio was used for a rest and recuperation facility for the jerries."

He smiled broadly. "The idea of launching a surprise attack behind enemy lines seems to have worked."

Sergeant Hollister, Section 2 leader, broke in. "Blimey! Do ya mean we've pulled off this lunatic operation?"

Hargreaves arched his eyebrows and nodded tentatively. "It seems that way. We're trying to *find* our enemies, and that's our mission. But keep in mind, we're not looking for engagement. When we encounter them, we'll break contact and return.

"Get your men ready. Take extra rations and water. Make sure the hand grenade and ammo bins are full. Check all weapons, and be ready to depart in an hour."

He stood and looked around at the grim faces. "Chaps, we're going to Rome."

The carrier patrol set out as the sun climbed higher in the early morning sky. The vehicles necessarily followed each other in a column resulting from the width of the main road cutting through Anzio and leading northeast out of town. Every man in the platoon was wide awake as they set out, fully geared and armed, and observing their surroundings for anything untoward.

Overcast weather, and trees bare of foliage for the winter, subdued the town's charm, but it was surprisingly clean and the temperature was mild, a far cry from the freezing cold in the mountains south of the Gustav Line. Most notably, there were no signs of fierce combat or an enemy force. No rubble, no bombed-out buildings, no artillery craters.

The people along the way appeared cautiously friendly. Given that this new force driving through their midst in strange war machines had just hours ago terrorized them out of their sleep with ferocious salvoes that had pulverized their coastline, Anzio's residents regarded the soldiers with surprising, albeit guarded, warmth. They came out of their houses to observe with startled eagerness. After satisfying their curiosity, the adults looked about furtively, as if concerned about who might be watching, and disappeared back into their homes. The children, however, remained, smiling and waving until snatched roughly out of sight by their parents.

The tree-lined road led to the northern edge of town and then opened out to cultivated fields spreading for miles across their front, and to their right, the Alban Hills rose blue and magnificent into the morning haze, stretching away from the northwest to the southeast. Horton was taken with the breathtaking beauty before him and surprised by the abundance of green foliage despite the time of year and many bare trees.

Twenty miles on, they came to Aprilia, the village with a key intersection that Hargreaves had mentioned. It appeared to have been evacuated. No villagers stirred. The troops immediately dubbed it "the Factory" for its resemblance to a three-story manufacturing plant complete with two tall towers that, from a distance, looked like industrial smokestacks. The buildings around it were low, bunched together, and with rectangular windows spaced at regular intervals.

The shorter of the two towers turned out to be a church bell tower, and the taller one belonged to the House of Fascism. "This was supposed to be a model city," Hargreaves explained during a rest break. "Mussolini had this idea to build it and three others like it in areas with sparse populations: Littoria, Sabaudia, and Pontina. He insisted that the designers use modern approaches to Roman architecture." He glanced around at the village. "I find it austere and quite unattractive. I don't see anything grand about it at all."

He shifted his gaze and swept his hand around to take in the wide-open fields. "This was all marshland. *Il Duce* had it drained and prepared for agriculture." He grunted. "Maybe he did one or two good things."

"The people seem happy he's gone," Horton noted.

"Of course," Hargreaves said sarcastically, "cuz like any dictator, he did it all for the good of the people." He started back toward his vehicle. "Let's crack on, shall we?"

The clouds parted, the sun shone down, and the troops relished the relative warmth. They drove on due north four miles through Campoleone, a collection of dwellings and outbuildings barely large enough to be called a village. Not seeing anything that might be militarily significant, and having seen nothing of the enemy, they pressed on to climb narrow roads leading up through Castel Gandolfo. The road rose sharply into the Alban Hills, and as the carriers approached the crest, they saw, clustered among innumerable stately buildings, a white dome gleaming in the sunlight.

"The pope's summer palace." Horton chuckled. "When ya's got big responsibilities, ya's need big houses."

The patrol maneuvered its way through the narrow roads to where they looked down on Lake Albano and across to the papal palace perched on the rim of the volcanic crater. Taking time to admire the beauty and once more noting the cautious friendliness of the Italian people, they prepared to continue on.

"Where to now?" Horton asked the lieutenant as they re-mounted their carriers.

"We're going straight up the Appian Way to the gate in the Aurelian Wall. Next stop, Rome."

14

January 23, 1944
Bletchley Park, England

"I'm afraid the news is not very good, sir," Claire told Travis, "but you should hear it."

The commander waved her into her usual seat in front of his desk. "Let's have it."

Claire started her report as she sat down. "Berlin is abuzz with what's going on in Italy, particularly around Anzio. The fact is that they had only two battalions in the vicinity when our forces went ashore.

"Kesselring is burning up the wires to get regiments, battalions, divisions—any *Wehrmacht* or *SS* combat troops not currently engaged elsewhere—and he's moving them toward Anzio at lightning speed. He's ordered units from as far away as France, Germany, and Yugoslavia, and they're moving to reinforce at Anzio. He received a message from the *führer* to 'lance that boil,' and he's been given a free hand.

"Kesselring is puzzled by our actions at Anzio. We executed an effective surprise landing, but then, instead of pressing inland, General Lucas concentrated on bringing more troops and equipment ashore and securing his beachhead.

"You'll recall that Germany had established a very detailed plan, Operation *Achse,* to occupy Italy if Italy switched sides, which of course it did. He's using the provisions and authorities of that plan to move troops just as he did at Salerno."

Travis shook his head grimly. "I'm not fully read in on Allied plans there, but I thought that our attacks around Monte Cassino were meant to draw German troops away from Anzio to allow for a successful landing there. Operations at Anzio were then to have drawn German units back north from Salerno, alleviating pressure in the south. Then our southern units would attack the German rear and link up with our Anzio forces.

"You're saying that hasn't happened. Instead, the *Wehrmacht* reinforced in the south, and now they're reinforcing in the north from other units. We've precipitated drawing in more German strength at Anzio. That was supposed to have been an easy march into Rome, and we've blown it."

Claire took a deep breath and let it out. "That's beyond my level, sir, but I can tell you that the Germans think we've made a terrific error in consolidating at Anzio, one that offers them an opportunity. In fact, the 3rd *Panzer-Grenadier* Division is on its way now to mount an aggressive defense in a village that commands key terrain at a major crossroads." She looked down at her notes. "The name of the village is Aprilia."

She paused a moment while she took a sheet of paper from a folder in her lap. "And then there's this."

She handed it to Travis. "We intercepted this message from Adolf Hitler. It is verbatim what the *führer* sent to his senior commanders this morning."

Travis took the paper and studied Hitler's words, his expression hardening. His attention was drawn to two phrases: "The Gustav Line must be held at all costs... The *Führer* expects the bitterest struggle for every yard."

Travis furrowed his brow. "I see. Now, instead of an easy march on Rome, we're poised for a bloody fight along the beach at Anzio and more carnage at Monte Cassino."

Claire's mind flew to Paul. The last she had heard from him, he was in the Cassino area. And Sergeant Horton, now as dear to her as any of her family members, was somewhere in the bitter fighting along Italy's boot. Cousin Zack too. She had received word that he was assigned to the US 36th

Infantry Division. The newspapers were full of reports about the massacre that division had suffered in its attempt to assault across the Gari or the Rapido Rivers. Varying reports cited both rivers. Americans and Britons alike were appalled and ready to hang General Clark from the highest, nearest yardarm.

Ironically, besides herself, the safest family member at the moment appeared to be Jeremy, now operating behind enemy lines in France to prep Resistance fighters for the coming invasion in France. Then again, there was Lance, locked away in a German POW camp where anything could happen, and her stepfather, Stephen Hathaway, now held in a German detention prison.

"Yes, sir," she whispered in a hollow response to Travis' observation about the fierce fighting in Italy. "God help our troops." She pulled another sheet of paper from a file on her lap. "There's another matter just as pressing that I must bring to your attention." She handed the paper across to him.

He read it. A look of consternation crossed his face. "Are you sure of this?"

"As sure as anything we've ever reported," Claire replied. Lines from stress creased the fine features of her face. "Our bombing run more than a year ago failed to take out the Norsk Hydro power plant at Vemork, Norway. Operation Gunnerside by Norwegian commandos succeeded in destroying its heavy water production machinery, but the Germans replaced it and returned it to full production in two months. Then the Americans had a go at it with another bombing run, with no more success than we had. The plant is too well defended by mountainous terrain. But, with four major attacks against the facility, the Germans know that we understand its significance.

"Messages intercepted from Berlin's high command tell us that since our Norwegian commando raid, the plant has produced almost enough heavy water to complete building a nuclear reactor, a necessary next step for creating an atomic bomb. Our three Allied attacks against the location rattled them, so they've ordered the plant and the heavy water moved to a place in Bavaria, where the bomb will be assembled. The production machinery will be re-installed there to generate more of the substance. If the Nazis succeed, they'll complete the reactor and fabricate the bomb."

"We can't let that happen," Travis said resolutely.

"Agreed, sir. But there's more on the subject."

Travis sucked in his breath, preparing himself for more disturbing news. "Go ahead, Miss Littlefield. Let's have it."

She frowned. "Other communications we've intercepted indicate that the Germans know of some project in the United States—they refer to it as the Manhattan Project—to build a similar reactor for the same purpose. They see development of the technology as a race, with the first to fabricate an atomic bomb being the winner and able to dominate the other. For that reason, they intend to escalate their effort and increase the production of deuterium oxide by five hundred times there in Bavaria."

Travis' eyes bulged, and he leaned forward. "Do I understand that they don't yet have enough deuterium oxide—that's heavy water, right?"

"Yes, sir. The *Wehrmacht* refers to it as SH200. That's actually a shipping number, and they'll camouflage the barrels by marking them as 'potash lye.'"

Travis nodded his comprehension. "Hmm. To summarize, they need enough of this heavy water to build their atomic reactor. If they succeed in transferring the plant machinery to Bavaria along with the amount of the substance they have on hand, then they will be able to generate the rest of what's needed to complete the reactor. Is that right? To that end, they intend to accelerate their effort five-hundredfold out of a belief that the Americans are developing a similar capability? Do I understand correctly?"

"That's what their communiques indicate, sir."

"I see." Travis thumped his desk with his thumb while he pondered. Then he leaped to his feet, grabbed his phone, and dialed a number. "I'm pushing this upstairs. Now." While waiting for his call to go through, he told Claire, "Get all relevant documentation on this to me immediately."

"Of course, sir."

As she headed to the door, Travis spoke into the phone. "Please put me through. This is Commander Travis." Moments later, he said, "I must see you at once. We still have a critical situation at Vemork—What's that? Yes, in Norway. Pardon? Right, sir. I'll come with the latest on Italy as well."

Claire was about to close the door when Travis hung up. He called to her. "You heard my side of the conversation?"

"Yes, sir."

"Bring me the latest on Italy."

15

January 24, 1944
Anzio Beachhead, Italy

"Gather round," Lieutenant Hargreaves told his section sergeants. "We've got a mission, and this time it's likely to get hot."

He remained standing while the noncoms sat down cross-legged in the sand in a circle around him. They were at the northern end of the beachhead, Horton among them. "Here's the situation," Hargreaves continued when all were seated. "We arrived back from our foray to Rome the other day in the nick of time. Word from intelligence was that the 3rd *Panzergrenadier* Division was on its way to occupy Aprilia and its vicinity while we were still en route from the north.

"Nothin' like livin' on the edge, I say," Sergeant Horton joked to the laughter of his comrades.

"It's good to be lucky," Hargreaves replied, nodding and chuckling agreeably. Then he became serious. "But I'm sure you heard that while we were traipsing across the countryside, the *Luftwaffe* bombed and strafed our beachhead, so we didn't get off scot-free. Despite that, VI Corps secured a beachhead fifteen miles wide and seven miles deep." He pursed his lips with a comical face. "Not bad for a day's work.

"In the British sector that same evening, the 1st Battalion, Loyal Regiment of the 2nd Infantry Brigade spotted the German division digging in at Aprilia, or as we've dubbed it, 'the Factory.' They're fortifying, and you might recall that when I briefed in front of the towers there, I stressed that the town is critical ground. Apparently, the Germans think so too. The crossroad there is crucial."

Hargreaves paced as he spoke. "As an aside, you should know that while we were on our pleasure ride, the Loyal Regiment moved northwest along the coast road out seven miles from Anzio. They encountered no opposition either. On our right flank, the Scots Guards scouted on the main road to Anzio, with the same result. And in the center, the 1st North Staffordshires and the 6th Gordons came behind us as far as Aprilia, again with no sign of the enemy. That is, until the Loyals spotted them at the Factory that evening.

"Then, earlier today, we sent a strong mobile reconnaissance force up the Albano. It surprised an enemy outpost at Carroceto, a village a mile south of the Factory. The patrol continued four more miles inland to a place north of Campoleone. A fighting patrol is going out this evening to probe weaknesses in enemy lines there."

"What about the Yanks," Corporal Tobler, #2 Section leader, asked. "What are they doin'?"

"They've had their hands full too," Hargreaves replied. "They landed three regiments south of Nettuno at two beaches on our division's right flank. In the center, they've got the 6615th Ranger Force, the 83rd Chemical Battalion, and the 509th Parachute Infantry Battalion. The 509th seized the port. They were supposed to clear out coastal defense batteries too, but like us, they met no resistance. Since the landing, they've pushed out to the Mussolini Canal facing Cisterna, which is their objective, but they're stalled."

"So what's our mission?" Tobler pressed. "Go up to Carroceto and throw the *Panzer* buggers out?" He exchanged jocular glances with his peers.

"Something like that," the lieutenant responded. "But we'll have plenty of help. Before we get to that, let me tell you what we're up against. We've been getting quite a bit of intelligence.

"By all accounts, the Germans have been busy since our arrival. They've emplaced a defensive perimeter beyond our own to contain us, and it's being constantly reinforced. So far, we know that the *Wehrmacht's* 1 Parachute Corps re-established a headquarters south of Rome. They're sending their reserves from the southern front and diverting any that are en route there. They're moving to Anzio as fast as they can. The units we know about are the 3rd *Panzer* Grenadiers and the 71st Infantry Divisions. A large piece of the Hermann Goering *Panzer* Division is also heading this way. The intel chaps tell us that Kesselring is grabbing every unit he can, even from France, Germany, and Yugoslavia, and sending them here."

"So much for an easy march on Rome," Corporal Mansfield from #4 Section remarked.

Horton jabbed him in the ribs. "We already did that. Now we gots to pay the piper."

Hargreaves tossed them a rueful glance. "Shall we continue?" He paused to gather his thoughts. "Our division's mission is to parallel 3rd Division, drive up the Albano to Campoleone, and secure the road and railway junction—it's also key terrain. It'll be used as a launch point for future operations.

"Our brigade has been released from the reserve force—the 179th Regimental Combat Team made it to shore and will replace us in that role. So, the entire 24th Guards Brigade with a squadron of the 46th Royal Tanks and one medium and two field regiments of artillery will push up to Carroceto.

"The 1st Scots Guards and 1st Irish Guards will go ahead of us to clear a mine field. And then, gentlemen"—Hargreaves bowed with a mock flourish —"this platoon's duty and honor will be to close on and seize the Factory. It's a stepping stone to the Albans and controls that key intersection."

If he had expected an enthusiastic reception of his announcement, Hargreaves was woefully disappointed at the stone faces and silence that greeted it.

"How did we come by that 'honor,' sir, if I may ask?" Horton said, his face deadpan.

"C'mon, Horton, you know how. By the trip we made to Rome. That was considered epic in some quarters. We get to be the tip of a spear."

Horton pursed his lips and blew out a breath of air. As the lieutenant had said they would two days earlier, after leaving Lake Albano and Castel

Gandolfo on their foray, they had patrolled into Rome's suburbs and, indeed, to the very gate of the Appian Way on the Aurelian Wall. They had been mesmerized by the colossal ruins, the broken marble columns and statues, the intricate stone structure of the thousands-year-old road, and the greenery lining both sides. The relics conjured up imaginings of Roman grandeur that had since receded into history's mists. Horton would have liked to stay longer, but everyone on the patrol knew they had probably pushed their luck past good reason, and they returned, warily but uneventfully, forty miles to the relative safety of the Allied perimeter at Anzio.

"That was two days ago, and does the corps CG even know we did it?" Horton replied to Hargreaves' remark. "We were trying to *find* the enemy then, and we were unopposed. That would have been the time to go out there in force, but you just told us that the 3rd *Panzergrenadier* Division came into the Factory right behind us. That *Panzer* Group isn't there for child's play, and they've had two days to set up and reinforce. You said that two platoons will need to clear a minefield before we go through. Those mines weren't there two days ago."

He gestured at their carriers, lined up under a stand of trees. "We're lightly armed and protected by thin metal. Our usual purpose is reconnaissance, not frontal assault against a major command with heavy weapons. That village is on a flat field with miles of visibility and fields of fire.

"Two days ago, we could have had it for the taking. Since then, the jerries have moved in a whole division around the Factory and enough troops near Anzio to put a perimeter around our own. Who knows what more they'll do overnight? Do we attack tomorrow?"

Hargreaves nodded with a dismayed expression. "I've had the same reservations, and believe me we're not alone." He had voiced them at the division mission brief, pointing out that word spreading among soldiers would inform them of their grim odds beyond what came from briefings. He had flatly stated that the exhilaration following the success of the "Great Surprise Landing" had dissipated.

He rubbed the back of his neck. "To answer your question about enemy strength, intelligence tells us that in addition to what's already come in, roughly forty thousand troops are expected to arrive by tomorrow. The

good news is that they'll be spread around the whole Anzio defensive position and they'll need some time to set up. We don't know what we'll find at
Carroceto." He looked around at the men sitting on the ground, exchanging
glances with each one. "There's no way to sugar this up, chaps. The Factory
—or Aprilia, I should say—is our designated objective."

The four section leaders looked among themselves. Then Horton spoke
up again. "You lead, sir; we'll follow." He clambered to his feet and saluted.
The other three section leaders followed suit.

The attack began at dawn the next morning. Major General Penny
dispatched the 24th Guards Brigade, two field artillery regiments, a
squadron of the 46th Royal Tanks, a platoon each of the 1st Scots and 1st
Irish, and Lieutenant Hargreaves' 5th Grenadier Guards' Carrier Platoon to
advance on Carroceto.

The units had moved to their forward assembly area in the dark of
night. At dawn, they set out along the Albano Road, also known as Via
Anziati, with Hargreaves' carrier platoon in the lead. Following them on
foot, the 1st Scots and 1st Irish lined both sides of the road, and behind them
were the squadron from the 46th Royal Tanks, the field artillery, light and
heavy, and then the bulk of the 24th Guards Brigade. Once the objective at
Carroceto had been secured, the three named platoons would advance to
seize the Factory.

By virtue of his position, that of sergeant of #1 Section in the carrier
platoon, Horton rode in the lead vehicle. He found the honor to be dubious, and unnerving. With the unseen enemy spread out to his front and a
full brigade with attachments behind him including heavy armor and
artillery, he saw himself as the lead in a swarm of red ants going forward to
confront a bulldozer in motion and coming their way. He purged the image,
noticing that groups of farmers had gathered and lined the roadway ahead
of them.

The morning was cold enough that ice had formed at the road's edges,
and the farmers stood in the damp soil. As the military procession passed
by, they waved and clapped. Horton put on his best smile under strain and

waved back as his eyes roved over the bystanders and the terrain ahead. He expected that contact would come at an unanticipated time and place somewhere beyond where curious civilians congregated. They seemed to have sixth senses about where pitched battles would take place, and steered clear.

As they approached Carroceto, gunships offshore launched a salvo joined by the brigade's heavy artillery. Horton heard their booms and the hiss of projectiles slicing through the air. Glad that they were arcing over him, he watched as the rounds struck their targets in the village with concussive impact. A similar enemy response would occur at any moment and he could only hope to be missed as a target.

When they reached open fields, the carriers spread out, two sections heading to the left side of the road, the other two to the right. Their tracked vehicles easily handled the ground, prepared as it was for winter and hardened by weeks of freezing temperatures.

The rest of the brigade also spread across the fields; the tanks moved forward and kept paced with the dismounted infantry. Hargreaves too was careful to monitor the distance between his platoon and trailing units to ensure the lead vehicles did not outrun their support. Allied fighters rotated overhead, prepared to pounce on *Luftwaffe* counterparts even as German anti-aircraft guns tracked them through the skies, their tracers glistening and revealing their flightpaths and origins.

The *Wehrmacht* artillery opened up. Their heavy guns concentrated firepower on their counterparts at the rear of the brigade.

The light artillery rained their lethal projectiles on the troops advancing across the fields toward Carroceto.

Two *Luftwaffe* fighters evaded their Allied foes. They descended low over the fields and let loose with volleys of machine gun fire, strafing soldiers and tanks.

Infantrymen fell.

Two tanks ceased forward movement. Black smoke spiraled up from their turrets, and first one and then the other erupted as their ammunition exploded, killing their crews and sending shrapnel flying across their immediate vicinity, creating more dead and wounded.

From his lead position, Horton heard the sounds. He turned momentarily and sucked in his breath as he caught glimpses of the destruction taking place behind him.

Then the sound of bullets whizzed by in close proximity. Enemy direct fire had engaged, followed by the thunderous, rhythmic beat of German machine guns.

Horton ducked as far below the rim of the carrier's thin armor plating as he could. Just as he did, his signaler, a corporal, grabbed him from the rear and yelled in his ear, "Hargreaves is down. He took one in the temple. It just came over the radio."

Horton stared at the corporal in disbelief, his mind momentarily frozen. Then an extra surge of adrenalin coursed through his body. He tapped the man's helmet.

"You stay here," he yelled over the cacophony. "I'm sending Tobler over to command this vehicle. Call back to the lieutenant's vehicle and tell them to pick me up. I'll wave so they'll see me."

He jostled the driver's shoulder. "I'm taking command of the platoon," he called. "This section is now under Corporal Tobler. Do you understand?"

Wide-eyed, the driver, a private, nodded.

"Good. When I get out, slow down but don't stop. We continue the mission."

The driver nodded with a grim expression. The implication of Horton's intended actions were clear, and meanwhile the deafening battlefield chaos continued.

Horton scanned the field to identify Corporal Tobler's carrier, waited for a break in gunfire, and dived out of the carrier. Then, he ran to Tobler's vehicle. "The lieutenant is down," he yelled to the corporal. "You move to my carrier and take over the section. Put your signaler in charge of this one. One of his riflemen will have to operate his wireless. I'll be up on the platoon net in a minute. We keep moving to the objective. Got it? My vehicle is right there." He pointed. "It's slowed down for you. Get it back up to speed."

Tobler stared only a moment and nodded, his face already streaked with mud, smoke, and sweat. He took a moment to issue instructions, then clambered out of the carrier and ran to #1.

Horton watched only long enough to see that his instructions were in motion without any vehicle halting before running to Hargreaves' carrier. The lieutenant's blood-spattered seat had been cleared, his body shoved into one of the gunner seats in the rear. The displaced rifleman followed on foot behind the carrier, using it as a shield.

Gunfire had started up again. Horton clambered aboard quickly. Out of breath and gasping, he croaked to the signaler, "Get me the brigade."

"I have them now," the corporal replied, and handed Horton the mic.

"Our lieutenant is down," Horton gasped into it. "I've taken command. Mission proceeds."

The wireless squawked, and a disembodied voice inquired, "Do you need a medic?"

Horton glanced back at the body slumped in the right rear seat. "Negative."

The radio was silent for an extended moment, and then crackled again. "Understood. Proceed."

That done, Horton called on the platoon wireless to the other two sections. His words were succinct. "I've taken command. Proceed as planned."

Carroceto appeared across flat, open fields, a small set of stone buildings at an intersection. As they drew closer, Horton noticed that they appeared to be not as well defended as previously thought. The Allied air forces had chased the *Luftwaffe* away, the heavy artillery fire must have come from much farther back, and the light artillery rounds were fired from just a few guns in the vicinity of the village. Even the direct fire, now that it could be seen and heard within the context of the firefight, was not as voluminous as it had seemed at first.

The 46th Royal Tanks moved their Shermans forward and shelled the village until it had been all but pulverized. The field artillery joined in the effort, and the infantry maneuvered under their fiery umbrella, drawing ever closer under dwindling enemy fire.

"Hold back," Horton ordered his platoon. "Take cover."

When the platoon was in relative safety behind a stand of rocks, he met with his team leaders. "We'll wait here until the armor and infantry have completed their missions. Once Carroceto is secured, we'll do our job. We can't do it if we're all shot up or dead."

By mid-afternoon, the German forces in the tiny village had been subdued. "Now it's our turn," Horton muttered.

The afternoon sun began its descent. The men of Horton's platoon sat in their carriers or stood near them, awaiting the order to advance on the strange village that looked more like a factory than a place where people resided. The soldiers imagined that within hours, Aprilia would look like neither.

Horton had coordinated with the leadership of the Scots and Irish platoons. He understood the elements of their task and the danger—clearing a live minefield while under enemy fire was no mean feat. "You'll get no pressure from me," he told them. "If the tanks and artillery do their jobs with suppressing fire, you should have a go. I'll watch for the signal that you're done, and then we'll go in."

He had pulled his section leaders together for a last briefing. "Let's keep this simple. That's elements of the 3rd Battalion, 29th *Panzer* Grenadiers in there. They're good fighters, but they've cornered themselves. They seem not to have much support from their higher headquarters, or we would have seen it. Sections 1 and 2, you go in first and take up positions on either side of the buildings. Number 2, you'll start the attack on my order by lobbing mortars into the center of the building. Adjust fire as you see signs of enemy activity. Number 1, when 2 is set, you go in behind them where you can watch anything trying to escape through the rear, and take it out with your PIAT. Number 4, you do the same behind #1, and be ready to take down any Germans trying to run. Number 3, you stay in reserve and be ready to support on my order. When it looks like the jerries are subdued, all but #2 will dismount and move in tactically on foot to clear the buildings. Be careful, use your cover and concealment, don't get into crossfires. Are we clear?"

The section leaders nodded, and then Mansfield cut in, "Maybe they should leave you in charge when this is all over. You're fillin' those shoes right well, I should say."

"It's not a job I want," Horton responded grimly. "We were lucky. We haven't lost anyone else, but we got a mission, an' we're goin' against a determined enemy. Let's coordinate our limits of fire, get whatever questions you have answered, and then get to your vehicles and be ready to roll."

An hour later, Horton received the order to move to his attack position. Almost immediately, artillery shells deluged the Factory. At first, heavy return fire blasted back from inside the village, but then two Sherman tanks rolled into a safe range and systematically destroyed the walls of the main buildings. They ceased when the enemy shot only sporadic small-arms volleys and the machine guns fell silent.

"Our turn," Horton intoned as he gave the signal for the platoon to execute. When all were loaded into the carriers, the drivers set them into gear, and the four sections headed to their designated positions.

The Bren machine guns fired their barrages as the carriers careened into place. The mortar team set up and lobbed their 2.6 lb. explosive rounds into the buildings.

Resistance appeared to shift inside the building toward the rear exit.

While #2 Section held its position, the rest of the platoon dismounted and closed in, moving from one covered position to the next and providing suppression fire to their teammates as they progressed.

A group of German soldiers broke for freedom at the rear in a *kübelwagen*. A shot from #2's man-portable anti-tank weapon ended their flight with no survivors.

"Look there, Sergeant," Tobler called out.

Horton glanced to where the corporal pointed. A white piece of cloth on a stick protruded through a shattered window. "Cease fire!" he yelled. "Cease fire!"

The order took a minute to spread, but then a pall descended over Aprilia. Only muted sounds of continued battle in the distance floated across the field. For a second, Horton mulled the irony of a place with such a pretty name for a stark set of buildings constructed by fascists to be a community of residents. It now lay in rubble, with the smoke and smell of battle still swirling over it.

"Keep down," he ordered his troops, and then raised his hand to motion the surrendering soldiers forward.

The first came out alone. He held his hands high, resignation and exhaustion on his soot-covered face.

Horton motioned him toward Tobler. "Find out how many are in there," he called to the corporal. "Get Becker up here. He knows a little Ger—"

"I speak English perfectly," the captive said calmly. "I'm from New York."

Horton stared in disbelief.

"I came to fight for the motherland at my father's insistence. I am Corporal Albus." He stood awaiting further instruction while Horton took in the turn of events. "Including myself, we are a hundred and eleven," Albus added.

"Blimey," Horton exclaimed. "Did you say one hundred and eleven?"

Albus nodded. "We were ordered to fight to the last bullet, and we've done that. We are out of food, water, and ammunition."

Horton took a deep breath and let it out. "All right. Tell your mates to stay where they are until I order otherwise."

Albus complied, shouting instructions back to the men still inside the buildings.

"Are there any wounded needing immediate attention?" Horton asked.

Albus nodded. "Sadly, yes. And some dead comrades we hope to bury."

"We'll worry about the living first." Horton redirected his attention to Tobler. "Position two of the carriers facing that entry," he called out. "They'll come out one at a time, drop their weapons to the right of the door, and come forward with hands up. Have 'em pass between the two carriers and then escorted to a holding area out of sight of the entrance. Set 'em on the ground, cross-legged, hands behind their backs, and keep 'em silent. No talking between each other. Put some observation posts out, keeping an eye forward of the battlefield, but otherwise put every available man on guard around the prisoners. Use my wireless and call back to brigade immediately for medics and guidance for what to do with our prisoners. Did ya get all that?"

"Affirmative, Sergeant."

"Let me know when it's all set up." He turned back to Albus. "You stay with me. I'll need you to translate."

"I am authorized by each man inside to give our parole," the German corporal replied. "On our individual word of honor, we will offer no resistance."

16

January 25, 1944
The Vercors, France

The message from Madame Fourcade confirming Jeremy's assignment to the Vercors had arrived three days ago, sooner than expected. Ladybird had immediately placed the phone call that set Jeremy on a journey southeast to the Vercors. He took a train to Grenoble, the stately prefecture and ancient city in the Isère department in the Auvergne-Rhône-Alpes region at the confluence of the Drac and Isère Rivers.

Jeremy arrived there that same evening and met his guide without incident, then the two men drove by backstreets and roads for twenty minutes to Montaud, a picturesque mountain town above the foothills on the northern edge of the Vercors. On seeing Jeremy admiring the magnificent scenery, the guide told him, "Don't fall in love with the view. You'll learn to hate it during the next two days and nights. Do you understand?"

Jeremy nodded.

"Ah, you speak French." The man grimaced. "I'm sorry to say that tonight, you go through frozen hell."

The man's words were prophetic and accurate. At Montaud, Jeremy was handed over to another guide who took him to a shed behind a house, outfitted him with mountain clothes, a backpack with snowshoes strapped to it, and gear stuffed inside. The two men set out at a stiff pace into the bluffs and crags, over weather-worn boulders, and into the snows of the high mountains. When they stopped only long enough to put on snow shoes, the guide told him, "*Les boches* never come this way. It's too dangerous."

All night they trudged. Freezing, gale-force winds howled over the mountain crest, bringing with it large, thick snowflakes. They blanketed the ground, already thick with previous snowfalls, and impeded eyesight. At times, Jeremy held onto the guide's jacket to keep from being separated in the blizzard.

At dawn, the *résistant* led him to a small cabin on the western crest of the ridge. It was stocked with firewood and a little food. "Stay here. Don't go outside. The Germans don't patrol here. Two men in a beige bread truck will come for you sometime before the end of the day. Stay hidden until they arrive." He told Jeremy how to identity the men.

"If anyone else comes for you..." He drew his hand across his throat in a knife-like gesture. "Throw the body over the cliff. No one will find it."

Seeing Jeremy's questioning expression, the man said, "No one else knows you're here. So if anyone besides those two come looking for you, you've been compromised." He shrugged. "It's your life."

"I have one question before you go. Why did we come this way? Surely, not everyone who comes into the Vercors hikes the mountain crest through blizzards at night."

The man grunted. "Our orders were to make sure you got to the plateau with the least likelihood of encountering German soldiers at checkpoints." He gestured toward the way they had come. "This was it."

Too tired to say anything other than thank you, Jeremy waved goodbye, but he looked across the crest and saw that the cabin was, indeed, near a precipice. After closing the door, he built a fire. As the cabin warmed, he rummaged in a cabinet for food. Soon he had eaten and was snug in his sleeping bag.

The door crashing against a wall and a rush of freezing air awakened Jeremy with a start. He opened his eyes wide to find a blurred face staring down at him.

"Hurry," the man said. "We must leave before it gets too late in the day." He shook Jeremy's shoulder. "If it snows again like last night, we won't make it down the mountain. We almost couldn't get here."

Jeremy forced himself awake. "I wasn't expecting you until later." He squirmed out of the sleeping bag and started dressing.

"We have to leave before the weather closes in," the guide said. He gestured across the room. "I am Matis. My friend there is Gervais."

Only then did Jeremy notice another male figure standing by the door. He was a boy really, probably in his mid-teens with scruffy, dirty-blond hair and alert green eyes. He carried a Sten gun, and it was loaded.

Jeremy tried to remember what his last guide had said about how to identify his new escorts, but his mind was too fogged with fatigue and cold —the door was still open. He acknowledged Gervais with a nod while still continuing to dress, and when his gear was packed, the three went out to a beige bread truck. Matis waved Jeremy into the front passenger seat, and Gervais loaded into the rear.

"Be warned," Matis said as they started off, "we are near a place called Rencurel. Some people find the way there to be scary, even in summer."

Irrespective of Matis' words, nothing could have prepared Jeremy for the most extraordinary road he had ever seen. It resembled a miles-long balcony leading through a succession of tunnels carved into the solid rock face of vertical cliffs. When inside a tunnel, millions of tons of rock rested overhead. And when not in a tunnel, the road was within feet of the precipice.

Despite the shock of what he was seeing, Jeremy could not help admiring the view. The day was bright, the sky blue; and notwithstanding the freezing temperatures and jagged icicles hanging from rocky edges, the sight before him lifted his spirit, bestowing a sense of well-being. High ridges, steep forested slopes, and limestone cliffs and outcroppings lined both sides of a deep gorge, much of it covered in snow.

Matis glanced across and saw Jeremy craning his neck trying to see the bottom of the chasm. "*C'est magnifique, non*? We call it *Les Gorges de la Bourne,* for the river. The road has the same name."

Jeremy sat back in awe. With switchbacks and hairpin turns visible in the road ahead, the sight was unparalleled. Soon they reached Rencurel. "After this village, we should be safe from the weather. We'll cross through a pass and descend into lower country that's sheltered. But I'll stop at a place where you can see a big part of the Vercors."

Suddenly realizing that he had not firmly established Matis and Gervais as the right contacts, Jeremy stiffened slightly. "Where are we stopping?"

"At an overlook, just for a minute or two."

Jeremy shifted uneasily, felt for the pistol strapped on his belt inside his trousers, and cursed himself. He had not moved the weapon for easier access while wearing his thick winter jacket. And Gervais was behind him with a Sten.

Matis slowed down and steered the van into the overlook. Jeremy sucked in his breath at the grandeur of the lofty mountains overlooking a high, snow-covered plateau stretching out as far as he could see. In the far distance, he just made out the majesty of yet more snow-capped mountains.

Matis smiled happily and pointed through the windshield. "This is the best place to see the full plateau—well, a lot of it. The gorges cut the Vercors into its north and south halves. From here you can see the ski country to the north and the farmland to the south. The whole of the Vercors is about forty kilometers across and sixty kilometers long."

He watched as Jeremy gazed over the magnificent scenery. "All of the Vercors is ringed by these mountains. It's a natural fortress, very difficult to get into. That's why we can defend against the Germans. We have water, we grow our own crops, raise our own meat. We're essentially self-sufficient, so we can hold off a siege if the *Wehrmacht* tries to starve us out."

Jeremy had been on enough missions with *résistants* to know the furtiveness that usually characterized them, resulting from constant worry over being betrayed and arrested. He had also dealt with the enemy up close and knew the look of enmity common in their eyes. By contrast, Matis exuded conviviality, although with an underlying air of sadness. Jeremy could not conjecture about Gervais, who remained silent behind him.

Matis put the car in gear and started on the road again.

Jeremy breathed easier but maintained his guard. "You seem very relaxed compared to your countrymen," he observed.

"Things are different here," Matis replied. His pride in the Vercors resonated in his voice and on his face. He raised a brow to make his point. "I told you why. Life hasn't been easy, and of course we worry about our friends and families in the rest of France. We've had things much better than they have." The sadness Jeremy had noted increased a notch. "But *les boches* haven't left us untouched."

Matis gestured through the windshield. "As you can see, the Vercors has a wide plateau that sits roughly a thousand meters in altitude. The mountain wall rises up to two hundred meters higher along a seventy-kilometer perimeter, so we're well defended on most sides. The northern section, Montagne de Lans, faces Grenoble, which is where the *Wehrmacht* has its area headquarters; and the Vercors proper spreads out from *les* Grands Goulets, another piece of our defenses, to Royans.

"Only eight roads enter the Vercors, some of them like balconies tunneled through rock as you saw, but the mountains have thousands of footpaths, well known to the people who live here, so if we need to move in or out secretly, we can do that."

Matis closed his eyes momentarily and breathed in deeply. "The air is so pure and fresh here. In the spring and summer, you can smell the thyme everywhere."

He made a sweeping gesture across the landscape. "The plateau looks barren now, but when everything is green and the crops are growing..." He kissed the tips of his fingers and brought his hand up sharply in the air, a perennial French gesture of sublime pleasure. "*C'est magnifique.* The Germans don't like to come here. They know we have hundreds of *maquisards* all over the Vercors, and we are accustomed to natural dangers—wild animals, rockslides, snow avalanches. We rotate watchers posted on every access road, day and night, and we see everything that could cause us harm, including German patrols entering our fortress."

Suddenly awed by the tenacity and resourcefulness of the farmers, shepherds, foresters, and mountaineers who had whittled out a degree of independence in the midst of merciless Nazi tyranny, Jeremy looked across at Matis. "You've done well," he said. He savored the air, and then spoke cautiously. "I've heard things about an attack on a village here last January. Échevis. Tell me what happened there."

Matis' face grew red with fury, and he nodded while struggling with agonizing emotions. He did not answer immediately, concentrating instead on the road ahead. When Matis finally spoke again, his voice broke. "You should ask Roger."

Jeremy breathed easier on hearing his contact's codename, but he maintained his guard. Matis drove on in silence for a few minutes, then he glanced at Jeremy and reached over to grasp his shoulder. "I'm sorry, my friend, it's too painful."

In the rear of the van, Gervais remained silent.

After a while, Matis said, "You'll meet with Roger at Valchevrière. We'll be there in less than an hour."

As they passed through villages along the way, people saw Matis and waved enthusiastically, and he waved back. The hamlets were nestled into the sides of the mountains with stone houses and often dominated by church spires.

The road continued west, turned south, and went through Pont-en-Royans, the town at the junction of the River Bourne and its tributary, Vernaison. Jeremy almost felt like a tourist for turning his head to see homes and shops built into cliffs down to the water's edge. And again, people who saw Matis go through waved to catch his eye.

"You're popular in these towns," Jeremy observed.

Matis shrugged. "I've lived here all my life and delivered bread to all the villages for years. I have lots of friends." He gestured ahead. "We've almost arrived. One more village to go through, Saint Julien."

The village was as picturesque as any he had ever seen, and Jeremy could only smile at the villagers greeting Matis as they drove through Saint Julien. Then the road became more winding, ascended again, and wrapped around the base of bare cliffs. Thick trees lined low hills, narrowing the field of view. They were once more driving beneath intermittent limestone overhangs arching halfway over the road. The grade steepened and traversed through another short tunnel carved into the rock.

"You live in a hidden world," Jeremy murmured. "This place is spectacular."

"We wish it would stay hidden," Matis said mournfully, "at least from *les boches*."

With snow piles lining both sides of the road, it climbed and narrowed into a single lane with intermittent wide spots for passing oncoming vehicles. A final plunge in elevation brought the trio to their destination, Valchevrière.

It was a tiny village set on relatively flat ground on a hillside in the heart of an evergreen forest surrounded by snow-covered mountains. Like the towns they had passed through on their circuitous route, it was neat, its buildings constructed with care. Its homes, shops, and barns were spread a comfortable distance apart on either side of the only lane. At the street's end, a stone building larger than the others housed a gathering place that served as a café and tavern, and on a knoll at Valchevrière's northern edge, a small stone church commanded a break in the wall of mountains with a prominent view of distant ridgelines overlooking hidden valleys.

The van came to a halt outside the café, and Jeremy alighted with Matis and Gervais. "We'll wait inside," Matis said. "Roger doesn't make appointments, and no one comes to him. He'll come to you when he decides that security is sufficient."

Taken aback, Jeremy stopped and stared, slightly irritated. "Does Roger know that I came across France under orders to meet with him? I'm not here on a lark."

"I assure you he doesn't think what he does is a lark either," Matis replied matter-of-factly. "Come inside. We'll drink some wine, and I'll explain."

Rankled, Jeremy followed Matis with Gervais. The café was well lit by daylight streaming through windows, but Jeremy saw that as the day wore on, the lighting would be inadequate, relying on candles and kerosene lamps. A roaring fire at the far end warmed the single large room that had one table at the center capable of seating twenty and smaller tables around the periphery with chairs.

About twenty men and a few women lounged together, some involved in deep conversation, while others laughed, presumably at jokes or funny stories. The atmosphere was friendly and pleasant, but strange for a gathering of *résistants* living under the Nazi gun, and Jeremy realized that only the unique topography of the Vercors Massif allowed such freedom with the Nazi totalitarian boot hovering so close by.

"Two glasses of house wine," Matis called to the proprietor. "We have a guest."

For a moment, the room quieted as people paused in conversation and turned to appraise the newcomer. Matis waved them off, calling out, "Give me a few minutes and then I'll introduce my new friend, but I need to speak with him first."

He and Jeremy took seats at a table in a corner near the fireplace. Jeremy welcomed the warmth as well as the wine.

"I need to explain about Roger," Matis began. "He was nearly arrested twice by the *Gestapo*, and avoided capture by his own instincts and wit. Some of his friends were taken, tortured, and killed. They were done in by poor planning, betrayal, and bad luck."

He lit a cigarette and took a moment to savor it. "So Roger takes no chances and does things his own way. He won't make you wait longer than necessary, but he's survived a long time in his position while others have been killed or captured after only a few weeks or months."

Jeremy sighed and nodded. "Understood," he said. He raised a glass. "To the Vercors, the *Maquis,* and all your *maquisards*."

"I'll drink to that. They are all very brave."

After the toast, Jeremy asked, "Matis, what can you tell me about Roger? I know nothing about him."

Matis grunted. "You know the rules. I can't tell you much."

"No argument, but obviously I'm going to meet him. What's he like to work with? That's what I'm here for."

Matis pursed his lips. "What can I tell you?" He leaned back in thought. Then he gazed around the room, paying attention to the various groups and individual faces. "He is much loved here. There is not a man or woman in this room—or on the whole of the Vercors—who would not take a bullet for him."

Jeremy could not hide his surprise. "But he's an Englishman. Why would your people care so deeply about him?"

"Because he would do the same for us," came the ready reply. "We know that's the case by the respect he demonstrates, the affection he shows us, and by the things he teaches us to stay alive. He never sleeps in the same place twice in a row, and no one knows where he'll go next. He'll show up at a farmhouse, introduce himself politely to the residents, state that he's a British intelligence officer, and request to stay the night. Word about him circulates among French patriots. They willingly provide food and shelter knowing two things: that he'll leave the next morning with no fuss, and that they put their lives and their families at risk by helping him. But they do it willingly because he fights for us. He fights for France. He's been in fire-fights alongside the *Maquis*."

Jeremy listened, awed by the depth of feeling that Matis expressed for the mysterious Roger. Then he chuckled. "I was supposed to be here to offer him backup and my experience, for what it's worth. From the sound of things, he doesn't need my help or advice."

Matis arched his eyebrows and shrugged, as if to say, "I have no idea about that." Then he remarked, "I'm sure he'll know what to do."

A man approached their table and requested a moment alone with Matis. Together they moved off into a corner of the tavern and engaged in whispered conversation. When Matis returned, his shoulders sagged, and his face had drawn tight in anguish. "*Les boches* hit us again, in Les Barraques, a village near Échevis." He rubbed his face. "I know those people, all of them. The Germans burned all their houses down this morning, probably while we were making our way down to Rencurel."

"I'm so sor—"

Matis gritted his teeth. "There's a Free French army officer on the plateau, a cavalryman, *Capitaine* Geyer. He brought his 11th Cuirassieres to the Vercors, and he camps above Saint-Martin. He thinks he's better than everyone, and he treats this war like a game. But right now, he's the military commander here. At the beginning of the month, he raided several small

German garrisons around Grenoble. He leads his men on horseback; they strike and then gallop away. He's proud that he came away with three hundred kilos of dynamite, a truck, and some horses and telephone wire, but the Germans are retaliating. With the invasion coming this spring or summer, they can't lock down too much manpower or equipment, so they don't stay. But they're killing our people, and they don't care if they're men, women, or children." He sighed deeply. "That's two villages so far, and I promise you, they're not done."

Jeremy suddenly noticed that everyone in the café had gone silent and now stood or sat around with gloomy faces. Matis grunted. "The man who brought me that news had another message." He took a folded piece of paper from his pocket. "This came from Roger. The weather did not favor us. His flight from London was cancelled and he has no chance of arriving for at least two more weeks. Drink up, my friend; you'll be a guest here for a while before your work begins."

Matis' words were prophetic. Three days later, the Germans struck again at Malleval. A group of French Alpine veterans had decided to keep themselves separate from the rest of the Vercors *Maquis*. They had established both a base outside of the protective ring of mountains and a round-the-clock sentry.

The *Wehrmacht Gebirgsjäger*, mountain troops, surprised the guard, cut communications lines, and mowed down the veterans with machine guns. Then they locked the village inhabitants in their homes and set the houses on fire. Only five of the Alpine veterans escaped.

"That's three villages and hundreds of deaths," Matis growled when telling Jeremy the news. "I'm sure they're not finished. They're sending us a message: 'Stay out of our way, or else.'"

17

February 10, 1944

A very tall man approached the table where Jeremy breakfasted with Matis at the lodge. He had been sitting within shadows in the opposite corner. Jeremy had noticed him, but knew not to ask questions about anyone he saw without a tacit invitation. As the man crossed the room toward them, he greeted Matis with a warm smile and turned to Jeremy. "Monsieur, I see that you've ripped your trousers."

Jeremy stared up at him. "And I heard that your daughter was late for school last Tuesday. Roger?"

Roger nodded. "It's silly, the things headquarters thinks up for us to say to ID each other, but it works. Labrador?"

Jeremy nodded. "Labrador" was the codename Fourcade had bestowed on him two years earlier. "I'm relieved to finally meet you."

"Finish your breakfast. I've arranged a place where we can speak freely." He thanked Matis for retrieving Jeremy, and then crossed the room to visit with other patrons.

Jeremy took a moment to observe the quiet icon. He guessed that Roger must stand at least six and a half feet tall. His face was narrow and long. His shoulders sloped, and his skin was weathered. He combed his dark hair close to the scalp and sported a groomed mustache that grew to the corners of his mouth.

Jeremy's meal finished, he approached Roger, who excused himself from the men standing around him, saying, "I have to go over some things with my new friend."

Jeremy noticed that the eyes of the partisans had modified from the neutral and curious expressions he had seen when he first arrived to warm and accepting. Roger raised his hand in a friendly gesture. "I'll be back with you later."

Being a keen observer for most of the nearly two weeks since arriving at Valchevrière, Jeremy had watched and listened. Since his position within Jockey was unknown even to him, he had initially kept his distance. But as days passed and he became a familiar figure and was known to speak French with an impeccable southern accent, he was regarded with less suspicion and more friendliness. Then, when he offered tips on aiming and shooting to individual *maquisards* with positive results, he became a respected figure.

He was impressed with the *maquisards*, most of them barely beyond boyhood. They had fled to the Vercors and other mountainous regions ahead of German sweeps to grab military-age males for forced labor in Germany's arms manufacturing plants. Organized into a loose confederation, they were known collectively as the *Maquis* for the scrubland on which they lived. Their intent was to recapture their country.

Despite scarce funds, insufficient weaponry, living off the land in many cases, and being short on supplies, the *maquisards* were training seriously to become a fighting force. Many had already carried out acts of sabotage against the *Wehrmacht*, but Jeremy noted that, at least here in the Vercors, they had only one rifle to share between every five *maquisards*, and the bearer of that weapon had to earn the privilege. They had uniforms of a sort; however, they drilled, they maneuvered, and they threw their hearts into training for the real fight they knew would come against battle-hardened *Wehrmacht* soldiers.

After a short walk through the snow and entering a nearby dwelling that was warmed by a large fireplace, Roger told Jeremy, "We have the loan of this house for a few hours and a security group keeping watch, so we won't be disturbed." He grunted. "We don't know when the jerries might try something, but we'll get plenty of warning. And by the way, sorry about the route you took to get here and keeping you here in Valchevrière these past two weeks. I couldn't be sure I would be here on your arrival, and I didn't want you exposed to too many people until we had met and discussed our working relationship and plans, so I brought you to the remotest location by the route that was the least likely to be compromised. We'll be moving closer to Saint-Martin where the civilian leader of the Vercors has his head-quarters. His name is Eugène Chavant."

"No problem. I'm here, and I quite enjoyed myself," Jeremy replied. As he took a seat on a wooden stool in a corner that served as a kitchen in the single room, he said, "I don't quite understand why I'm here. I was told that I might help train the *Maquis* in tactics or intelligence-gathering, but what I'm seeing is that you have things in hand. You're a local legend."

Roger laughed. "You were brought here under false pretenses," he said. "You're here to be my deputy."

Jeremy stared in surprise. "I'm what?"

Roger chuckled. "I came through Paris on my way here and spoke directly with Georges Lamarque, and he's all for the arrangement. If something happened to me, we didn't have anyone here to take my place. A large part of the job is to liaise with SOE and get more guns, ammunition, money, and supplies for my network. For that to happen, we have to show results, which means we have to train hard and execute aggressively to help the Resistance in our area meet its objectives.

"I'm supposed to prepare you to do exactly that in my absence, but there's another reason too. I'll get to that in a minute, but first you need to understand the scale of what we're talking about.

"I'll make it simple. Right now, there are roughly fifteen hundred *maquisards* in the Vercors. But beyond here, running from the Mediter-ranean north to Lyon, and across the country to the Swiss and Italian borders, we've built a larger organization, the Jockey Network. We're in Alpes-Maritime, Basses-Alpes, Bouche du Rhône, Haute Alpes, Isère,

Rhône, Drôme, Vaucluse, Gard, Ardèche—and I could go on. We operate over seventy clandestine airfields, and we have roughly twenty thousand *maquisards* in our organization."

Jeremy's eyes widened in admiration. "What you've done is incredible."

"I'll explain more, but one point to understand is that I command nothing. I'm the link between Jockey and London. I'm an adviser and a coordinator for bringing in resources, and while I carry influence, the command decisions belong to the Resistance commanders. And I have to tell you that the French Resistance is not confined to just the people doing the sabotage and ambushes.

"Keep in mind that when a country is occupied, the populations can still resist. Workers slow down engine production for military vehicles at Peugeot and other factories. Mothers risk themselves and their children to feed, shelter, and clothe Resistance fighters—they are part of the Resistance too. Farmers hide crops for the use of their own people and the *Maquis*. All of that goes to finally defeating the *Wehrmacht*.

"In the Vercors, Chavant is the recognized leader, the *patron*. He's code-named Clement, and you'll meet him later. He's pushing a concept, Plan Montagnard, to turn the Vercors into a vast base of operations from which to strike the Germans from their rear all over France. The plan is gaining support."

Jeremy listened, absorbed. "All of that's incredible," he said slowly, "but someone's made a big mistake. I don't have the experience to handle what you do."

Georges shook his head. "I don't think there's been a mistake, Jeremy. I know about you. I was in Britain when you escaped from Dunkirk and rescued that toddler from the *Lancastria* when that ship was bombed. The story was in all the papers when you made it home to England with the boy.

"I know you flew Spitfires and Hurricanes during the Battle of Britain and then nightfighters during the *blitz*. Then you helped organize the Resistance around Marseille, volunteered for the commandos, and were in the operation at Saint-Nazaire—there's never been a bigger raid or one more successful. You liaised with General Giraud when the Allies decided that he should lead the Vichy troops in North Africa, and you impersonated a *Gestapo* officer to help bring key documents safely out of Paris for the Allies."

When Roger finished speaking, Jeremy glanced at him awkwardly. "I did my job."

"Exactly. You're resourceful, effective, and you don't let your successes go to your head. You care about the people you serve with, and that's a crucial ingredient I require in anyone I work with closely." His eyes twinkled. "Winston Churchill himself endorsed you to me. He said you were 'respectfully insubordinate and utterly bound to keeping state secrets, even when being interrogated by no less a personage than the prime minister himself.' You apparently briefed him once, though he seems to be better acquainted with your brother Paul."

Jeremy sat red-faced for a moment without an adequate response. Finally, he stated flatly, "So I'm here to learn from you."

"You are, and I expect you to provide your experience fully to train the *maquisards*. You have a lot to teach them."

"I'll do the best I can, under your direction, of course."

"Of course," Roger said, chuckling. "I've been warned about Littlefield modesty. I was told that you could not shake it if your life depended on it."

Jeremy flushed red again. "That comes from my mother, sir. She always pressed on my siblings and me that the moment we take ourselves too seriously, we've set ourselves up for severe embarrassment or failure."

"And your mother would be the Dame of Sark?"

"Correct, sir. You seem to know a lot about me."

"I insisted on it. I met with Fourcade and your boss at MI-9, Major Crockatt, in London. She and Alliance are SOE assets, as you know, and of course Crockatt's main effort is to help escaping POWs get home. But the two of them cooperate on missions, and escapes are being discouraged now, pending the coming invasion. We were looking for someone to fill my deputy role, and I was particular about candidates. Phone calls flew between offices, and MI-9 offered you up. You've been transferred to SOE."

Roger leaned against a windowsill and crossed his arms, amused as he watched Jeremy absorb the information. "Now here's the thing," he continued. "As Georges told you, the invasion will happen. We just don't know where or when, but it could take place along either France's southern shore or anywhere along the Atlantic coast. We have to train to be ready for it.

"I'm expected to provide fifteen thousand *maquisards* to help sabotage roads, bridges, factories, power plants, communications centers, manufacturing facilities... The list goes on. In addition, and this is tricky, we have to safeguard certain assets in the ports and along the coast that the landing force will need on coming ashore."

Jeremy had remained on his feet, pacing slowly, arms folded. Now he sank back into his seat. "Sir, this is all a bit much. Have you thought that my supposed successes might have been blown out of proportion? This job might be too big for me."

Roger laughed. "I'll find out soon enough, and if that's the case, I'll send you packing. But consider this: two years ago, I was a schoolteacher and a pacifist."

Seeing Jeremy's surprise, Roger pressed on, "It's true. I opposed all war and declared myself to be a conscientious objector. As my government-mandated public service, I worked on a farm tending sheep for slaughter to feed the military."

He paused, and Jeremy noticed a somber expression cross Roger's face. "My brother was a fighter pilot and was killed," he said. "In that moment I recognized that evil truly exists, and that it must be stopped by whatever means." His voice rose slightly with emotion. "The Nazis have enslaved whole countries—almost the entire continent of Europe. They bombed us mercilessly in Great Britain. They round up women and children all over Europe and massacre them by the hundreds. They've utterly destroyed whole villages. And those are just the things we know about."

He stopped talking, and silence descended. It lingered a few moments, and then Roger chuckled wanly. "So if I can go from being a schoolteacher to being a major in His Majesty's army, organizing and leading the Jockey Network, then with your background, you can certainly learn enough from me to continue where I leave off. I hope that gives you some reassurance."

Jeremy shot him an admiring look. "That's all hard to believe, sir, but I'll take whatever reassurance I can get."

Roger waved aside the comment. "What are your questions?"

Jeremy thought a moment. "How did you build such a large organization so quickly? That is absolutely amazing."

"Perhaps crediting me is inaccurate. What I really did was unite organizations that already existed. Through SOE, I got them arms, supplies, and money and convinced these groups that we must unite to meet our common enemy."

"That can't have been easy for such a large network spread over so wide a territory."

"It wasn't. But much of the work was already done by a man called Jean Moulin. He was the heart and soul of building the Resistance. Have you heard of him?"

Jeremy shook his head.

"I wouldn't have expected you to. Unfortunately, he was captured and executed last July. He and Madame Fourcade were acquainted and shared mutual respect. Georges too. Moulin was charming, very young-looking, but quick-witted and brave; and he loved France with a passion. The people loved him for it."

Intrigued, Jeremy listened with rapt attention.

"He was arrested, tortured, nearly died, and was then released," Roger went on. "He went to Béziers near the southern coast, and there pretended to retire into being a connoisseur of modern art. In reality, he had taken on a pseudonym, Joseph Mercier, and he actively sought out contacts who could help build a Resistance movement.

"Before the first full year of the war was over, while you were flying in the Battle of Britain, he convinced the Gaullists, communists, anti-communists, disaffected ex-military, and others to set aside their political differences until after the war and fight to liberate France. That November, de Gaulle signed a directive appointing Moulin as his representative to the newly formed Committee of National Liberation. Moulin overcame suspicions between factions, and rather than focusing on counter-propaganda, he went across the country using his wits to initiate direct action against the *Wehrmacht*—acts of sabotage, with resources that started flowing through him."

Roger paused. When he spoke again, his voice lowered and became somber. "As I said, he was the heart and soul of the Resistance, and he inspires every *maquisard*. In fact, he approved Plan Montagnard months before he was captured."

"How was he taken?"

"We're not sure whether he was betrayed or if they caught him because of a security error. He chaired a meeting in Caluire, near Lyon, that was raided by the *Gestapo*. A particularly vicious *SS* commander there, Klaus Barbie, had Moulin beaten for days and then shipped to the *Gestapo* in Paris for further interrogation. Moulin died somewhere along the way, but he never gave up a single piece of Resistance intelligence, and he had it all in his head."

Roger remained reverentially quiet for a few moments and then drew in a deep breath. "When the history of this war is written, his name will figure prominently near the top of the list of heroes." He tossed his head. "Anyway, among our groups we have all the same types of people he brought together: Gaullists, libertarians, socialists, ex-military, communists, etcetera. Setting aside differences at least until after the war takes regular, tricky convincing, patience, and negotiations. But the arrangements have so far held. The chief point is that, if the factions don't unite, we'll have no France to save."

Jeremy absorbed Roger's words as his next question formed. "Are there any main groups here in the Vercors?"

"Three," Roger replied. "The first were people who heard General de Gaulle's call to arms over the radio from London right after Pétain surrendered France. That group recognized the advantages that the Vercors offers for both offensive and defensive operations. They gathered here but didn't organize well until 1942."

"When you arrived?"

Roger shook his head. "I won't take credit for what they did. They had no arms or money, yet they still took the fight to the enemy."

"And you talk about my modesty. What about the second group?"

"They called themselves *Le Movement Franc-Tireur Dauphinois*. Don't ask me the origin of the name. I don't know it. But it was formed by two doctors, Martin and Samuel, and a third patriot, Aimé Pupin. They set up in the forests around the Vercors.

"Members of the third group came from veterans of the French army, which was disbanded in November of last year. They were mainly from Lyon and trooped down here *toute-de-suite*. They are trained fighters, and many are combat veterans."

"Is that the group led by Captain Geyer? If so, I've picked up that the locals don't like him. They blame him for the German raids into the Vercors."

Roger sighed. "And they might be right. I believe a new commander will be arriving soon. Hopefully, he'll be able to tame Geyer." He furrowed his brow. "The man is a fighter, though. We'll need him."

Jeremy shook his head. "This is all quite incredible."

Roger smiled. "The people of the Vercors are proud of their *esprit* and capabilities, and rightfully so. The organization here is a significant part of the Jockey Network." He sat quietly again, and then asked, "What other questions do you have?"

Jeremy grunted. "I'll have many, I'm sure, but I have one now that Matis said I should address to you. What happened last year at Échevis?"

Roger suddenly looked tired, reluctant to speak. His voice remained subdued. "Any opposition can be overcome with sufficient resources, especially with better technology, which the Germans certainly have. So our position is still tenuous, even here in Fortress Vercors Massif."

He took in a deep breath and exhaled before continuing. "Échevis was a tiny village. It was built right into the cliffs. You must have passed near it on your way in. It's one of the only villages the Germans could get to relatively easily, even if opposed. It's not the only place the Germans have raided in the Vercors, but it was Matis' home.

"I should tell you that the *maquisards* here are anxious to fight. They're not a real fighting force yet, but they've gone out and blown up bridges, hit supply convoys, and the like. Back in November, three months ago, some *maquisards* attacked a German staff auto on one of our access roads, killing the driver and the officer inside.

"Matis was out on his delivery circuit when the *Wehrmacht* retaliated. They attacked up that road in force, and when they came to Échevis, they killed every man, woman, and child. Then they burned down the village. Matis' wife and little girl were among those slaughtered."

Jeremy took a deep breath, shaking off his shock at the horror. "That poor man."

Roger leaned against the wall. "I've been to see the ruins," he said, his lips quivering. "It's sickening. How anyone can do that to other people is beyond my comprehension. We're talking babies, young mothers..."

He stopped talking and breathed hard. "That's why I can't be a pacifist. There's no reasoning with evil which cares nothing for human beings." He sighed. "I'm not saying that all Germans are bad. I'd like to believe that most of them are good. But somehow, evil infiltrated them, cajoled them. It now rules them and is intent on subjugating or exterminating the rest of us. We can't let that happen."

When Roger finished speaking, Jeremy was at first quiet with his thoughts. Then he said, "I've seen the cruelty, the bombs falling on innocents during the Battle of Britain and the *blitz*. Was that the first assault into the Vercors?"

Roger shook his head. "Not the first, but it was the worst to date until Les Barraques and Malleval."

"So the people here have witnessed the murder of friends and family only recently."

Again, Roger nodded. "That's true, but coming from all over France as they do, many if not all of the *maquisards* have seen atrocity up close."

"I'm sure," Jeremy said, "but let me add another view. I was shot down twice during the Battle of Britain. The first time, I parachuted into a field a few meters from the German pilot who downed me. One of my mates got him in the same dogfight right after I was hit. After we both parachuted to the ground, we met, surrounded by British farmers pointing guns at the German. He surprised me completely by facing me and saluting before a constable took him away. I remember feeling sorry for him, given how he would likely spend the rest of the war.

"The second time, my Spitfire was shot up and I lost consciousness. My kite spun out of control. Fortunately, I came to and managed to get it back in hand and set it down in a field. As I was landing, two German fighters flew past me on either side. They had followed me after I was hit, and apparently, when they realized I had been incapacitated and then came to and landed the plane, they came by and saluted. They could have killed me easily. My point is that good German people are still to be found. We have to win this war and get the good ones back in charge of their country."

Roger listened attentively. When Jeremy had finished, he stepped forward and gripped Jeremy's hand. "Georges told me you'd be an excellent choice. Welcome."

A reflective look crossed Roger's face. "I should add to all I've said that few people outside of France understand how deeply the German occupation and the Vichy government broke French society and culture. The social organizations belong to the state now. Parents fear for the futures of their children growing up under totalitarian control. They don't even allow them to go to school or church because they don't want them to be corrupted. I'm sure the same is true in other countries the Nazis have conquered."

"I've seen that in Marseille, Lyon, and Paris," Jeremy replied somberly. Then he added through gritted teeth, "Let's win this thing."

18

February 14, 1944
Hardangervidda, Norway

Second Lieutenant Knut Haukelid stared caustically at the decoded message in his hand. Then he glanced across the table at his wireless telegrapher, Second Lieutenant Einar Skinnarland. "London wants us to sink the *Hydro*."

Einar nodded, eyes closed, while rubbing his temples. "Do they know the cost in lives?" he hissed. "Women. Children. Innocents."

Haukelid nodded. "They say the numbers will be thousands of times higher if we fail. Maybe millions."

"I know. I just don't know how I'll live with myself afterward."

The two men were the last members remaining in Norway of a commando raid, Operation Gunnerside, mounted almost a year ago on the steep mountain walls of Vestfjorddalen, a valley in Norway so deep that the sun never directly warmed its floor.

Norsk Hydro, a plant at Vemork producing ammonia for the manufacture of fertilizer, was perched on a plateau on the valley's northern wall and was surrounded by thick forest eight miles from the village of Rjukan. As a byproduct the facility also produced heavy water, known to scientists as deuterium oxide. The plant had been the only resource worldwide that could provide the substance in volumes sufficient to activate an atomic reactor, key to Nazi ambitions of building an atomic explosive device.

Two bombing raids, one British and one American, had failed to destroy Norsk Hydro, but the Gunnerside commandos, seven men in all, had succeeded in climbing the steep sides of the valley undetected, entering the plant, and placing small bombs inside the heavy water production machinery, destroying it. The deuterium oxide spilled onto the floor, rendering it useless.

All the commandos had escaped safely. The others had left Norway to engage in the war in other places. Haukelid and Einar had remained in Norway near the southern edge of the vast, frozen reaches of the Hardangervidda. The glacier-covered plateau, known across Norway as the "Vidda," incorporated nearly twenty-five-hundred square miles, and was the largest such plain in Europe.

Haukelid, born in New York City to Norwegian parents who returned to Oslo when he was still a child, was skilled at disappearing into crowds. He was able to do so because, at five foot ten and just thirty years of age, he subdued his appearance to be less than memorable. He worked at maintaining fitness, and thus had an impressive chest and muscled shoulders, but he masked them with loose clothing. Despite his blond hair, he bore a slight resemblance to Humphrey Bogart, and his blue eyes could fascinate equally with humor or cold hard determination.

Einar Skinnarland, the telegrapher, had grown up around Lake Møs, Norway's largest lake ensconced in the mountains at an altitude high above Vemork. The lake fed the plant's water supply. Now twenty-five years of age with flaming reddish-blond hair, his avid outdoor lifestyle had hardened his physique. Further, Einar was an engineer at Norsk Hydro. Before the successful Gunnerside raid, he had fed British intelligence with information regarding the quantity of heavy water produced and at what levels of purity. Never having raised suspicions about his involvement, he continued working at the plant after the fact.

Being thoroughly at home on the Vidda, Haukelid and Einar had enjoyed free range of it since their raid, and had used it as their sanctuary —German soldiers ventured no farther on the vast, frozen plain than they could safely return from before nightfall. From the Vidda, Haukelid could train and lead the Norwegian Resistance and strike at the *Wehrmacht* almost with impunity.

Besides being chronically short on supplies, only the threat of reprisals stayed his hand against the Nazis, who had punished whole villages for actions against the German occupiers. In a recent such retaliatory action, the German *Reichskommissar* Josef Terboven sent a busload of Norwegian residents from Dalen to a concentration camp in Grini because a local girl, Åse Hassel, had refused to go out with him. She had been among the detainees.

Her crime was that, when Terboven persisted, she had spit in his face.

Åse was fortunate. Other infractions in other places had resulted in massacre.

Shortly after the Gunnerside Operation had destroyed the deuterium oxide machinery at Norsk Hydro last year, Einar informed British intelligence that the Germans were intent on rebuilding the production facility and would complete its reconstruction within eighteen months. London directed Haukelid and his *résistants* to monitor the plant and keep British intelligence apprised.

Then in late November, the Americans once more bombed Vemork, this time with a flight of roughly two hundred B-17 Flying Fortresses and B-24 Liberators dropping nearly eight hundred tons of deadly bombs. The target, Vemork, had been hardened, and minimal damage was done. Tragically, a navigation error had resulted in massive ordnance being unleashed on Rjukan, killing twenty-two civilians: men, women, and children.

The mission had been seen as a failure, and the loss of innocent life a travesty. The Norwegian government-in-exile, which had not been consulted before the operation, was furious. However, more significantly, the raid had signaled to German High Command that the Allies grasped the significance of the work at Vemork, and that to preserve the plant's technology, it must be moved. They set about doing so immediately.

Einar learned that the *Wehrmacht* intended to move their heavy water to Bavaria, Germany. They would do so by railing it down the mountain to the Rjukan train station and on to an isolated ferry harbor at Mæl, to be loaded onto the SF *Hydro* for further transport. The cargo was designated as "SH200."

British intelligence sent word to Haukelid that the shipment must be stopped.

By any means.

This time around, a commando raid on the plant was out of the question. Besides the plant being hardened against bombs, the fence around it had been rebuilt and strengthened, the illumination increased such that it was bathed in light around the clock, and the guard unit had been replaced by crack combat veterans.

Two of the twelve flatbed cars were to be loaded with forty-three drums, each carrying a volume of one hundred and five gallons of heavy water. The required machinery would be loaded on the ten remaining cars. All of them would transfer onto the ferry, which would carry them across Lake Tinnsjå for overland passage down through Sweden and Denmark to Haigerloch-Hechigen in Bavaria.

"Through Sweden?" Haukelid asked, incredulously. "Will Stockholm allow that?"

"They're not being given much of a choice," Einar replied, "and the cargo is being billed as a harmless shipment. If the customs officials inspect, all they'll see is water."

Haukelid grunted. "Amazing that water could cause so much fuss."

He had determined that attacking the train as it transferred the shipment was not an alternative. A German ammo dump existed along the railway, but its security provisions were unknown. Haukelid estimated that at least fifteen minutes would be required to mount such an attack against the dump with questionable odds, particularly given that it would have to be detonated at the exact moment the train cars passed by.

Responsibility for moving the precious cargo out of Vemork had fallen to General Nikolaus von Falkenhorst, Commander-in-Chief of German forces in Norway. He had instructed his troops that, "When you have a chest of jewels like this, you plant yourself on the lid with a weapon in your hand," and he had followed through with the tightest security measures, to include orders for stationing troops on and around each flatbed car as well as along the entire eight-mile train route.

"Their plan has only one weakness," Haukelid told Einar. "The *Hydro*. We have one week to prepare. Let's get the team together to figure out how we do this."

Haukelid organized quickly. On learning of the mission to sink the ancient ferry with its passengers and cargo as it crossed Lake Tinnsjå, Norway's deepest inland body of water, his other team members' reactions were similar to Haukelid's and Einar's: horror and dread.

Among them was Rolf Sørlie, a construction engineer at Norsk Hydro and an active member of the Resistance. Last year, he had provided a marked-up map to the Gunnerside assault force for the commando raid on the plant.

In his mid-twenties when the Germans invaded Norway, Rolf was small in stature, fluent in their language, and had a physical condition that had left his left hand permanently in a half-clench, removing him from suspicion when soldiers searched his house. That had been fortunate because not only did Rolf hide two radios in his attic, but also, from the time the Gunnerside commandos landed to raid Norsk Hydro, he had run supplies to them, as well as information pertaining to the plant. Doing so had required strenuous treks up and down the mountain and into the Hardangervidda. Clearly, the Nazis had underestimated Rolf.

Einar had recruited another Hydro Norsk engineer to join the team, but due to the risk to the man's family from reprisals after mission completion, Haukelid declined the man's participation but accepted yet a third plant engineer, Knut Lier-Hansen.

Handsome with dark hair and fine features, Lier-Hansen was born in Rjukan and had been a Norwegian army sergeant who fought to oust the Germans at the invasion. He had avoided capture, staying just beyond their reach through wit and the help of friends, and went to work for Hydro Norsk without a hint of suspicion. He and Haukelid were of similar personality and became fast friends immediately, sharing the passion to free Norway from the Nazis.

Besides the assault team, Haukelid also recruited Ditlev Diseth, a most unlikely bomb-maker. At sixty-seven years of age, retired from Norsk Hydro, and living on a pension, Ditlev ran a clock-repair shop resembling that of a mad scientist. He had also fought the Germans, and had been captured, held, and tortured by the *Gestapo* for an extended time. Upon release, he had immediately joined the Resistance.

Cannibalized springs and gears lay among parts from other gadgets all over his shop, or they were stacked about in boxes or stuffed in drawers. His task was to devise how to accomplish a timed detonation.

"Can you wangle a reliable timer?" Haukelid asked him.

The old man looked over his wire-rimmed glasses under thinning gray hair. He sighed and shook his head. "I'd rather say no," he said glumly, "but I don't see another way." Then he nodded sadly. "I can do it."

"We'll need Alf Larsen to cooperate," Haukelid told the team as they closed on a plan. "Syverstad and Nielsen too. I'll take Rolf with me to meet with the three of them this evening. Meanwhile, continue preparations." He turned to Lier-Hansen. "Get the demolitions ready."

Lier-Hansen heaved a heavy sigh but assented.

Haukelid next turned to Rolf. "Arrange for a car and driver."

"I'm working on it," Rolf replied somberly. "That's going to be difficult since very few people are allowed cars these days."

Not part of the assault team but of equal importance were Alf Larsen, another engineer at the plant and the one who knew most about manufacturing heavy water; Gunnar Syverstad, a laboratory assistant and the man who had recommended Lier-Hansen; and Kjell Nielsen, the plant's transport manager.

While actively working with the Resistance, Larsen had, against all odds, maintained his job and the confidence of his Nazi masters. In that capacity, he had slowed down the work on rebuilding the heavy water production machinery after the Gunnerside sabotage, partly by allowing Syverstad to insert cod liver oil into the distillation process, seemingly from natural causes. That artifice, added to subtle actions by workers on the production line, had cut output at the required level of purity to less than half of the desired four kilograms per day.

Kjell Nielsen's participation was crucial to Haukelid's plan. As Norsk Hydro's transport manager, Nielsen would coordinate with the SF *Hydro's* operations manager at Mæl for the day SH200 would load onto the ferry to be carried across the lake.

When Haukelid knocked on the Norsk Hydro guest house door in Rjukan where Larsen was staying, a maid informed him that the engineer was suffering from flu but would like for Haukelid and Rolf to visit him for a few minutes. When they did so, Larsen assured them that he would do all in his power to ensure the success of the mission.

"There's one piece of news I'm sure you don't know about," he told Haukelid anxiously. "The Germans are becoming quite nervous about this move. They've received word through intelligence in Oslo to expect an attack. For that reason, once SH200 reaches Notoden, well south of Lake Tinnsjå, they've decided to send half of it overland by truck, and the other half by train to Bavaria."

Haukelid grunted. "Then we must get the job done here."

He explained what he needed Larsen to do, and then he and Rolf joined Syverstad and Nielsen in another room. "We have three options," he began. He watched their faces as the two men prepared for the enormity of what he was about to tell them. "None is satisfactory. Women and children will die. The fourth option is to do nothing, and then thousands, or maybe millions, will be killed."

"Just tell us," Syverstad growled. "We're well acquainted with funerals for friends and neighbors."

"We have to blow up the *Hydro* ferry as it transports the heavy water across the lake on Sunday."

The group sat in silence for a few moments. Then, Syverstad suddenly looked thunderstruck. "My mother is supposed to be on that ferry that day," he breathed.

Haukelid exhaled sharply. "Find a way to keep her off of it," he said grimly. He shifted his gaze to Nielsen, who glanced sympathetically at Syverstad and then nodded with obvious reluctance.

"Your part is as crucial as any," Haukelid told Nielsen. "The basic idea across all three options is to get the *Hydro* out over the deepest part of the lake. The bottom there is thirteen hundred feet down, far beyond the Nazis' ability to recover any cargo.

"I estimate that it takes forty-five minutes to get to the blast area after casting off from Mæl. At that point, the ferry would be too far from either shore to run aground. It cannot be allowed to be rescued. It must sink in water so deep that none of the barrels on the train cars can be retrieved. Do you understand?"

"Yes," Nielsen muttered gravely. "Fully."

"Good," Haukelid went on. "My assault team needs time to prepare. Today is Thursday. We need the ferry to embark with SH200 on Sunday. Can you make that happen?"

"It's a heavy load. We can pretend that we need to reinforce the ferry's structure or take on extra fuel. Whatever, you'll have the *Hydro* on Sunday. That's also the best day because the *Hydro* usually carries fewer passengers on Sundays."

Grim faces all around acknowledged the rationale.

Haukelid took a deep breath. "Each option is simple. The first is that we get the crew to open the seacocks and shut down the engine to scuttle the ferry. The problem will be that all the crew members must cooperate. If just one of them sounds the alarm, we could find ourselves in an onboard gunfight against the German guards without sufficient time to prevent the ferry from making it to shore. With the number of *Wehrmacht* soldiers aboard, we'd be overpowered easily."

Syverstad raised his brows. "How many are on the assault team?"

Haukelid gestured toward Rolf. "Just the two of us and Lier-Hansen."

Nielsen let out a low whistle. "I see the problem."

"The second option," Haukelid went on, "is that I go out on the boat and plant a small explosive sufficient to blow a hole in the bow below the waterline. The *Hydro* will take on water at the front. The added weight and drag will sink it. The advantage is that we gain more time for people to get off the ferry, but it also gives time for the *Hydro* to run aground close to shore, and saves the damned shipment."

Haukelid hesitated, steeling his emotions. "The third option is the one I'm afraid has the greatest chance of success." He took a deep breath and continued. "The assault team will board the ferry early on Sunday with the demolitions. We'll plant them on the bow as with the second option, but the explosion and the resulting hole will be much larger. The *Hydro* will sink quickly, but it gives enough time for *some* passengers to escape. With the lifeboat, a few people might be saved." He sighed. "But the water is very cold."

He sat for a moment in sad contemplation. Then he continued. "I'll set detonation to go off over the deepest part of Tinnsjå. Recovery of SH200 will be impossible."

Syverstad and Nielsen stared at Haukelid, silent and horror-stricken. At last, Nielsen asked, "Will you still be aboard?"

Haukelid shook his head. "Probably not. For this to work, we must board undetected, and hopefully we'll get off the same way."

"Through all that security?" Syverstad said skeptically.

"It's the only weak spot we've found in their plan," Haukelid replied. "They'll have guards on the rail cars and all along the train route. The plant at Vemork is now impregnable, so another commando raid won't succeed. Bombing runs do more damage to our people than to the enemy. I don't see a better solution."

The other two men shook their heads sadly. "We'll do our parts," Nielsen said.

"I'm counting on it," Haukelid replied. "The ferry will run its normal schedule tomorrow. I'll go aboard to look over the boat and find out how to access the bow."

"Are your identity papers that good? We have more Germans in the valley than Norwegians these days, and they're becoming uneasy. They control everything, and they stop every Norwegian, check their papers and packages, and question them."

For the first time, Haukelid smiled, slowly and enigmatically. "Fortunately, a folk concert is in town with celebrated musicians and an orchestra."

The next morning, well-groomed, sporting a borrowed blue suit, and carrying a violin case under his arm, Haukelid strolled through Rjukan. With a deliberately lighthearted nod and smile, he greeted residents glancing his way with suspicion, but his heart beat faster as he approached the checkpoint at the train station.

He started past it as if not expecting to be stopped. When the sentries diverted their eyes toward him from passengers cued in front of them for ID inspections, he called out, "I'm bored. We don't perform until tomorrow. I must see this magnificent Lake Tinnsjå while I have the chance."

Perceiving that he belonged to the visiting orchestra comprised of both German and Norwegian musicians and was visiting Rjukan for the pleasure of the German military presence, the soldiers half-smiled dully as though they understood boredom, and waved him through. Soon, Haukelid boarded the train for the short ride to Mæl. He grunted at the thought of the soldiers' reactions if they had discovered his Sten gun and clip inside the violin case.

The tiny harbor was nothing more than a flat piece of ground almost completely surrounded by foothills, with a slice of fjord leading onto Lake Tinnsjå. A single railroad track terminated at the edge of the only dock. A parallel road ran past the harbor into the distance. Two small red buildings were set in the space between the road and the rails. Beyond them, almost even with the wharf, several empty freight cars sat idle on a siderail next to the road.

The SF *Hydro* was berthed and waiting to receive passengers when the train arrived. Built thirty years earlier to ferry supplies in and out of Rjukan and Vemork, it was capable of transporting twelve rail cars and a hundred and twenty passengers. Today, she carried light cargo and only a few travelers. Her steam engine plowed her five hundred tons and the weight of her passengers and cargo through the usually placid waters, while twin funnels channeled her vapor into the atmosphere. The captain's bridge was located in a superstructure that spanned the width of the deck well above the height of any cargo.

The passengers, Haukelid among them, climbed down from the train and boarded the ferry via a gangway on its side. They waited in the third-class salon below the main deck while castoff preparations took place.

Observing closely while boarding, Haukelid saw that just before the dock's edge, a railroad switch allowed train cars to be rolled onto twin rails, six cars to each side, in the middle of the ferry.

Although the day's loading operations were fairly relaxed by German standards, the soldiers were still there, and Haukelid was sure that on Sunday, the combat veterans who would replace the regular guards temporarily were well versed in abiding by the letter of von Falkenhorst's admonition to treat the SH200 shipment as they would crown jewels. Guards would be on top of the freight cars for the entire trip.

The *Hydro* shoved off. Haukelid noted the time and climbed up the stairs leading to the main deck. A crewman approached him as he walked onto the flat surface but, on seeing the violin case and perceiving that Haukelid might be among the musicians sent to entertain the occupying army, he changed to a direction that avoided an encounter.

Haukelid reached the front of the vessel and lingered to view the landscape as the *Hydro* maneuvered down the fjord and out onto the lake. When he saw specific landmarks on either bank, and as the ferry passed them, he again glanced at his watch. *Forty-five minutes to the deepest point. Confirmed.*

As the *Hydro* made its return trip to Mæl, Haukelid scouted surreptitiously. Near the front of the third-class passenger compartment, he saw the final item he needed to locate: the hatch at the entry of the bilge at the forward end of the boat.

Early the next morning, back in the room where he had stayed the previous night, Haukelid awakened to two popping sounds. He leaped to his feet to find Einar and Ditlev enjoying his discomfiture. "They work," Ditlev enthused. "My timers work."

He showed Haukelid his invention. He had removed the bell from a regular alarm clock and replaced it with an electrical connection that closed when the striker touched it at the prescribed hour. "You'll need two of them," he explained, "just like the ones that woke you up. They'll be attached to the explosives." His face and tone grew serious. "You'll have to be very careful because the gap between the striker and the connection is tiny, only one-third of an inch. If you slip…" He shrugged and looked up at the ceiling while blowing out a breath of air to mimic an explosion.

"Let's get the rest of the team," Haukelid said. "I'll go over what I learned yesterday, and we'll make final coordination."

When Einar, Lier-Hansen, and Rolf had joined them, Haukelid briefed. "The time required to get above the deepest part of the lake is confirmed. The ferry leaves the dock at 10 o'clock. We'll set the clocks to detonate at 10:45.

"I know how to access the lower level from the upper decks, and I located the forepeak inside the bow where we'll place the explosives. It'll take some doing because obstacles are in the way of getting to it, but nothing we can't overcome.

"Arriving at Mæl early is imperative, long before the train with SH200. There's only regular security on the docks now, but that's likely to change."

He turned to Rolf. "Do we have a vehicle to get us there?"

Rolf shot him a worried look. "We do, but it's old and hasn't been driven in a while. We also asked two doctors about using theirs. Physicians are the only ones allowed to use their cars now, but neither of theirs is in working order. The owner of the one we got advised us that if we're caught, things would go better for him if the auto appeared to have been stolen. So we'll break into his garage.

"If we get stopped, particularly loaded down with weapons, grenades, and the explosives…" He let the thought linger, and then went on. "I hope the car doesn't give us a problem. I have a driver, Olav, from the Resistance. He's reliable if the vehicle is."

Haukelid pursed his lips and nodded. "We do the best we can. Eight miles is a long way on foot in the time available, even for us. Regardless, we can't be late. We'll go pick it up very early."

He turned to Einar. "You'll man the wireless on the Vidda."

Einar shifted in his seat, disgruntled. "Of course. As usual. One piece of news to share is that the rail cars have made it to the Rjukan train station. They came down from Vemork today. The Germans wanted to send them on to the ferry, but they bought the reason about why they must wait until tomorrow, whatever that was."

"That's a relief," Haukelid acknowledged. He glanced at Lier-Hansen.

"We'll be using Nobel 808 plastic explosives, nineteen pounds of it," Lier-Hansen said, unprompted. "We rolled it into a sausage shape yesterday. Per your calculations, that's enough to blow a hole eleven feet wide in the bow."

"That'll do the job," Haukelid replied hoarsely. He drove away images flitting across his mind of young mothers and children leaping for their lives and then succumbing to the freezing lake. Setting his jaw, he continued, "As water rushes in, the bow will be dragged down. The freight cars will shift forward. At some point, the weight will break the restraining chains, upend the ferry, and they'll either roll off the front into the water, or they'll be carried down while still onboard."

He looked across the faces of his teammates. "Let's go over our individual actions and escape routes."

19

February 19, 1944
Rjukan, Norway

Just before midnight, under a half-moon, myriad stars, and a clear sky, Haukelid and Rolf peeked over the crest of a foothill west of Rjukan. Below them, the Måna River ran by the train station, which was bathed with floodlights, illuminating twelve flatbed cars. Two of them were loaded with huge steel drums, and soldiers stood atop of and surrounded them.

"We'd need a whole company of commandos to destroy that freight," Haukelid growled to Rolf. "Blowing up the *Hydro is* the only option."

Angered by the prospect, the two stole down the steep slopes and through the back streets to the detached garage behind the house where the car they intended to use had been stored. Lier-Hansen was already there with Olav, the driver. Soon, Alf Larsen appeared, still suffering from the flu, but carrying skis and a rucksack of supplies needed for the escape to Sweden. He, Haukelid, and Lier-Hansen planned to take a train from Kongsberg to Oslo after the operation, and from there, to ski cross-country to the Swedish border. Rolf would stay behind and head back into Hardangervidda to rejoin Einar and the wireless link to London.

"How is it," Haukelid asked, indicating the ancient jalopy.

"Not good," Lier-Hansen replied. "We've checked the fuel, and it's clear. The battery is good. We must hand-crank to start it, but it turns over without catching."

"Keep working it." Haukelid turned to a coughing Larsen. "Are you all right?"

"Better than I'll be if I stay in Rjukan," Larsen replied while rubbing his eyes and nodding. "It's done. Syverstad and I oversaw hooking up the cars with the heavy water to the locomotive a few hours ago." He sighed. "I don't know how I managed to stay on at the plant after your raid last year. After this operation, I'll be the first one the Germans will look to arrest. If I stay, I won't survive."

"You can't stay in Norway anyway, Alf," Haukelid observed. "You're the last engineer remaining in the country who knows about the production of heavy water."

Larsen sighed and acknowledged his words with a nod.

"What excuse did you give to delay the train?" Haukelid asked.

Larsen grunted. "I told them I'm still suffering from the flu and needed yesterday off. I came in late to supervise the train hookups."

Haukelid chuckled. "What about Nielsen and Syverstad? Where are they now?"

"Nielsen is having an appendectomy at an Oslo hospital. He went in late Friday. The surgery will be on Monday. He shouldn't be suspected, but you never know."

Haukelid raised his eyebrows. "Did he need the operation?"

Larsen shrugged. "His sister arranged it. She's a nurse at the hospital."

Haukelid mulled the situation a moment. "And Syverstad?"

"He's at the plant. He's worried about his family. He thinks that being on the job will avert suspicion. That might work, but I'm doubtful. Remember, he helped me hook up the train cars to the locomotive."

"And his mother? Will she be on the ferry."

Larsen shook his head. "He mixed a laxative into her meal last night. She's in no condition to travel."

Haukelid grunted. "At least I can have that off my conscience."

Larsen stared at the garage floor and dragged the toe of one boot along it pensively. "You know if we don't succeed, we won't have another chance. This is it."

Their eyes met and Larsen noted that Haukelid looked haunted, the most solemn that he had ever seen him. "I know," was Haukelid's only reply.

He turned to check progress on starting the car. Olav applied the choke and turned the crank. The engine shook and coughed, but then it sputtered out.

"Keep trying," Haukelid said. "We're nearly an hour late."

He and Olav went back over the engine, checking each component. This time they opened the carburetor and found it coated with soot. They cleaned it out, replaced it, and Olav once more tried the engine. It roared to life and stayed running.

The forbidden little auto, old enough to require a hand crank and laden with the driver, four passengers, nineteen pounds of explosives, multiple weapons and ammunition, a pile of hand grenades, four sets of skis, and a rucksack of escape supplies, ground through the snow on tire chains. Olav drove along a road paralleling the railroad track that would soon carry a cargo of utmost importance for the Third *Reich*. Surprisingly, no sentries were yet posted along the route. Haukelid had expected to encounter heavily guarded checkpoints, but none materialized.

They rode in silence, absent the banter common among soldiers going into battle or on a covert operation. Among these five men, only Haukelid and Lier-Hansen were professional soldiers. The other three were civilians fighting in the limited ways they had available to save their beloved Norway. They understood that, in this case, the stakes went well beyond their country. Not comprehending how that could be, they accepted as sufficient evidence of the heavy water's potential destructive capability the massive effort that Germany extended to save it.

They rode with dread, not resulting from fear for their own demise, although that was also a visceral undertone. The thought of being stymied in their mission resided at the back of their minds as well, with visions of what tortures they might endure, should they be captured, before death released them from pain and guilt.

Their overriding horror, though, rose from the prospect of succeeding at what they had set out to do. They could not drive from their minds the images of bodies of fathers, mothers, and children, people whom they knew and loved, floating on a cold lake.

A mile before reaching Mæl, Haukelid told Olav to pull over behind a stand of trees. Accompanied by Rolf and Lier-Hansen, he got out of the car. Then he leaned back through the window and instructed the driver and Larsen, "If we're not back in two hours, leave. If you hear shooting, get the hell out."

Hugging the shadows from the trees overhanging the road opposite the docks, they approached the first red building. It was quiet. Nothing and no one stirred.

They approached the second building and heard laughter and loud conversation in German. The regular guards. But still no sign of the expected horde of special troops.

They moved on quietly, staying on the opposite side of the road until almost even with the docks. The *Hydro* floated there, quiet and peaceful, the lake in front of it glimmering in the half-moon. The foothills rose around the lake in silhouette against the moonlight and starlight. Far up the slopes, nocturnal creatures called to one another intermittently. Somewhere out on the water, a fish broke the surface and splashed, leaving ripples that spread across the surface and then smoothed out.

The trio sat in the dark, listening, and when no sign of a disturbance was sensed, Haukelid hurried across the frozen road as fast as his load of demolitions, grenades, and his Sten gun and ammo allowed, apprehensive all the way across that he made too much noise on the frozen road's crackling ice. He slunk, panting, into the shadow of the empty freight cars on the siderail. Staying in dark places, he moved close to the ferry and scoped it out. When he was sure that nothing yet was amiss, he stepped momentarily back into the moonlight and waved.

Lier-Hansen scurried across the road, followed seconds later by Rolf. Still expecting that at any moment German guards would accost them, they headed to the ferry, now only yards away. Still all was quiet, but as they drew near, they heard voices from inside, but no one was visible on the decks.

Taking measured breaths and with Haukelid leading, they crept aboard.

They headed down a companionway past a door to the crew quarters. As they hurried by, they glanced through a porthole and saw several members playing cards, the source of voices and laughter.

The crew remained oblivious. A few steps beyond was a door leading down a set of stairs to the third-class passenger compartment. That was where Haukelid had seen the hatch that led to the area below decks where they would place the explosives.

Lier-Hansen provided cover for Haukelid and Rolf to locate the hatch. Then, they heard footsteps, a light shone on Lier-Hansen, and a voice called, "Who's there?"

The three froze. If the man called out in alarm, the mission was over.

Without hesitation, Lier-Hansen stepped forward to where he could be seen plainly. "John, it's me."

"Knut?"

"Yes," Lier-Hansen replied. "What are you doing out this late?"

The heavy man sighed. "I'm on watch duty." He peered into the shadows. "Why are you here? Is someone with you?"

"Friends," Lier-Hansen said. As Haukelid and Rolf moved into the light, he indicated the watchman. "This is John Berg. We know each other from the Mæl Athletic Club on the north side of the lake. We're both members there. He's on the ferry crew..." Lier-Hansen paused in mid-sentence. "He's sympathetic to the Norwegian Resistance, a true patriot."

Before he could say more, John Berg demanded warily, "What are you doing here?" He eyed the trio's heavy overcoats, obviously covering bulky items.

"You know how things are, John," Lier-Hansen said. "We're expecting a *Gestapo* raid, and we have things to hide."

John continued to study the three men, and then broke into laughter. "We've hidden lots of stuff here before." He pointed his light at the hatch Haukelid had been searching for. "Down there. Don't forget where you put your stuff."

While Lier-Hansen continued to engage John Berg, Haukelid and Rolf opened the hatch and descended into the bilge. Freezing water sloshed on them as they proceeded on their hands and knees by flashlight until they reached the bow.

Rolf held the light while Haukelid carefully drew out and organized the two makeshift clock timers, their respective detonator fuses, electronic caps, batteries, and connecting wires, and finally, his two sausage-shaped Nobel 808 plastic explosives.

Drawing an end of one sausage to meet the end of the other, he placed a fuse between them, taped them together, and connected them to the detonator caps. Then he repeated the process with the opposite ends of the sausages.

Despite the cold, sweat beaded on Haukelid's brow. The most sensitive parts of his task still lay ahead. He steadied his hands and laid the Nobel 808 in a circle against the metal forepeak and attached the fuses to the ferry's ribs.

Taking the clocks out of their carrying bags, he wound them up and set the alarms. Then he connected the clocks to the battery packs and taped them to the hull.

Now came the trickiest part of the job, attaching the connecting wires between the clocks, the batteries, and the detonation caps, and ensuring that the connecting wires were not already electrified. With only a third of an inch between the striker and the electrical connection on the clocks, any jolt or slip...

Shivering, with fingers aching from the ice-cold water sloshing about, sweat blurring his eyes, and his breath coming in short gasps and forming thick vapor in front of him, Haukelid continued to work. Then, with barely six hours to go before detonation, he pushed a tiny switch on each clock, activating them to go off at 10:45.

He was through. The bomb was armed. Cold and pain disappeared, replaced by contentment that came from a job well done.

That sense lasted barely a second.

Haukelid and Rolf scrambled back along the bilge and up into the third-class compartment. Lier-Hansen was still there conversing with John Berg, but Haukelid was in no mood for talking.

"Thank you," he muttered in as appreciative a voice as he could manage and headed up the stairs to the main deck. Rolf and Lier-Hansen followed.

Two minutes before Olav and Larsen were to drive away, the rear passenger doors opened and the three men of the assault team tumbled in. "Go," Haukelid said. As the car rumbled back onto the road, he turned to Lier-Hansen. "John Berg is a friend?"

"Not a close one, but a friend nevertheless." Lier-Hansen looked away and muttered, "Maybe he'll make it safely to shore."

They had driven a short distance when Rolf called out, "This is where I get off." Olav pulled over. Rolf exited and grabbed one of the pairs of skis. A two-day journey would take him back onto the Vidda to meet up with Einar. He would ride out the aftermath there.

"I'll join you soon," Haukelid told him as they bade farewell, and then Rolf disappeared up a snow trail into trees.

After farewells and as Olav started off again, Lier-Hansen said, "Drop me in the woods near my house."

Haukelid glanced at him in surprise. "I thought you were going with us to Sweden."

Lier-Hansen shook his head. "I changed my mind. Rjukan is my home. I can't leave in the wake of the catastrophe I know is coming. I'd never forgive myself." He sighed. "Those clocks on the *Hydro* are ticking."

"So long, my friend," Haukelid said. "I'll see you soon."

Two hours later, Haukelid and Larsen boarded a train at Kongsberg, bound for Oslo and their escape on skis to Sweden.

At ten o'clock, Knut Lier-Hansen sat alone atop the foothill overlooking the *Hydro* at Mæl, the Måna River's mouth, and across the southern branch of Lake Tinnsjå. After being dropped off at home, he had climbed into higher country and hiked back overland, staying well away from the road and out of sight.

He had seen the train arrive at Mæl, as well as the flatbed cars loaded with their deadly cargoes. The railroad was now well guarded on both sides with lines of *Wehrmacht* soldiers brought there fully armed by roaring troop-transport trucks. They were reinforced with *panzers* and *kübelwagens* full of steely-eyed officers. And, he had seen the train's passenger cars full of people journeying to...

Lier-Hansen forced the thought from his beleaguered mind. He had come to be a silent witness and to pay tribute to those whose minutes were numbered.

The old ferry's whistle focused his attention. He stood for a better view, and watched as the *Hydro* started out on its ill-fated final voyage across Lake Tinnsjå. It left the docks, headed down the last mile of the Måna River to where the waterway widened and spilled into the lake. There the vessel turned onto the main body of water.

As the ferry continued, overwhelming guilt gripped Lier-Hansen as he recalled how he had kept John Berg engaged as a diversion while Haukelid and Rolf did the work that might seal the ferryman's doom. He looked at his watch, and almost counted down the remaining time. Ten-thirty. Ten-forty. Ten-forty-five.

Nothing happened.

And then a soft sound whispered across the water and up the hillside, like nothing more than a muffled puff of air. From this distance, the *Hydro* was little more than a blot. Lier-Hansen could make out only its shape.

Its stern lifted into the air.

Lier-Hansen could not stop his imagination from working overtime. He saw in his mind's eye the startled looks on people's faces as they heard the explosion. Panic spread as the nose of the ferry dipped and did not come aright. Men and women scrambled for the exits while children screamed in terror. Mothers and fathers grabbed them desperately and held them close as their inescapable fates were sealed.

Lier-Hansen imagined the twelve heavily loaded flatbeds on the deck, two of them carrying the deadly cargo of SH200, the ones in the rear ramming into the ones in front, wrenching their retaining chains apart, their combined weight forcing the ferry's bow down even farther, and then rolling off the end and splashing into the lake.

His mind continued to play havoc as he watched the small ferry across the waters. The *Hydro*'s stern rose until it was almost vertical. And then it disappeared below the surface. All was quiet.

20

February 20, 1944
Bletchley Park, England

"Sir, I'm sure this news has been picked up through operational channels," Claire said as she entered Commander Travis' office, "and it's all over the wires at Berlin's high command."

"About the ferry-sinking in Norway. Yes, I'd heard. The newspapers should have headlines out about it shortly. For the time being, that should be the end of that heavy water production—" He searched for words. "What's that scientific name?"

Claire looked down at her notes. "Deuterium oxide, sir."

"Yes, that. Good job on bringing that situation to our attention, Miss Littlefield. Do we know anything about casualties?"

Claire's expression fell. "I'm afraid we do, sir, although we have not yet confirmed them through Norwegian Resistance sources. The Germans claim that thirty-eight civilians were aboard, and that fourteen of them lost their lives."

"Hmm. That bad." Travis sighed and leaned back in his chair.

"The Nazis are already mounting patrols into the Hardangervidda to find the culprits. They're calling it a terrorist attack."

Travis reacted angrily. "Of course. They would. And they would just as easily have blown up London or New York if they had the means. Fortunately, we stopped them. This time. Rest assured that reprisals against civilians are underway now."

He rose from his seat and paced over to a window where he stood staring across the estate's gardens. "I suppose we can console ourselves with the rationale that there *really was no other way.*" His voice shook as he uttered the last phrase. "But dammit, I have a family too. I feel for those people." His eyes misted.

"I could use a drink," he said after a moment, and moved over to a cabinet on the opposite wall. "Would you care for one?"

"No thank you, sir. I'll be fine," Claire said while she quietly mused about her own responsibility in bringing about so many innocent deaths. The messages she had intercepted, analyzed, and delivered higher had played such a part in destroying the deadly heavy water, and with it, many innocent lives. She forced the thoughts from her mind.

"Ah yes. That irrepressible Littlefield equanimity." Travis poured a shot of bourbon and tossed it down his throat. "Well, I admire you for it."

Returning to his desk, he gestured for Claire to take her seat while he lowered himself into his chair. "Anything new on Italy?"

She shook her head. "It's a slog. 'Inching northward' would not be much of an exaggeration for our troops fighting up from Monte Cassino, and our chaps at Anzio are taking it in the shorts. Marshal Kesselring has little regard for General Lucas. He still sees the failure to exploit the initiative after landing on the beach unopposed as a colossal blunder. He seems to have resigned himself, however, that the *Wehrmacht* will give up Italy. His main intent now appears to be to inflict as much damage and provide as much time as possible to build up Germany's interior defenses." She paused to take a deep breath. "The casualty figures on both fronts are truly horrific."

Travis grunted. "Yes, they are."

He remained silent with an expression indicating that he had something else to say, but when he did not speak, Claire started to take her leave.

"One moment," he said, and she settled back in her chair.

"I'm reluctant to discuss another matter with you, but I feel I owe it to you."

Claire sat forward now, her senses taut. "What is it, sir? My parents—"

"No, no." Travis waylaid that concern with a wave of his hand. "Well, perhaps your father, but the one to worry about right now is your brother Lance. As you know, he's been identified and held as a *prominente*. As invasion worries grow at Berlin's high command, they're gathering together more of these people, those of high birth or high office, and they're holding them in various places across Germany. I think the obvious intent is to use them for ransom if they find themselves suing for a settled peace.

"Churchill and Roosevelt already announced that nothing less than an unconditional surrender is acceptable. That does not bode well for the *prominentes*."

Claire took her time to reply. "I know, sir. I lose sleep thinking of that."

Travis studied her face sympathetically. "Advisories have gone out telling the senior British officers in the POW camps to discourage escape activities. They cannot be allowed to interfere with preparations for the invasion. That's where Resistance efforts will be focused until it takes place.

"Lance has no good alternatives. If he escapes, he'll be largely on his own, unassisted by the Resistance. But if he waits out the war, the Nazis might execute him with the other *prominentes* as Hitler's revenge."

Claire leaned forward and rested her face in her hands. Then she straightened her back and stood. "I do best when I don't dwell on those matters, and I keep my mind diverted by keeping busy. Will that be all, sir?"

Startled at her brusqueness, Travis also stood. "I apologize. I didn't mean to upset you."

"You didn't, sir, no more than this bloody war already has." Seeing his concerned face, her expression softened. "You were being kind, sir. I appreciate that."

"Thank you for that. Well, changing the subject, I know this isn't in your bailiwick, but I'm wondering about communications between Germany and Japan. I recall that in '41, they exchanged quite a bit of information. For instance, the Japanese sent observers to Berlin to study the tactics we used with our Swordfish biplane torpedo bombers to knock out the Italian navy at Taranto. At the end of the year, they used the same tactics against the US at Pearl Harbor. Are they still cooperating that closely?"

Claire cocked her head to one side, and her mouth opened in mild surprise. "Now that you mention it, sir, communications between them do seem to have dropped off. They never got much beyond the propaganda stage—Taranto was an exception. They're too far separated geographically to do each other much good."

She paused for a thought to germinate. "I do recall from conversations with the American team that was here in mid-1942—they had broken the Japanese codes and wanted to exchange cryptographic methods with us—"

"Oh yes. I remember. Go on."

"They learned that the Soviets had a spy in Tokyo posing as a German. His name was Richard Sorje, and he reported that the Japanese had made the decision not to attack Soviet targets. Consequently, Moscow could free up troops in the far east and move them to defend in the west."

Travis leaned back in his chair with an admiring glance at Claire. "You have a marvelous memory, Miss Littlefield. I had forgotten that tidbit. That decision made things a lot easier for us on this side of the planet."

Claire continued thinking. "Some German warships have docked at Japanese ports, but beyond that, aid between the two countries hasn't amounted to much that I know of. Japan is barely mentioned if at all in the German communiques we intercept. With Italy flipping to our side, and both countries forced into defensive postures, they must be looking at each other with jaundiced eyes." She added as an afterthought, "As you say, that isn't in my bailiwick."

Travis leaned forward with a dismissive gesture. "Oh well, the subject was a curiosity, nothing more. A lot is going on in the Pacific, but with all that we do here, keeping up is difficult." He half smiled, as if in jest. "You don't have a brother in that theater, do you?"

"No, sir. I have a cousin there, though, whom I've never met. Josh Littlefield, an American. He's a fighter pilot, and I believe he's a lieutenant commander. His brother and sister spent Christmas here with me. The youngest, Zack, is an infantryman in Italy now, and Sherry is a flight nurse."

"Oh bother," Travis said, grimacing. "A close family member. I shouldn't have asked."

"That's all right, sir," Claire said, smiling in strained amusement. "I appreciate your concern."

When Claire arrived home that evening, Timmy met her at the end of the garden path leading to the front door. "Gigi," he cried, and ran to throw his arms around her legs. She picked him up and kissed his cheek, then the two walked hand in hand into the house.

Later, when Claire played with Timmy before supper, she was absent-minded. Thoughts of her family members, including her cousin Josh, plagued her. Though she had never met him, she cared for him for knowing and caring for his siblings. She had become close to Zack and Sherry while they were with her at Christmas, and of course, concern for her parents was constant. Beyond that was a sense of guilt she could not shake regarding the casualties aboard the ferry in Norway. Knowing she had done nothing to cause the situation that brought about the deaths of innocents offered little solace. From her intercepts and analysis had come the decision to destroy the heavy water irrespective of collateral casualties.

While reading a story to Timmy at bedtime, she stumbled over words and cleared moisture from her eyes. He sensed her melancholy. "I love you, Gigi," he told her, looking into her face with big eyes and wrapping his arms around her neck. "Things will get better, you'll see."

Hearing him say those words that had been her characterizing maxim while growing up, Claire let out a small gasp of laughter. Then, with a broken smile, she hugged the little boy tightly. Looking into his eyes, she tweaked his nose with a forefinger.

He squealed with laughter.

"You are absolutely correct, my little man," she said as she kissed him goodnight.

21

Sixteen Days Earlier, February 4, 1944
Fifth Fleet, Somewhere on the Pacific Ocean

Lieutenant Commander Josh Littlefield exulted at the roar and vibration of his Grumman F6F Hellcat fighter, powered by a two-thousand-horsepower Pratt & Whitney R-2800 Double Wasp engine with a four-blade prop. The bulky fighter plane was new to the Navy inventory, and all evidence was that it significantly outclassed the Japanese fighter workhorse, the Mitsubishi A6M Zero. America's design prowess and industrial might had placed in Josh's control a fighter significantly superior to any he would face, while Japanese pilots still flew outdated, aging aircraft.

Josh was familiar with the target. He had insisted on flying this reconnaissance mission over the Truk Atoll. Being short of pilots and knowing Josh's propensity to push against higher authority successfully, his superiors aboard the USS *Enterprise* had objected only nominally. Most of them found pointless any attempt to argue against this officer who had trained pilots for the Doolittle raid, flown a dive-bomber and sunk an enemy ship at Midway, survived being shot down twice, and fought alongside Marine infantrymen against a bloody Japanese ground assault at Edson's Ridge on Guadalcanal. Added to that were hushed rumors that he had been instrumental in helping General Clark convince the Vichy French forces in North Africa to desert the *Wehrmacht* and join the Allies. The result of his exploits was that Josh had become a favorite of Admiral "Bull" Halsey and a legend among Pacific Theater pilots and crews.

Josh was mesmerized at the breathtaking beauty of Truk Lagoon. Its coral crest rose to the ocean's surface, appearing as a string of pearls against royal blue velvet. He had chosen a gorgeous day to make his first flight over the atoll, and he had flown his Hellcat on the basis of needing aircraft familiarization time. Cruising just above the waves from the east at dawn, he had little fear of being detected, either by electronics or by observers at Truk looking into the sun. Other pilots had noticed that Japanese radar was either not working or incapable of detecting low-level flights.

"If you come up against Zeros, don't dogfight 'em," the operations chief had warned Josh on his way out. "They're more maneuverable than your Hellcat. Your advantage is in speed, climbing rate, and firepower." He had grunted and chuckled. "That and the fact that a lot of the good Jap pilots have checked out to *Paradaisu,* if you get my drift. The replacements aren't well trained.

"But you're going on a recon run. If you get into a fix, your buddies won't be around to swoop in and bail you out. Keep that in mind."

As Josh headed out the door, the ops chief called after him with a sardonic note, "Be sure to get that Hellcat back here. We need the aircraft."

As he flew toward the atoll, Josh noted the eastern segment of the coral perimeter and the mountains within its ring rising out of the ocean much as Hawaiian islands would appear, green, lush, and peaceful. He flew over a saddle ridge at Dublon, site of the Japanese Combined Fleet's headquarters and its communications buildings. Many ships, most of them merchant marine supply vessels, lolled in a large anchorage to the south. Another anchorage of similar size was immediately to the west.

Then he spotted an unbelievable construction he had heard about but scarcely believed could exist, until he saw it: a twenty-five-hundred-ton floating dry dock. Intelligence reported that it was able to service any of Japan's warships.

Cruising ahead and back over water, he saw to his right Moen, the largest island with an airfield on its near side. Pilots from previous recon flights reported an airstrip, hangars, and fuel oil storage facilities on the island's north side as well, but Josh couldn't see it. Shifting his view to the south, he picked out yet a third airfield on Eten. Param was now just ahead, and as he flew over, he spotted a fourth fully functional airfield. Reportedly, there was a fifth one, but Josh did not spot it.

As he passed over the anchorages, he made note of the ships, their types, estimated numbers, and any that he specifically recognized. Then, edging his nose up, he started to climb, but refrained from doing so too quickly—he wanted to see the far edge of the coral necklace. The atoll was thirty miles wide at this point, its perimeter a hundred and forty miles in circumference, and the coral gleamed white as waves broke over it, their spray sparkling in the sun.

Deciding that he had seen enough and was pushing his fuel consumption if he hoped to return safely to the *Enterprise*, Josh turned south toward a bank of clouds. He rolled slightly so he could see across the atoll through the top of his canopy and spotted the sun's reflections glinting off of three fast-moving objects coming his way.

Uh-oh.

He opened the throttle and climbed toward a mist transforming into clouds. Though thin, the white curtain floated near the ocean's surface, and was close enough that he should reach it long before the pursuing Zeros could angle in.

He climbed higher, mindful that he could now be acquired by enemy radar and watchful for ack-ack positions. The Japanese guns were nothing to trifle with: 127 mm barrel, five-pound rounds, accurate out to twenty-five thousand feet.

Just before reaching the mist, he rolled his aircraft to glance back through the top of his canopy to locate the three nearest Zeros. They flew in formation well north of him, but with his steep climb, they could close the horizontal distance.

As soon as he was behind the curtain of vapor, Josh dropped his nose and veered south toward the thickest part of the clouds. Then he descended almost to the ocean's surface. Leveling out, he checked again through the canopy toward the atoll. He could not see the Zeros, which meant that they could not see him, and at this low altitude, enemy radar would apparently not detect him.

He had to get to the other side of Truk where he had made his entry, but if he continued his current path, he would break from the clouds and be exposed along the southeast quadrant. He expected that more Zeros would launch if they had not already done so, and he needed to head east before his fuel level became critical.

That he would be detected had been anticipated. Most recon flights were. However, he could not lead his pursuers to the vast armada cruising toward them. The Fifth Fleet's location and intentions was a secret not to be revealed by leaving a trail that could be followed.

Besides the USS *Enterprise*, Task Force 50, organized for the upcoming Operation Hailstone, incorporated four *Essex*-class fleet carriers, including the *Yorktown*, named for the carrier lost at Midway. With four more *Independence*-class light carriers, they supported five hundred and sixty aircraft. They were screened against Japanese attack by seven battleships, including the USS *New Jersey*, commissioned less than a year ago and having joined the fleet last month. Ten cruisers, twenty-eight destroyers, and ten submarines rounded out the force. Absent from this formation were troop carriers; the objective was to destroy the ships and shore facilities within Truk Lagoon, not to occupy it.

Josh's quandary now was how to get to the other side of the lagoon.

Do the unexpected. The ack-ack gunners won't crossfire over the lagoon.

Dropping his nose into a steep dive, Josh allowed gravity to accelerate his speed as he headed to a position southwest of Truk. Then, below fifty feet, he pulled the aircraft into a hard left toward the islands, leveled out, opened the throttle, and skimmed the waves.

Although he believed he now flew below radar, the base was alerted. The anti-aircraft crews would watch for him. More Zeros would join the chase.

Near the center of the atoll, Josh pulled his stick back. The nose turned up, and the Hellcat soared, screaming skyward, climbing vertically. Buffeted by rapid acceleration and mindful of the anti-aircraft guns, Josh rolled the fighter every few seconds, altering his path enough to evade enemy fire.

He labored under G-forces, his breathing difficult and deliberate, and he jammed his knees into his chest to stem the drain of oxygen from his lungs. As he passed through five thousand feet, flak burst around him, jarring the Hellcat and reminding Josh that they only had to explode close to him. Nearby concussions could knock him out of the sky.

He glanced at his altimeter. It indicated a rate of climb near its maximum of twenty-six-hundred feet per minute. Fortunately, he could fly above the AA guns' maximum range, but until he passed that limit, he was still vulnerable, and the Zeros would continue pursuit.

The Hellcat's vibration increased as the air thinned and the engine struggled for sufficient oxygen. Josh drove it to reach the aircraft's design apex and leveled out, belly up, so that he could see down through the canopy and try to locate the Zeros. He could not see them, but for a second, he marveled at the view he beheld. The atoll's coral crest was strung out, glistening in the sun against the deep blue sea, and arranged in a rough circle like a necklace around its islands.

Josh shook off the dreamlike state that beckoned him and set a course for the *Enterprise*. The radio crackled. "Wannabe, status, over."

Josh smirked. "Wannabe" had been pinned on him for a nickname since he fought with the Marines at Guadalcanal. After the battle, he had been kidded that he really wanted to be a Marine. The nickname stuck and became his call sign.

"On return leg. Zeros in pursuit."

"Roger. Shake 'em. Don't bring 'em this way."

"Wilco. Out."

Heading into more clouds farther east, Josh stayed on his course for several minutes at full throttle. Just before entering the haze, he pulled a hard right, rolled such that his tail rudder was parallel to the ocean's surface, and scanned his back trail. Seeing no sign of the Zeros, he righted the aircraft, resumed his heading, and entered the clouds.

They were thick and blustery but not particularly unnerving, and Josh immediately throttled back and dove, leveling out just above the wavetops. Then he set a new course and cruised.

Although he maintained wariness, the flying was relatively easy now. Josh used the time to reflect over events that had brought him here. He recalled the horror of Pearl Harbor and seeing the devastation left in the wake of the Japanese surprise attack just over two years ago. The US response had been fast and furious with Colonel Doolittle's raid over Tokyo, undertaken to douse Japanese morale, sting its Imperial Navy, and inform the world that the Land of the Rising Sun was not impregnable.

By then, Admiral Halsey had made lightning strikes at isolated Japanese island outposts, but at that juncture in the war, the inescapable reality was that Japan's navy dominated the entire Pacific Ocean, and the US was powerless to do much about it in the immediate future, aside from defending against Japan's eastern advance toward the US western shore. However, even protecting the US continental west coast had proven beyond American capability as Japan had attacked the far islands of the Aleutians. Fighting continued there even now, two years later, as well as in General MacArthur's Southwest Pacific Theater.

Looking back over events since the dark, early days of the war, Josh perceived the outlines of Admiral Chester Nimitz' strategy. As Commander of the US Pacific Fleet, the admiral had first set out to halt the Japanese advance in the face of losses at Pearl Harbor that included battleships, fighters, bombers, destroyers, cruisers, and support ships. Josh found unfathomable the challenge that Nimitz faced.

Bull Halsey's harassing forays in the Gilbert and Marshall islands and Doolittle's raid over Tokyo had blunted Japan's eastward advance. However, in addition to their pre-Pearl Harbor conquests of Burma and parts of China, Japan had since then forcefully occupied Guam, Wake Island, and various other islands. The most prominent American losses to the Japanese were the Philippine Islands, forcing General MacArthur to flee with his staff and family for Melbourne, Australia, via Mindanao. Britain had also lost Singapore, its singular greatest defeat in history.

Then, battles fought in the Coral Sea brought the Japanese navy's offensive operations to a standstill and allowed Nimitz to move into the next phase of his strategy in which he continued primarily on defense, but he could also begin to engage in offensive operations. That culminated in a battle at Midway. Victory there had blunted Japan's eastward thrust. Having participated in that action, Josh recalled the confusion and the inescapable conclusion that triumph for the US in that clash of titan navies had resulted from being luckier than the Japanese.

Regardless, revived spirits and the arrival of new ships and weaponry to rebuild from the materiel losses at Pearl Harbor allowed Nimitz to look ahead to more aggressive operations. However, despite victories in the Coral Sea and at Midway, the US was compelled to defend its gains against an unremitting enemy, and thus its actions were constrained.

Josh remembered that the public had been advised of a decision at the Casablanca Conference early last year to pummel the enemy into unconditional surrender in both the European and Pacific theaters. That meant destroying its capacity to fight faster than its resources could be replaced. In the Pacific, the strategy translated into the imperative of keeping Japan under constant pressure, forcing the empire to expend all of its reserves. To that end, Nimitz defined his strategic objectives as precluding Japan from strengthening its current positions; safeguarding Allied gains and embarking on new large-scale offensive operations; and using land, air, and sea forces to defeat enemy re-supply capability by attrition.

Josh shook his head at the thought of the enormous task the strategy had imposed on Allied military forces in the Pacific. It had meant fighting across twelve thousand miles, from the Bering Sea through Hawaii, Samoa, Fiji, New Guinea, and Northwest Australia to Singapore. Japan, on the other hand, had developed secure lines of communication within its perimeter of occupied territories, allowing it to counter Allied operations quickly with economies of force.

Josh had often wondered about the wisdom of striking in so many places at once, but the reason suddenly became clear why that was done. If the Allies hoped to destroy Japan's military power, they had no choice but to keep pressure on enemy forces by striking everywhere at once with overwhelming firepower. Japan would thus be unable to consolidate any gains, harden its positions, or replace lost materiel.

His new insight cleared a question about "island hopping," a tactic that had bothered Josh. Those in the assault forces, primarily Marines, often grumbled at making frontal assaults on heavily fortified targets.

Josh had heard Halsey mutter more than once on the *Enterprise's* bridge,

"We've got to jump over the enemy's strong points, blockade them, and leave them to starve."

Now, reflecting on operations as the US advanced across the ocean, Josh saw that all actions of land, air, and sea forces had been coordinated to do exactly what Halsey had said. Some islands had been seized, but only when, following their conquests, they had been used by Allied forces for airfields, harbor facilities, amassing troops, building up supplies, or providing some other critical support.

He perceived that a primary objective had always been to move Allied assets farther west until the Japanese homeland could be threatened by land-based bomber attacks; but he also realized that such a strategy alone would take too long and consume enormous resources. To speed up the process, destroying enemy supply lines was crucial, and had thus been intensified; and direct pressure on Japanese positions behind its defensive perimeter had to be undertaken.

The reason for combat operations in Burma and increased support in China for Generalissimo Chiang Kai-shek became clear. Constant pressure on Japan and recent victories in the Marshalls allowed Allied forces to advance to the Mariannas and provided the latitude for more offensive operations. Greater Allied support for the generalissimo required Japan to commit more resources to defend across a wider front.

Despite three Zeros possibly still chasing him, thrill seized Josh as realization dawned: the US was entering its final offensive phase. The door to attacking Japan was opening without threatening Allied gains. With the island nation pressed to maintain large-scale combat operations all the way from Burma to New Guinea, Japan would be unable to adequately maintain a defensive garrison in its home chain of islands. With victories also in General MacArthur's Southwest Pacific Theater, the US Navy now advanced aggressively across the Central Pacific.

The island of Japan was becoming vulnerable. Its combined fleet was divided and could not marshal sufficient forces to meet the US fleet. It had begun withdrawing, and the Allies had shifted to all-out offense.

Josh took in a deep breath at the thought. He believed he now understood the rationale behind the initiative to overrun Truk. The reason had eluded him. Only weeks before, the Japanese had been pushed out of the

Marshall Islands. The Caroline Islands in which Truk was located was the next step across the Pacific, bringing closer the objective of threatening Tokyo with land-based bombers. To that end, the US had only recently attacked and occupied Japanese forces at Eniwetok, an atoll of forty islands located seven hundred miles to the northeast of Truk. It contained a deep anchorage protected within its coral reefs and thus opened a gateway to Guam and the Mariannas. From there, the main island of Japan was within bomber-striking range.

But Truk Lagoon also represented another almost obscure but strategic opportunity. Josh had taken time to learn the atoll's history, and so he understood its significance. It had been discovered and claimed for Spain by explorers in 1528. It was sold to Germany in 1899 at the end of the Spanish-American War, which surrendered it as a condition of the WWI Armistice. By then, it had already been occupied by the Japanese for six years.

Its strategic attraction for Tokyo lay in its position away from Japan and far out in the Pacific, but within the country's defensive perimeter of occupied territories. Besides the atoll's natural defenses provided by its coral-encrusted, wide circumference, Truk had many islands able to house troops, support airfields, and provide space for fuel depots.

Most crucial of all were its two deep-water anchorages capable of servicing large ships. With only three easily defended entries into the atoll's interior, it was an ideal place for locating the Japanese Imperial Navy's headquarters and bringing its ships in for repair and replenishment. Hence the mammoth floating dry dock Josh had spotted.

After taking possession of the atoll, Japan had immediately based its 4th Imperial Fleet there, and it had used the location to strike at Burma. As the war progressed and the probability of war with the US rose, Japan merged the 4th Fleet into its Combined Fleet and located the headquarters there. By striking Truk and destroying the Japanese naval headquarters, or by driving them out, the Allies would have denied them the crown jewel of their naval defense system.

Within the US Navy, Truk had become known as the Pacific Gibraltar. Naval intelligence had reported twenty years of buildup, to include land-based heavy guns, thousands of combat troops, and extensive radar systems. Josh now puzzled over that characterization. To him it seemed an exaggeration of Truk's defenses.

The radio interrupted his thoughts. "Wannabe, sitrep. Over."

"Inbound. Dodged behind some clouds. Left bandits behind."

"Roger. We see you on radar. Your back trail is clear."

22

"The admiral wants to see you ASAP," a crewman told Josh when he had touched down, taxied to a spot directed by the deck handlers, and climbed down. The *Enterprise* traversed through heavy waves, so Josh had gone from being buffeted in the air to unsteady legs on the carrier's pitching deck.

He groaned, tossed the crewman an appreciative salute, and headed toward the ship's island. Moments later, he entered the bridge and was immediately directed to the admiral's quarters. Admiral Raymond Spruance sat at a desk. Josh entered, stood at attention, and saluted. "Lieutenant Commander Littlefield reports, sir."

Per an arrangement worked out with Admiral Nimitz' approval, Halsey and Spruance alternated command of the fleet. While one conducted an operation, the other planned the next. When Halsey had command, the fleet was designated as the Third Fleet, and when Spruance had it, the Fifth. In that way, they could move from one operation to the next with little loss of time. The technique had proven highly effective.

Admiral Spruance and the Fifth Fleet would carry out Operation Hailstone. He was slender, dark-haired, had a no-nonsense demeanor, and was known to be usually on his feet, roaming around the ships he commanded to engage with his sailors. He frequently conducted business with senior subordinates while on these walks. To be summoned to his office was a sure sign of his displeasure.

He returned Josh's salute and looked up at him with a furrowed brow. "What did you see, hotshot?" From Spruance's demeanor, his seeming attempt at humor bordered on sarcasm. "When you get done reporting, you can explain to me why you risked one of my flight leaders and a very expensive Hellcat to take a jaunt over Truk. That's a fortified enemy position. I need my leaders and my planes for combat missions. You went far too low for a recon mission."

"I didn't believe the intelligence, sir."

The admiral looked askance at him. "What was it you didn't believe?"

"That Truk was as fortified as we've been told."

"What are you talking about?"

"Sir, I studied the aerial photos from previous missions. I know what naval intelligence reported, but I didn't see evidence of heavy fortifications in the pictures."

"Heavy fortifications weren't in the photos for Tarawa either," Spruance retorted, his voice rising.

"Naval intelligence had that wrong too."

Spruance stood abruptly and folded his arms. "We don't need another Tarawa," he growled. "Before we went in there, we were told that defenses were light, and now you're telling me the same thing about Truk."

The battle at Tarawa had been bloody and costly. At its outset, Marines had been dropped in the water on a coral shelf far from shore, and they had waded into blistering machine gun fire. They won the battle, but with nowhere to find cover or concealment, their casualties had been the highest by far of any assault in the war to date.

Before Josh could respond, Spruance added, "We know Japan's navy has been on high alert since we made our recon flights over Truk back in December."

"I'm not telling you defenses at Truk are light or that the base isn't on high alert, but I think their fortifications have been exaggerated. I was in the battle at Tarawa, sir. I saw it at ground level."

"Don't you mean sea level, Commander. As I recall, you were shot down there."

"True, sir, but I was low enough over land before hitting the water that I could see what naval intelligence missed." Josh took a breath. "Please, sir, hear me out."

Spruance sighed and re-took his seat. "All right, let's hear it. At ease. Relax."

Josh spread his feet apart and held his palms together behind his back.

"Relax, Commander," Spruance growled. "That's an order." He grunted and allowed a quick smile. "That's the best I can do for humor at the moment. Tell me what you saw and why intelligence has it wrong." He indicated a chair in front of his desk.

Josh sat down. "I went over all the aerial photos, sir, and I just didn't see anything that looked like heavy gun positions or large-scale troop housing. I'd estimate manpower levels between ten and fifteen thousand soldiers and sailors, not the forty thousand that's been reported.

"After we took Tarawa, I walked the coastal defenses the Japs had built there. They were discernible in the intel photos. I studied the Truk photos before I went on my recon, and I saw nothing that looked like what was on Tarawa. One of my chief objectives for going was that I wanted to see in person if I was missing something. I wanted to draw fire and probe their defenses."

"You certainly did that," Spruance said sternly. He thought intently. "I'll buy what you say for the moment. You told me what you didn't see. Now tell me what you saw."

Josh nodded. "I spotted the headquarters, fuel storage facilities, both anchorages, anti-aircraft gun positions, and four of the airfields. I scanned the harbors. I couldn't count the ships, but I think there are fewer of them now than back in December. And I identified the battleship *Musashi*, several carriers, and a torpedo boat. There were quite a few merchant ships, maybe thirty or more, scattered in several anchorages around the lagoon."

Spruance stared at him dubiously. "That's it? What about the *Yamoto*."

Josh shook his head. "Wasn't there."

Spruance arched his brows. "Hmm. I'm having a difficult time believing that they would leave Truk so weakly defended. All of Japan's Combined Fleet offensive operations were run out of Truk including combat at Wake Island. They countered our initiatives at New Guinea and the Solomon and

Gilbert Islands from there. We thought they'd use 'em against us in the Mariannas.

"And *Yamoto* is the biggest warship that's ever been built. Admiral Yamamoto had his headquarters on that ship before we shot him down. If the ship's not at Truk, where is it?" He paused and glanced up. "That's a rhetorical question."

"Sir, Truk's defense was the Japanese offense spread across the Pacific east of the lagoon. That defense is gone now. I kept looking for anything that would indicate otherwise, but I haven't seen it.

"I did see a number of ships being serviced at the docks. They won't be able to move. And it looked like only about half of the aircraft on the fields are ready to fly. The rest are lined up for service." Josh pursed his lips. "I only made one pass, but I came in low from the east over a saddle at daybreak. The lagoon and its shore facilities were laid out in front of me."

Josh's eyes suddenly widened. "I almost forgot. I saw the floating dry dock that's been reported. That thing is a monster. Ingenious, really. I have to hand it to the Japanese for their ingenuity.

"And I'm positive now that their radar can't see down close to sea level. The spotters couldn't see me when I came in because of the sun in their eyes, and there was no sign I was detected by radar before I flew over that saddle. I came out right above their headquarters. I saw no major radar installations, and I was all the way to the other side of the atoll before any bandits were on me. If I had to guess, those anti-aircraft batteries are shooting without radar." He shook his head. "Sir, if that atoll were as heavily defended as intelligence says, I would've been a sitting duck."

He grinned as a thought struck him. "Now, if we could hit the target at night guided by radar—"

Spruance interrupted Josh, his expression implacable. "Anything else?"

Josh took a deep breath. "You mentioned Tarawa. No one wants to see another one, but if we consider that event too much, we're likely to go in less aggressively, possibly fail, and maybe take more casualties than we should. If the Japs are on high alert and really intend to defend Truk, they're slow on the trigger. I saw no sign that they're expecting an attack. My gut tells me they're pulling out. We can catch them with their pants down."

Spruance stifled a chuckle. "That saying is a little worn, Commander."

"Yes, sir, but it applies. I think we can navigate in with our radar, under theirs, and come up on target with all guns blazing. I know for a fact now that our Hellcats outperform their Zeros, at least in speed and firepower. If we avoid dogfights and just shoot right through any of their formations, we'll kill off their overhead protection.

"In fact, if we go in with our torpedo bombers first, we'll hit the ships before their Zeros can organize into air formations. We'll—" Josh paused, searching for words. Then he grinned. "We'll take them by surprise, knock them from the skies, destroy their warships and merchant ships, and instead of being called the Pacific Gibraltar, Truk Lagoon will become known as the Japanese Pearl Harbor."

Spruance laughed in spite of himself. "I'll consider your views, Commander. I can tell you this: your observation about fewer ships in the anchorage lines up with another event today. Our submarine *Skate* spotted and killed a Japanese light cruiser just after it left the atoll through the northern break in the coral perimeter. It looked like it was on a course back to Japan. We've had other reports from submarines of ships steaming toward Japan, but most of them are supply ships. That's not out of the ordinary.

"If we find more of their warships headed that way, I'll redesignate the *New Jersey* as my flagship and give chase. I'm a cruiser officer by training, not a carrier man. We just might see a real shooting battle between warships on the west side of Truk before all this is over." He grunted. "It might be the only time that *Iowa*-class battleships fire at enemy warships in this conflict."

The admiral leaned back in his chair, seemingly studying the ceiling. Josh waited silently, his heart beating rapidly.

At last, Spruance spoke again. "We'll get the staff to analyze Truk's defenses again—get more pilots to tell us what they've seen. We can't do any more flyovers. We're too close to execution, and we can't let the Japanese learn our position and direction. With the size of this fleet, they'd guess immediately what we intend to do.

"And just so ya know, by going straight for Truk, we'll bypass the Japanese stronghold at Rabaul and isolate it. Japan won't be able to re-supply it." He drummed his fingers on his desk as he reflected. "Our loss there two years ago was a tough pill, but now it'll be like a lodestone around Japan's neck. It's got strong forces there that it won't be able to use or resupply. We'll starve 'em out."

He dropped into pensive meditation a few moments, and when he looked up again, he rose to his feet, a signal that the meeting was ending. "Good report, Commander. We'll study your observations for our planning. Meanwhile"—his voice rose and he glared at Josh—"you're grounded until we execute Operation Hailstone."

Josh flushed red. He stood and saluted. "Yes, sir."

The two men regarded each other in silence. Then a slow smile spread across Josh's face. "Sir, you said 'until we execute.' Does that mean I get to fly the mission?"

Spruance chuckled. "Littlefield, you sure know how to push the boundaries and do it respectfully." He smacked his lips in mock sarcasm. "Hell, you're going to lead Hailstone."

23

February 17, 1944
One Hundred Miles Northeast of Truk Lagoon

Josh revved the Wright R-2600-20 Twin Cyclone fourteen-cylinder radial engine on his TBF Avenger torpedo bomber. It was the heaviest of any single-engine fighter in the navy's inventory, but generating nineteen hundred horsepower, it was equal to today's mission. As advantageous as the powerful engine, the plane navigated by radar.

As opposed to his Hellcat, flown by a lone pilot, the Avenger carried a crew of three: a pilot, bombardier, and turret gunner. Josh's bombardier, Petty Officer Third Class Charlie Kettle, the man who would release the torpedo and also operate the radar and radio, sat behind him. While cruising, Kettle sat on a bench in the tail section and monitored the radio and radar screen. During combat, he stood to acquire the target and release the torpedo. However, if the aircraft came under attack from below and to the rear, he would defend with a 7.62 mm machine gun mounted under the tail.

The third crewman, Seaman Eddie Baucus, sat behind Kettle in a rear-facing, electrically powered turret. He operated a .50 caliber machine gun, covering against hostiles to the sides and rear above the tail.

Josh spoke over his intercom to his bombardier and turret gunner. "Are y'all ready for this?"

Receiving two affirmative responses, Josh thought through the defense at his own disposal. His control stick included triggers to fire twin Browning AN/M2 0.50 caliber light-barrel guns, one in each wing outboard of the propeller's arc.

Josh had thought he would be flying a Hellcat on this mission, but two days after his tête-à-tête with Admiral Spruance, he had been eating breakfast in the mess hall when he was summoned to the bridge. He was met there by smiling faces, and then, with no other warning and little fanfare, an orderly called the deck to attention, and Admiral Spruance strode out of his office and stood next to Josh.

"Proceed," he said.

To Josh's shock, a personnel officer stepped forward and read orders promoting Josh one grade, from lieutenant commander to commander. When the man had finished, the admiral removed Josh's gold oak leaves and replaced them with silver ones. Then he shook Josh's hand and told him, "You've got work to do, Commander, planning your part of the raid on Truk. You'll be leading in the TBFs."

"The Avengers, sir? I thought I'd be flying a Hellcat?"

Spruance chuckled. "It was your idea to lead with the Torpedo bombers. I think it's a good one. Do you want to bow out?"

Josh exhaled. "No, sir. I still think it's a good idea."

"Fine. Then you'll transfer to the *Intrepid* and prepare the Avenger pilots." Spruance gripped Josh's shoulder. "And don't worry, Commander," he said with an amused smile, "your Hellcat buddies'll be around to pull your butt out of the fire if things get too dicey."

Josh had laughed off the comment uneasily. His task suddenly seemed formidable. He had never flown an Avenger torpedo bomber, but since one of its crew was a bombardier, Josh's main function on the aircraft would be to fly into position. The bombardier would release the tube. And, Josh reminded himself, he had not flown a Dauntless dive bomber before jumping into one and taking off to join in attacking ships at Midway. With almost two weeks to go before mission execution against Truk, he had time to familiarize himself with the Avenger and meld with his own flight crew as well as the pilots and crews of his new command.

Among Avenger pilots, the aircraft had a terrific reputation despite a common comment that, "It flies like a truck, for better or worse." Its bomb bay was large, allowing for a Bliss-Leavitt Mark 13 torpedo and a single two-thousand-pound bomb, or up to four five-hundred-pound bombs. It was easy to handle, and its long range of nine hundred miles, fully loaded, and its thirty-thousand-foot ceiling made it the best US torpedo bomber in the war thus far, and superior to its Japanese opposite. Rugged and stable, it came with solid radio equipment. Better yet, those in Josh's squadron contained onboard radar.

Josh's pilots, among the twelve best aboard the *Intrepid,* were assigned for this specific mission. They would fly with Mk 13 torpedoes and a two-thousand-pound bomb loaded into their bays, and deliver them to explode below the waterline of their targets, creating massive holes in the hulls and sinking their targets, the ships anchored at Truk Lagoon.

At one point a few days after taking command, Lieutenant John Marsh, one of the squadron's flight leaders, approached Josh. "Sir, may I have a minute."

"Shoot, what's on your mind?"

"I've been a torpedo pilot since Pearl Harbor. I haven't flown anything else."

"Got it, Lieutenant. Is that a complaint?"

"No, sir. I'm making the point that I know my aircraft and its weapon system."

"Do you have a concern?"

"Yes, sir, I do."

Josh studied Marsh. He was big for a pilot, with a large head, curly hair, and intelligent eyes. Before Josh could ask further about the concern, Marsh interjected, "From what I've heard, there's a lot of coral in that lagoon."

"True enough. Does it affect the torpedoes?"

"It'll make them porpoise—you know, surface and submerge unpredictably and uncontrollably."

"Hmm. You got any suggestions?"

Marsh nodded. "We should fly in at masthead level; and right when we lose sight of the target ship's side under our aircraft's noses, that's when we release the torpedoes. They'll skip across the surface and sink just before hitting their targets, which is right where we want them."

Astonished at the suggestion, Josh whistled. "Are you serious? You've got to be half-crazy to be a torpedo pilot in the first place, but you're sayin' we should almost crawl down the Japs' throats to drop our tubes. You'd need nerves of steel for that."

Marsh laughed. "Yes, sir. If we don't do it that way, we're playin' roulette. If we do, we're still gamblin' but we got a better shot. If I hit a good target, I don't mind dyin', but I'll be ticked off if I check out for nothin' when I had a better way." He cocked his head to one side. "Ask around to the other pilots. They'll mostly agree."

"Have you done it before?"

"More than once or twice. We call it skip bombing."

Josh sized up Marsh. He had a gregarious personality and was trusted among his fellow pilots. "Let me give it some thought," he replied. Later, after interviewing his flight leaders and their subordinate pilots, Josh had one more question. "We'll have radar, but will we be able to physically see the specific ships at night?"

"Yes, sir," came the response. "We've tested it."

"But you've never done it operationally at night?"

"That is correct."

"How will we know we're at mast height in the dark?"

"We know the ships' characteristics. The pilot aims for the side, the radar operator tells him the correct altitude. He'll know when to drop. But then you've got to pull up fast and steep."

With gut-level misgivings, but trusting his pilots, Josh had run the concept up the chain of command with his own positive recommendation. He received approval.

Early this morning, an hour before mission launch and after the typical send-off breakfast of steak and eggs, the pilots had gathered in the *Intrepid's* ready room. Admiral Spruance addressed them via a public address system, his message also carried to Hellcat pilots preparing to launch from the *Enterprise* and to the Dauntless pilots readying for launch aboard the *Essex.*

"Our mission," Spruance intoned, "is to destroy enemy ships at anchor, shoot their fighters out of the air, crater their airfields, bomb their headquarters, set fire to their fuel depots, and destroy parked bombers and fighters. If an object is man-made, we'll hit it. If you do your jobs well and thoroughly, and I know you will, we'll remove Truk as the central base for Japanese offensive operations. They need the lagoon. We don't. It's their turn to be on full defense. We go on full offense.

"Our Avengers will lead this time, going after the ships. That's a bit unusual, but the tactical reasoning is sound. The Hellcats will be right behind them, knocking out Zeros before they have a chance to organize in the sky and dropping bombs on targets of opportunity. And our Dauntless dive bombers will go in and destroy the headquarters, the fuel installations, supply and ammo depots, the airfields, and any aircraft still on the ground. We'll crater the runways to make them unusable, and hit anything still floating in the anchorages after the torpedoes have done their jobs.

"Hailstone is a crucial mission, men. Bring havoc down on our enemies' heads."

In the *Intrepid's* ready room, when the admiral finished speaking, all eyes shifted to Josh. "I've got nothing to add," he said. "You know your targets."

The *Intrepid* pitched in ten-foot swells, and it had turned into a stiff wind blowing from the west. Once again, as Josh waited for the flagman to wave him into action, a combined sense of excitement and trepidation gripped him.

Strangely, he had not only become accustomed to the mixed smells of salt water, aviation fuel, and exhaust fumes, but he had also learned to welcome them, particularly on this morning. The roar, clamor, and clang of the aircraft carrier, muffled by his helmet and closed canopy, tended to increase his nervous energy.

He reveled in the powerful thrust of the aircraft straining against his pressure on the brakes. This would be the first such raid, guided by onboard radar, at night. And the target was only one hundred miles away.

Far down the deck to the left, the aircraft handling officer leaned against the wind, watching for the right moment as the ship's bow plowed the waves. Then he swooshed a checkered signal flag.

Josh released the brakes.

The Avenger pounced. Guided by a white stripe painted along the left side for the full length of the deck, it accelerated and rushed into the wind. Lifting its nose, it cleared the end of the *Intrepid*, took a slight dip, and soared.

The aircraft gained altitude, circled around the ship, and continued orbiting as the other Avengers took off in turn. The squadron formed up. Josh checked his azimuth against a giant lighted sign on the ship's island displaying the correct direction and squawked his radio. "Let's roll," he called to his squadron.

The twelve Avengers dropped down, skimming the water's surface, heading west, with the bombardiers monitoring their radar screens. As Josh flew, he wondered how the *blitz* must have been for his cousin Jeremy. The two had never met, but his cousin Paul had related that Jeremy was among the early nightfighters flying Beaufighters against the *Luftwaffe* over London when waves of bombers had dropped tons of flaming destruction on British cities. At the time, the Royal Air Force had mastered the use of ground-to-air radar for command and control, but air-to-air and air-to-ground radar were in their infancy. The radar operator guided the pilot to an enemy bomber based on audible blips crossing a small screen with no geographic indicators.

Now, with the radar system aboard the Avenger, Kettle could identify targets, navigate to them, and see obstacles in their path, all from a simple screen that outlined dry land like a map. *The wonders of modern technology!*

Flying at a cruising speed of two hundred and fifteen miles per hour at a height of fifty feet, the distance closed very quickly. Peering through his windshield, Josh saw nothing but black sky. The stars were blotted out by a blanket of thick clouds. Feeling like he had barely settled into his seat, Kettle surprised him by calling over the intercom, "Ten minutes out."

Josh's buttocks tightened. In each of the twelve Avengers, the bombardier would advise their pilots the same way Kettle had. The squadron flew on under radio silence.

Shortly, Kettle called on the intercom, "Five minutes," and then, "Climb to five hundred."

Josh's hands became moist, his mind fully concentrated as he nudged the Avenger's nose up. "We'll cross the saddle in two," Kettle said.

Using maps and mock-ups, Josh had drilled his pilots on the positions of the targets relative to the saddle as their main reference. From there, they would fan out with two flights to the left and two to the right, and Josh's plane at the center. The flights would further separate so that each Avenger had exclusive responsibility for a section of the atoll that extended to its far side. They would strike the largest target in the water in their respective sections with the Mk 13, using Marsh's skip bombing technique, and then drop the two-thousand-pound bomb on the next available target.

The Avengers would continue straight on to form up beyond the coral perimeter on the far side of the atoll. From there, they would swing to the south, flying in a wide arc for their return to the *Intrepid,* outside the flight paths of the inbound Hellcat fighters and Dauntless dive bombers.

"Over the saddle," Kettle intoned. "Target spotted. Start smooth descent to fifty."

Josh nudged his nose down and throttled back, disbelieving that he was flying in a black night at the Avenger's maximum speed and taking directional instructions from a man three feet behind him staring into a green-lit screen.

"A little steeper. Adjust two degrees to the right."

The plane vibrated roughly as it descended, pulled by gravity to greater velocity.

Trying to pierce the darkness outside his canopy, Josh strained his eyes to no avail. He glanced at the altimeter. The needle fell past three hundred feet, then two hundred. As it passed one hundred, his breath came in short gasps.

"Level out," Kettle called anxiously.

Josh pulled the stick back and reset his trim.

"On my mark," Kettle exclaimed. "Five, four, three, two, NOW!"

The Avenger shook and bounced higher as the heavy Mk 13 torpedo dropped away. In the same instant, Josh pulled the nose of the aircraft up and opened the throttle. The engine roared, the wind rattled the canopy, and heavy G-forces pulled the crew hard into their seats.

"We're clear," Josh yelled.

A flash of light momentarily illuminated the cockpit. Behind them, an explosion erupted. Baucus shouted over the intercom from his turret, "We got a direct hit. The sky's lit up. The other torpedoes are hitting too."

For fear of colliding with one of his own Avengers, Josh resisted an urge to bank the plane for a look. He re-set his course along his designated section. "What's next?"

"We got a freighter straight ahead. It's a good-sized one. If you hold at a hundred, we'll fly right over the top of it and I'll cut loose when I'm ready."

"Roger. Do it."

Moments later, the Avenger once again lifted higher as the two-thousand-pound bomb dropped away. The concussions joined a chorus of eruptions from the left and right, illuminating the sky with the totality of massive explosions and shipboard fires. "I'd say our mission's a success. What do you guys think?"

Baucus whooped, and Kettle said, "I'd say so, and still no bandits in sight."

With no longer any reason for radio silence, Josh keyed his mic and called the flight leaders. "Report."

"This is Red Dog. All primary targets hit. Two of three secondaries."

The next two flights called in with similar results.

The last one reported, "I still got one out. Popeye. His primary target was not there, but he spotted it on radar outside the atoll to the west. He's going after it."

"Roger. Form up as planned. We'll wait outside ack-ack range. Out." Elation for mission success abated as Josh waited anxiously to hear about Popeye. That was Lieutenant James Bridges. He was a quiet man, but friendly and thorough. Hardly a maverick, he broke from the popular image of fighter pilots. He listened attentively at briefings, took notes, and studied maps, sketches, and photos of his specific targets. He had studied the lagoon in detail.

The Avengers circled and met five miles out, to the southeast of the coral necklace, and out of the way of the next waves of incoming friendly fighters and bombers. From this perch, the silhouette of the islands' hills were clearly visible against a sky illuminated by flames. Zeros flew up from the west side pursuing the Avengers.

No dogfights took place. The Hellcats intercepted the Zeros, engaged with greater firepower from a longer range, flew through the disorganized formations, and knocked the Zeros from the skies in twos and threes.

The Dauntless dive bombers flew in under the Hellcats' protective umbrella. When they were past the failing Japanese defensive screen, they gained height, crossed over the mountains, and dove down to deliver their lethal payloads.

Josh's radio crackled. "Wannabe, this is Swordfish. Popeye has acquired his target. Will strike momentarily. It's the *Aikoku Maru*."

Josh gulped. The *Aikoku Maru* was a huge freighter known for transporting explosives and ammunition. If it blew...

Only seconds later, an explosion of volcanic proportions erupted to the southwest, lighting up the sky even brighter than the fires inside the atoll. It reverberated across the ocean like rolling thunder.

Swordfish called in, "Wannabe, target hit." Anguish in the flight leader's voice was unmistakable. "Popeye down. Caught in the explosion."

24

Oflag IV-C POW Camp, Colditz Castle, Germany

"You do realize that I probably have no chance of surviving if I'm still here in the closing days of the war." Lieutenant Lance Littlefield addressed his remark to the members of the escape committee. "Hitler takes revenge. When he's convinced that Churchill and Roosevelt really mean unconditional surrender, and we *prominentes* are of no further value to him, we're dead. Simple as that."

They sat in a day room in the upper reaches of the castle within the barracks area, with stooges set out at strategic points on the castle's stone stairways and corridors to provide early warning in case the guards decided to enact a no-notice search. Captain Richard Howe stood near an outside window overlooking the quad three stories below while Lance sat across a table from him. The committee being composed of five officers, and Lance himself being a member, only three other men attended the meeting.

As though a stray thought had flashed through Lance's mind, he asked, "What constitutes a *prominente* in the first place? Captain Arundell is the bona fide 16th Baron of Wardour. He's a blue blood, but he's not classified as a *prominente*.

"Or how about Captain the Lord of Hopetoun, Lothian and the Border

Horse, son of Marquis of Linlithgow?" Lance enunciated each part of the aristocratic titles. "He's certainly prominent. I'm not." He added quickly, "Not that I wish this dubious status on anyone. I'm just curious. Why me? I'm sure more *prominentes* will arrive before it's all settled and done."

Howe, a tall blond officer and head of the escape committee, responded. "We've wondered about the same things, Lance. We've reached a conclusion. Mind you it's speculative and not pleasant, but it lines up with your own inference.

"Arundell is not married, has no siblings, and no heirs. His line dies with him unless he gets home safely, takes a wife, and has male children. He's not close enough to royalty or anyone of influence. As a result, his value as a bargaining chip is remote, and apparently, the Germans see him that way too."

"You've almost described my own situation, sir," Lance insisted vehemently. His ire had already been piqued at an unexpected negative reception to his request to be placed at or near the front of the queue for another escape attempt of his own. "My family is in no danger of passing into history, but I'm from a tiny plateau of barely two-square miles sitting atop an eighty-foot-high rock in the Channel. It's hardly of significance to anyone."

Howe nodded. "Ah, but the difference is that your rock is not only a gun platform defending France's western coast in Normandy, but Sark and the other nearby Channel Islands also compose the only British soil that Hitler occupies. They're of great propaganda value to him, and in that regard, he considers them to be significant.

"So, your island and your family are known to Churchill and probably to King George as well. Hitler knows this. If he hopes to use *prominentes* as bargaining chips, you'll be among them.

"I should add that the difference between how you and Arundell are treated supports our conclusion about what the Third *Reich* intends for *prominentes*."

"Which is exactly the reason I must escape," Lance said, exasperated. "Besides," he added with a dour look, "it's every officer's responsibility to try to escape."

Howe inhaled sharply. "Agreed, but you do realize the reason why

London's asked us to discourage attempts right now. The Allied invasion of France is coming, and preparations are underway."

He crossed his arms as he watched Lance's face. "As I recall, the last time you escaped, you were aided for a number of weeks by a network in the Loire Valley after you got through Switzerland."

Lance nodded, but did not speak.

"Your risk will be higher this time. We won't have the usual French Resistance networks to help you get through to Switzerland or Spain. They'll be sabotaging targets. Escapees could interfere with their efforts or get caught in crossfires. We'd do all we can for you, supply you with forged travel papers, maps, money, and food to last a few days, but once over the wall, you'll be on your own."

Lance closed his eyes, leaned back in his seat, and blew out a breath. When he leaned forward again, his voice took on a beseeching tone. "I was on my own for a time in every attempt I've made." His voice changed to stubbornness. "The fact is, I can go over the wall on my own without anyone's permission."

Howe's expression turned grave. "That's not a good idea, Lieutenant. If you do that, you'll do it without the maps, money, etcetera that we provide. Furthermore, if you're recaptured and returned here, you might be subjected to Hitler's mandated treatment for captured commandos—death —and we'd be in poor position to intercede on your behalf with *Komman-dant* Prawwit. Even if he meted out nothing more than the standard term of solitary confinement for making the attempt, you'd still face Colonel Tod, and he would be likely to add to your punishment."

Lance sat without speaking as he contemplated. All eyes focused on him.

Lieutenant-colonel Willie Tod, a Scotsman, was the senior British officer or SBO. He was a fair man. By dint of his seniority among officers, he had assumed the position of authority over British POWs at Colditz on his arrival in November. He had left the escape committee intact as it had been prior to his arrival. Like his predecessors, he stayed apart from their proceedings so that he could truthfully report to Prawwit that he knew of no escapes in the offing. However, owing to the expected invasion of France, he refrained from encouraging attempts and instructed Howe to approve only those plans that had a strong probability of succeeding. Further, on the basis of military professionalism and respecting foes, he took measures to end the inmates' habit of disparaging the guards.

Despite Tod's added strictures, he had quickly won the hearts of his fellow inmates, particularly when they learned through intelligence channels from London that, shortly after his arrival, Tod's son had been killed in combat. Tod had never mentioned the fact, and when Howe asked him about it, he said with introspection evidenced in a momentary far-off glance, "These things happen to soldiers."

Tod continued policies of behavior inherited from his predecessors intended to lessen strife among men in forced confinement. The rules aimed to lessen military decorum while insisting on maintaining respect. Also, in the early days of Colditz as a POW camp, too many escapes had exposed other plans being executed concurrently. The participants had not known of the other attempts. As a result, Tod was rigid on enforcing protocol for escape planning, coordination, and execution, and he had little sympathy for recaptured escapees who had tried their getaways without coordinating through the escape committee.

At last, Lance spoke, exasperated. "I can't just sit and wait for the end of the war. Who knows how long that will take? Allied victory is far from assured. Every fiber in my being screams for escape. Every second I'm awake, I look for a way out."

"Every man here dreams of freedom—" Howe began.

"But not everyone wants to take the risk," Lance interrupted. "Some have resigned themselves to whatever comes—from my perspective, they're barely alive. Others feel like they've taken their share of danger and just want to ride the war out. So they take university courses, do painting or sketching, or engage in some other activity. Most are willing to help escape plans, but the group of men who feel in their bones that they must escape is rather small."

He glanced across the room at an average-sized, red-haired lieutenant who might have been stocky under normal circumstances but whose physique had, like everyone's in the room, been emaciated by the ravages of the living conditions and poor nutrition of a Nazi POW camp. "Tell him, Mike," Lance said. "You know what I mean. You've made what now, six attempts?"

"I do know," Lieutenant Michael Sinclair said somberly. He had been dubbed the Red Fox by the Germans for his multiple ingenious methods, including an attempt nearly a year earlier in which he had impersonated the most noticeable German sergeant in the castle. That plan had anticipated freeing more than fifty POWs and had nearly succeeded. Disguised as the German sergeant, Sinclair had ordered a sentry at the front gate to return to the guardhouse. For unknown reasons, the sentry had refused.

Sinclair's disguised identity had not been questioned, and he could have walked out of Colditz Castle unhindered, but he risked his own freedom to try to gain that of this comrades. Thus he had repeated his order to the sentry with rising anger until suspicions were aroused. His escape was blown when the sergeant whom Sinclair had impersonated showed up at the gate to investigate the row.

Sinclair had tried yet again last month. He had been released from solitary confinement for that attempt just days ago. He turned his sunken eyes on Howe. "Believe me when I say that I'm already thinking about my next try."

Howe grunted. "I wouldn't expect anything less."

Sinclair turned back to Lance. "Let me remind you that with only a few exceptions, every POW present at Colditz is here because somewhere, he escaped or tried to escape from a German prison camp. So you and I are not unique." He gestured toward Howe. "And you should recall too that Dick is still here because continuity in the escape officer position is important. The SBO asked him to fill that role, and he accepted, even under the constraint that he would make no such attempts himself. That's quite selfless. He has his own admirable record of escaping."

Lance took his time to respond, and when he spoke again, he took a softer tone. "Sir," he began, addressing Howe, "I understand the situation fully, I assure you of that. But my time is limited because I've been named a *prominente.*

"Bill Millar escaped two weeks ago, and he hasn't returned. No word's come out that he's been recaptured and taken elsewhere. Chances are, he scored a home run."

"Could be. I'll ask London to confirm," Howe replied. "Regardless, that doesn't change anything here and now. The Resistance is busy preparing for the invasion; the Germans know it's coming, and security is tightening. I won't have another Giles Romilly situation, and I can't handle another Errol Flynn."

Giles Romilly, a British civilian journalist, had been detained during Germany's invasion of Norway. He had the distinction of being the first *prominente* by virtue of being Winston Churchill's nephew, and he had been incarcerated at Colditz because it was considered to be the Third *Reich's* most secure POW camp.

Last July, he had tried a spur-of-the-moment escape that had almost succeeded but with near disastrous consequences. The German army had decided that managing POWs could be done more easily if they could be segregated by nationality. Until then, Colditz housed primarily British, French, Dutch, and Polish prisoners. Giles and one other man were the odd civilians among the prison population. The other non-military prisoner had been captured while attempting to cross Europe to fight for Finland in its war against the Soviet Union at the time that Moscow and Berlin were still allies.

In the past year, German High Command developed a new concept of high-security containment for those with a propensity for escape. Instead of interning all the high-risk prisoners together, they moved them to other camps, separated by nationality, leaving only the British at Colditz. As the French POWs packed to leave, Romilly noticed an empty packing crate. He convinced a departing inmate to cut air holes in the lid and nail it closed with him inside. Romilly carried only a penknife and a flask of water.

He succeeded in being transported to the train station. The plan failed when the crate was thrown upside down onto the platform, and his penknife proved inadequate for its intended task. Besides being tossed about, Romilly nearly suffocated, and after being found out, he was returned to Colditz.

Frank "Errol" Flynn, so nicknamed for his resemblance to and bearing the last name of the famous actor, took a different approach. Relying on a

Geneva Convention provision that allowed cooperation between opposing combatants through the Red Cross to repatriate prisoners who were beyond recovery either mentally or physically, he had decided to convince a medical commission that he had gone insane.

To accomplish his objective, Flynn began carrying out deliberate acts of extreme irrationality. In one instance, he had been sitting at a table with several companions. Without a word, he left his seat, went to a nearby table where two other inmates were playing chess, scattered the pieces, grabbed the board, and brought it down on the head of one of the players. He then walked back calmly to his seat and resumed conversation without explanation.

Howe's dilemma with regard to Flynn had been that he was not sure that the man had not driven himself into real insanity. Flynn's actions had been increasingly disruptive and difficult for other POWs to forgive.

Two weeks ago, that consideration ended. Flynn had apparently tried to hang himself, although his positioning made dubious his intent to actually do so—he had placed himself such that he could have easily stepped onto a toilet rim to save himself. Nevertheless, he was discovered with a noose and a deep red mark around his neck. The guards rushed to save him, and he was removed from Colditz. However, he was not repatriated or moved to another camp. Instead, he was taken to a concentration camp of unknown identity and was not heard from again.

Howe locked eyes with Lance.

Anticipating the captain's thoughts, Lance pleaded, "Will you at least hear my plan?"

The captain pursed his lips and sighed. He leaned back against the wall and searched the ceiling as if hoping for divine wisdom to descend. Finally, he faced Lance directly and shook his head. "Not now."

Lance started to protest, but Howe stopped him with an upraised palm. "Listen to me. I want you to take more time to think this through thoroughly. I'm sure you already have, but double-check yourself. Do you have someone traveling with you?"

Lance shook his head.

"That's a flag. A man traveling alone stands out and is suspect, particularly in an area where a POW has escaped. You know that. You're thinner than most of the population you'll travel through. Let's face it, you're gaunt, like the rest of us. Malnourished. And we're far into Germany's east side."

Lance closed his eyes. "It's winter," he growled. "I'll wear a heavy overcoat—"

"Which will hang on you like a scarecrow's. I'm not trying to be unkind, just realistic. I'm not saying no, but I am insisting on an extra layer of precaution."

"I'll go as a migrant worker from the east. I speak German and French fluently."

"That might work, and your fluency is an advantage, but it's not fool-proof. I still won't listen or approve until you've had time to think through every aspect completely and bring back a detailed plan. There's too much risk."

"Only to myself, and it's my life." Lance stood, barely able to contain his anger.

"Which I treasure," Howe said steadily.

The two men stared stonily into each other's eyes. Then Lance's glare softened. "I know. I appreciate you, sir." He stepped back and left the room.

An hour before curfew, Lance entered the *prominente* quarters, hoping to speak with Giles Romilly. He found the journalist alone in the cell shared with Michael Alexander, the second ever *prominente*.

Alexander had been captured during an operation in North Africa. His mission had been thrown together so rapidly that he had not had time to change out of civilian clothes and had thus been taken for a spy when he was captured, which would have mandated his execution. He had avoided that end by implying that he was nephew to Supreme Allied Commander Mediterranean, General Sir Harold Alexander. As such, the ostensible nephew had been remanded for safekeeping in Colditz Castle.

Finding Romilly alone, Lance asked for a word with him. Known to be irascible and friendly in equal measures but on an unpredictable basis, Romilly looked beleaguered even by the standard of anyone who had endured long periods of isolation, hunger, confinement, and the deprava-tions of freezing weather and damp conditions with inadequate warmth. This evening, he seemed in reasonable spirits.

The room was barely large enough for two beds, two writing tables, and two chairs. Romilly was sitting on his bed reading when Lance entered.

"How's my friend, the escape artist," Romilly greeted him, opening to garrulous conversation for which he was known. He arched his eyebrows. "You know you're the most successful one here. You scored a home run and came back." He smirked. "Why would you do that?"

Lance chuckled. "That wasn't my intention, I promise you."

During his previous stint as a POW, Lance had escaped four times before finally, on the fifth attempt, evading capture and getting all the way home to England. He had then joined the commandos and was captured again on a sabotage mission to Norway, and was once more returned to Colditz.

"What can I do for you?" Romilly asked.

"Do you mind talking about what happened during your escape?"

"Do you mean how I ended up in such a silly predicament with no air to breathe?" Without waiting for a response, he continued. "It's not as if I planned things to go that way. The truth is, I did no planning at all. I saw the opportunity and took it. But I was done in by the Law of Unintended Consequences. It always lurks with its black magic, creating havoc.

"I thought that the same people who nailed me into the crate would let me out on the train platform. As far as I can determine, once all the baggage was loaded onto trucks to go to the station, it fell under the handling of orderlies, and they didn't know the contents of my box from any other. It ended upside down, my air cut off, and then my knife was too small to cut through the crate. When I started banging..." He shrugged.

"I get the picture," Lance said. "Will you try again? Aren't you concerned about what might happen if using us to bargain doesn't work?"

Romilly shook his head. "I'm done. I took my chances. I don't mind saying that I was terrified. But we've taken North Africa and Sicily. The Allies are rolling up Italy, however slowly. An invasion of France is in the offing." He glanced through his window that overlooked the basketball-court-sized POW quad surrounded by the tall stone walls of Colditz' prisoner barracks. "I'll bide my time. The Allies will win this war by dint of vastly superior resources coming from America if by no other means.

"The balance of power is shifting away from the Germans. They know it, even in here. So as to whether I worry about what will happen to us, of course I'm concerned, but neither the guards nor their commanders want to be tried for war crimes after final victory. I'll rely on that."

Lance barely slept that night, his mind churning with the improbable escape plan Mike Sinclair had devised. Sinclair had intended to use it himself, but given Lance's urgency for being a *prominente* and the suspicions over the tragic result if and when Hitler perceived that he could not win the war, Sinclair had passed the plan on to Lance.

The odds of surviving the initial scamper to and over the wall were not great. Succeeding that, Lance faced the dubious prospect of traveling through Germany's hostile population to either Switzerland or Occupied France. If he managed to cross into Switzerland, he faced being confined to a town called Davos until the end of the war. A provision of the Geneva Convention allowed for that to prevent escaped combatants from rejoining the war, although several had been repatriated to England, including six from Colditz.

Alternatively, if Lance fled into France, he could not count on local support to get him either south into Spain or across the Channel. And Howe had adequately described his fate should he be recaptured and returned to Colditz.

Lance's mind churned over the risk of staying versus escaping. The *kommandant* had recently warned that, as opposed to past policy, guards would shoot at escaping prisoners. Conventional wisdom growing among inmates was that the best bet of surviving the war was to rest in place and await liberation. That notion was buttressed by advice coming from London dissuading future attempts. Of course, no one could predict when, or even if, the long-sought invasion would occur, or how soon after that, if it succeeded, liberation would reach this far east.

That evening, after leaving the escape committee meeting, Lance had wandered across the courtyard. Being cold and late in the day, few men were out, but in three of the four corners, lone prisoners lurked. He did not greet or speak with them, and they ignored him as he passed by.

By unwritten rule, when a prisoner entered one of these corners, no one bothered them. These darker places were usually occupied by men of Lance's own mindset—to escape whatever the cost. They went there to think through their plans unmolested. However, at any time, the occupants could be just seeking a few moments to themselves, to meditate in the only place of solitude available to them. Privacy elsewhere was nigh impossible.

While passing this time, Lance allowed his glance to linger a few moments longer, taking in the lined, worn faces, the scrawny physiques, the eyes either glimmering with faint hope or fading into despair.

He continued past the courtyard and entered the "silence room" where men went ostensibly to read. Some probably did, but many stared at open books without turning a page, their minds floating numbly, overtaken by boredom, despair, and having nothing else to do. An overturned chair might stay that way—no hurry, the war would go on interminably, leaving plenty of time to right the chair when someone made use of it, or to read a book if ambition struck again, however feebly.

Lance studied his comrades furtively as he ambled through. Many sat against the walls staring into nowhere. A man in a corner shifted his eyes up as if concerned that Lance might occupy the floor next to him, thus shrinking the man's own space.

Lance left the silence room, entered the main door of the barracks, and climbed the twisting stairs to the room he had shared with eight other men before being named a *prominente*. Several were already asleep, others were engaged in card games or rested on their bunks, reading, writing, or drawing, waiting until lights-out at nine-thirty.

Once again, Lance paid attention to oddities that he had never much considered, like mounds of tin cans in various places in the room, the result of hoarding anything and everything that might be useful or alleviate the suffering and hunger experienced on arrival and before the Red Cross packages began to arrive.

Each man had his bunk, some lower, some upper, some closer to the windows (great in summertime, terrible in winter), others closer to the stove (a reverse situation), with items collected over the duration of their stays arranged as neatly as practicality and inclination allowed. Letters and pictures from home were prominent, tacked to bedframes or the sides of boxes serving as shelves and wardrobes of sorts, sometimes with articles of hanging clothing obscuring those beloved reminders that a bigger world lay beyond the stone walls.

"Do you need something?" one of the men asked.

Lance shook his head. "I was looking for Mike Sinclair."

"He's out and about, but I don't know where," came the reply.

Lance bade goodnight and headed down the stairs, across the court-yard, and back to his own quarters. He breathed deeply as he settled onto his cot. "We live like rats here," he muttered. "We've become rats. I must get out."

25

The next morning Lance stood by the window watching *appell*, the first of four accountability parades conducted each day in the courtyard. *Prominentes* were not required to attend, but they had to be in their rooms, and their presence was reported by the guard just outside their doors. Each of their entries had a spy hole cut into it large enough for the guard to be able to see them anywhere in their cells at any time.

Usually, when Lance studied his surroundings, he looked for anomalies in the castle's structure that had been overlooked and might provide a way out, or he watched the guards for procedural weaknesses that might offer an advantage. Sinclair had already identified vulnerabilities of both types that offered a possibility for his escape, so today, mindful of his heated argument with Howe before the escape committee yesterday, Lance concentrated on watching his fellow prisoners.

They were, as Howe had said, gaunt, every one of them. Their clothes hung on them, their eyes were deep-set, and their facial bones protruded under loose, sallow skin. Although some still walked with a semblance of a spring in their step, most dragged their feet, and their shoulders drooped.

Lance observed almost as if making a discovery. He wondered how he had spent so much time in this accursed place and interacted with most of these soldiers, yet he had not internalized the state of depravity in which they were forced to live. With too many men sharing toilets and crowded barracks, with too little food becoming more meager between deliveries of Red Cross parcels, and many of those hoarded under Tod's order to provide for POWs making escapes as well as to hedge against times when food could become even more scarce, that any spirit of resistance remained at all among the prisoners was remarkable. Yet that spirit, hardly detectable by a quick scan of the dirty masses lined up for the German guards to count, was precisely what had landed these particular POWs in this desolate place. Their determined resistance was nourished daily by furtive activity carried out under the noses of their jailers within the byzantine passages and hidden rooms of the ancient castle.

The earliest POWs here had seized on the notion that they had nothing to do but explore the bastion while the sentries were occupied with guarding them inside Colditz' walls—and its fortifications had been built to keep enemies out, not keep anyone in. Given that these prisoners were some of the most intelligent, creative, and daring of British servicemen, they set their minds to acquiring materials and setting up rooms for printing documents, forging signatures, building makeshift sewing machines, fabricating uniforms and civilian clothing for escapees, manufacturing weapons facsimiles, and developing all manner of items needed to provide a hope of completing a home run.

The POWs' pluck manifested in loud demonstrations, such as when Germany invaded Russia. Polish, French, and Dutch prisoners had been present then, and they had all jeered at their guards, creating such a furor that a security platoon had entered the area to reinforce, and it had fired indiscriminately into the windows of the barracks. Fortunately, the POWs had ducked behind the heavy stone walls, and no one was seriously injured.

Many similar protests had taken place on the slightest provocation, and the guards had been further subjected to loud and profane insults during much of their daily tours of duties. However, in recent months, hostility between guards and prisoners had dissipated to sullen acceptance of each other's roles as security measures within the castle tightened, even as Germany's fortunes in the war turned for the worse. That such was the case was plainly visible for all to see other than the most blithely ignorant or those fervently deluded by Nazi dogma.

Lance waited until *appell* had been dismissed, and then made his way through the half-sunken dungeon to the room of Captain Michael "Micky" Burn. The captain was a most unusual chap with aristocratic good looks, and he was the most genuinely prominent of the *prominentes* in that his father was solicitor for the British royal family. He had grown up in a house near Buckingham Palace, courtesy of the king.

Word among the POWs was that he was a commando, saved from execution as was Lance by his protected status. Micky had participated in the raid at the French port of Saint-Nazaire nearly two years ago, undertaken to deny the *Kriegsmarine* battleship, *Tirpitz*, a place to berth for refitting along the French Atlantic coast. Without that facility, she could not operate against Allied shipping in the Atlantic.

Micky's mission, as part of the two-hundred-and-fifty-man commando raid, had been to lead his twenty-eight fighters to destroy a heavy machine gun position, but his motor launch had been struck and exploded by a German artillery round. Half of Micky's men perished immediately.

He had swum ashore under fire, reached the objective alone, and assaulted the position. By the time he was captured, he had been shot through his arm and thigh, and a piece of shrapnel had lodged in his back. He had arrived at Colditz not because he had tried to escape, nor even because of his status—that was found out later. The Germans had sent him from his previous POW camp to the castle because he had publicly destroyed Nazi propaganda fliers in a fire.

Lance found him sitting at his table eating a biscuit from a Red Cross parcel. "Is that breakfast?"

Micky laughed. "It's about as good as it gets on the fly. Have a seat. What can I do for you?"

"You're always in such an upbeat mood," Lance said. "How do you do that?"

"It's not difficult. I just refuse to be otherwise."

"And you have no intention to escape. Why is that? Your exploits are known. You can't possibly like it here—"

"My 'exploits,' if that is the term to be used, should be singular, not plural. One exploit, and I led no one. As you must know, everyone in my command was killed. I couldn't protect my men, and I destroyed nothing."

"Well, some say that you'll be awarded the Military Cross, so you must have accomplished something."

"Nothing to speak of, and they should save that MC for someone who's earned it. Now what did you come to see me about? Wait. Before we go there, I've been meaning to tell you that I knew your brother Jeremy. Corran Purdon told me Jeremy was related to you. Your brother is quite a chap. I must say, he looks just like you. He was missing for a time, as I recall, but Corran said that he made it safely home. I'm glad to hear that."

Lieutenant Corran Purdon had been Jeremy's team leader during the commando raid at Saint-Nazaire. Along with Burn, Corran was captured and brought to Colditz.

"I thought you might know Jeremy," Lance replied. "He did get home. We spent Christmas of '42 together at my sister's house."

Micky chuckled. "That must have been before you decided to come back here."

Lance laughed. "I suppose your description of how I arrived back at this bloody castle is as good as any." As he spoke, he glanced around the cell and out the window. The courtyard was at eye level, and already, men were starting up a game of stoolball.

"You want to know why I don't care to escape," Micky said. "The answer is probably not one you'd anticipate." He took his own glance at their surroundings and laughed. "I'm living in a bloody castle, pitiful though it is. That's what all the best people do this time of year." He pointed to a stack of papers sitting on his table. "Besides, I'm writing a novel, and I need to finish it before the war is over."

Surprised, Lance said, "That's interesting, and a good way to spend your time. You can travel to far-off places without ever leaving your chair."

"I'm not the only one doing it," Micky replied. "At least fifty books have been started in this castle. I'd love to know at some point how many are finished."

"Does yours have a title?"

Micky nodded. "Yes, *Farewell*."

Surprised again, Lance started to rise from his seat. "Are you telling me to leave? Did I say something wrong?"

Micky guffawed. "No. That's the title of the novel. *Yes, Farewell.*"

Lance sat back down with a sheepish look on his face. "So will you now please tell me what is so attractive about this place that keeps you here, apparently willingly?"

Micky tossed his head to one side. "It's a challenge. I was a journalist before the war. Here, daily, I visit our secret room where our radio is hidden away. I listen to the BBC, take my notes, and distribute the news to the other blokes." He pursed his lips. "My novel incorporates an accurate description of this place, not just the layout and structure but the ethos, its utter wretchedness. I couldn't ask to be in a better place to do the research. I must finish, though, before the war is over. And it *will* end. Only time will tell when, but my sense is that the fortunes of war are tilting in our favor."

He looked quizzically at Lance. "Does that answer your question?"

Lance thought a moment. "It does, but I have another. Are you concerned at all about what will happen to us, the *prominentes*, when Hitler determines that the Allies are hard over on 'unconditional surrender?'"

For the first time, Micky dropped his smile and became serious. "Of course it's a concern, and that's the direction events are headed." Then his face brightened again. "But I've always lived by my wits, and I feel certain that they will carry me through again. Why did you ask those questions?"

Lance rose from his chair. "Just curious, I suppose. I had to ask. You don't lack for energy or creativity, and your courage is proven. I thought perhaps I was missing something."

"And what did you conclude?"

Lance grinned. "My own instincts are to keep finding a way out. It's a compulsion."

Micky observed Lance through studious eyes, as though reading him. "I wish you luck, my friend."

Lance left and mounted the stairs into the courtyard. The stoolball game was in full swing, with at least fifteen members on each side crashing into each other as opposing team members, while carrying a ball, tried to unseat the man sitting on a stool at the opposite end of the court. The sport had come out of medieval England and had been modified to suit the peculiar character of Colditz' POW population.

Other men sat around the narrow periphery, soaking up what sun they could in the frigid winter air. Some read, some dozed, others cheered on players in the game.

Lance searched the crowd and finally spotted Mike Sinclair in the middle of the shoving, grunting, hitting players. When a break finally occurred, Lance caught his eye. Sinclair motioned to someone on the sidelines to take his place and joined Lance among yet another group of men walking the circuit, around and around the quad.

"That was quite an argument you had with Howe yesterday," Sinclair said.

"I don't know what he wants from me. He knows I'm careful. Every escape I've made has succeeded, at least in getting me out of Colditz. And my last one got me all the way home."

Sinclair clapped his hand on Lance's back. "He'll let you go. Security is tighter now, and the German population is skittish since the Allies started bombing their cities. Howe just wants to be sure that you've considered every possible detail. He knows that every plan goes out the window the moment it's executed."

They reached the far end of the courtyard, passed the delousing hut, and turned in front of the chapel. The theater where Lance had begun his first escape from Colditz was three stories above them.

"It's a good plan," Sinclair said. "I'm only letting you have it because your situation is more dire than mine. But with any luck, I'll get to execute the same plan in a few weeks."

"That's very good of you. What about the ghost? Is he willing and able."

"He is. We'll give him extra rations from the Red Cross parcels. He's about your build, and we'll color his hair to match yours. I'll walk into the *prominente* quarters with him an hour or so before your curfew. He's practiced your voice and mannerisms, so we should put on a pretty good show."

"Ghosts" were prisoners who faked escapes. They hid out in secret places within the castle. The guards believed that the men who had transformed to ghosts had made successful escapes. When a real escape took place, one of the ghosts stood in formation on behalf of the missing POW for a few days. The ghosts' everyday task of hiding inside an already dismal situation took an emotional and mental toll on them, so much effort by the POW leadership went into maintaining their morale and keeping them fed, safe, and mentally stable.

Lance blew into his hands to warm them. "The guards were on high alert after Romilly's escape. Prawwit's head would have rolled if Romilly had got clean away."

"Some weeks have passed since then," Sinclair observed. "The guards have relaxed into normal routine. At best, they won't find out you're gone until the following night when you don't show up for curfew. At worst you'll have a six-hour head start."

They had walked a complete circuit, crossing past the main gate and the punishment cells, rounding the far end in front of the *prominente* quarters, and then passing in front of the canteen just ahead of where they had started.

"How will the ghost get out of my cell?" Lance asked.

"He'll make early morning noises just before *appell*, and then more noises like he's sick. I'll go down around mid-morning and walk him back out. Then he'll disappear again. If that works, the guards will assume correctly that you escaped, but they'll believe you somehow did it during the day. They'll estimate you got out by a few hours rather than roughly eighteen hours."

"Good. And may I know the name of this ghost?"

Sinclair shook his head. "You may not. If you're recaptured, that name should not be in your head."

"Please extend my warmest gratitude."

"Tell me your cover story again."

"I'm originally from Aschaffenburg, a town southeast of Frankfurt. I've been a supervisor in a munitions factory close to Germany's eastern border with Poland. I was injured in an explosion, treated in a hospital for several weeks, and sent home for a month of recuperation."

"That story works to get you to Frankfurt, but what about west of there, going toward France?"

"I'll use the same story, but shift the location of the factory to a place near the French coast. I have travel documents to reflect that. I'll destroy the first set in Frankfurt."

"That works. Now, why don't you have visible wounds?"

"I was thrown in the explosion's blast. My injuries were internal. I couldn't take in solid food for weeks and had to be fed intravenously."

"Good. You'll have doctors' certificates, medical records from the hospital, orders sending you home, etc. Now, tell me all of that again in German."

Lance did.

"All right," Mike said when Lance was done. "To get past Howe's review, we'll have to pick a date, a route, and establish contingency plans. Your documents must line up with your travel dates and train schedules. Let's go over it all again."

26

February 23, 1944

Lance's heart beat furiously as he looked down through the barred window at the thirty-foot vertical plunge that he would take in a few minutes. He would descend on a long rope made from blankets and sheets to a twenty-five-foot-wide stone terrace below. An additional drop to a garden beyond the terrace was estimated at only fifteen feet, but in case that estimation was off, he would wrap a shorter rope around one of the balusters, use it to climb down, and then pull it out of sight.

The initial part of the plan had been rehearsed many times, with other members of his escape team practicing their actions until they could do them with clockwork precision. He turned to glance around the dark room. Mike was there, as were two men stationed on either side of the window. At the right moment, they would bend the two pre-cut bars out of the way to each side of the opening. They had come to the room a few days earlier to cut through them at the top.

A pair of stooges were stationed two stories up keeping lookout across the castle but paying particular attention to the immediate area. One would give the signal to go.

Others were stationed at strategic places along stairways and corridors to warn of anything untoward that might interrupt the escape. Disconcerting at the moment was that a guard could be heard haranguing a maintenance worker just outside this room where Lance and his companions now prepared for the escape.

Lance was already dressed in black clothing made large enough to cover a full set of civilian clothes, provided courtesy of the POWs' secret tailor shop. A black balaclava covered his head and face, leaving only his eyes showing. Dark socks covered his shoes.

A nine-foot-long trestle had been built against the wall under the window, with a wide surface to form a table that was even with the sill. Lance was to lie flat on his stomach just before plan execution. Two more men held onto the long rope secured to the bottom of one window bar. Their job was to feed the cord out rapidly as Lance dropped, apply tension to ease his landing, and then raise it quickly once Lance was on the terrace and released it. The other end was already looped around Lance's waist and tied off to the shorter rope and a suitcase—a lone individual traveling without luggage would be immediately suspect.

Once Lance was on the table, two additional POWs would be positioned near his head. They would tilt the trestle surface steeply so that Lance could easily slide through the window. "We only have one minute to get you down and out of sight," Mike had told him when explaining the plan. "That's enough time for you to crawl through and scale down the wall fast, and you'll need enough clearance so that you're not banging into hard stone."

By ambient light coming through the window, Lance made out one individual at the back of the room: a photographer to record the occasion.

Less than an hour ago, Lance had gathered for a hot meal with Mike, Dick Howe, and the other members of the escape team. By prison standards, it was a feast, consisting of heated Spam, a shared tin of biscuits, both from a Red Cross package, and POW-produced wine distilled in one of the hidden outer reaches of the castle.

Lance had lost his appetite, but not knowing when he would see his next full meal, he forced himself to eat. Then, as the time approached to depart, strange sadness set in for the comrades he would leave behind, men who at this moment risked solitary confinement to aid him. Men with whom he had shared misery for many months.

"I'll inform Colonel Tod shortly after the guards discover your absence," Howe said in parting. "I assure you of his best wishes, and of course you have mine as well."

Completing farewells with others at the dinner, Lance and his team had gone to their various posts. Now his breath came in short bursts while he waited in the dark. In the hall on the other side of the wall, the guard continued to berate the maintenance worker. Lance wondered what could possibly have occurred to draw such ire at this place and at this hour.

He glanced at a second window. Mike was there, seen now only in silhouette, watching for the signal from the stooge two stories up. He and Lance had already said their goodbyes.

Lance climbed onto the table and lay there on his stomach, holding onto the rope, his feet toward the opening. A pair of wire cutters strapped to one leg dug into his skin. He shifted. And waited.

Outside in the hall, the guard continued yelling at his victim.

Mike had spent months reconnoitering for this particular escape. He had noticed that the changing of the guard was precisely at the same time each day. When that occurred in the evening, the new shift turned on the floodlights. At this time of year, full darkness descended only moments before the sentries were relieved.

That left a minute during which the outside walls were in full darkness.

The next guard detail would switch the lights on.

Lance would have just enough time to get to the terrace, over the balustrade, and down to the garden.

"Go!" Sinclair hissed.

Lance gripped the rope tighter. With his head down, he could not see. He had to trust that the two men responsible for the bars were now bending them out of the way. The table inclined and his body started sliding.

Mike ran to him. "Good luck, mate. See you in London." With that, he reached over the end of the table and shoved Lance by the shoulders.

Lance's feet cleared the edge, and then he was in the air and free-falling.

He held fast to his rope. It tightened, the slack was taken out, and he lowered smoothly to the hard stone surface of the terrace.

Taking no time for relief, he jerked free his luggage and short rope. The long one immediately disappeared, pulled out of sight back into the room above.

His heart pounded as he ran to the balustrade. His breath heaved in gasps now. He lashed the handle of the case to one end of the cord, lowered it to the garden level, looped the other end under the top of the balustrade, flung it below, and, holding both segments, clambered down to the garden.

Retrieving his briefcase, he took a moment to pull the rope down and shove it out of sight behind a bush. Then he settled into the deepest shadows.

At that moment, the floodlights above the terrace flipped on, bathing the castle walls in white, piercing light. It illuminated the garden, but cast a shadow along its base.

Lance pressed his body into the darkness and waited, listening.

Hearing no alarms, he crept along the base of the wall for thirty yards, occasionally tripping over segments of a barbed wire field barrier stretched over the barren garden to his left. At the end of the terrace's retaining wall, he encountered another low wall running across his front. A shoulder-high barbed-wire barrier stood in his way. He extracted the wire cutters taped to his leg, and began cutting.

Minutes ticked by. He pressed the handles of the cutters, and finally snipped through the first wire with an audible twang.

Lance glanced over his shoulder. He was sure that anyone looking over the balustrade of the terrace would see him, but he heard no sounds of alarm.

Twang. The second wire gave way. One more to go.

He shrank into the shadow and waited, but all was quiet.

Twang. He snipped through the third wire and scrambled under the barrier, pushing his briefcase ahead of him and tearing his clothes on the barbs.

Emerging on the other side, he found that the height of the stone outer wall was over his head. By stretching, he could grasp the top.

He tossed the briefcase over, reached up, grasped the crest, and tried to pull himself up.

He was too weak, the result of months of malnutrition.

Sweat poured from his brow, and his biceps ached as he demanded that they pull his body up, but to no avail. They shook as his weight pulled him back down.

From the terrace, he heard sounds of guards moving about, barking orders. He shrank again into the shadows.

The sounds abated. He waited, resting, gathering his strength.

Finally, he stood and faced the wall, his jaw set. Then he rushed it, planted one foot firmly against it, and sprang up, landing with his elbows over the top.

Now he was in the light. Anyone looking out from the terrace could see him.

He stayed there, panting, once more gathering his strength until he could swing one leg up and over. Then, by inches and minutes, always with an ear listening for shouts and cries from the guards, he pulled himself across the top and spilled to the ground on the other side.

He lay there panting.

Lance found himself in the back yard of a house that abutted the outer castle wall. A low glow of a lantern revealed a frail old lady with streaming white hair who stood at her back door. She stared in Lance's direction.

He held his breath, unsure of whether she had seen him or not. Then she hurried into the house, slamming the door behind her. The suitcase lay below her window. Perhaps she had heard it tumble across the ground. Perhaps she had also heard Lance's grunting and panting as he struggled over the wall. *What will she do now?*

Spurred by the possibility of having been found out, Lance sprinted, retrieved the briefcase, ran headlong to the far end of the yard, and vaulted over a low fence. Recalling from a previous escape a row of houses nearby with an alley running behind them, he made his way there, and by the dim light of a cigarette and using a needle and thread in his kit, he mended two tears in his trousers. He stuffed his black outer garments and balaclava in a trash bin, put on a heavy overcoat from his luggage, and headed out on an overland hike.

Once before when he had escaped, he had gone directly to the local railway station, but he had waited hours in freezing weather to board a train to Leipzig. He had made a clean getaway from the local area, but in retrospect, his sense was that he had greatly increased his probability of early recapture. Currently, his plan of achieving an eighteen-hour head start seemed to have worked, but he must make best use of that time to put the greatest distance between himself and Colditz. Waiting in the local area would be a waste of time.

Instead, Lance set out on foot toward Borsdorf, about twenty miles northwest. He should arrive there within eight or nine hours. Given that darkness had fallen over the castle at roughly six o'clock, he should arrive in the early hours after midnight with plenty of time to rest in some unsuspecting farmer's barn before joining the crowds heading to the town's train terminal.

The map he followed was in his head, memorized at Mike's insistence. Lance knew that the road ahead of him was straight enough for most of the way that he would have warning of approaching vehicles from either direction. Nevertheless, he clung to the shadows.

He stopped suddenly as another sensation swept over him, one that he welcomed. It manifested in the bright stars against a cloudless sky, in the scent of a field adjacent to the road, in fresh air and other fragrances of the country.

He left the road, though keeping it in sight, and wandered across meadows, pushing through hedges, checking his direction against a compass, and exulting in his solitude, in motion uninhibited by the proximity of other bodies. And then, just for the feel of it, he ran through the darkness, tripping, losing his balance, straightening, and continuing to run until he all but collapsed, panting but smiling broadly. For a time, he lay in the dirt, watching the stars and soaking in freedom—for however long it lasted.

Lance boarded the train in Borsdorf at six-thirty the next morning, gently pressing to the center of a crowd. He had put on a suit carried in his luggage, bought a newspaper that he carried under his arm, and now appeared as a tired business traveler. The guards at the checkpoints, looking about as wide-awake as the sleepy, early morning passengers, inspected travel documents cursorily. Lance moved through with no inter-ference.

The train chugged out of the station bound for Leipzig, where Lance planned to transfer to the main line headed to Frankfurt. He settled into his seat, opened the newspaper, and started reading. Then, as happened with many train passengers traveling in early morning, his eyelids fluttered, his newspaper fell across his face, and his eyes closed.

He awakened with a jolt. The train pulled into Leipzig and halted amid screeching wheels braking on steel rails and shrieking locomotive whistles. Lance sensed a disturbance among passengers. Looking through the crowd when the doors opened, he saw standing next to them two serious, plain-clothed men bristling with authority. Obviously *Gestapo*. They were accom-panied by *SS* soldiers in black uniforms.

All around him, people pulled out their travel documents to have them ready when asked. Taking a quiet, deep breath to maintain composure despite a racing heart, Lance reached inside his overcoat to take out his own documents, ambling slowly so as to appear lethargic.

The *Gestapo* officers stationed themselves at the exits while the *SS* blocked passage on both ends of the carriage. As passengers left the train, the *Gestapo* scrutinized their identification papers. At the other exits up and down the length of the train, other *Gestapo* officers performed the same function.

Lance stood in line behind other travelers. He took long, quiet breaths to quell his beating heart, but feared he was losing the battle of nerves. Then he remembered an article he had read about the British-born Amer-ican comedian Bob Hope. The star had said that to control his nervousness when going on stage, he would wiggle his toes, and doing so amused him. The urge to laugh calmed him.

Lance tried the maneuver and found that the act did, indeed, create amusement. So as he moved closer to the *Gestapo* officers, he wiggled his toes furiously, hoping that his smile did not appear forced.

The line continued through the exit.

Lance's heart pounded in his ears.

He wiggled his toes non-stop.

When his turn came, he stepped in front of one of the officers.

"You look pleased this early in the morning," the *Gestapo* man said.

"Yes, and why not? I'm going home for a month. I'll be there in a few hours." Lance handed the man his papers.

The officer flipped through them in a practiced manner, looking at specific spaces on the various forms. "You're from—" He left the sentence unfinished.

"Aschaffenburg," Lance replied in German. "I grew up there, but I've been away for some time, as you can see."

"Aschaffenburg," the man crooned, "I've been there. As I recall, there's an ancient castle on the west side of the river across from the town's center."

Lance furrowed his brow. "Hmm. I don't know that one. There's *Schloss* Aschaffenburg on the east side of the river right downtown, but it was built in the early 1600s, I believe. The architect was a man named Ridinger."

"You seem well acquainted with it."

"Yes, yes. My mother insisted that my siblings and I knew about our local history." He looked thoughtful. "You might be referring to another castle on the west bank farther south toward Obernau. That one is very old and in ruins."

"You're probably right," the officer said. He had been studying Lance's face closely during the exchange, and now he further scrutinized the papers. "What do you do at this factory?"

"I'm a munitions engineer. I check for quality at the end of my production line, which manufactures hand grenades." He let out a small laugh. "We want to be sure they go off at the right times, and never before."

"I see." The officer showed no compunction toward humor. He indicated a particular document. "It says here that you were released from a doctor's care, at the hospital indicated here, to go home to recuperate following an explosion. Hopefully, that was not from one of your hand grenades."

"Certainly not," Lance responded indignantly. "We were hit by Allied bombs. Fortunately, they didn't hit my section. I had just reached the facility for my shift and was in the entryway when the bomb struck. I had heard the warning siren and ran as fast as I could, but didn't make it to the bunker." He shook his head. "My luck."

"All right," the officer said. He folded the papers back to their original form and handed them back to Lance. "May I see your arm?"

Surprised, Lance stared. "Sir?"

"Your papers include a doctor's statement that you were fed intravenously for nearly a month. That's a long time with a needle in your arm. It must have left a mark." His voice took on a steely quality. "Take your coat off and show me your arm."

"Here?" Lance glanced around. Behind him, passengers looked grim, but remained silent. In the other line, people glanced at him nervously and looked relieved as they showed their papers and were released to continue on about their business.

"Is there a problem?"

Lance shifted his attention back to the officer in front of him. He shook his head. "It's just that I'll need to take my shirt off as well."

The *Gestapo* man smirked. "No need to be embarrassed," he said in silky tones. "These people have all seen a man's chest."

Lance locked eyes with the officer. Then, slowly, he set his suitcase down and removed his coat. That done, he opened his shirt and took it half off to expose his left arm. A large bandage covered part of it just above the elbow.

The Gestapo man took a close look. "Let me see under there," he ordered.

Controlling his emotions, which now tended toward anger, Lance complied. He reached up with his right hand, tugged at the bottom of the bandage, and pushed it gingerly back from a black and blue area of skin with a distinct reddish puncture mark at its center. "The nurses had difficulty finding a vein," he said tersely, "and that happened every time they had to refresh the IV tube. I was left with this. My right arm looks identical if you'd like to see that one too."

The *Gestapo* officer looked into his eyes steadily. Then he shook his head. "That won't be necessary. You serve the motherland well. You may go."

Lance's mind swirled with relief. He steadied his legs, which suddenly threatened to give way beneath him. "*Vielen dank,*" he managed. "I know you have a tough job."

Minutes later, having put his shirt and coat back on, he boarded the train to Frankfurt while silently thanking his mother, Dame Marian of Sark, for taking him and his siblings on annual vacations to Aschaffenburg when he was young; and Mike Sinclair for paying close attention to details, like pricking his upper arms with needles and bruising them to resemble poorly treated sores from intravenous feeding tubes.

27

Saarbrücken, Germany

This evasion journey had been more difficult for Lance than his last escape when he had crossed into Switzerland with two comrades a few hours after leaving Colditz. This time, his cover had held up all the way to Saarbrücken, just east of the French-German border. But he had no story or travel documents to take him into France, nor was a contact available and ready to rendezvous with him and escort him through the backroads of Germany, across the border, and then south to Montrichard, his intended destination.

This phase had been the acknowledged weakness in his plan, but one that was unavoidable within the stone confines of Colditz Castle—the escape committee had insufficient information to forge reliable documents providing passage across the border. However, it had acquired a sizeable sum of Vichy French franc notes and provided some to Lance along with some *reichsmarks*. He had secreted the currency in the heels of his shoes.

The train ride across Germany's heartland had been an eye-opener. Leipzig had been bombed, and so had Frankfurt and other towns and villages along the train route. Many of the towns' commercial buildings,

factories, and dwellings lay in rubble, and as the train pulled into Saarbrücken, he saw that it had also been hit with massive damage.

Lance had also noticed a pensiveness among passengers. He had
avoided conversation, but he had heard low-voiced murmurs about
concerns with a coming invasion of France and the prospects of having to
defend the motherland at its borders.

As he left the station, the sun descended, casting long shadows. He
glanced at his watch, and his stomach tightened. In another three hours, he
would be due back in his cell for curfew at Colditz; the ghost would be back
in hiding, and Lance's absence would be discovered. The alarm would go
out across Germany at once with his description, followed soon thereafter
by his photograph.

The physical search would start in the immediate vicinity of Colditz,
but when he was not found, it would widen. Checkpoint guards would be
more attentive and scrutinize his face and ID more closely. The civilian
population would be alerted as well.

Word might also follow him into France, but there, at least, civilians
who spotted and identified him might be friendly. He must cross over
before the Colditz curfew.

He spotted a battered farm truck rumbling by the station and waved it
down. "I'm trying to get to my cousin's house," he told the driver. "It's not
far. It's on the main road to Forbach. I'll pay you." He held out several
reichsmark notes.

"The German town?" the farmer growled. "That's quite a distance. If
you mean the French one, I can't take you into France."

"Don't worry," Lance replied in a reassuring voice. "I'm visiting a cousin
who lives on a farm along that road, the one to France, but it's within our
German border. I'll point out the turnoff."

The farmer studied Lance's face and then stared at the wad of money in
Lance's hand. He nodded and gestured for Lance to get in.

As Lance settled in the seat, the farmer reached across with an open
palm. "The money?"

Lance nodded, and handed it over. The truck wound through Saarbrücken and then started southwest. Lance watched the passing landscape
carefully as they drove. Within minutes, he saw what he knew had to be

there on the left: a two-kilometer stretch of road that paralleled the border with France. More accurately, the boundary was that of Alsace-Lorraine, the highly productive textile region of a previously autonomous French province with deep Germanic roots that had been tossed back and forth between France and Germany at the end of wars going back to the 1600s. It was now governed by *Gauleiter* Robert Heinrich Wagner, who reported directly to Adolf Hitler.

Lance studied the immediate terrain carefully. It consisted of rolling hills, steep on the right side of the truck, with some flat ground bisected by the road, and then more forested hills on the left—but those hills had to be in Alsace-Lorraine, and few buildings existed along this stretch.

Several minutes later, the driver called over, "Did we pass the turnoff? We're coming to the border crossing."

Lance peered ahead through the windshield. Dusk was settling in. The road was narrow, but ahead a circle of light appeared, and a guard station. Apparently, this crossing point was rarely used, for no traffic currently awaited clearance, and a single guard lounged at its front smoking a cigarette.

For a moment, Lance was tempted to bluff or barrel his way through. On second thought, doing so would set off alarms that could quickly provide a likely place to start for those who would soon be hunting him. "Sorry, I must have missed it," he replied. "I'm not from here. The only directions I got were to come on this road and look for a long driveway lined with trees. It'll be the second to the last before the frontier."

"Ah, the Schultz farm," the man exclaimed. "Why didn't you say so?" He maneuvered the vehicle around, waved at the sentry in passing, and headed back the way they had come.

"I wasn't sure you'd know the family," Lance replied, thanking fortune that the farmer had mentioned a name before Lance had been asked for one. "But yes, the Schultz place."

"You must be the cousin from Hanover. I think I've met all the others."

"Are you a close friend?" Lance hoped concern had not seeped into his voice.

"An acquaintance. I've had business dealings with various members of the family over the years. Here we are." The farmer turned left onto a gravel road. "I'll take you up and say hello to Albert. I haven't seen him in a while."

Lance's mind whirled. He was about to be found out.

Tall trees covered the road with wide canopies, which intensified the darkness ahead as the last rays of the sun disappeared. On impulse, Lance reached into his pocket and withdrew one of his forged documents.

"Pull over," he ordered harshly.

Stung by the stern command, the farmer half-looked over at him. "What?"

"Pull over," Lance demanded. "Now. I won't tell you again."

The truck lurched to the side of the road and halted. The farmer glared at Lance through uncertain eyes.

"Listen to me very carefully and follow my instructions exactly," Lance growled. He thrust the document in the man's face and withdrew it, leaving the driver no time to read any part of it. "I'm a *Gestapo* officer on an under-cover assignment. Your friend Shultz is under investigation for assisting the *Maquis*. He's been stealing from our armories and smuggling the weapons across the border. We need to catch him in the act so we can also capture his collaborators. Do you understand?"

"A traitor?" the driver gasped through fear and disgust.

Lance nodded. "I'm getting out of your truck now. My colleagues will come when I call them. You are to go back to town and never say anything of this to anyone. Am I clear? I know where to find you..."

He let the implied threat ride.

The man shook with fear, but he nodded. "I won't even tell my wife."

"Good." Grabbing his suitcase, Lance stepped out of the car and into the woods. Then he watched and listened as the truck drove away. He continued to listen as his eyes became accustomed to the gathering night. Stillness settled over the forest, broken by intermittent calls of nocturnal animals.

Watching and listening for any sign of human activity, Lance stole back to the main road and crossed it. This part of the border had jogged north and east such that, for a short distance, Alsace-Lorraine was to the east. Because it had been occupied and annexed, and was not neutral like Switzerland, he counted on the notion that this section would be lightly defended, if at all, and he could slip through unobserved. He was almost there.

He moved as quietly between the trees as possible, stopping to listen each time he stumbled and holding onto his suitcase as best he could. He reached the bottom of the small valley and started up the other side. Somewhere between him and the crest lay the border.

Coming to a fence and feeling along it, Lance determined it to be wire mesh with barbed wire along the bottom. Backing off, he found a flat piece of ground, sat down, and pulled his greatcoat tightly around him against a slight wind and the late February cold air. After an interval, and hearing no dogs or sounds of a roving patrol, he eased back to the fence and extracted his wire-cutters. Fifteen minutes later, having snipped the wires and reconnected them as best he could, he stood in Alsace-Lorraine.

His trek was easier after that. He was sure that he had beaten the time of discovery at Colditz and that word would not yet have spread as far west as Saarbrücken.

Now to find warmth.

Under a cloudy sky, he headed overland, avoiding roads except as a means to try to spot farm buildings, specifically a barn with hay stored inside where he could rest in warmth. Deep fatigue set in from the hike of the night before and again this evening. He had slept on the train, but the clackety-clack of the cars and rumble of the locomotive, the frequent stops with screeching brakes as they entered another town, and the constant shuffle of passengers boarding and leaving all aggravated raw nerves resulting from possible discovery and made restful sleep impossible. As a result, he had not eaten, and now with the relief of escaping Germany and finding himself in a relatively benign environment, if not a friendly one, hunger clawed at his gut.

He came upon a wide, open hilltop. The clouds cleared and a half-moon shone brightly against a star-strewn sky. He imagined how the countryside might appear absent blackout provisions against bombing raids, with lights of farmhouses scattered over the rolling landscape adding to the celestial illumination. An occasional dog barked, answered by another, but neither snarled or seemed to have detected him.

He pulled out a tin of sardines, provided courtesy of the Red Cross, and downed them quickly. Then he trudged on, hoping fleetingly for a last winter storm to erase any vestige of his cross-country trek. Coming to a small brook, he drank his fill while entertaining the idea of wading downstream to cover his scent, but decided that the immediate dangers of frostbite or hypothermia were much greater, particularly in his weakened state.

Hours passed, and he lumbered on, his feet now like blocks of ice, his hands freezing. His breath created clouds of vapor, and his mind had numbed. By degrees, the sky lightened the way ahead. The sun cast a golden sheen across the horizon. Dogs yelped, and roosters crowed their welcome of another day.

As Lance approached a road, an engine sputtered to life. A farmhouse appeared nearby through an early morning haze. A door slammed, and a panel truck rumbled onto the road.

Lance stumbled directly in front of it.

The small truck screeched to a halt.

Lance tried to raise his arms, but he was too weak. He collapsed.

He awoke to a loud argument. Through bleary eyes, he looked about. He was alone, lying on a sofa near a fire, and covered with blankets. Every part of his body ached and he still shivered from cold. He wondered how long he had been there.

Shouting continued between a man and a woman in another room. After a few moments, Lance could make out the words.

"We can't keep him here," the woman insisted. "How many times do I have to say it? The Germans will be looking for him. If they find him here, they will shoot us and take our children to be raised as good Germans."

"We can't turn him in," the man replied vehemently. "The invasion is coming. I feel it. Remember Dunkirk? The British fought for us. The least we can do is hide him."

"How do you know he's British?"

"I found his identification disc on a cord around his neck."

A momentary silence ensued, broken by the desperate mother. "We will be found out." Her voice became shriller, filled with fear. "And we hardly have enough food to feed ourselves, much less another adult."

Lance raised himself to a sitting position. He was still fully clothed, including his shoes. Slowly, painfully, he swung his legs around, placed his feet on the floor, and pulled himself upright. Then, he stumbled across to a door and opened it a crack.

Immediately, the argument ceased. Lance creaked the door open further and peered into the farmhouse kitchen.

The man and woman stared back at him, wide-eyed. She appeared in her late twenties, thin, her face lined, her blond hair fastened behind her head and showing gray strands. The man, also thin, with sinewy arms, dark hair brushed back, and a small mustache, moved briskly across the floor to support Lance.

"Come," he said, "sit." He turned to his wife. "Angeline, bring some coffee."

Angeline continued staring. As Lance proceeded across the room, her expression softened. She covered her face with her hands as tears ran down her cheeks. Then she ran across the room to pour the hot beverage.

Lance sank into the chair. His eyes expressed his gratitude when she brought the coffee, and he wrapped his fingers around the cup, savoring the warmth and the aroma. He took a sip, breathed in deeply, and sank back in the chair. Then he raised his eyes to Angeline's.

"I won't stay, Madame," he rasped. "I have food in my suitcase. It's not much, but it's yours. I just need to warm up. Then I'll go."

Angeline's shoulders drooped and she once more covered her face with her hands. "You can't," she whispered in a broken voice. "Not like that. It's too cold. You're too weak. You'd be picked up immediately." She turned to her husband with terrified eyes. "Milàn, what are we going to do?"

Milàn crossed the room and embraced his wife. "We'll be careful," he soothed. "No one saw him come in. Our friends will help with food."

Still with his arm around Angeline, Milàn turned back to Lance. "Your French is very good. Where did you learn it?"

The couple joined Lance at the table, and he gave a brief run-down of his life. When he had finished, Milàn regarded him, dumbfounded. "So you speak French, German, and English fluently, and you're a commando and an escaped POW?"

Lance nodded tiredly. "I'm trying to get to Montrichard, by the Rivière Cher. I worked with the Resistance there for a few weeks. They'll know how to help me." He grinned wryly. "To tell you the truth, I'm not sure where I am. On the map I memorized, I saw a lot of French villages with German-sounding names, so I set an azimuth toward a village called Henriville. I thought I might find a better reception there. When I stumbled in front of your truck, I was too cold and tired to care who found me. All night, I looked for a barn to sleep in, but I just never came across one."

"You need rest," Angeline blurted out, now viewing Lance with sympathy. "We'll make a bed for you."

"Let's think this through," Milàn cut in.

"You think it through," Angeline said. "I'm going to make our new friend breakfast and then prepare his bed."

While she moved about the kitchen, Milàn reflected. "A word of warning. In this area both French and German are spoken, but the primary language is a dialect, Alsation. If you addressed a stranger on the street in French, you'd be immediately identified as an outsider. Depending on whom you encountered, you might be reported."

"Good to know," Lance muttered.

Milàn nodded absently. "This area was last annexed by the Germans after the War of 1870. It was returned to France in 1918 at the end of the last war, but the Germans annexed it again in 1940. So technically, you're still in Germany.

"German rule has always been tyrannical here. They've built four concentration camps nearby, forced their language on us, and mandated where we sell our textiles. So you'd probably have been all right even if you'd gone to one of the villages with a German name. But some people support the Nazis, so I'm glad we found you."

With drooping eyes, Lance sat up straight and nodded. Across the room, Angeline worked over a counter and then a stove, and soon the aroma and sizzle of frying eggs filled the room along with toasting bread.

"Madame, please. I don't want to take your food," Lance protested.

"We'll manage," she replied with a slight smile. "Keep talking to my husband."

"The Germans don't patrol here much," Milàn continued. "We're not near any factories, railroads, or other military targets, and in winter, we have no crops to plunder."

Bitterness seeped into Milàn's voice as he uttered the last phrase. He rose, went to a cabinet, and pulled out a Michelin roadmap. "You did a good job of navigating," he said, re-taking his seat. "We're near Henriville, and it's historically a French town."

He spread the map out on the table. After studying it, he found Henriville and traced an index finger south into the Loire Valley and then to Val de Cher. "Here's Montrichard. It's about six hundred kilometers from here. That's roughly three hundred and sixty miles."

Tossing his head, he looked up and saw Lance struggling to stay awake. "Angeline is right," he remarked. "You need sleep. Lots of it."

Lance forced his eyes wide open. He started to say something, but exhaustion overcame him, his eyes closed, and his head dropped to the table.

28

March 15, 1944
Isle of Sark, Guernsey Bailiwick, Channel Islands

Amid the labored barking of her two white skeletal poodles, Marian Littlefield made her way through the hall of her medieval mansion, La Seigneurie, which also served as Sark's seat of government. She opened the door and greeted Joseph Wakley, the courier who had faithfully brought GUNS, the illegal newsletter, to Sark from Guernsey since shortly after the German occupation had begun. With Wakley was Hubert Lanyon, the local baker and shopkeeper who had secretly distributed GUNS to confidential subscribers across Sark.

Although anxiety on the men's faces was plain to see, so were their attempts to maintain outward calm. Marian escorted them into her sitting room. "What's wrong? You both appear to have met the Grim Reaper himself."

"And well we might," Wakley broke in anxiously. "Charles Machon was arrested."

Marian sat back in her chair in shock. Machon was the linotype operator at the *Guernsey Star* who had produced GUNS. He was a frail man, always in poor health with ulcers and requiring a special diet, but he also had not let his physical condition stop him from carrying on the fight against German occupation in the only way he could, by publishing his newsletter. "How did that come about?"

"It was that scoundrel, Peter Doyle, what done him in," Wakley replied. "He led the police right up the walkway and into Machon's house."

"I thought Doyle was Machon's friend," Marian exclaimed.

"So did Machon," Wakley said.

"And us too," Lanyon interjected. "Doyle's a black marketeer, though. He's acquiring merchandise somehow and selling it at a high price to people who have nothing left. He's gouging them. In retrospect, he never should have been trusted."

Marian listened in alarm. "Has Machon revealed any of his helpers or subscribers?"

"Not so that we can tell," Wakley replied. "They've had him for two days, but so far there've been no more arrests. When the *Gestapo* came to Machon's house, Doyle had already given them a copy of the most recent newsletter. Paper was in his typewriter with the GUNS masthead on it, ready for the next edition. I waited two days to come here so as not to bring suspicion onto Sark."

"It's good that you did," Marian said. "I feel terrible about Machon, though. He's such a good man, and obviously very brave."

"I brought a copy of the last newsletter, the one that caused his arrest. Would you like to see it?"

"Of course. We should see the evidence of his deed that is so dastardly he now sits in a *Gestapo* cell under a death sentence."

Just then, the white poodles started barking again. "They are my alarm system," Marian explained to the two men. "Someone is arriving at my door."

A very thin servant girl thrust her head into the sitting room. "The *kommandant* is at the door, mum."

The two men reacted with consternation.

"Muller?" Marian exclaimed. "Are you sure it's Major General Muller? He was too afraid to confront me in person about the electric generators breaking down."

The girl shook her head. "I'm not sure. It's that officer who came about the generators and shouted at you."

Marian chuckled. "Oh, you mean Captain Zachau. He was speechless when I explained to him calmly that we English do not shout at each other when conducting business. I told him that if he wished to conduct business with me, he must modify his tone. He left without another word, and we haven't heard from him since."

She turned to Wakley and Lanyon. "Stay in here until he leaves." Then she instructed the servant, "Show the captain into the library. I'll see him there."

Zachau was gazing at the books lining the shelves when Marian entered. "Madame," he said in German, "we meet again."

"Yes," she replied stiffly, also in German. "My pleasure." She held out her hand to him in the posture of expecting it to be kissed.

The captain stared at it. Then he smiled punctiliously, clicked his heels, bowed slightly, took her hand, and obliged.

"Now, what can I do for you?" Marian asked.

"We've had an incident on Guernsey," he replied. "We arrested a terrorist who was publishing an illegal news—"

"A terrorist? Here? In the Guernsey Bailiwick?" Marian tossed her head. "The only terrorists I'm aware of here are quite open about their activities, and they all wear *Wehrmacht* uniforms."

Anger crossed Zachau's face, but he held it in check. "The *kommandant* insisted that I come so that you can warn your people. We will not tolerate the spread of lies and propaganda. Anyone in possession of such material will be considered to be distributors of it, and will be dealt with to the full extent of the law."

"You mean you will execute them," Marian said flatly. "You will kill people for the simple act of reporting news events. We understand that." She took a step toward the door. "Is there something else, Captain? I know of no civilian terrorist activity on Sark, but I will be sure to pass along the *kommandant's* remarks to our people."

Visibly flustered, the captain departed, and Marian returned to the sitting room. "You were going to show me the latest newsletter," she said to Wakley.

"Yes, mum." He removed his left shoe and twisted off its heel. From there, he extracted three thin sheets of paper, unfolded them, and handed them to Marian.

She scanned them. "Yes," she muttered with thick sarcasm. "I can certainly see why someone would merit death for reading or distributing these articles."

She held up the first page. It contained, in tiny print, a series of headlines:

March 6, 1944

- American bombers mount daylight raid on Berlin.
- Soviet forces take Volochysk.
- Finland rejects Soviet peace offer, objecting to Soviet demand that German troops in the country be interned and 1940 borders be restored.

March 7, 1944

- Japan begins offensive operation on Indian-Burmese border.

March 8, 1944

- Fighting commences in northeast India.
- The British government announced plans to build 300,000 houses after the war.
- General strike in Italian Socialist Republic ends after eight days. Germans arrest and deport 1,200 workers.

March 9, 1944

- US Marine Regiment take Talasea in New Britain.
- American destroyer-escort *Leopold* torpedoed and heavily damaged in the North Atlantic by German submarine.

March 10, 1944

- Ireland rejects US request to expel Axis diplomats from country.
- Kriegsmarine loses four U-boats to Allied action.
- "Fighting Seabees" released, starring John Wayne & Susan Hayward.

March 11, 1944

- British forces take Buthidaung in Burma.
- Church of the Eremitani hit by American bombers in Padua.
- German submarines bombed and sunk at Toulon in an American air raid.

March 12, 1944

- US Marines occupy Wotje Atoll.
- Soviets reach Bug River at Gayvoron.
- Pope Pius XII asks belligerents to spare City of Rome.
- Hitler orders German occupation of Hungary.

Below each headline was a brief summary of the pertinent event.

"What shall we do?" Wakley asked.

"Do?" Marian replied. "Continue as we have. The truth will come out, one way or another. The Germans can't hope to keep news from the people indefinitely. Tyrants fall, and this one in Berlin most assuredly will. If he were secure, he'd have no need to stifle news.

"I doubt the other newsletters will stop operations, and some will fill the vacuum left by GUNS. I worry about poor Mr. Machon, though. The *Gestapo* won't be merciful."

29

April 16, 1944
Vassieux-en-Vercors, France

Jeremy listened intently to the high-pitched grind of military vehicles ascending the road to the pass at Col de Rousset, one of the eight approaches into the Vercors. This way climbed the heights by a circuitous route from Die in the southeast. Already, spotters had identified twenty-five vehicles that composed a well-armed patrol of trucks and half-tracks carrying roughly two hundred *miliciens* of the Vichy France government's militia, the *Milice*. The raid was announced as additional punishment for the attack on the *Wehrmacht* staff automobile, which had resulted in the attack on Les Barraques.

Jeremy had never before encountered the *Milice*. Certainly, he had heard of them, and the *Maquis* were always wary of being infiltrated by *miliciens*, considering them to be even more dangerous than the *SS* or the *Gestapo*.

The *miliciens* were Frenchmen, seen as traitors by many of their countrymen. They not only spoke the native language, but they also knew the accents and variations in dialects that identified people as coming from elsewhere. Often, they would be acquainted with the residents in areas where they worked and could notice strangers or unusual activity. And because they worked with the Germans to apprehend, torture, and execute their fellow citizens, they were even more hated than *les boches*.

Formed in January of the previous year, the *Milice* had grown quickly to twenty-five thousand to thirty thousand members spread across France, recruited with the incentives of keeping their current jobs and acting in official capacity for several hours each week. In addition, they received ample food rations, they did not fear being taken for labor in Germany, and their families were protected. They even had their own uniforms consisting of dark blue trousers with a matching jacket over a brown shirt; and indeed, they functioned much as the Nazi Brown Shirts who had been instrumental in regimenting the German population in the early days of the Third *Reich*.

The paramilitary organization had been created by the Vichy regime under Prime Minister Pierre Laval, with Party Secretary General Joseph Darnand leading it in his capacity as the *Milice's* chief of operations. Furthermore, the *miliciens* were well trained and equipped; and they were chartered to function outside of civilian law, to counter Resistance activity. Thus an individual *Milice* member's authority was limitless within specific instructions up to and including on-the-spot executions. In pursuit of fulfilling their missions, they had already murdered many of their countrymen throughout France.

Jeremy suspected that the reason for their advance into the Vercors this morning was related to the arrest a few weeks earlier of *maquisard* Pierre Agapov. The man had been a key leader in Roger's network prior to Jeremy's arrival. Standard protocol for all Resistance members was that, if captured, they should provide only their names and rank, and to tell their inquisitor, "...you know I can't say more than that." They were to resist divulging information for forty-eight hours, even under torture, giving time for their comrades to move headquarters, relocate communications equipment, and vacate the areas of operations known to the prisoner prior to arrest.

Roger had no idea how Agapov had been identified but suspected that the man might have been working with the Germans from the start; several days after being detained, Agapov was seen riding with his captors, unhurt and in good health. That happenstance required Roger to notify the entire Jockey network to take immediate action to avoid arrest. Within the same timeframe, General de Gaulle, as the recognized Free French leader, had mandated that any captured *miliciens* should be executed immediately.

Spotters at the Vercors passes had seen the *Milice* vehicles begin their long and arduous ascent and had spread the alarm. However, the Vercors *maquisards* were still poorly armed. Nevertheless, they set out to meet the *Milice* patrol, hoping to stop them at the southeastern pass.

Jeremy joined them.

Roger had gone to another part of his region to train other *maquisards*.

Once having climbed onto the plateau, the *Milice* unit would make faster progress. Stopping them before they arrived at any of the towns was imperative.

As Jeremy headed toward the inevitable confrontation, thoughts of Échevis, Malleval, and Les Barraques crossed his mind. He hoped to avoid a repetition of those tragedies.

He had drilled the *maquisards* in fire and maneuver techniques and coached them on effective firing skills, but they were not heavily combat experienced, only having engaged in light raids, nor did they have sufficient arms and ammunition. Despite his best efforts and promises from London, no supplies had been dropped.

The small *Maquis* group had driven through Vassieux in trucks and southeast up to the pass. The *Milice* continued their ascent on the steep, winding, narrow road from Die.

The *maquisards* had learned from earlier combat engagements, particularly at Les Barraques. That had been a three-hour skirmish in a constricted passage. The partisan strategy was to hit hard, do as much damage as possible, and then pull back. They had not understood, though, that in addition to raiding for the purpose of inflicting punishment, the enemy was also probing defenses. In Les Barraques, although the *Wehrmacht* had lost thirty men to the *Maquis'* single casualty, the enemy had gained valuable intelligence regarding how well the Vercors *maquisards* were armed.

Letting the leader of this contingent do his job, Jeremy stayed out of the way and made himself available for questions. But he carried a Sten gun and had a few rounds to fire when the time came, the same as the other fighters.

They set up an ambush at a curve in the road looking down the passage. The vertical sides were formed from hard, rough rock. Jeremy sighed. Among supplies he had requested from London was dynamite, which could have closed the pass.

The three hundred pounds of explosives that Geyer had acquired in the raid that had set off the retributive patrols had been used on sabotage missions of the captain's choosing in the plains outside of Vercors. The *maquisards* at this pass had only a limited supply of plastic explosives, which was great for derailing trains and knocking out bridges but was no contest against solid rock.

The leader positioned his men on either side of the road. Jeremy sensed an undercurrent of futility. Only half the men carried rifles, each having fewer than twenty rounds, insufficient to stop a force as large as the one described. They hoped to do as they had done in the past, inflict damage until the enemy withdrew.

At this point in the road, the slope was fairly gentle. The *Milice* could gain speed, and if they broke past the *maquisards*, the enemy patrol would be on flat ground. Within minutes, they would enter Vassieux.

The skirmish was short-lived. The *Milice* unit came with mortars and anti-tank weapons and blasted away at any place they identified as a firing position. Before reaching the plateau, they stopped at a farmhouse and demanded of a woman there to be informed of the locations of the residences of various people. When she said she did not know, they stripped her naked, tied her to the back of a vehicle, and dragged her for several miles. She did not survive.

Arriving in Vassieux a short while later, the *Miliciens* occupied Hôtel Breyton, and immediately arrested twelve random men to be executed. Only the intervention of the local priest stayed their hands. He convinced the district chief that the men had nothing to do with the *maquisards'* attack on the staff car.

The *Milice* chief had brought along his mistress, a sadistic woman who enjoyed the power that her lover's position extended to her. Quickly dubbed as "Colonel Maude," she held court in the hotel and La Chapelle, prosecuting the cases, deciding what types of torture to use, and meting out sentences at her whim. In one instance, she caused the owner of the Breyton to sit in a red-hot frying pan. At least one man, a Pole, died from beatings after being interrogated, and another could not walk.

The brutality continued, and a week after arriving in Vassieux, a tribunal for three men was held at the Hôtel Allard in Vassieux. Disguised as an old man, Jeremy stood in the horrified audience with other residents of the Vercors.

The defendants were stripped naked, one was tortured, and Maude pronounced sentence: death by firing squad. The priest again intervened, but this time he was refused, granted permission only to take the condemned men's confessions before sentence was carried out.

People wept. Some, including the accused, lost control of their bodily functions. One of the prisoners begged the priest, "Please comfort my wife and children, and watch out for them. Our fourth infant is on the way."

Minutes later, without benefit of blindfolds, the men were executed in front of the Hôtel Allard before a weeping crowd, with the shots echoing off the stone walls of the close buildings. As the sound died down, the engine of a truck started up. It transported six more men, tried at an earlier tribunal, to a concentration camp at Dachau, Germany.

The chief departed the Vercors the next day, taking Maude with him, but not before warning the residents in Vassieux, "You've witnessed what happens to terrorists. Let it be a warning to you and others."

Even the cavalry officer, *Capitaine* Geyer, deciding that a lower profile was in order that did not provoke the *Wehrmacht* or the *Milice*, ceased his raids on German garrisons in the plains. He moved his camp to *La Forêt de Lente,* the largest virginal forest in France, located on the high plateau in the western part of the Vercors.

With the *Milice* gone, Jeremy joined with the grieving families. He consoled where he could, helped with burials, and toured the passes to ensure that they were manned, the warning system functioned, and that morale did not dip too far. And he begged London again for materiel support.

All the while, he could not rid himself of worry for Amélie and Chantal, his own siblings, and particularly, his parents. At night, alone in the dark, he noticed a change that had come over him unnoticed in the mayhem of the past eight days. He had developed a grim determination that the perpetrators of the atrocities he had witnessed would be made to pay for their crimes, regardless of how long that took.

30

April 25, 1944
Paris, France

"I can't think of a single reason why anyone in London would wish to speak with me, the least being Prime Minister Churchill." Jeannie Rousseau stood at the end of the sofa in Georges' sitting room, facing him and Amélie. "I don't even understand most of what I write down. I'm a human tape recorder, not a technical genius."

"Nevertheless, Churchill personally invited you," Georges replied. "His scientists believe that if they ask you questions—"

"You mean interrogate me."

"I'm sure they don't think of it that way. You are held in the highest regard there. Your drawings and annotations have been so accurate that the British made significant breakthroughs based on them. They think if you go there and speak with them, they might be able to get greater depth."

"Do they know who I am?"

"No, your identity has been carefully hidden, even from the prime minister."

Amélie stood listening quietly, but now she spoke up. "It'll be a chance for you to get out of this pressure. You've been gathering intelligence at the heart of German High Command in France for three years, under the most stressful conditions. The invasion is coming. We all know it. Maybe it's time to leave, rest, and enjoy life for a change."

"That can't be the reason I'd do it," Jeannie replied stubbornly. Her elegant face with her turned-up nose, perfectly aligned chin, and bright eyes had acquired fine lines, and her coiffed hair had lost a bit of luster. "As long as France is occupied and I can do something here, then I must do it. It's a moral obligation."

"Your moral obligation was met long ago," Georges interjected with a mock chiding tone. "I'd go so far as to say that you might have made the single greatest intelligence coup of the war. You must know that the strike at Peenemünde resulted from the information you provided. And you've continued to provide detailed reports in the months since then from facilities all over Germany."

Jeannie shook her head. "Don't heap undeserved praise on my head. I'm neither a great spy nor brave. Most of the time I'm terrified almost into paralysis. Fear lances all over my body like thousands of needles piercing all at once."

She contemplated a moment. "I'm just a girl who uses her brain. I was put into a situation where I could be useful in this vicious war, and so I did. I could not do otherwise. I don't see how that warrants a trip to London while the war is still ongoing."

Georges chuckled. "You're one in a million, Jeannie Rousseau. Think of it this way: you're being put in a position to meet with great scientists who will query, not interrogate you, to learn if there are any more details in that magnificent mind of yours that might help end this war earlier."

Jeannie stared at him with a slightly reproachful expression. "You're using semantics against me now."

Georges walked over and took her hands. "I shall miss you, Jeannie, if you go. You were my finest student and you're my friend. You've provided France with the most honorable service. Perhaps this is how you'll finish for this war."

Tears welled in Jeannie's eyes. She leaned against Georges and grasped his shoulders. "I fear that if I go, I shall never see you again."

Georges put his arms around Jeannie and squeezed her. "Of course you'll see me." He spoke softly. "When the Allies take Paris, we'll walk the *Champs-Élysées* and celebrate together under *l'Arc de Triomphe.*"

Jeannie stepped back, kissed his cheek, and looked across at Amélie. "While you're being so generous with praise," she told Georges, "let's not forget my dearest friend." She gestured toward Amélie. "She rescued me out of Dinard; she was my distant and constant companion throughout all these months here in Paris. Whenever I saw her, despite that we couldn't speak, I knew that good people watched out for me. She gave me courage to continue. And she took such risks to deliver my documents to the Allies."

Amélie had listened, her cheeks turning bright red. "What I did was nothing—"

"Jeannie is right," Georges interrupted. He crossed the room, kissed Amélie on both cheeks, and embraced her. "The two of you made an indomitable team."

Quiet descended on the room.

Georges broke the silence. "This is too somber," he said. "Let's toast to a job well done and Jeannie's trip to London."

"I haven't yet said that I'd go," Jeannie protested.

"Then indulge my hope that you will," Georges replied. He crossed to the cabinet, poured three glasses of sherry, and handed them out. He faced Jeannie. "To you and a safe trip," he declared, and lifted his glass in the air.

"Wait," Jeannie interrupted. "I'll agree on one condition." While Georges tossed her a wondering look, she turned to Amélie. "I want to take Amélie with me."

Startled, Amélie started to protest. "I can't. I'm sure Madame Fourcade—"

"Nonsense. You've been here long enough too." Jeannie's face took on a sly expression. "Where is your Jeremy right now? Do you know?"

Amélie shook her head. "I try not to think of it. I haven't heard—"

"I don't know where he is either, but likely, the next place you'll see him will be in London." She spun on her heel toward Georges and lifted her chin impishly. "That's my condition. Either Amélie goes with me, or I don't go."

Georges furrowed his brow and allowed a smile. "Amélie? What do you say?"

"What about Chantal?"

"I'll get a report on Chantal delivered to you when you arrive."

Amélie took a deep breath. "All right then, I'll go. When do we leave?"

"In three days."

April 28, 1944

Amélie disliked the feel of the travel arrangements to transport her and Jeannie to London. Her disquiet was undefined, an element that she could not yet qualify.

She had traveled to England twice before, once by submarine and once on a Lysander moonlight flight. She had returned once by parachute and once by Lysander. Despite the danger, she had been calmed by the pilots on the flights. Their quiet confidence had reinforced her own, and the crews at both ends of the Lysander flights had moved about their tasks in a practiced manner. She had been fully briefed on what to expect, and the transports had gone like clockwork.

She knew that such was not always the case. Storms brewed unexpectedly while crossing the Channel. Flights blew off course. Engines sputtered out. Infiltrators and collaborators betrayed landing sites. All manner of tragic events had cost the lives of more than a few who took to the air at night during the week before and the week after a full moon. The pilots navigated by compass, stars, and ghostly landmarks in reflected moonlight. They flew to small dirt fields marked only by Resistance members holding flashlights, illuminated when they heard the aircrafts' engines.

There would be no flight for this trip. The moon was at the dark end of its waxing and waning period, and the scientists in London were anxious to confer with Jeannie, currently known to them only as "a young girl, the most remarkable of her generation." They knew only that she had provided incredible intelligence notes and sketches of high technical quality accompanied by key information on troop movements, strategies, and leadership profiles. Aside from curiosity about this marvelous creature, the scientists' urgency stemmed from the approaching D-Day and what they might learn from this girl in her early twenties that might help in the cross-Channel invasion of France.

Instead of a Lysander, a boat would meet them off the coast of the Bay of Saint-Brieuc in the Gulf of Saint-Malo, roughly a hundred and forty miles from England. In addition to the danger of boarding in hostile waters and crossing the treacherous Channel at night, Jeannie and Amélie would need to travel overland from Paris to Tréguier, and from there, to be ushered to the rendezvous point by unknown escorts.

Just the thought of the boat was unnerving for Amélie. She recalled her seasickness and embarrassment aboard the submarine for several days during which it was attacked. The boat's tossing had made her horribly sick and only a thin curtain had separated her and the noises of her illness from the crew.

Although this trip over the stormy waterway was expected to take only hours, not days, the area was hostile and the waves and currents were treacherous. Nevertheless, rendezvous points were established to meet those who would escort the two women out to sea to meet the British vessel.

Keeping a practiced eye out for anyone paying more than cursory attention to them, the two women boarded the train at rush hour, expecting a four- to five-hour ride to Saint-Brieuc. Partisans would pick them up in the town and transport them via backroads to a house in Tréguier. There, they would meet two other agents traveling back to England, and the four of them would be led to a marina and the boat that would carry them to the waiting British motor launch in the bay.

To Amélie, the arrangement felt complex with more variables than usual and beyond her comfort. Her travel documents now showed her as Simone Lavigne, and Jeannie as Madeleine Chauffour. They were ostensibly cousins on their way to Saint-Brieuc for a family reunion. With Jeannie's perfect German ability and practiced charm, they had no trouble at the checkpoints in Paris and settled in their carriage for a trip as pleasant as could be had under German occupation.

Jeannie was her normal vivacious self, her eyes barely concealing her excitement. Watching her, though, Amélie sensed an undercurrent of apprehension or perhaps wistfulness, manifested in moments of quietly staring at nothing. But Jeannie shook them off, smiled brightly, checked her hair and makeup, and once the locomotive had pulled out of the station, she watched the passing countryside.

Amélie thought Jeannie a marvel, unreal but for her physical presence that could be touched and felt. Always exuding supreme confidence and charm, fluent in multiple languages, she met every challenge with just the right expression of interest, respect, courtesy, or even disdain if the occasion arose. She wore fine clothes, although some had faded and showed signs of having been mended. Yet she mixed with average people as gracefully as she did with members of high society. Her courage was unbounded, yet she admitted to being terrified much of the time; and when praised for her accomplishments, she invariably said, "I do what I must do. It's an obligation."

The train traversed flat farmland as it headed southwest out of Paris through Chartres toward Le Mans. What crops they saw were green and half-grown as they should be at this time of year, but many fields were fallow and untended, the result of so many young men having been shipped to Germany to work in the arms factories or having fled to the mountains to join the *Maquis*.

After passing through Vitré, Châteaubourg, and dozens of quaint villages and towns with stone houses and neat shops, some with thatched roofs, they stopped briefly at Rennes. "Have you ever visited here?" Jeannie asked.

Amélie shook her head.

"Then you must at some time. It's a beautiful town, over two thousand years old, and the buildings are so stately. The Lile and Vilaine rivers join here—" She stopped talking as her voice turned momentarily hoarse.

Amélie glanced at her sharply. "Are you all right?"

Jeannie nodded but did not speak. The train continued its journey, and soon they once again passed through open fields. Then she stirred. "I don't believe I've told you about this town where we get off the train, Saint-Brieuc. I was born there."

"I didn't know that," Amélie exclaimed. "What's it like?"

"A wonderful town. Before the war, our family would go back there as often as possible." She lapsed back into silence, and then murmured, "We have such a beautiful country. Despite the plunder and the atrocities, it remains what it has always been, France." Her jaw tightened and her eyes narrowed. "And so it must remain."

Anticipating her thoughts, Amélie grasped Jeannie's hand and squeezed it. "I've been to England and back twice in this war," she said softly. "You'll be back."

Jeannie bit her lip and forced a smile. "I know. At least I hope." Then she smiled primly. "Look what I've brought." She pulled a bag from her coat and showed a dozen sets of nylon stockings. "I thought Jeremy's sister might like to have them as a welcome gift. I've heard they're scarce in England. I acquired them on the black market. Those and a few other things in my suitcase. Perfumes, and such."

"How thoughtful," Amélie exclaimed, pleased but also alarmed. "I hope you didn't take on more danger to acquire them."

"Hardly," Jeannie replied with a tone of having been reproached. "Buying on the black market is a necessity in Paris these days, to survive. You know that. The *Gestapo* knows that too and ignores it within limits."

"But nylons? Perfume?"

"Given the social events I've gone to with the *Wehrmacht* high command, they would not be seen as unusual for me. In fact, some of the officers bring such things to me as gifts, trying to get closer." She smiled coyly. "But I keep them at a distance. If I'd let any of them into my bedroom, jealousies would have developed between them, and I would have lost effectiveness."

Amélie laughed softly. "Ah, my friend, you are a wonder."

After two more hours, they rolled into Saint-Brieuc. Jeannie regained her full composure, and they once again maneuvered through the checkpoints on the strength of excellent forgeries, Amélie's skill at knowing how to move through crowds and checkpoints, and Jeannie's charisma.

They arrived as the afternoon waned. After leaving the station, they made their way to a café across from the entrance and sipped coffee until shadows had lengthened and dusk descended. Then they followed memorized instructions to a small grocer's a few blocks away, keeping watch on their back trail, to the sides, and ahead of them for anything indicating that they were being surveilled.

Seeing nothing untoward, they entered the grocery store near closing time. Two other people, an old man and woman, chatted with the store-keeper. Jeannie and Amélie browsed a meager fruit bin that spilled into the display window.

"How fresh are the grapes?" Amélie called out.

The grocer looked up as if startled that she had spoken to him. His voice broke with nervousness. "They came in this morning. Try the purple ones. They're very juicy." He glanced at his watch. "Time to close," he told the old couple, ushering them toward the door. "Let me handle these ladies, and then I'll lock up."

As soon as his customers had gone, he pulled the sash down and put up the "*Fermé*" sign. "This way," he instructed.

Without further conversation, the women followed him through the store, past a storage room, and out a door to an alley. A car and driver waited there, the engine already running. The introductions consisted of innocuous phrases exchanged to establish identity, and when the doors were closed, the driver said, "We have to pick up the other two passengers, and then we have an hour's drive."

As nighttime deepened, they drove a short distance through Saint-Brieuc's streets and halted behind a row of houses. The driver rolled down his window, spoke a few words, and received a soft-spoken reply.

The front passenger and rear driver's side doors opened. A man climbed into the front and a woman slid into the back, leaving Amélie sitting in the middle. No one spoke as the car wound its way through back roads with only dim blackout lights. Even Jeannie, normally lively around anyone, remained silent.

Amélie's trepidation grew. To her, this operation seemed loose. Accustomed to having the assurance of a team watching over her movements, the thought that a driver she did not know was taking her and Jeannie with two other people, whose faces she had not seen, to a rendezvous for transport out to sea on an unknown boat to meet a British vessel on a moonless night seemed the height of folly.

The road led into a hilly area with steep slopes and curves, throwing the vehicle's passengers uncomfortably against each other. Amélie's unease increased when, an hour later, they descended from a high plateau into

Tréguier and approached the waterfront. The fishy smell of the coast rode the air.

They drove through darkened back alleys with rows of widely separated houses, crossed over a bridge, and emerged on a road next to the west side of a canal leading to the bay. The distance between homes and other buildings widened with hills and steep bluffs between them.

The automobile finally came to a halt across the road from a large house near the canal that stood out in the dark because of its large white frame. "I'd suggest you go in one at a time," the driver said. "The rest of you should wait in the shadows until it's safe. I have to go."

Jeannie spoke up. "I'll go in."

Amélie's sense of foreboding took a leap. "I don't like this," she said. She spoke to the driver. "Pull down the road a ways. We can walk back."

Jeannie had already alighted and leaned back in. "I'll be all right, and I'll see you inside in a few minutes."

"All out," the driver said. "I really must go. Those are my instructions." When at first no one moved, he said impatiently, "This is dangerous for me too."

The woman to Amélie's left opened the door and clambered out. Amélie followed. The man in the front also climbed out and circled around the back of the car while Jeannie walked up the concrete path to the front door.

The vehicle drove away. Amélie ducked behind some bushes with her unknown companions.

"This doesn't look good," the man said, reflecting her own apprehension. "We should spread out."

Amélie agreed and, staying in the shadows, crept to the base of a hill off to the side. When she turned back around, the man and woman had disappeared. Jeannie, seen now only as a dark figure in the ambient light, had reached the door and knocked.

It opened, and Jeannie stepped inside.

Minutes passed. Then suddenly, the door flew open, and three dark figures emerged. Two of them seemed to be dragging the third one between them. Jeannie's musical voice was loud and distraught. "Why are you arresting me? I'm a black-market vendor trying to make a living. Check my coat pockets. You'll find the nylons I came to sell. Someone called my home and asked me to bring them here."

She spoke in German. Amélie understood none of it, but she comprehended immediately that by her choice of language, her friend had sent a warning.

Jeannie struggled against her captors as they continued to force her to the opposite side of the house. "Look at my ID," she yelled. "My name is Madeleine Chauffour…"

And then Jeannie was in the shadows with her captors, out of sight, and her voice suddenly silenced. Car doors slammed, and moments later, a large sedan emerged. It turned out of the driveway and sped away toward town.

Horror-stricken, Amélie watched it disappear as she absorbed the implication. Jeannie had been taken by the *Gestapo*.

Five Days Later, April 30, 1944
Lyon, France

Amélie restrained herself from pounding frantically on Ladybird's door. Instead, she took a deep breath, tried to stop shaking, and knocked quietly and in the specific rhythm that informed those inside the apartment that a Resistance member awaited.

The door opened, and Madame Fourcade stood there. She gazed momentarily at Amélie and then snatched her hand, pulled her inside, and closed the door.

Amélie no longer controlled her shaking. Her ashen face had grown thinner; her hair, wrapped in a scarf, was unkempt; and her clothes hung from her emaciated frame.

"You poor child," Fourcade cried, and threw her arms around Amélie, who shuddered, weeping and wobbling on unsteady legs. "This way," Fourcade soothed, and led her straight into a bedroom.

Amélie collapsed into the sheets. "I'm dirty," she protested in a whisper.

"We'll worry about that later. You need sleep. Now."

Amélie shook her head. "I can't sleep." She sobbed again. "Jeannie—"

"Shh. We know. We're all upset over the news. We were worried for you too."

"Where did they take her?"

Fourcade shook her head. "We don't know. When the *Gestapo* arrested her, we lost track of her."

Amélie's body trembled with grief. Fourcade held her until her sobs subsided.

"There was a man and another woman with us. I never knew who they were. I don't know what happened to them."

"The contact at the house was expecting them. Fortunately, he was not expecting you or Jeannie."

Amélie absorbed that tidbit. "The *Gestapo* was already in the house," she gasped. "We were betrayed."

Fourcade nodded. "And the contact there has been dealt with. He won't betray anyone again."

Amélie glanced up at Fourcade's face, her eyes hardening. "Good." She dropped her head onto the pillow and her eyes closed momentarily. Then they flashed back open. "What happened to those people? Did they get away?"

Fourcade sighed. "Maybe you should sleep. You've been through an ordeal."

Amélie struggled to sit up. "I want to know," she rasped.

Fourcade took a deep breath. "All right. The woman got away. She's safe. The man had got away too, but he's from Saint-Brieuc. He feared retaliation against the village and his family, so he turned himself in. He was executed."

Amélie rocked from side to side, fighting tears. "And where's Chantal. Please tell me my little sister is all right."

Fourcade smiled and pushed a strand of hair from Amélie's face. "She is. My last report on her activities came in early this morning. The project she's working on has proceeded unimpeded, and the remarks about her contributions are excellent."

Amélie exhaled slowly while nodding. "At least there's that."

"Now will you get some sleep?"

Amélie shook her head. "I'm too restless now. I won't sleep."

"Then come into the kitchen and I'll get you some food and something hot to drink. You need it. You can tell me how you escaped."

Over a single fried egg, a few slices of cold cuts, and some bread with tea, Amélie related her ordeal after seeing the *Gestapo* sedan drive off with Jeannie. "I froze in place for a time, but then I thought the *Gestapo* would likely be back or there might be more of them in the house. I never saw the man or the woman again."

Keeping to the shadows, Amélie had climbed the hill behind her leading away from the road. It had been a rugged ascent, but that seemed wiser than taking her chances on the single vehicular route away from the canal. She had found a barn and spent a sleepless night there agonizing over Jeannie's capture. "I'm so afraid for her. What they'll do to her if they find out who she is and what she's done—it's unimaginable."

"She kept her wits about her," Fourcade said by way of offering solace. "That was plain in the way she warned you."

Amélie sniffed and agreed. "She is a real friend. If she's alive at the end of this war, I will find her. I won't rest again until that's done."

Fourcade squeezed Amélie's hand. "That's something to live for, so let's make sure you get plenty of food and rest so you can do that."

Amélie sat staring into space for a few moments. Then, suddenly, she took more interest in her food.

"How did you get from Saint-Brieuc to here?" Fourcade asked.

"I'm not sure I even remember it all," Amélie replied wearily. "I walked for miles. I stayed away from the trains and skirted around checkpoints. I begged. I caught rides with farmers and others. I slept in barns. When I couldn't avoid soldiers, they treated me with disgust. They perceived me as being no threat at all, and not worth their bother to check my papers." She sniffed and gestured to indicate her figure. "I mean, look at me."

"Hmph. There's irony in that," Fourcade said. "Thankfully, their brains are not as sharp as their bayonets. If they had known the things you've done..." She shook her head. "Let's get you cleaned up and rested. You'll stay here out of sight until we find a safer place."

31

May 2, 1944
Hameau de Fontenay, France

"So that's it," Chantal asked. "*Fait accompli?*"

Robert Douin nodded wearily. "All but the delivery," he said. "And none too soon." He glanced toward a dark sedan parked on a hillock near a farmhouse two hundred meters to their rear. "Don't look," he warned. "We've gathered sustained interest."

"I've noticed," Chantal said. "They've had someone watching us almost daily for the past two weeks. It's made delivery to the dead drop difficult."

Douin looked across the stunning view where he sat at his easel facing east toward the English Channel. The water glimmered in the distance. The late afternoon tide had begun to recede, and the waves lapped gently along the shoreline less than a hundred meters to his front.

"Listen," he told Chantal, "I want you to dance and prance in front of me like a little girl. I'll keep talking, and then we'll go down to the beach. I'll leave my easel up here with one of our unfinished drawings showing. It's right beneath the real sketch I just finished. But before we go, I need you to move behind me, blocking the view from that sedan. I'll pull off the top drawing and roll it up. You keep jumping up and down and acting like you're trying to convince me to take you down to the beach. Then, you'll grasp my arm and walk close to me until we get to where the ground becomes steeper.

"At that point, you take off, still acting like the little girl, but you'll be carrying the sketch. I need you to find a place to hide it while I stay in plain sight. Make sure you put it where you can find it later. Do you understand?"

"I think so," Chantal said, and began pulling at his shoulder, prancing behind him, and pointing out to sea. "Why is today different?" she asked as she kept up the pantomime. "They've been observing us for at least two weeks."

"It's a feeling," Douin said as Chantal moved behind him. "We've been pushing our luck." He quickly removed the sketch from the easel, rolled it up tightly, and stuffed it in a long pocket in his white smock. He left in its place one of his prepared sketches for anyone to see. "Now start pulling against my shoulder."

Chantal complied, and after a few repeated jabs, he stood, half-turned toward her, nodded, and stretched, lifting both arms in the air as if in frustration. She came back around in front of him, took his hand, and they started walking toward the beach.

In the weeks that Chantal worked with Douin and Rémy, she had become fond of them. For the most part, the job had been fun, riding bicycles along roads paralleling the coast and where the *Wehrmacht* allowed civilian traffic. Then, the trio had turned onto roads taking them closer to the beach. They were careful to move past German facilities without showing more than cursory curiosity, always waving to the sentries and showing no hostility.

As the weeks passed, Chantal had noticed a change in Douin's attitude. She suspected that the daily toil of climbing stairs of church belltowers or hiking miles to the next location over the course of many months had taken its physical toll. In addition, she was sure that he paid a mental and emotional price as they traversed Normandy's coastline, always within sight of Hitler's vaunted Atlantic Wall.

She had been astounded at Douin's artistic skill. With each motion of his hand, he brought the smallest detail to life, drawing sections of the coastline just as it appeared when she observed the real beach. He added the massive gun emplacements that Dragon had mentioned; the miles of thick barbed wire stretched anywhere where a landing vessel could drop off troops. He sketched in each and every steel obstacle, their shapes and orientation just as they actually appeared, as well as any other detail that might be of military significance.

Chantal and Rémy had scouted their respective areas and brought back information on locations of headquarters, troop housing, ammo storage facilities, supply routes, and roads accessing the beaches. Douin had included those features.

At odd times when she could, Chantal watched Douin work, entranced by his talent and attention to detail; and when in any of the church towers, she compared his rendition against the reality and was amazed at the accuracy. He had enjoyed her interest in his artwork, and when time permitted, he had provided instruction and allowed her to try her own hand.

Thrilled at showing a talent she had been unaware of, she paid close attention to how Douin held his pencils, the types of strokes he made, and the technique he used to scale objects against each other, how to give the illusion of leaves on trees or sand on the beach, or add in mood by using shadowing.

She had also been on many forays with Rémy, and for the most part, they were pleasant outings, doing nothing more than riding to a location, sitting out of sight, and observing Normandy's beaches. Passing through checkpoints had become a routine function, and they had become practiced at it.

Fortunately, Rémy had needed no forgeries. As he had explained on the day she arrived, he was often taken to be older than his age, and his ID had been scrutinized carefully to confirm his birth year. On those occasions, instead of Chantal feigning being younger than she was, she reverted to acting her age, then treating Rémy as an annoying younger cousin.

So far, the various ruses had worked, and Chantal began to regard Rémy fondly as a younger brother and Douin as an endearing, if sometimes irascible, uncle, maybe even as a surrogate father. Her relations with the two of them had become familial to the extent that, late at night when lying awake, she felt guilty over how well she was living life while Amélie was in Paris, doing what? Chantal hardly dared guess. Then her mind drifted to Horton, and her heart skipped beats.

"Where's Rémy now?" she asked Douin as she walked toward the beach holding onto his arm. "He should have been back from the village."

"That's what's troubling me," Douin replied. He had sent Rémy on the legitimate errand of buying bread and whatever he could find in the grocer's to make the evening meal. "The distance wasn't far. He should have been back more than an hour ago."

They reached the edge of the gentle slope where it descended more steeply and started down. "I'm going to drop the sketch onto the ground in front of me. You take my hand and pull me like you want me to go down to the beach with you. I'll shake my head and wave you to go on. You start down, but as soon as you are sure you're out of sight, duck down, come around, get the drawing, and take it to a safe place. Then go to the beach and pretend to play. When you come back up, bring some rocks and seashells to show me."

Chantal locked her eyes with his. "You know this is moronic, the way we have to live." Wrinkling her forehead, she said, "By the way, why is this section open down to the beach?"

Douin shrugged. "I haven't a clue. Perhaps they just haven't got here yet, or maybe this area has a lower priority. Doesn't matter. I draw what I see. Run along now."

Chantal made a show of pulling on his arm a few times. He pulled it away, waved her off, and she headed toward the beach.

As she turned away, she was sure she heard a car door slam.

Spurred by adrenaline, she flew down the hillside a few feet, turned to check line of sight, and circled back in a crouch below the crest. The rolled-up sketch lay on the ground. She grabbed it without looking up at Douin and headed back downhill.

A distant voice called out. Chantal ran down the hill as fast as the rough ground allowed, looking for a place to hide the sketch. A series of fissures appeared in the dirt, apparently made by the wind and rain. As she ran, she searched for one long enough and deep enough to obscure the roll.

She tried one. Too short. Another was too shallow. At last, she found one that barely served the purpose. She shoved it in and whirled around to find landmarks to establish its place. Seeing nothing other than Douin himself standing near the crest looking out to sea, she fastened in her mind where he was relative to his easel still sitting in the field, and how far down the steeper slope she had come.

She glanced uphill once again, seeing Douin standing there in silhouette with his wide-brimmed hat flopping in the breeze. He turned slightly, and then two men appeared next to him. Reverting to role, Chantal waved, called out to him, and bounded down the remaining distance to the sandy beach.

Douin stood with his hands in his pockets, watching Chantal. He smiled distantly, thinking that she was indeed a lovely girl, as much for her character as for her looks. She had amazed him at her ability to move so easily between little girl and mature older sister roles, and he had felt flattered that she had taken such an interest in his drawings. For a fleeting second, he thought wistfully about what life would have been with her as his daughter, Rémy's sister. The two got along so well.

He heard the padding of feet over soft ground behind him, and turned. Two men in suits and slouch hats came toward him.

"*Monsieur* Douin," one of them called.

"Yes." He turned the rest of the way to face them. "Do I know you?"

"No, but you'd know of us. We're *Gestapo* officers."

Douin pulled himself up into a non-committal posture. "To what do I owe this pleasure?" His effort to keep sarcasm out of his voice succeeded only partially.

"We heard that the famous Robert Douin was doing a series of drawings along Normandy's coast and thought, what a great opportunity to watch a real artist at work."

"Landscape drawing is one of my specialties, and this stretch of coastline is so picturesque. I've been wanting to do it for a long time. Did you see my work? You must have passed it on the way down."

"We did," the apparent senior of the two officers said. "It's quite impressive. We just needed to be sure that you're drawing only the landscape, and not any of the military installations."

"Gentlemen, do I look like a fool?" Douin replied brusquely. "You are free to look through my portfolio. I draw my art to sell. Who is going to be interested in buying sketches of landscapes overrun by an occupying army?"

The officer raised his eyebrows but did not respond. Instead, he looked down the hill and watched Chantal playing in the shallow water of the receding tide. "Your daughter?"

Douin shook his head. "My niece. She's here for the summer. She wanted to spend time with me to learn how to draw."

As they watched, Chantal waded in the surf. Then she crouched and searched for shells in the wet sand. Finding some that seemed to interest her, she stood and examined them in her hand. After a few minutes, she hurried up the hillside with a beaming smile. "Uncle Robert," she called, arriving breathless and forcing exuberance into her voice. "Look at these shells I've found."

"You have a very pretty niece," the senior officer said unctuously. "Maybe she'll turn out to be as talented as her uncle." He doffed his hat. "Good day, sir."

Fury filled Douin's eyes as he watched the two *Gestapo* men walk away. Chantal noticed. "I'm just as angry," she said in a low voice.

"We can't leave the sketch there," he said. "If we do and it rains, it's gone. Go retrieve it now, but don't come back up until they're gone. I'll stay here and signal when it's safe."

He watched as the two officers reached their sedan and drove off. Only when they were out of sight and the sound of their engine had died away did he signal to Chantal to come up.

A short while later, Rémy appeared. "I stayed out of sight when I saw that *Gestapo* sedan. They were asking about you in the village. The only thing anyone told them was that you're a famous artist and they were proud to have you here."

Douin turned and hugged his son. Then, as if the thought had just occurred to him, he wrapped his arms around Chantal. "We're family now," he said, his voice quivering. Then he growled, "It's not just moronic the way we live. It's monstrous."

They returned that evening, without incident, to a guest house at the church where they had stayed the previous night. "Our time together comes to an end," he told Chantal sadly. "You must take that last drawing straight to the farm where all the others have gone and wait there for it to be attached to the others. Then you'll take the entire roll to Dragon."

Sensing that her life might be changing in unpredictable ways for the worse, Chantal barely slept that night, and when she came into the kitchen for breakfast the next morning, she was overcome with dejection. Douin noticed. "What's wrong, *Papillon*?" he asked.

Chantal stared at him and then shifted her gaze to Rémy sitting across the table. "I'm afraid I'll never see either of you again. I couldn't bear to think—" She choked back a sob. "The *Gestapo* is watching you."

Douin stood in front of her, his arms crossed, smiling beneath his wide mustache. He studied her face, and then reached out and rubbed her cheek. "You'll see us again, *Papillon*. Every time you see my drawings, you'll see me, and you'll see Rémy. And if Fortune smiles on us, we'll come back after the war and re-do these landscapes minus the German accouterments."

Chantal threw her arms around his neck and held on, shaking. When finally she let go, she did the same with Rémy. He held her tightly.

"I should go with her," Rémy said.

"No," his father said emphatically. Seeing a sullen, defiant look on Rémy's face, Douin softened his stance. "You're already known to the *Gestapo* and they're inquiring about me. We need to keep you out of sight. If they decide to bring me in, your birth year will be disregarded. You'll go off to a labor camp."

"But that hasn't happened yet," Rémy insisted. "Why should she risk herself if I can't do the same?"

Douin studied his son and grunted. "You've risked plenty all these months. The fact is that *Papillon* plays the part of a young girl very well, and she knows how to throw the guards off. If you're with her, all we need is for one of them to decide that either of your IDs or travel papers should be looked into—they don't need a reason. They might look more closely at her and what she's carrying. Not only could her arrest destroy our mission, but an investigation would lead back to me. You'd be at much greater risk of being taken to Germany for labor."

Rémy nodded glumly. He wrapped his arm around Chantal's shoulder, hung his head, and exhaled.

"You've got a long ride," Douin told Chantal. "About sixty kilometers, but you won't be alone. Members of the Resistance are spaced along the way to watch over you. They know that what you're carrying must reach its destination. They're prepared to protect you if an attempt is made to stop or arrest you, even if their interference means reprisals against the local population." He chuckled. "So you won't need to use those deadly fists to take out anyone today."

Chantal could not help a small laugh.

"Are you armed?"

Chantal nodded.

"Let me see."

She produced a small pistol from one skirt pocket and a knife from the other. "I've practiced pulling them out quickly, and I know how to use them."

Douin tossed his head and chuckled. "I have no doubt that you do."

"Where's the sketch?" she asked.

"In the cross-bar of your bicycle. If you're stopped, it's unlikely to be found. The route I've outlined takes you on back roads, through forests on narrow paths, and along farm lanes. You should get there unmolested. You'll receive final instructions on arrival. Once you've finished there, you won't have far to go."

―――――――――――

The ride to the farm turned out to be more pleasant than Chantal had anticipated. The route was circuitous, but given a fresh breeze blowing in from the Channel, the brilliant green foliage and bright flowers resulting from April rains, and the pleasant sense derived from riding a bicycle through breathtaking countryside, she soon found her spirits lifted. Tall hedges lined many of the lanes, shielding her from view, and her path had been carefully planned such that she avoided main roads and their checkpoints.

At various places along the way, a man or a woman, some of them old, some very young, stepped out as she passed by to wave and wish her well. She waved back with a smile while noticing that several had straps looped over their shoulders supporting Sten guns. The sight reminded her of her somber mission.

Thus she arrived at the farm four hours after having left Douin and Rémy. More accurately, she arrived at a point in the woods away from the farm. A man identified only by the exchange-of-phrase method met her there. He took the bicycle and told Chantal to wait. Forty minutes later, he reappeared leading a donkey burdened with a bale of hay and some firewood. He gave no explanation, but outlined the route to take to reach Dragon's farm. "You should be there within forty-five minutes." Then he smiled for the first time. "Douin sent word to provide you with the best care and security. He said that you're a true daughter of France."

Chantal's chest welled even as she choked back emotion. She thanked the man and started off with the donkey. It was a small animal, probably indistinguishable among a herd with its dark brown color, white snout, and complacent attitude. It flicked its tail but followed Chantal without protest.

Shortly before coming to the main road to cross on the last leg of her journey, she heard voices ahead around a bend. Quickly, she stepped off the path, but not before two German soldiers appeared coming her way, obviously on patrol.

They saw her.

"*Anhalten!*" one commanded.

Chantal froze as they strode up to her.

"Papers," the other demanded.

She produced her fake documents. One of the soldiers scrutinized them. The other leaned his rifle against a stump, took a bayonet from his belt, and prodded the donkey's load with it.

Chantal watched him carefully. He thrust the blade into the hay, pulled it out, thrust it in again in a different place, and repeated the process several times. Suddenly, he called to his companion.

Chantal could not understand what he said, but his message was clear. He had found something.

"*Bleib hier,*" the soldier inspecting her papers commanded.

Chantal understood him to mean to stay put. He threw her documents on the ground and went to help investigate the donkey's load.

Deftly, Chantal reached into her skirt, drew her pistol, and shot twice, aiming first for center mass of the nearest soldier's back and then his head. He dropped.

The other soldier stared at her in shock. He glanced at his rifle leaning against the stump a few feet away, and then at his bayonet, but before he could move, Chantal shot him twice in the same manner. The two men lay in the dirt path, their bodies twitching out their last signs of life while the donkey munched on a patch of grass.

Nausea overcame Chantal. She leaned over and retched. Her mind clouded, and she found herself unable to think.

Then she sensed that she was not alone. A man stood in front of her in civilian clothes. He held his palms out in a calming gesture. "I am Lucien," he said, "a friend."

Hearing rustling noises behind her, Chantal turned. Four other men dragged the corpses away. Two more seized the dead soldiers' weapons and cleaned blood spills.

"You must leave here," Lucien said.

Her head pounding, Chantal realized that she still had the pistol in her hand. She returned it to her pocket while nodding at Lucien, seeing him through listless eyes. Then she staggered over to grasp the donkey's lead rope.

"I'll handle the donkey," Lucien said. "Follow me."

Several hundred feet ahead, he turned onto a different path that led to a small clearing. "Rest," he said. He held out a canteen. "Would you like some water?"

Sinking to a sitting position, Chantal buried her face in her hands. Lucien crouched next to her. "I am so sorry, *Papillon,*" he said. "Those soldiers came from a side path. We didn't see them until you did. My comrades are erasing any sign that you came that way."

Chantal heard him as if from a distance, but she nodded.

"Those bodies will never be seen by anyone," Lucien went on. "Desertions are rising in the German ranks. We'll spread rumors in the villages that two of them have been trying to get partisan transportation south to Spain."

She reached out her hand. "Water."

Lucien opened the canteen. "We can't stay long," he said as he handed it to her. "Their unit will be looking for them and will come this way. We're moving to another route."

Chantal nodded and took a few swallows. Then she struggled to stand up. "I've never shot anyone before," she muttered. "Let's go. I'll be all right."

Lucien regarded her admiringly. "Are you sure?"

"I'm sure. Let's go."

Word had reached Dragon about the shooting before Chantal arrived late that night, and he treated her solicitously. "You were perfect," he told her, but noticed that she only acknowledged him with a distant smile. "We have the compiled sketches, and I'll get them to *Hérisson* tomorrow night. The arrangements are set. Now you sleep."

The aroma of hot coffee greeted Chantal when she staggered into the kitchen the next morning. "You're a hero of the French Resistance," Dragon greeted her enthusiastically. "The men who brought you saw the whole episode. You're a legend."

"Hmph. I don't feel like a legend," Chantal said, scraping a chair out from the table. After sitting down, she rested her head in her hand and leaned her elbow on the tabletop. "I have a headache and my body feels numb." She raised her head and looked about curiously. "Where did you get fresh coffee?"

"Those men brought it and some other food they've all been hoarding. They wanted to be sure that you ate well this morning."

Chantal pursed her lips and shook her head. "Please thank them for me. I didn't plan for things to go the way they did. Believe me. I did what I had to do, and that's not being heroic." As images of yesterday's skirmish flashed through her mind, intense regret momentarily overtook her. She gasped. "I'd practiced shooting a lot. I didn't expect to really ever shoot anyone."

"You saved the mission and probably your own life," Dragon said with finality. "Nothing more to consider.

"Here's the situation. The Gestapo is asking a lot of questions about Douin. They're closing in on him. But they're asking questions about Rémy too, and about you."

"No surprise there," Chantal replied. "They'll investigate everyone close to him."

"That means we have to move you out of here. I'm taking you with me to deliver the sketches to *Hérisson*."

Chantal's head popped up. "I'm going back to Lyon?"

Dragon smiled as though about to reveal a secret. "You are. And I have more good news."

"Tell me. I need all the good news I can hear."

"Your sister is there, healthy, well, and waiting for you."

Chantal's eyes opened wide and suddenly regained their mischievous sparkle. She let out a shriek and sprang from her chair, knocking it to the floor as she rushed to hug Dragon. "*Merci, merci, merci!*"

32

May 5, 1944
Écully, France

Chantal stared dully around her cell in the town's jail, reviling herself for having been so stupid. She and Dragon had maneuvered through the countryside from his farm so carefully, using all his Resistance resources to scout ahead on their route to ensure no surprises. There had been none until they arrived at this suburb roughly seven miles northwest of Lyon.

They had traveled by backroads all night in a farmer's truck, and were supposed to wait out the day until afternoon rush hour when a vegetable van would deliver them to the front door of Ladybird's apartment building. Scouts posted in the vicinity would let them know when they could go there and carry the heavy roll of Douin's sketches safely into the building.

Chantal had let her anticipation of seeing Amélie overcome her good sense, and she had dropped her guard. She had become impatient, desiring to take a public bus early to surprise her sister. Nothing untoward occurred until she waited at the bus stop.

Then, as she stood in line to board, two overzealous young *gendarmes* appeared and began checking identity papers. Forgetting that she had travel papers for going to Caen, but none to return, she presented hers, and then stood in shock as realization dawned over what she had just done. She tried to bluff and charm her way through the ordeal by claiming to have lost the return document, but the officers were having none of it. They pulled her from the queue and escorted her to the police station.

"If your story checks out," they told her, "you'll be released."

As they led her away, she glanced toward the street where the safehouse was located. Dragon stood within sight below a café awning, watching, expressionless.

Now in the cell, Chantal's mind went into overdrive. Her identification and travel documents had been good enough to get her through checkpoints without a second glance, but when calls were made to confirm the information they contained, she would be found out. Worse still, they would connect her to Robert Douin. Possibly as bad, she had overheard remarks between the booking officer and the arresting officers to the effect that Chantal resembled the description mentioned in a bulletin that directed authorities to watch for a woman in connection with an incident at Tréguier on the Gulf of Saint-Malo.

The *gendarmes* did not mistreat her. In mid-afternoon, they even brought her a few slices of bread and some water. She was careful to display only cooperative behavior, making much ado about her missing travel document. However, as daylight waned, dread set in at the prospect of spending the night in the cell on one of two cold steel cots secured on opposite walls, each with a threadbare mattress and a thin blanket. She shuddered to think of what tomorrow might bring.

Night fell. The lights in the confinement area flicked off. Illumination spilled through a barred window above Chantal's head. Its framed glass slanted outward, held in place by a lever on the wall. More dim light came from down the hall in the administrative area, but all was quiet. She wondered how many *gendarmes* were on night watch. Then, snoring echoed through the hall.

She stood and paced with a growing sense of foreboding that tomorrow she would face either the SS or the *Gestapo*. Absently fingering the pills sewn into her sleeve, she wondered if she would be brave enough to take them.

Sitting on the cot opposite the window, she rested her elbows on her thighs and dropped her face into her hands. Despair seeped in. To fight it off, she leaned back and took a deep breath, her eyes drawn to the window.

She sat up and studied it. Overcome by curiosity, she stood on the cot immediately beneath it. Reaching up to grasp the bars, she managed to pull herself up high enough to look out. A floodlight at the corner of the jail cast its beam along the outside wall, but otherwise all was dark beyond the pool of light.

Chantal lowered herself and studied the bars, positive that she had noticed an oddity. Taking her belt from around her waist, she used it to compare distances between bars.

Excitement welled when she confirmed what she thought she had noticed. Only two bars were embedded in the concrete that formed the window frame. However, while the distance between the left side and its nearest bar was equidistant to the corresponding gap on the right side, the space between the two bars was wider. By about two inches.

If she could get her head through, her shoulders would also fit.

She looked around for something to stand on. Only the mattresses and blankets could be moved. Chantal rolled up the pads and rested one atop the other against the wall. Then she stood on them, gaining several inches.

The slanted window pane could present a problem. It was made of heavy glass, and probably not broken easily, but its frame appeared weak, made of thin strips of metal. Its designers never expected it to hold the weight of a person.

Chantal pulled herself up by the bars again. Her head fit narrowly. She let herself back down. Then she jumped, reached as high as she could, grasped the bars, and pulled herself higher, determining two things: that she had to get her feet onto the base of the window, and that her clothes were too thick to allow her through.

Lowering herself once more, Chantal studied the opening. An idea formed, and she almost laughed at how ridiculous it seemed, but she had no other alternative. Reaching down, she slid her shoes off and stood on the concrete floor. Next she removed her coat, her skirt and blouse, and finally her underwear. Rolling everything into a bundle, she reached up high and forced them into the space to the left between the bar and the window glass.

Then, once again standing on the rolled-up mattresses, she jumped high, grabbed the bars, and immediately pulled her lower body up at the waist. Her right knee caught on the window sill. Straining, wanting to cry out, she gasped as she forced her body up, her arms and torso shaking.

But she got an arm around the right bar. Her knee moved farther onto the sill, and then her calf. Finally, her right big toe clung on its side atop the sill. She rested there a moment, panting.

Down the hall, the snoring stopped.

***

Saint-Martin-en-Vercors, France

Jeremy stared in horror at the decoded message in his hand. It had come marked "emergency," and once read, its routing was obvious: it had originated with Fourcade in Lyon barely two hours ago. It had flashed to London, and then to Roger at the Vercors. It read, "*Papillon*, top agent with critical intel, arrested vicinity Lyon. Rescue imperative." With the message came a description.

Jeremy swung around to Roger, who had taken the message from his wireless telegraph operator, read it, and handed it back. Roger then immediately picked up the telephone and dialed a number. Reading Jeremy's face, he held his hand over the microphone end of the receiver while he waited for someone to answer. "Do you know something about this?"

Jeremy nodded, his face intense, his mind obviously whirling. "*Papillon*. That's one of Fourcade's agents. She was trained in the UK."

At that moment, he heard a voice in the phone's receiver. Roger pressed it close to his ear, read the message out, and then issued rapid instructions.

"That was Chevalier, the head of the Jockey cell in Lyon," he said when he had hung up. "He's putting together his best men to locate and free *Papillon*. We'll forward the description to him." Seeing Jeremy's concentrated expression, he said, "Tell me anything you know that can help us."

"The prisoner is Chantal, my fiancée's younger sister. If the *Gestapo* ever learns what's in her head, it could be catastrophic for the Allies; and if they get an inkling of it, the way they'll torture her to get the rest of what she knows is unthinkable." A sudden thought crossed his mind. "And she's carrying cyanide pills sewn into her sleeve."

Roger remained calm. "Let's hope things don't go that far. We don't have any particulars yet. I instructed Chevalier to find out where she's being held. Hopefully, she's in one of the *gendarmeries* on some minor charge. We routinely have people watching all stations just in case something like this happens. We'll find her. One element we have going for us is that the Germans still don't fathom the notion that women can be spies, so they won't immediately think she is one. Maybe the *gendarmes* won't either."

He stopped talking abruptly, and then mused aloud, "On the other hand, there's a particularly vicious SS officer in Lyon, Klaus Barbie—"

Jeremy's muscles went taut and his head swung around. "The one you told me about when I arrived? The man who had Jean Moulin beaten to death?"

Roger nodded with doleful eyes. "One and the same."

"I'm going there," Jeremy said flatly. "She's one of ours, and she's already sacrificed a lot."

"Let's not get carried away," Roger warned. "If we leave right now, it'll take us five hours to get there. We have things set in motion by men who know what they're doing."

"Roger, she's eighteen," Jeremy insisted. "Maybe nineteen by now. I've lost track, but the point is, she's very young. She's lost—"

"I thought she was a top agent," Roger interjected. He picked up the scrap of paper with the message and read it again.

"She is," Jeremy retorted emphatically. "The things she's done for the Resistance are beyond words. As I was saying, she and Amélie were already motherless, and they lost their father to this war. War is all that Chantal's known since she was fourteen. She's already killed a man; maybe more by now. She deserves an all-out effort, but it's also in the Resistance's interest to rescue her. I need to be there. We can't stop until—" He paused, and when he spoke again, his voice had dropped an octave. "Until there's no reason to continue."

He watched Roger's face. "She's never been captured before. She's probably terrified. She knows about holding out for at least forty-eight hours—"

"All right," Roger broke in. "We'll go, but we'll do things my way to get there. I'll take you to the contact and establish your credentials, but then I'll recede into the background and monitor from a distance. Is that understood?"

Jeremy nodded. "Call ahead and inform your men that I'll need a *Gestapo* uniform. Let's go."

Early the next morning, Jeremy strode up the walkway of the *gendarmerie* before the station opened for business. He tried the front door and, finding it locked, banged it loudly. From inside, he heard sleepy grumbling, and then the patter of feet hurrying to the entrance accompanied by the sound of jangling keys.

When the door opened, the eyes of the *gendarme* on duty widened with surprise and fright. Standing before him, he beheld a man in black uniform, red armband with black swastika, jackboots, and a flat service cap bearing the silver skull of the *Gestapo*. He carried a briefcase under one arm.

"You are holding a woman here, I believe. Young, slight build." Jeremy pushed past the jailer, entered the foyer, and looked around. "Take me to her," he ordered while slapping a pair of gloves into his left palm with his right hand. He raised his voice. "Now. *Schnell!*"

The *gendarme* bobbed from the waist obsequiously. "At once, sir. Follow me."

"Show me the way, then get her transfer paperwork ready. I'm taking her with me to be interrogated."

"Of course, sir. Take the hall to the right. She's in the fourth cell, the only one occupied at present."

"I'll find her. Get the papers ready." Jeremy started away, and then added, "Make sure you include all her documents, including her ID and travel papers."

The *gendarme* headed straight to his desk and began flipping through a file and pulling out forms. Suddenly he heard a loud shout, and Jeremy stormed out of the hall. He stalked over to the desk and bent low over the cowering officer. "Are you playing games with me? The cell is empty. So are the others. What have you done with her?"

Wide-eyed, the officer gaped at Jeremy, rounded his desk, and hurried through the hall. Coming to the cell, he stared in disbelief. Only the rolled-up mattresses gave a hint of what could have happened.

Jeremy followed and now stood behind the hapless jailer.

"She was here," the man gasped. "Last night. I swear it."

"Then you let her escape? Are you a *résistant*?"

"No," the *gendarme* exclaimed, his eyes pleading. "I saw her here last night. No one else has been in or out all night."

"I don't have time to waste with fools," Jeremy said in his harshest voice. "Write down your name and your contact information. I shall have to make a report."

The officer, now almost sobbing, scurried to his desk and provided the needed information. Observing him, Jeremy took pity. "Where are those transfer forms?"

He took them from the terrified man's hand, filled them in, and signed off. "This is a matter of highest security," he said. "I'll take responsibility to find her. You are to mention this affair to no one except to say that you made the transfer. As far as you are concerned, the matter is closed. Next time be more careful."

"Yes, sir. Yes, sir. *Merci*."

As Jeremy left the *gendarmeries*, he glanced back at the row of windows along the outside wall of the cells. All but one slanted out from their bases. Counting them off, he was certain that the one that differed from the others was outside the cell that had held Chantal. Its frame and glass hung down vertically.

Stifling fleeting hope, Jeremy hurried out of sight into a nearby alley. There, stripping out of the *Gestapo* uniform, he left on a set of civilian workman's clothes he had worn underneath. Dumping the uniform and boots in a trash bin, he put on a pair of scuffed shoes taken from his briefcase and made his way to a specific café. Ten minutes later, a sedan picked him up, drove into Lyon, and dropped him off down the street from Ladybird's apartment.

A small gathering greeted Jeremy with joyous faces and muted celebration when Ladybird led him into the sitting room. Fourcade was there, and Dragon and Roger. Amélie and Chantal sat next to each other on a sofa. The sisters bounced to their feet and ran to him, arms outstretched, tears of relief streaming down their faces.

"I can't believe we're all together," Chantal cried. "And safe."

Dumbfounded, Jeremy peered at her. "Are you all right? Did you squeeze through that jail window? I saw that the slat was down."

Chantal nodded. "It took hours and I kept being afraid that I'd either get stuck or someone would come along and see me. The guard had been snoring in the other room. He stopped, and I was so scared, but then he started up again. I kept kicking the frame until it finally broke under my weight, and I fell to the ground. It wasn't a long drop."

"She had to strip off her clothes," Amélie teased. "She was naked in the street."

"Just for a minute or two," Chantal retorted ruefully, "until I put my clothes back on—in the shadows." She turned her attention back to Jeremy. "Then I waited until first light, took the first bus into Lyon, and walked over."

"Amazing," Jeremy observed. "So you didn't need me after all." He pulled her papers from a pocket and handed them to her.

"You got them," she cried, astonished. "How?"

Jeremy related the events at the *gendarmeries*. "I don't think anyone will be looking for you."

Chantal hugged him tightly. "Thanks for coming after me. That's comforting." She suddenly stood back. "How's Horton?"

Jeremy shook his head. "Sadly, I have no news." Looking into her somber eyes, he added, "I'm sure he's all right."

Chantal nodded, unconvinced, and wandered back into the sitting room. While the others conversed, Jeremy and Amélie moved to the balcony where they could be alone. She told him about Jeannie and what had happened at Tréguier.

Jeremy listened in silence, his anger building. "That's terrible," he said when Amélie had finished. Then, seeing the anguish on her face, he soothed her. "I know how close you became. I love her too."

"I'll find her," Amélie swore. "I won't stop until I've brought her home."

In the sitting room, Roger turned to Fourcade. "We can't all stay here," he said softly. "It's too risky."

Fourcade agreed. "If we were raided now, the Nazis would decapitate two major networks." She left unsaid the damage that might be inflicted on Allied invasion plans if Douin's sketches were seized. The roll had been deposited in her office/bedroom. She had studied them with Dragon, awed by the intricacy of the drawings and what they revealed about German coastal defenses along Normandy's beaches.

"These are incredible," she exclaimed. "Douin's talent and diligence are beyond words." They had continued viewing the drawings, rolling them like ancient scrolls. "From these, the Allies will know where every ant hill is located."

Now, she gestured toward the balcony where Amélie and Jeremy sat close together. "I'm sorry to say that we'll have to break that up. Let's let them have a few minutes, though." Turning to Dragon, she said, "I need a private conference with you."

He followed into her room, and they sat at the table. "I received a message from London after your arrival," she began. "They're sending a Lysander tonight to pick up the sketches. Whoever takes them to the landing site will need to carry them on to London. Should that be you?"

Dragon shook his head. "No. The person here who knows the most about them is Chantal. She should take them. There'll be questions, and she's the most qualified to respond. I'll escort her to the landing site and make sure she gets off all right."

"That makes sense. Chantal insists that she wants to go back to Normandy. She's convinced that's where the invasion will take place, and she wants to see it and be part of the sabotage activity."

"That sounds like her," Dragon said with a slight laugh. "She's proven herself. If she'll do the courier run, we'll arrange to bring her out on her return."

"That'll work." Fourcade started to speak again but hesitated. "There's another issue that she brought up, and it's one of our own making."

Dragon eyed Fourcade expectantly.

"Chantal's travel papers connect her directly to Douin," she said. "If anyone took note of that at the *gendarmeries*, the Germans would watch him even more closely."

"Hmm. We'll get word to him at once."

"Good. There's one more matter. Chantal overheard the booking *gendarme* say that a bulletin was out on Amélie. It didn't mention Amélie by name, but the officer said that a woman was being sought in connection with an incident at Tréguier and that Chantal fit the description. That bulletin must be about Amélie. She was in Tréguier."

"She and Chantal look nearly identical, and there's a search on." She thought a moment. "We might have to do something about the grocer in Saint-Brieuc or the driver who took Amélie and the others to Tréguier. Amélie says that no one besides those two saw her face. They're the only ones who could have given them away."

Dragon nodded in sober agreement. "We'll deal with it," he said grimly. "We'll have to change Chantal's appearance, papers, and develop a background story that goes nowhere near Tréguier. We can keep her out of sight for the most part. Most of our work is done at night these days anyway. Is she trained in demolitions?"

"She is," Fourcade affirmed. "They both are."

"Then she'll be even more valuable. What will you do with Amélie?"

"I'll have to think on that. Sending her with you is not an option. We'd double the chances of one of the sisters being captured. She could go to the Vercors with Jeremy, but Roger might object. Amélie is already upset over the capture of another agent at Tréguier." Fourcade sat back and rubbed her face. "Let's get Roger in here. He might have some ideas."

After hearing the details of the situation, Roger said, "I agree that bringing Amélie to the Vercors is not a good idea. We have enough problems with husbands and wives protecting each other with horrible consequences. We don't need to add to that." He directed a question to Fourcade. "Why not send her back to London?"

Fourcade shook her head. "She won't go. She says her place is in France until it's free."

"That's admirable, but creates a dilemma." Roger thought a moment longer. "Can you keep her here?"

"I can, but Lyon is a hotbed of *Gestapo* activity."

"But Tréguier is over five hundred miles to the northwest. They wouldn't be looking for her here. Jeremy doused Chantal's trail when he grabbed her papers from the *gendarme*. All anyone in that station knows now is that a *Gestapo* officer took custody of Chantal, who fit the Tréguier description."

"Good point." Fourcade mulled a few moments. "Let's do this: I'll keep Amélie here for at least a few weeks. She needs rest anyway; she's been under the gun too long. I'll make her my assistant and keep her indoors as much as possible. Jeremy goes back with you to the Vercors, Roger. And Dragon, you'll take Chantal on her return from London."

Stoic farewells followed the announcement of Amélie's elevation to Fourcade's assistant. Chantal balked about the trip to London and again being separated from her sister, but she was mollified when the importance of her presence at the presentation of Douin's sketches in London was explained, and upon the promise of returning to Normandy. She and Dragon departed first to allow ample time to meet the Lysander flight at an isolated field north of Lyon.

"You've become quite the agent," Amélie remarked as she and Chantal said their goodbyes. "I'm proud of you."

"Now we're both jailbreakers," Chantal replied, chuckling. "I shall miss you."

After the door closed, Amélie and Jeremy returned to the terrace for their goodbyes. All too soon, Roger knocked on the door, opened it a crack, and called softly, "I'm sorry, old boy. It's time."

As the couple kissed farewell, Jeremy murmured to her, "I'm glad you're staying here. A lot of *résistants* are watching over Fourcade."

"But you'll be in constant danger," Amélie replied mournfully.

Jeremy chuckled and gestured toward Roger. "I'll be fine. I'm learning personal security from the best."

When all had gone, leaving only Amélie, Fourcade, and Ladybird, the three retired to the living room. When they were seated, Amélie told Fourcade in a steady voice, "You don't need to patronize me."

"Excuse me?"

"I don't need to be handled with kid gloves," Amelie replied. "I appreciate you, Madame. You've done more for France than anyone. Working with you is an honor. If you need me to do something, just tell me. I'll do it."

Her throat caught and she wiped her eyes. "I'm worried about Jeannie, but I'm not broken. I'm tired, but I'm not fragile. I know I need rest, and I'm sure that's why you're keeping me here. Thank you. But I mend quickly, and I expect to be back in the thick of things. Now, please tell me, how do we go about finding Jeannie?"

Fourcade listened in stunned silence. Then she rose from her seat and went to sit beside Amélie on the sofa. Taking her hand, she said, "I'm properly chastened." She exhaled. "I don't know how to find Jeannie, but we'll move heaven and earth."

Amélie squeezed Fourcade's hand and regarded her with steady eyes. "And I'll help you find Léon Faye," she said softly.

Fourcade froze. She closed her eyes and bit her lip. Then she let go of Amélie's hand and stood. Alternating her gaze between Amélie and Ladybird, she said hoarsely, "Would you ladies join me in a drink? I could use one."

33

April 29, 1944
Truk Lagoon, Central Pacific Ocean

Josh Littlefield revved his Hellcat's engine, watched for the signal flag, and roared skyward into the dawn from the bow of the USS *Enterprise*. Shortly after the battle at Truk Lagoon back in February, his specially organized squadron had been disbanded and their pilots returned to their regular units.

Josh, per his request and his heart's desire, had been transferred back to the *Enterprise*, and he had taken command of a Hellcat squadron. The assignment had been sweet-and-sour: he had replaced a squadron commander lost at Truk on the day of that battle.

Recent intelligence reconnaissance over the atoll had revealed a disturbing development: left unoccupied by the Allies, and apparently intent on rebuilding its offensive capability, Japan had re-occupied Truk's islands, repaired its airfields, and installed many more anti-aircraft guns. And this time many of them were radar-guided.

Warships and supply vessels, in particular large fuel oil tankers, once again anchored in its lagoon. Very soon, they would be poised to resume offensive operations in the Central Pacific.

Eniwetok, the US-occupied atoll with similar strategic attributes of forward location, anchorage facilities, and airfields, was within striking distance to the northeast less than two hours' flight time from Japanese fighters and bombers. Further build-up at Truk must be stopped, its repairs and improvements destroyed, its availability as a Japanese strategic offensive platform removed forever—or at least for the duration of this war, with hope that another would never occur.

With three months of additional fighting since Truk, Josh had grown weary of combat, having seen enough death and destruction to last a lifetime. Some of his dreams had turned nightmarish as he had led more men into aerial battle and returned to the *Enterprise* with some lost. Mealtimes had become somber events as empty spaces at the table became profound announcements of lost comrades.

The Avengers from the *Intrepid* would not lead this time. The Japanese expected an attack, and were on full alert. Josh found himself in the lead again, his squadron's task to clear the airspace above the lagoon so that the torpedo and dive bombers could do their jobs of sinking ships and destroying airfields, headquarters, barracks, and other support structures.

Even before he had circled behind the *Enterprise*, the next Hellcat behind him launched, and then another, until the full squadron was airborne, formed up behind him, their azimuth checked, and on their way.

"Remember, gentlemen," Josh had warned his pilots at the early morning mission brief, "our advantage is speed, flight range, climbing ability, firepower, and training. Do not dogfight the Zeros. You will likely lose. They're more maneuverable and their pilots have gained experience. We'll open up out of range of their weapons, and fly through their formations with guns blazing. Let 'em follow us if they want to. We'll outrun them, climb high, circle around, and hit 'em out of the sun again.

"Hold your bombs for the end of our second run. By then, the airspace should have been cleared out quite a bit. We'll drop down, hit targets of opportunity, and then head for home. Any questions?"

There had been none of significance, so Josh finished by reading a message from Rear Admiral Marc Mitscher, a US naval aviation pioneer and now commander of Admiral Spruance's 5th Fleet carriers. He had signaled to all the pilots in the attack, "Plaster Truk with everything you have including empty beer bottles if you've got 'em."

The briefings had become even more sobering for Josh than they had been before his promotion as he had learned to brace himself against wondering which faces would be absent at the next gathering. The pilots had been over the plan several times and knew their tasks, so the questions were few and of a coordination confirmation nature. Grim-faced, they had headed to their fighters and taken to the skies.

They approached high, hoping to catch the Zeros off-guard but knowing the probability that the Japs would see them on radar and be in the sky, organized and ascending to meet them. Zack and his Hellcats and the other fighter squadrons flying close behind, guided by their own ship-based radar, intended to descend from above and cut a hole through their formation on their first pass. Follow-on squadrons would engage the Zeros that flew in to fill the gaps, keeping them occupied while the Avengers and Dauntlesses flew beneath the melee and sought out targets at anchor or on land.

"Wannabe, they're five miles out," the *Enterprise* radar operator intoned. "They're roughly five hundred feet below you and climbing at two-seventy degrees."

Josh scanned his instruments, noted the direction, and dipped his nose slightly for a better view of the direction and altitude. He saw tiny specks in the far distance against a blue horizon. "Roger. I see the lead elements." He thumbed his mic and called to his flight leaders, "Bandits at two-seventy, down three hundred. Acknowledge."

Within seconds, he had heard from his flight leaders. "Arrow formation," he called. "Let's roll."

In addition to his own plane, Josh's squadron was organized into two flights of eight aircraft each. They positioned themselves around Josh in a formation intended to concentrate maximum firepower to the front while minimizing the risk of having several Avengers taken out by a tight burst of enemy fire.

As soon as they were through the Japanese formation, they would dive, break left and right respectively, and then climb into the western sky. By the time they came around for a second attack, follow-on Hellcats would be in the attack, and the Avengers and Dauntlesses would be approaching their stations for release to bring havoc on the surface targets.

Josh dipped his nose further. The Zeros had already enlarged from specks to dots, and within seconds, their wings and tails were discernible. "They're within our range. Pick your targets. Fire at will."

Immediately, he pressed the trigger on his stick. The Hellcat shook as its twin .30 mm machine guns in his wings spat out trails of bright tracers racing ahead of his aircraft toward a Zero centered in his range finder. From above, below, and to his sides, Josh heard the eruption of gunfire joining his own, and streams of tracers streaked across the sky, each toward a different target.

Bright flames and thick black clouds erupted in the air as bullets struck home. Zeros exploded, some spun out of control, and some plunged nose first toward the ocean. Before any of them splashed, Josh heard plinking against the skin of his aircraft and the hiss of many rounds whooshing by. Then the Japanese planes loomed large in front of him, and he had to maneuver to avoid collision. For the space of a second, he saw a helmeted face with white goggles tilted toward him.

Then he was past the swarm and into open air space. But glancing down, he saw another horde headed his way. "Second wave climbing to meet us," he called over his radio. "Fire at will."

Once again, he chose a target, fingered his trigger, and saw the tracers stream out. The Hellcat bolted through the air, gunfire erupted all around, and more Zeros fell away in front of him.

Then he was through, once again in clear airspace, though still in a dive. He leveled out and started his climb. "Report."

"Hawkeye, no casualties. One heading back home with shot-up wing."

"DoubleDee. One lost."

Josh sucked in his breath. "Roger. Reform. Orbit. Prepare for second run. Out."

The second run was similar to the first except that Josh's squadron flew to a position where it could enter the attack zone behind the trailing squadron. By the time they reached their assault position, the number of Zeros flying up to meet his Hellcats had greatly diminished.

Josh's squadron engaged more targets, saw more enemy fighters fall to the sea, and then headed within Truk Lagoon's circle of coral to drop their two-thousand-pound bombs on any ship or facility that presented itself.

The destruction already laid out in front of Josh was profound. When he had flown the Avenger during the first attack on Truk, he had felt his torpedo drop away but had not seen it nor the damage it caused. The same was true for the bomb he dropped on a ship as it tried to rush for an entrance.

This time, he had circled and come in after waves of dive bombers and torpedo bombers had made their first strikes, and everywhere was destruction. Flame and smoke spewed into the sky from enormous oil tankers, adding the smell of burning fuel to the omnipresent stench of spent ammunition.

The enormous floating dry dock that had so mesmerized him during his recon run at the beginning of February now lay partly submerged in water at a steep angle to port. On dry land, the headquarters and barracks were cauldrons; black clouds rose above ammo depots; fuel supply facilities shot flames hundreds of feet high; the airfields were pocked with craters; and uniformed men ran in every direction, seeking shelter. Even from this height and distance, Josh made out crimson blotches where volumes of blood had spilled.

He spotted a freighter heading to the northern pass out of the coral necklace. Maneuvering behind it, he lined up, and swooped in. As he closed in, he made out the faces of terrified sailors jumping into the water. Then, as his propeller passed beyond its stern, he dropped his bomb. Climbing steeply to avoid the concussion, he gained altitude and rolled to see his result.

A direct hit.

He felt empty. No exultation.

Climbing higher, he started a wide turn to the south and then east, out of the way of incoming fighters and those still engaged. "Report," he called, deliberately keeping his voice steady.

"Wannabe, Hawkeye. One down. One on the surface awaiting rescue. No aircraft unscathed."

Josh took a deep breath. "Roger. Out. DoubleDee, report."

"Wannabe, DoubleDee. Two more down. One more crippled. Headed for base."

"Roger. Hawkeye, DoubleDee, form up. Let's go home."

With his pilots, Josh sat in the squadron day room listening to battle reports as they came in. The day had produced a huge US victory. A third of the total destruction had been the result of attacks flown from the *Enterprise*.

Enemy losses were staggering. Three light cruisers. Four destroyers. Three patrol craft. Thirty-six merchant ships and auxiliaries. Two hundred and seventy aircraft. An unknown number of Japanese soldiers, sailors, pilots, civilians; undoubtedly numbering in the thousands. Two-hundred-thousand tons of commercial shipping and cargo. The airfields and supporting infrastructure left unusable.

Noticeably absent from the atoll had been battleships and aircraft carriers.

On the American side, one aircraft carrier had been damaged. Twenty-five aircraft had been downed. Forty sailors and aircrewmen had lost their lives.

Josh grimaced as he studied the reports and the names of those lost. Slowly, he made his way out of the day room and back to his quarters. He had one last duty to perform before he could call it a day. Three of the downed pilots had been his. Now he would write letters to inform the next of kin, be they mothers, fathers, or wives; people whose lives had just been inexorably changed, and they did not yet know it.

He finished the task late that night, but although exhausted, he could not sleep. Tossing his sheets aside, he crossed to a small desk built into the wall and flipped on a lamp. Then he sat to write a letter to his brother.

"Dear Zack, I can only hope you are alive and well. The news coming out of Italy is sobering to say the least, and the last I heard, you're in the thick of fighting. I have to tell you, little brother, that I hate war. The cause and the people who fight might be noble, but a war by its nature is evil. You should be home courting Sonja. I should be out finding a girl who will have me. (Stop it. I see that grin.) Sherry should be nursing people who are sick, and not because they've been shot up or bombed. Some of the best years of our lives are draining away when we could otherwise be getting to know our cousins on Sark or in London. I envy that you've met Jeremy and Claire. Paul is a great guy. I'm so glad we got to serve together for a while in N. Africa. And I hope Lance comes home safely from Colditz. I'm not sure the Germans will be able to hold him that long. I don't mean to leave you despondent, and I hope I don't. I lost three good pilots today, and it hurts. We're at war because of evil that wants to control people's lives. I know that, and if I had to do all this over again to save our country, I'd do it in a heartbeat. But I have to say, there's no glory in it. Stay safe, my brother. I love you, I'm proud of you, and I can't wait until we're together again, you, me, Sherry...and let's throw in our cousins too. Love, Josh."

34

May 13, 1944
Qualiano, Italy

Zack Littlefield sat on the ground scratching out a letter on a soiled scrap of paper with a broken pencil. He wrote to his sister Sherry in response to a missive he had just received from her. Hers had been dated and posted three months earlier. She had written that she hoped his internal wounds and concussion incurred at San Pietro late last year had fully healed, that she missed him and wished him well.

He had not heard from Josh in many weeks. Knowing only that his older brother was somewhere in the Central Pacific, Zack hoped that he was alive and healthy. He wanted to write to Josh also, but that would have to come later.

He wrote, "Dearest Sister, Sorry for the late reply. I just received your letter. Hopefully you'll get this one within a few months. I'm well because of you, and you know it. I couldn't have been more surprised to wake up and find you tending to me in the hospital than you were shocked to see me on the medical evacuation flight. I'm so proud of you and what you do: a nurse, a captain, and flying into combat areas to tend to badly wounded soldiers on their flights back to hospital care in the rear. Amazing! You and the other flight nurses truly are Flying Angels. This is a weird war. Do you remember how we used to fight as kids? And now I get all weepy-eyed just thinking about you and hoping you're well and out of danger. On top of that, would you believe I had lunch today with Marlene Dietrich? It's true. She came wearing olive drabs and a GI wool cap to entertain troops up close to the front. She went through the chow line just like we did and sat right down on the ground to eat with us, not more than three feet from me. It was funny because some of the soldiers got all tongue-tied and red-faced. Others tried to act cool, like that was going to get them a date with her. She's as beautiful in real life as her pictures, and very nice, but don't tell Sonja I said that she was beautiful! I mean don't tell Sonja that I said Miss Dietrich was beautiful. Sonja is too. You can tell her I said that. (I don't have an eraser, so I can't fix what I already wrote.) I worry about Josh and our cousins. This war has our family spread all over, and keeping up with everyone is an impossibility. I hope we all survive intact. We've had our share of close calls. If I were to guess, I'm sure that Josh was in that battle at Truk. People are calling it Japan's Pearl Harbor. I think Paul is somewhere here in Italy, and Chantal's boyfriend, Sergeant Horton, too. I miss Sonja. I got a letter from her last week, and from the sound of it, she's still my girl. Can't wait for this war to be over so we can get home and get on with our lives. The way we live here is not the way anybody should live. Oh well. Gotta go. I love you, sis, always, Zack."

With Monte Cassino nearly vanquished, the abbey obliterated, the Germans escaping north, and the Liri Valley secure, the 36th Division had been pulled back south to Qualiano, a town a few miles north of Naples, to rest, replenish, and await further orders. Word had come down that the unit would be shipping out to Anzio. Zack felt tired just thinking about going back into combat.

He comprehended dully that the battle around Monte Cassino was over for the 36th with some skirmishes taking place as the Germans retreated north, but the reality of it had yet to seep into his inner core. When he had swum across the freezing river back in January dragging the wounded and unconscious Smitty, he had thought they were both goners. But they were carried downstream by the current, somehow made it to the friendly side, and two medics had spotted them and pulled them up onto the riverbank.

An ambulance had taken them both away. Zack spent a night in a warm hospital tent recovering from hypothermia and was returned to the division headquarters for reassignment. He never knew what happened to Smitty, whether the soldier lived or died. Thinking about Smitty, Zack grunted. "A whole squad—more than a squad—died to save him," he muttered to himself, "and I never even knew his real name."

Stifling the thought, Zack pondered his dilemma now, four months later. The 36th (Texas) Division had lost so many men attempting to cross the river over those two days that larger numbers of replacements than normal filled the ranks. The combat veterans had been reshuffled to provide leadership and experience for the raw replacements. Zack found himself once again leading a squad of men he did not know, and somehow word leaked out that he was the only survivor of his unit for the fourth time.

Soldiers being peculiarly superstitious at times, his squad members treated him with respect and even liked him, but Zack thought he recognized doubts behind their eyes about their survivability with him as their leader. The notion had first formed as he prepared his new squad for combat shortly after it had been created. Fortunately, four subsequent months in combat with few wounded and no fatalities had restored his confidence and that of his men.

Nevertheless, some doubts persisted. *Four months! Whoever heard of a battle lasting that long in this war? And it still goes on.*

Fearing that the Germans were using St. Benedict abbey on Monte Cassino as an observation post despite protestations to the contrary, the Allies had bombed the ancient monastery into rubble. Ironically, with historical considerations removed, the *Wehrmacht* occupied it after the bombing. Its basements had proved impregnable to Allied ordnance, so the Germans used it as an unequalled surveillance station with an unobstructed view across the landscape to the east, south, and north up the Liri Valley.

Many attempts were made to storm the heights of the mountain with many lives lost. French units circled around to try coming in from the northeast without positive result. General Clark finally ordered the 36th Division to attack again exactly where and how General Walker had first suggested. The German lines had been broken, but the stronghold at the abbey still held. Then, the 36th had been relieved and transferred south for a much-needed rest.

Four months! A battle lasting that long with so much destruction and carnage boggled Zack's mind despite that he had participated and survived in seizing nearly every forward inch of it.

Shortly after the first dismal attempt at crossing the river back in January, a group of 36th Division soldiers held a meeting and invited Zack along. They were furious at what they perceived to have been reckless actions ordered by General Clark resulting in a needless waste of thousands of lives. They planned to bring formal charges against him after the war.

At the time of the meeting, Zack was still dazed from his ordeal and could not analyze objectively, so he refrained from committing to be one of those accusing the general, but he promised to give the matter serious thought when his mind had cleared. Since then, the division had been in almost constant combat, inching up Italy's boot, and he had heard no more about the issue.

He tucked the letter to his sister in his shirt pocket, clambered up from the ground, and headed toward his squad's area in the bivouac to start his men packing for transport to Naples. There, they would board ships bound for Anzio.

May 19, 1944
VI Corps Headquarters, Nettuno, Italy

Major General Walker gripped Lieutenant General Truscott's hand warmly. An affinity had flourished between the two men on their first meeting near the beginning of the month when Walker had visited Truscott's headquarters to prepare to transfer the 36th Division to Anzio.

"Good to see you again, General," Walker said, "and I'm pleased that my Texas Division is part of your command."

Truscott smiled. "We Texans are doing our share in this war. I'm glad to see that the 36th is fully ashore and in position."

He guided Walker through the spacious villa where he had taken up temporary residence, stopping on a terrace to look out from atop the high cliffs where the house was situated across the town and the Tyrrhenian Sea. "I hate to see all the destruction left behind," he said with a sigh. "The Germans muck it up, and we come behind them and make it worse. Ya have to give the Italians credit. They give us a warm welcome and get to cleaning up the mess quickly."

Gesturing across the town at cathedrals, castles, fortresses, and imposing government structures built in classical style and interspersed among the concrete and stone houses, he remarked, "Look at those ancient buildings. They're magnificent, and some go back hundreds of years, a few maybe from Roman times. Fortunately, most of them are largely untouched."

After a moment, he crossed the room to a cabinet, poured two drinks, and offered one to Walker, who accepted it and took a sip. Truscott was a plain-spoken man with a square jaw and perceptive eyes who was known for his compassion and love of his soldiers, but he asked no quarter in combat and gave none.

Walker picked up the conversation. "Those smoke generators on the Anzio beach must be working overtime. It was thick as we came through. That must be tough on the soldiers stationed on the beach."

"It is," Truscott agreed, "but necessary. The Germans can't see our dispositions there, not even with aerial reconnaissance. But as you say, our soldiers pay a price." He swallowed a sip, and when he spoke again, he did so with obvious reluctance. "General Lucas didn't exploit the initiative and push on toward Rome, and for the life of me, I can't figure out why. Germany had nothing there when he put VI Corps onshore at Anzio."

The intended effect of drawing German forces to Anzio from Monte Cassino to relieve pressure on Clark's divisions in the south had been lost. Under Kesselring's command, the Germans had pulled units from France and the Balkans to defend around Anzio, with formidable firepower. Clark had selected Truscott to replace Lucas.

Exhaling through pursed lips, Truscott went on. "You know we're only thirty-seven miles south of Rome?" He shook his head. "I like John Lucas. He's a competent general and he executed the Anzio landing perfectly, but his decision to stay put on the beach cost us time, materiel, and lives.

"Within two days, we found ourselves facing forces here just as strong as those around Monte Cassino. And do you know what the most ironic part of the fiasco was?" He turned to face Walker. "On the day after the landing, a British lieutenant led a reconnaissance mission all the way to Aurelian Wall inside Rome. He was unopposed the entire way there and back." He grunted. "Unfortunately, that lieutenant, Hargreaves was his name, was killed two days later in the first few minutes of our first skirmish with a sizeable German force at Carroceto." He sighed. "Like I said, not seizing that opportunity cost us dearly."

He took another sip of his drink. "Then again, I wasn't in Lucas' shoes." He turned abruptly and headed toward the dining room. "Let's eat and get to business."

"I'm holding your division in reserve, Fred," Truscott told Walker after orderlies had cleared the dinner dishes from the table, leaving a pot of freshly brewed coffee. "Yours is the most experienced and strongest division in the corps. I'm confident that you can achieve any objective I give you."

Walker lifted his eyebrows. "I'm honored, sir, but are you sure? General Clark doesn't share your confidence."

Truscott chuckled. "Let me worry about that. He runs Fifth Army, but I run VI Corps. I know what went on. I'm interested in your comments."

"Are we talking about the events at Rapido? And by the way, I don't know why everyone keeps referring to the Rapido. That river was a little farther down. Where we crossed was the Garigliano. Is that what we're discussing?"

Taking a swig of coffee, Truscott nodded. "Speak freely. I'd like to know your perspective of what went on."

"What went on, General," Walker began, stifling rising anger, "is the foolhardiest military adventure ever undertaken in this war. I told Clark so just before the operation. I understand the need to bog Germany down in

Italy, and I accept that. But to throw lives away in pursuit of that stalemate is—" Walker took a deep breath. "Is—"

"Go on."

"I'd rather not further characterize it, sir. Let's just say there were other ways to accomplish that end, and my senior staff took the fall for the failure. General Clark stripped them from me and replaced them with men I didn't know. I'm not complaining about the new staff. They've served competently and well. But if the general thought my division failed because of poor execution, then he should have relieved me."

Truscott grunted. "Are you asking to be relieved?"

"No, sir," Walker replied without hesitation. "I brought these boys over from Texas, and I'll see this war through and take as many home as is humanly possible."

Truscott studied Walker with steady eyes. "And you don't mind that I'm several years your junior in age?"

For the first time, Walker broke a smile and chuckled. "Sir, you've proven yourself in combat. I'm your subordinate. I'll move heaven and earth to meet your lawful orders."

"Good," Truscott replied gruffly. "Let's go over plans."

May 28, 1944
36ᵗʰ Division Headquarters, Torrechia Nuova, Italy

General Walker studied his new orders with dismay. He had already spent hours spread over several days in a cramped reconnaissance plane crisscrossing his area of operations. The combination of what he saw on the ground and the requirements of his new orders appeared to set up his command for a repeat of the deadly debacle of the Garigliano River.

Clark had previously ordered Truscott to advance VI Corps on Valmontone, a town that straddled the route that the escaping *Wehrmacht* divisions from the south must take to continue their withdrawal to a position east of Rome. There, they would link up with their fellow units for the drive into the "Eternal City."

Starting five days ago, Truscott had hurled the 3rd Infantry and the 1st Armored Divisions against the Germans defending the route along the base of the Alban Hills to Valmontone. The town was an important junction on Via Casilina, the German 10th Army's main line of communications to Rome. It was that very army, coming north from Monte Cassino, that most of General Clark's Fifth Army was intent on destroying or capturing before they could link up with the *Wehrmacht* forces northeast of Rome.

Truscott had held Walker's 36th Division in reserve. However, the *Wehrmacht* had fought fiercely and well, and in two days of fighting, the two American divisions were exhausted, their equipment and ammunition nearly depleted.

Then, a day later, against the orders of Supreme Allied Commander Mediterranean, Field Marshal Henry Wilson, Clark ordered Truscott to pivot the VI Corps to the north, a maneuver that, if successful, could result in an early liberation of Rome. Clark left only two major commands, the 3rd Infantry Division and a brigade-strength commando unit, the 1st Special Service Force, assisted by an armored combat team from the 1st Armored Division, to continue toward the original objective at Valmontone.

The 36th Division being in reserve, Walker had spent his time of relative quiet monitoring progress, overflying the battle area, and visiting forward positions. Then, this morning, he was ordered to relieve the beleaguered 1st Armored Division at the base of a mountain. He was instructed not to engage in serious combat, and further, to prepare to withdraw on short notice and move to exploit a breakthrough anywhere along VI Corps' front.

Walker ordered his headquarters to be set up in a barn at a dairy farm two miles from Cisterna and then became curious that he received no enemy artillery fire despite the position being a good target. Taking to his reconnaissance plane again, he directed the pilot north over the mountain. On the other side, a few miles beyond his front line, nestled the small town of Velletri.

As the little plane passed over the area, Walker spotted, via a map in his lap, several villages he had heard about besides Cisterna. They included Campoleone, Aprilia, and even the pope's summer residence at Castel Gandolfo. He snorted in disgust and shook his head. These were the same villages that Lieutenant Hargreaves had patrolled unopposed four months ago. "How many lives lost because we didn't press on past Anzio in January?" he muttered to himself.

On the outbound and inbound legs, Walker neither saw enemy positions nor received incoming fire. After several repeat trips with the same result, he landed, called in his division engineer, Major Oran Stovall, and asked if a temporary road capable of supporting tanks could be built across the mountain. Stovall flew up for his own reconnaissance and reported back that, yes, such a road was feasible.

"Plan for it," Walker ordered. That night, tossing on his cot, unable to sleep, he became convinced that attacking against the entrenched enemy to the east would thrust his soldiers into another Garigliano situation. He reflected on the possible route free of enemy troops to his immediate north, a weak point overlooked by both opposing forces until he had discovered it. The route was thus one that should be exploited. Further, this alternative could expedite Clark's Fifth Army's entry into Rome.

At a commanders' conference the next morning to iron out plans for additional assaults to seize Valmontone, Walker listened in dismay. At the end of it, he was sure that he was being ordered to send his men into a meat grinder once more. Rather than make an issue during the meeting, he chose to see Truscott privately afterward.

The VI Corps commanding general was in no mood to make changes. "I've issued orders," he snapped. "You're proposing a major change. It can't be done."

"But sir, we've found a safe passage that cuts off time. Major Stovall, my engineer, has reconned the mountain. He commands the 11th Engineer Battalion. We have the men and equipment to do it." He took a deep breath. "We don't have to send our men into another cauldron."

Truscott faced Walker, his fists on his hips. "General, you have your orders."

May 30, 1944

Snatching breakfast in his operations section amid a flurry of activity in the dairy barn the next morning, Walker was surprised to see Truscott standing in front of him. "I want to go over your alternative plan again," Truscott said. "I couldn't sleep last night."

The two moved to a map where Walker briefed in detail, showing the enemy and friendly positions, the nature of the terrain, and the threat coming from the south in the form of the German 10th Army. "We can get to Rome before that army can, unopposed most of the way, and avoid that fight."

"We're supposed to block that army," Truscott said, "and either capture or kill it."

Walker grunted. "With all due respect, sir, that horse has left the barn. General Clark let it out when he ordered us to pivot north and sent a reduced combat task force to confront the German 10th at Valmontone." He reached up and slapped the map. "This is the way."

Truscott strode toward the exit. "I'll pass it by Clark. He'll have to approve. Stay near your commo."

Two hours later, Truscott growled over the phone, "Execute your alternative plan. My headquarters will direct coordination with your adjacent units. And General, you'd better make this work."

35

Knockinaam Lodge, Scotland

"Did you have any trouble getting in?" Prime Minister Churchill asked.

General Dwight Eisenhower, Supreme Allied Commander Europe, shook his head. "It was fairly easy. And that was a nice drive down the coast from Turnberry. You picked a beautiful spot for this confab." He looked around at the bluffs surrounding them on three sides. "I've never seen any place more lush or green."

The sixteenth-century lodge evoked strength and endurance with its stone walls, steepled slate roof, large chimneys, and multiple bay windows and dormers. It rested on a lawn next to a strip of sandy beach in a private cove spilling into the calm blue waters of Port of Spittal Bay off the Irish Sea. Yellow wildflowers dotted the steep slopes interspersed among scrub trees and bushes. The nearest town, Portpatrick, lay six miles to the east.

"This is one of my favorite holiday spots," Churchill said. "The ocean views are marvelous, and the people here not only respect privacy, but they know better than to spread word about who visits.

"I'm glad you called our rendezvous a confab because that is exactly what I intend, a frank, friendly conversation without the interruptions of staffs and meetings. With our normal security precautions, we should be able to speak freely; and given that the cross-Channel invasion is imminent, I thought we should compare notes one more time before execution. That's particularly true as I won't be able to meet with President Roosevelt again before we launch Overlord."

They had descended from the lodge to the beach where the prime minister removed his shoes, cuffed his trousers, and exulted in the feel of sand between his toes. "I know your president is very tied up with his re-election campaign," he continued, "but how is his health? I noticed the last time we were together that he seemed a bit piqued, and he tired easily."

Eisenhower smiled gently. "I'm not sure I should be speaking about the health of our president—"

"Mr. Roosevelt is my friend," Churchill interrupted. "I should be able to ask about his health without ulterior motives being inferred. We're all aging, and we've been under tremendous stress. I just want to know that he's all right."

Looking fleetingly chastened, Eisenhower proffered a non-committal smile. "Of course, sir. He has a lot on his plate, including this war and the election. But he's a fighter. Even if his health were failing, I'm probably one of the last people he'd inform. But he's keeping on with his campaign, so I'd say his health is good enough to serve another term—at least he thinks it is."

Churchill chuckled. "We hired you into your job for your formidable diplomatic talents, which you just demonstrated once again."

Eisenhower displayed his famous sphinxlike smile. "Who hired me, sir?"

Churchill let loose a belly laugh. "You're not going to give me an inch, are you, General. Let's put it this way: your president put you up for the job, stressing your ambassadorial skills. I consented, doing so heartily and without objection. Did I adequately describe the situation?"

The general chuckled. "That's as I know it to be, although I'm a commander, not an ambassador."

"At last, we're agreed." Churchill contemplated the waves rolling to shore as he gathered his thoughts. "General, you're about to command the greatest armada that's ever been assembled to transport the largest amphibious operation ever undertaken. I've made plain to your president that I will support that invasion as long as I am convinced that we've pulled together sufficient manpower, landing craft, supply stockpiles, aircraft, ammunition—you know the picture. I told Mr. Roosevelt that I won't have another Dieppe. If we were facing such a prospect, I'd pull my support and remove all the soldiers of the British Empire from the operation. Mind you, that includes Canada, Australia, New Zealand, India, and other outliers of the empire."

Operation Jubilee, an Allied raid on the port city of Dieppe on the French Atlantic coast nearly two years ago, was a horrific memory for the prime minister. Primarily Canadian forces had carried out the raid at the initiative of Lord Louis Mountbatten, the chief of combined operations. It realized over sixty percent casualties, the result of the wrong kind of landing craft, inadequate numbers of them, and inexperienced leadership for amphibious operations.

Yet, some military reviewers argued, it pointed out the very weaknesses that had since then led to better preparedness and amphibious successes from North Africa to Sicily, and even at Salerno and Anzio. Furthermore, unknown to the public, a unit in the raid had seized German radar technology, putting the RAF at a considerable advantage over the *Luftwaffe*. Nevertheless, the huge number of casualties had soured public support, particularly in Canada where Mountbatten had been figuratively pilloried.

While breathing in the fresh breeze blowing across the bay from the Irish Sea, Eisenhower took his time to respond to Churchill's last remark. At last he said, "I understand about Dieppe, Mr. Prime Minister, but you drive a hard bargain."

He inhaled. "How shall I say this, sir? Mistakes were made in this war, including some of my own. I guarantee no results. That said, your guidance through the campaigns has always been well considered if not always welcomed. I don't know what percentage of your input has been enacted compared to anyone else's, but it's enough that our American war staff believes—"

Churchill cut him off impatiently. "Yes, yes, I know. They believe that the president is on my leash. But nothing could be further from the truth. We've discussed openly and directly just as you and I are doing now. If the president and I had competing ideas, and we went with mine, that was because he decided, independently, that mine was the better concept. Keep in mind that when he entered the war, Britain had been fighting for three years. My thinking was tempered by war experience. His is now, but not then.

"And let me remind you that at Tehran last year, a theme came out of that conference regarding the Alliance. Before then, the three leading Allied countries in the war—the US, the Soviets, and the UK—were referred to as the Big Three. After that, it was quietly referred to as the Big Two and a Half. Need I point out which country was considered the 'Half?'"

Eisenhower shook his head. "I heard about that, sir. I'm sorry. That is certainly not the official view of the US as I know it."

"It's neither here nor there at the moment. The main point is that staff's impressions are not always accurate."

"So how can I help you?"

Churchill pulled two cigars from his pocket and offered one to Eisenhower, who declined. The prime minister lit his own and puffed on it until its far end glowed. Then he spun on his heel and faced the general directly. "Convince me, General. In a few days, you'll order many thousands of men into a battle like no other. They will include thousands of troops from the British Empire over whom I wield sovereign authority. Should I delegate our forces to the Allies for Overlord, they will deploy into combat on your authority alone."

He paused. "Ike, I cannot fathom the responsibility that imposes on you. If I didn't consider you qualified for the task, I would never consider such delegation. But I'd be remiss in my own responsibilities if I did not double-check the thinking, planning, and preparations that must take place to have an inkling of success."

"I'll answer your questions as well as I can," Eisenhower said. "Shoot."

Churchill nodded and took a drag on his cigar. "Here we go then. Do you have confidence in the plan?"

Eisenhower chuckled. "That's a trap, sir. If I say yes, and we have a significant failure, I could be seen as incompetent, despite that the breakdown could be for weather, bad intelligence, poor execution at the ground level, or any other myriad events beyond my control. On the other hand, if I say no, the obvious question is, why are we doing it, or why am I in command?

"So let me answer this way: do we have enough soldiers to create a foothold in France that will not be pushed back easily into the sea on the first day? Yes.

"Do we have sufficient men in a follow-on force to proceed into the French countryside and press the invasion inland so it can't be repulsed? Again, yes."

Churchill broke in. "You know those are two of my main concerns."

"Yes, I do, sir, and rightfully so. We were almost routed at Salerno, and at Anzio we lacked overwhelming force to continue inland. Both became months-long slugfests after successful landings. We won't do that again."

"Exactly. Go on."

"You'll want to know if we have sufficient supplies and logistics to support our men in the initial assault and in the follow-on actions, including enough ships and landing craft to carry them to the battle."

"And your answer?"

"Emphatically yes."

"What about intelligence and air superiority?"

"Did you see that ground sketch that came out of Normandy? It was done by a French artist in the Resistance along with his son and a girl posing as his niece."

"I had heard that. I think the artist's name was Douin," Churchill replied. "An amazing piece of work. It's fifty feet long, two feet high, and more detailed than any photographs we've had. It's probably the best ground-level scouting report we could provide to our front-line troops."

"Yes, sir, and accurate too, from comparisons to air reconnaissance photos. It is the best information we have on enemy dispositions, gun emplacements, obstacles, and the like along the critical eighty miles of Normandy's coast. We've made great use of it, and of course your MI departments and SOE along with our OSS feed us constant streams of fresh intelligence coming from the Resistance networks all across Europe. Our sources will never be perfect, but for the most part, they've been reliable."

Eisenhower continued. "Then there's the prep work that the Resistance networks are doing across France. We have your SOE operatives there training the *Maquis* on how to blow up trains, power stations, bridges—anything that will slow down *Wehrmacht* units sent to reinforce along the Atlantic coast. They'll be joined by our own special OSS units, starting just before zero hour."

Churchill wandered down to the water and let it run over the top of his feet. "What about the Mulberries? Will they work?"

Eisenhower pursed his lips. "The floating docks? I think so, sir. We've tested them extensively and they've been equal to the task so far."

"They *must* work, General. The port cities are too far apart on Normandy's coast for units landing there to support each other. Furthermore, the Germans will aggregate their forces in those cities."

"Agreed. We'll bypass the seaports and tow the Mulberries to empty beaches between the port cities, attach the pieces together to form docks able to service large ships, and effectively create new harbors within hours. They'll be reinforced and expanded as we bring more manpower and supplies ashore. That will be a real surprise to the enemy. The main town we're looking at is Arromanches."

"And you have confidence that those docks will serve their purpose?"

"Good enough to order their deployment as it makes sense after we execute Operation Overlord."

"Good. That's what I wanted to hear." Churchill pointed east, over the horizon. "You know those docks are manufactured about forty miles that way, at Mulberry Harbor in Garlieston Bay. That's how they came to be nicknamed Mulberries."

Eisenhower nodded. "I've been there. Beautiful town. The views of the harbor are spectacular in spite of being clogged with those tall floating cubes—the dock sections. They're moored all around. But the workers are doing a terrific job."

"I'll pass along those words. They'll appreciate hearing that from you."

"Do I need to talk more about our air forces?"

Churchill shook his head. "Not really. I'm satisfied that we enjoy air superiority sufficiently. The *Luftwaffe* has depleted its forces almost to the point of not being a factor. Just make sure we maintain that advantage."

"Will do. What else?"

"What about those rolled-up pipelines that are supposed to be strung along the Channel's floor to transport petrol to our troops at the landing sites?"

Eisenhower grunted. "I'll admit to less confidence in that regard."

"Oh?"

"The system works in theory and to a degree in practice, but it falls short over distance. The problem comes down to pumps needed to maintain correct pressure for the length of the pipelines.

"We have fuel tankers among the assault fleet capable of pumping out six hundred gallons per hour to the shore. They'll make sure our forces have all the fuel they need, irrespective of the pipelines. We'll keep working the pipeline issue. If we can get them to work reliably, they'll provide a tremendous advantage as we head inland."

"Hmph. I'm glad you're on top of that." Churchill blew out a cloud of cigar smoke. "You know what's been one of my biggest concerns since Dieppe? Do we have *enough* landing craft of the *right type* to ensure that our chaps at least make it to shore?"

Eisenhower took in a deep breath and exhaled. "You'd think that machines as large as landing crafts would be easy to keep track of, but they're not. With old ones being shot up, sunk, worn out, damaged and repaired, shipped to the Pacific and then re-shipped to Great Britain after intensive combat, matching men and landing craft is a constant challenge. The difficulty almost doubles when we have the same kind of situation with similar vessels for tanks."

He considered his next words carefully before proceeding. "President Roosevelt passed on a promise he made to you not to allow any landing craft transfers to the Pacific from the European Theater until Operation Overlord is fully executed."

Churchill sniffed. "A simple yes or no would have sufficed."

Eisenhower chuckled. "Sir, you know that's not the case."

The prime minister cast a sideways glance at him and puffed on his cigar, but offered no comment.

"I can tell you this," the general continued, "we have faithfully fulfilled the president's promise, and we've transported huge numbers of new landing craft straight from our factories and many more used ones from the

Pacific Theater." He dug his toe into the sand. "You asked about confidence, Mr. Prime Minister? I can say this with confidence. We have sufficient landing vessels of the right types. We'll get our boys ashore, and we'll throw our all into the fight."

"Of course that's good to hear, but what about the weather?"

Eisenhower let out a small laugh. "When we've learned to control that, all other aspects will fall into line with no problem. The weather is the weather, unpredictably stormy across the Channel."

Churchill harrumphed. "You and I both know that the weather was a major factor, among others, that prevented Germany from invading here in 1940."

"Understood. I didn't mean to imply otherwise." The general paused in thought. "You know better than I that seasonal storms and routine violent currents in the Channel drove selection of the period for Overlord. I receive regular meteorological reports. Based on historical data, we've chosen a time window that provides the best opportunity, as near as we can predict. Beyond that, Mother Nature dictates."

They walked in the sand for a distance, taking in the peace and beauty. After a while, Eisenhower said, "Prime Minister, I've got a feeling there's something else you want to discuss."

Churchill chuckled. "You're perceptive, General. Whatever gave you that notion?"

"Well, you didn't invite me to toast to our meeting of the minds or to see the sights. We walked on in silence, so I figured—"

"I'd like your perceptions of Italy."

"That's not my theater, sir. Your General Wilson is doing a fine job as supreme commander there."

"Yes, yes, but you must have some opinion," Churchill insisted.

"I think the Italian campaign's worth will be debated for years to come. Could this invasion into France have succeeded without the Italian campaign? I don't know. We haven't done it yet. But assuming we do succeed in Normandy, the question remains open. The element that makes it such a profound debate is the number of casualties and used-up resources. May I ask for your own assessment?"

The PM stopped and looked out to sea. "It might not be what you expect to hear."

"I doubt there's anything you could ever say that would disinterest me, sir."

Churchill laughed. "The diplomat re-emerges. All right. From my perspective, it was one of the deftest moves of the war. The *Wehrmacht* was forced to transfer many divisions from the Soviet Union to Italy. Those units were insignificant to their Russian front, but had they been left in place, they could easily have been shifted to France to reinforce against our cross-Channel invasion. They could have made the difference between success and failure for Operation Overlord.

"Now those divisions are pinned down in Italy and cannot be transferred without opening a door to start the ground campaign against Germany itself. Add in that their divisions in western Europe must defend behind the Atlantic Wall all the way from Norway to southern France, that leaves the *Wehrmacht* with insufficient troops to reinforce at any given point to rebuff our invasion. They have only the XII Panzer Group left to be their reserve.

"Our chaps will quickly outnumber theirs. Throw in Allied air superiority and your work in marshalling and staging resources, and we're set for a successful invasion."

"I see all of that, sir. The counter-argument is the sheer number of casualties coming out of Italy. Were they necessary and were they worth it?"

Churchill sighed and nodded. "I know. I feel every one of them, I assure you. The compensation—if that is an acceptable term to describe the horror of the Italian campaign—is that the other side has seen similar numbers, which would have been thrown against us during Operation Overlord. Would we have suffered more or fewer overall casualties by invading France first without the Italian campaign? I don't pretend to know. I do know that we are near the end of that campaign, we're emerging victorious, and our chaps in Normandy will face fewer of the enemy."

Eisenhower joined the prime minister wading in the shallows. "All good points," he remarked. "We'll see how things turn out. Since I was involved only peripherally in the planning for Italy and not at all in its execution, I'm not qualified to provide a definitive opinion."

Churchill remained silent a moment, then he said, "I fear that our friend, Mark Clark, is in for heavy criticism."

Eisenhower took a deep breath. "I don't feel comfortable discussing him, sir."

Churchill puffed on his cigar. "You know, when I first met the two of you, he was your senior."

"I remember. We met you at the White House. He took my promotions over him in stride and did a wonderful job of bringing the French to our side in North Africa."

"He did at that, and when you consider that his job in Italy was to keep the enemy pinned down, I hope history will not be too harsh with him. Time will tell. I'm a bit annoyed with him right now."

Eisenhower glanced sharply at the prime minister. "Oh?"

Churchill puffed on his cigar and nodded. "Clark's orders were to take control of the highway leading north through Valmontone and cut off the German units escaping from the south. Word reached me shortly after midday today that he is now executing an operation to take a shortcut that will put him in Rome sooner than expected."

Eisenhower laughed softly. "I give you credit, sir. Your intelligence apparatus is swift and on the job."

Churchill harrumphed. "Someone has to keep you Americans in line or you'd run over the lot of us." He blew out a few smoke rings. "As I was saying, if Clark succeeds, we'll take Rome earlier than expected. If he fails, we'll fight hard going in there against *Wehrmacht* divisions that have linked up. Either way, instead of destroying or capturing those units from the south, they'll escape north of Rome to fight another day. That would be a calamity, and perhaps an avoidable one."

"If I may say, sir, it's no secret that you want Rome and that Clark wants to get there before D-Day."

Churchill smacked his lips in annoyance. "Winning a war is as much a mental effort as it is a physical one," he retorted, clearly agitated. "Yes, I want Rome, and I'll admit that gaining it will stoke my pride. But it will also demoralize the *Wehrmacht*. Taking Rome will demonstrate to the German people that their *Reich* is crumbling. Every German soldier from there to the Soviet Union, to Norway, and all along the Atlantic Wall to the south of

France will feel the loss to his toes. Clark is right to try to seize that trophy before our soldiers set foot on Normandy beach. The Germans shooting at them will wonder how soon they will take bullets from their rear."

The two men ambled along in silence. Then, Churchill continued, "In any event, I gather that none of our British soldiers are among the attack force heading into Rome. I hope Clark isn't excluding British units to snub them or brandish American superiority. Or worse, burnish his reputation. The situation begs the question of whether excluding our chaps occurred by happenstance or design."

Eisenhower grimaced. "I have no comment on that, sir."

Churchill shrugged. "If it had been Patton, I would be sure that both elements are at play. Patton deliberately upstaged General Montgomery at Messina."

"Then again, sir, by putting Patton's army in Sicily in a purely support role, an argument could be made that Monty was both burnishing his own ego and upstaging Patton."

Churchill chuckled and sighed. "You might be right. The effects of generals allowing personal considerations to color their actions is not one I care to consider at the moment. On balance, the Allied leaders have exercised restraint in that regard. I'll give Clark the benefit of the doubt that there might be a military imperative at play that is unknown to me.

"The fact is that one of your division commanders, General Walker, proposed the alternative plan after conducting a personal aerial reconnaissance of the new route when VI Corps units bogged down while pursuing the Germans. The corps commander, Truscott, heard Walker out and called Clark to discuss the situation over the phone. Clark approved Walker's plan. As you Americans say, here's the kicker: Clark and Walker are known to be at odds with each other much of the time."

Eisenhower took his time to respond. "Then you approve of the new route?"

Churchill laughed. "It's positively brilliant. In any event, the new plan is already in motion, so there's little I can do about it now. There's just one more question I'd like to ask on a completely different subject. Have you heard anything concerning an agent codenamed Nimrod?"

Eisenhower's face turned grim, and he shook his head. "Nothing."

Churchill sighed. "Well I suppose we deal with what we have in hand." He turned to look up at the lodge. "I think we've hit the essential subjects, General. Would you join me for tea?" He glanced up at the sun, still high in the sky but heading toward the horizon. "That's a euphemism for something stronger at this time of day."

"Will that be to celebrate our meeting of the minds?"

Churchill chuckled. "I suppose it is. I seem to have talked myself into final commitment for Operation Overlord."

"That's good, sir. I'd hate to think that I'd had to convince you."

"Ahh, General Eisenhower, you *are* the consummate diplomat. Some might call you a politician. I will properly inform the president that I'm fully committed. The invasion is in your hands now."

The general's brow furrowed. He leaned back as if absorbing the enormous implications and briefly cast his eyes heavenward. "God help us," he breathed.

36

June 5, 1944
Rome, Italy

Zack's heart pounded as he entered a dark, narrow street shortly after 02:00 hours. He could not believe where he was patrolling. Rome. The capital of the Caesars; the "Eternal City"; the city on seven hills; the seat of power for centuries. It was the place of architectural wonders: the Forum, the Parthenon, the Colosseum where gladiators had battled to their deaths, Hadrian's Tomb, the catacombs, the massive Tomb of the Unknown Soldier, site of Vatican City... The place where Benito Mussolini had hoped to rebuild the Roman Empire.

The familiar edifices seen in magazines and photographs flashed through Zack's mind, but now he saw nothing of the city other than the cobblestones on the street's surface reflecting ambient light, and the white walls of closely built dwellings that silhouetted his squad members as they moved deeper into an urban neighborhood.

A door creaked.

Zack whirled. His breath caught.

His men crouched, searching around, their M-1 rifles ready.

A minute passed. Zack raised his hand and signaled to continue. With them was a guide, provided courtesy of and at the initiative of Colonel Lynch, the 142nd Brigade commander who, upon arrival at the city's edge, had recruited locals to lead his command through the maze of cross streets and alleys while avoiding dead ends. The 141st and 143rd Brigades had followed and would spread out cautiously in adjacent neighborhoods and commercial areas, seeking the enemy.

Zack's squad crept forward again, following orders to patrol through the city by whatever route their guide indicated, engage the enemy where they encountered him, and link up with their own battalion and company head-quarters on reaching the far side. They had taken only a few steps when they heard more hinges creak, and they were uncertain of whether they had heard doors or windows opening.

Again they crouched and stayed down, but then they heard a soft patter, like two hands clapping together. At first unsure of what he heard, Zack stayed put and whispered to his men to do the same. But the sound grew louder and was joined by others, and now it was unmistakable—people at dark windows and doors applauding their incoming liberators.

The guide, Antonio, sidled up next to Zack. "It's all right," he whispered. "The people are happy to see you."

Pleasantly surprised, Zack moved forward, followed by his squad. As they crept deeper into the neighborhood, more doors opened and more people clapped, and when the conclusion became inescapable that the Germans had deserted the area, they poured out of their dwellings into the night, bringing candles, lanterns, and flashlights with them. They danced in the street, seized the soldiers to hug and kiss them, welcoming them and thanking them for their deliverance.

At first wary, the soldiers submitted to the good feeling by degrees. "What do we do, Sarge?" one asked. "They want to feed us."

"Keep going," Zack said. Bestowing his friendliest smile on the rows of shining eyes now watching him in awe as the acknowledged leader of this rough squad of armed saviors, he called out, "*Grazie, grazie.*" Then he turned to Antonio. "Please tell them that we have to move on to clear the way through the rest of the city."

A subdued, appreciative cacophony rose from the crowd as Antonio translated, and heads bobbed as the residents nodded at him with serious eyes. Then they pressed bread and fruit on their liberators. One man entered into conversation with Antonio, who relayed the remarks to Zack.

"He says that they will call ahead to friends and family, and let them know you are coming by, so they can tell you if any Germans are ahead of you."

Zack smiled and thanked the man. As the squad continued forward, the people behind them cheered and celebrated in the street. They were replaced farther on by more throngs crowding around to thank the soldiers. The pattern continued through the night, and as the squad progressed, they heard similar celebrations in adjacent streets.

As dawn broke, the news spread that the Germans had deserted the city and the Americans had entered Rome. As the exhausted combatants continued through the streets, their smiles became irrepressible, the tension of months relieved. Girls flocked around them, kissing them, sometimes passionately. Men offered handshakes, bear hugs, and cigarettes.

A Sherman tank creaked up behind them, the rumble of its tracks vibrating through the streets. The crowd parted, and Zack's squad moved out of the way.

The tank halted. The commander grinned down at Zack. "General Walker directed all his war machines to drive through the city," he called. "He ordered every vehicle to pick up and carry as many soldiers as they could. The Germans are gone. Climb aboard."

The soldiers stared. Exhaustion forgotten, they leaped into the air, pounded each other's backs, and when girls once again kissed them, the men did not hold back. But they eventually clambered onto the tank, one sitting on the barrel, two on either side of the driver, Zack next to the commander's cupola, and the others spread along the back.

The crowds grew bigger, now offering wine, tearing down the hated red flags with swastikas, and waving the Stars and Stripes. Army units converged at intersections and melded into processions of vehicles burdened with soldiers interspersed with girls with happy smiles, heading to the far city limit.

They rode on every conceivable vehicle propelled on tracks or wheels, with soldiers sitting atop howitzer barrels, inside trailers, packed into the back of jeeps, holding on for dear life on overcrowded two-and-a-half-ton trucks. Some troop trucks drove through, their canvases down, the soldiers onboard looking worn and spent, ready for a long rest. They rode to the opposite side of town, where supply units quickly prepared hot breakfasts for the exhausted troops—including real beer, shipped from home.

Skirmishes occurred against determined defenders on the western edge of the city—apparently not all German forces in the area had received word to vacate. But by nightfall, they had been subdued, either captured, escaped, or no longer of this world.

Later, having found their battalion, company, platoon, and squad area, and having cleaned their equipment, Zack's men spent the afternoon basking in Rome's warm sun. Zack was about to lean against a truck's tire to brace his back as he added to the letter he had written to his sister days before. He had been on the move ever since and had forgotten to mail it. His assistant squad leader ran up.

"President Roosevelt is about to speak," he called excitedly. "It's on the BBC."

The men grouped around a radio to listen. Soon, they heard the president's well-known voice amid electronic crackling.

"My Friends: Yesterday, on June 4, 1944, Rome fell to American and Allied troops. The first of the Axis capitals is now in our hands."

"Yesterday?" a squad member broke in. "Today's the 5th. I thought we were in first. This morning."

"A reconnaissance troop of the 88th Division came in yesterday," another man replied.

"Big deal," yet another soldier called. "The 36th was the first full division to go all the way through Rome. We liberated it."

"Yeah, but did you hear? The brass already put Rome off-limits to combat soldiers." He snorted. "They're busy downtown picking out their luxury digs."

"Shh. I wanna hear."

The group settled down to listen to the president.

"It is perhaps significant that the first of these capitals to fall should have the longest history of all of them. The story of Rome goes back to the time of the foundations of our civilization. We can still see there monuments of the time when Rome and the Romans controlled..."

"Hey, what's with the history lesson," a soldier broke in. "Ya think he'll mention us?"

"Quiet. Let's hear."

The president droned on, speaking in grandiloquent terms about the suffering of war-torn Italians, the dedication of the Allies, and the need to press on. Many soldiers dozed or moved away for other pursuits.

After fifteen minutes of speaking, Roosevelt approached the end of his "fireside chat."

"And so I extend the congratulations and thanks tonight of the American people to General Alexander, who has been in command of the whole Italian operation; to our General Clark and General Leese of the Fifth and the Eighth Armies; to General Wilson, the Supreme Allied Commander of the Mediterranean Theater, and to General Devers his American Deputy; to Lieutenant General Eaker; to Admirals Cunningham and Hewitt; and to all their brave officers and men. May God bless them and watch over them and over all of our gallant, fighting men."

"At least we got a mention."

Additional comments matched the sarcasm.

"Nice to be appreciated."

"That's fifteen minutes I'll never get back."

"Oh, the glory of Rome."

Zack chuckled, keeping in mind the age-old adage about a soldier's right to gripe. He went back to his letter. Retrieving it from his pocket, he unfolded it and wrote, "PS—You won't believe where I am now. Rome."

Early the next morning, jostled by his assistant squad leader, Zack awoke with a start. "You're gonna want to hear this, Sergeant," the corporal said with palpable excitement. "Ike just broadcasted. It's on the BBC. They're playing it over and over."

Reluctantly, Zack squirmed out of his sleeping bag and followed the corporal through the dark pre-dawn to a group of soldiers gathered around the same radio they had listened to earlier. One of his squad members nudged him and extended a metal canteen cup toward him. "You want some coffee, Sergeant?"

"Is it any good?"

The man grunted and chuckled. "It's hot."

Someone in the dark announced, "They're getting ready to play Ike's broadcast again."

The soldiers fell silent. Then the clear, soft, familiar voice of General Eisenhower said, "People of Western Europe: A landing was made this morning on the coast of France by troops of the Allied Expeditionary Force. This landing is part of the concerted United Nations' plan for the liberation of Europe, made in conjunction with our great Russian allies...

"I call upon all who love freedom to stand with us now. Together we shall achieve victory."

Zack listened in stunned disbelief. A soldier sitting nearby put words to Zack's own thoughts. "We've invaded France?"

"Sounds like it," a voice in the darkness replied. "But that was about as inspiring as the president's speech. Or uninspiring, I should say. Does anyone higher than platoon sergeant know what we do out here?"

"Wait," a third voice broke in. "Ike's made another speech. For the troops. It should play in a minute." Moments later, they heard again their supreme commander's voice.

"Soldiers, Sailors and Airmen of the Allied Expeditionary Force!

"You are about to embark upon the Great Crusade, toward which we have striven these many months. The eyes of the world are upon you. The hopes and prayers of liberty-loving people everywhere march with you. In company with our brave Allies and brothers-in-arms on other Fronts, you will bring about the destruction of the German war machine, the elimination of Nazi tyranny over the oppressed peoples of Europe, and security for ourselves in a free world.

"Your task will not be an easy one. Your enemy is well trained, well equipped and battle-hardened. He will fight savagely.

"But this is the year 1944. Much has happened since the Nazi triumphs of 1940-41. The United Nations have inflicted upon the Germans great defeats, in open battle, man-to-man. Our air offensive has seriously reduced their strength in the air and their capacity to wage war on the ground.

"Our Home Fronts have given us a superiority in weapons and munitions of war, and placed at our disposal great reserves of trained fighting men. The tide has turned! The free men of the world are marching together to Victory!

"I have full confidence in your devotion to duty and skill in battle. We will accept nothing less than full Victory!

"Good Luck! And let us all beseech the blessing of Almighty God upon this great and noble undertaking."

Zack had listened carefully. He strolled back to his squad area and leaned back on the same truck tire where he had finished his letter to Sherry. Several of his members joined him, sitting cross-legged in a half-circle in front of him. Once again, the soldiers voiced their thoughts, summed up in the utterance of one of them.

"It's good that he's saying nice things about those guys in Normandy, but does he know we just took Rome?"

One queried Zack, "What do you think, Sergeant?"

Zack scanned the tired, grimy faces looking back at him. They seemed so old yet so young. "If you're a praying man, I'd say do it. Those guys landing in France are in for pure hell, a cauldron, probably worse than this division faced at the Garigliano."

37

One Week Earlier, May 30, 1944
Bletchley Park, England

Claire knocked on Travis' door and opened it. "Sir, you asked to see me straight away?"

"Yes, thank you for coming. Have a seat." He kept talking as Claire sat down before his desk. "There are some goings-on that I can't speak about at length, but I need you to keep me apprised immediately of anything that comes across German wireless messaging regarding someone codenamed Nimrod."

"Nimrod, sir? That's an interesting choice. As I recall from religious studies, Nimrod was a great hunter. He was the son of Cush who took over several cities in Babylonia, including Babel, among others that I don't remember.

"As it happens, we've already had one such mention. I remember the message clearly because of the codename and because the content was so unusual. It was from the *Wehrmacht's* 7th Army headquarters, and it ordered an immediate increase in investigative patrols, to be conducted around the clock. The purpose is to apprehend an agent, Nimrod, who is believed to have arrived in their area. He is not to be harmed or mistreated, and he is to be escorted under armed guard to Army Group B headquarters for interrogation immediately.

"The message went on to say—and this is the other part that caught my attention—that the commanding officer in the area where Nimrod is detained would be held responsible, personally, for the agent's safety."

"That sounds like the man we're looking for. Good. I'm glad you're handling it." He paused and then mused aloud, "Army Group B. Isn't that Field Marshal Rommel's command?"

"Yes, sir. It is."

"All right then. Classify as Ultra anything to do with Nimrod, and inform me immediately when something comes in. That'll be all."

June 2, 1944
La Roche Guyon, France

Stephen Rigby stared over the side of a canvas-topped *kübelwagen* through an early morning drizzle. Ahead of him, a vertical promontory jutted into the River Seine. A high, round tower dominated its summit.

Rigby was an athletic young man, muscular, with blond hair and blue eyes. He spoke English, French, and German fluently. Sitting next to him in the rear was a lieutenant with his left arm looped through the detainee's right arm. The officer's opposite hand held a pistol aimed at Rigby's stomach.

Hauptman Arngross, a pudgy German captain in the front passenger seat, was the acting corps intelligence officer while his boss was on a short leave. Arngross' task, almost completed, was to escort Rigby to La Roche Guyon from his own headquarters south of Paris. His demeanor indicated a belief of being overdue for promotion. He was also armed, as was his driver.

Despite his frustration on not yet achieving his next rank, Arngross was in a jovial mood, and Rigby quickly discerned the reason: word had gone out to be on the lookout for Rigby, and the captain had the pleasure of detaining him. From the German officer's view, that event should be career-enhancing. He had intercepted the message of Rigby's landing in France, ostensibly as an SOE agent codenamed Nimrod, a wireless expert sent to assist the local Resistance organization experiencing radio difficulties.

Arngross had ordered the doubling of ground patrols, pushing out the word to be diligent in searching for a German agent traveling with a false ID showing him to be Stephane Dubillier among Resistance members. When found, he would identify himself by his codename and request to be brought to corps headquarters.

One of the patrols had raided a farm where Rigby had been brought after flying to France on a British intelligence Lysander night-flight. Rigby had immediately identified himself as Nimrod and demanded to be brought to the highest-level German intelligence officer. Per instruction, the patrol had brought him to *Hauptman* Arngross.

A Resistance member, furious at the obvious betrayal, had taken a shot at Rigby. The soldiers on the patrol dispatched him with a fusillade.

Irrespective of the circumstances and the stormy weather, as the *kübelwagen* crossed a bridge over the Seine, Rigby had to admit to the beauty of his surroundings. Deep green foliage adorned the crest of the cliffs towering over the picturesque town on the river's west bank. Dark mouths of caves opened on the cliff face. The stone tower rose from the summit with a few yellowing houses resting on rocky outcrops.

An enormous castle, appearing as a manor house to rival Versailles, appeared below the face of the cliff. Four hundred years earlier, the Duke de la Rochefoucauld had built the castle, and his descendants had lived there ever since. German occupation notwithstanding, the current duke, his duchess, and their family lived in the upper stories. The remaining floors and rooms had been taken over by Field Marshal Rommel to be his home and his headquarters for Army Group B. To that end, he had directed his engineers to drill back into the cliff and construct tunnels, office spaces, conference rooms, and a communications center impregnable to bombing raids.

German sentries guarded key points, with two of them posted at a secure portal along Rue d' Audience. They opened the high wrought-iron gates for the *kübelwagen* and quickly closed them once it had entered. Another lieutenant met the party inside a vast courtyard to escort them into the castle and to the proper office.

Rigby had never before seen such finery. The French doors at the entry were thirty-five feet high, and the foyer was elegantly ornate with classical artistry and statuary. The guide led them through a maze of rooms and corridors of equal opulence, and then stopped and knocked on a polished oaken door. On hearing a call to enter, he opened it, gestured the three men through, closed the door behind them, and left.

A colonel rose from behind a desk. Seated to one side was an older civilian with a menacing countenance. He stared at Rigby intently through horn-rimmed glasses, studying every line of his face.

The captain presented himself at attention to the colonel with a salute. "*Hauptman* Arngross reports, sir, with Nimrod."

The colonel returned the captain's salute with a perfunctory Nazi salute and turned to gaze at Rigby. "So, you are Nimrod? I am *Oberst* Ritter." He motioned to a chair. "Please, have a seat."

Rigby sat in the chair indicated, and the captain and lieutenant stood behind him. Ritter took his seat behind his desk. For a few moments, all was quiet while the colonel gazed at Rigby quizzically and the civilian's eyes bored into him.

"Excuse me," Ritter said after a time. He indicated the old man. "This is *Herr* Mannheim. He's followed your activities in England. He says that you sought out and provided valuable intelligence through Weber, one of our agents there."

"I've tried. I hope it's been helpful." Rigby lapsed back into his first language easier than expected, even comfortably.

Mannheim broke in for the first time, his tone tinged with skepticism. "But you are *not* German?"

"I am, sir. I was born in Frankfurt but spent much of my life in England."

"How did you come to us? Is this your first time in France?"

"The first time since 1939. This was my first opportunity since then."

Ritter held up his palm to stop him. "I want to hear your background, but I want to make a record of our conversation." He rang a bell, and a clerk appeared from an interior office. Ritter instructed him to take notes and then turned back to Rigby. "'We understand you've been working in Lord

Mountbatten's Combined Operations office and with the SOE on Baker Street in London? Is that correct?"

Rigby affirmed with a nod. "That's true, but it's been a part-time effort, not steady." He related his activities in England including his work with Weber.

Mannheim cut in abrasively. "So where do you have lunch when working at the Baker Street office." His manner confirmed Rigby's sense that the two men would question Rigby on known details and that he could expect attempts to trip him up.

"Usually at the Wallace Head," he replied. "It's fairly close by."

"I'm not familiar with it," Ritter interjected. "I worked at our embassy in London. I ate out often, but I don't recall that place."

"It's on Blandford Street, a bit far from where the embassy was."

And so it went, including questions about what was written on the identifying plaque outside of SOE headquarters, "Inter-Service Liaison Department."

"How did you come about the information already transmitted and that you're bringing to us now?"

"I was a member of No. 10 Commando. As such, I was occasionally assigned staff work, and so I moved between headquarters and, at every opportunity, I seized intelligence that I thought would interest Germany."

Ritter and Mannheim exchanged glances. The questions came less rapidly. Mannheim softened slightly in his approach. Rigby had time to take a breath and marvel at where he was: in the headquarters of Field Marshal Rommel, the most famous of all German senior commanders. The Desert Fox.

Also crossing Rigby's mind was the sense that he could not equivocate on any answers. Otherwise, he might find himself in a dank cell in the bowels of this castle, being interrogated by experts determined to learn if he had lied to them.

"Tell me about Weber," Mannheim said. "How do you know him?"

"He taught me piano when I was younger. His name was Werner then. He changed it to Duncan, and then to Weber, probably because of the work he does for you."

Ritter chuckled. "That's a good guess. How do the two of you communicate?"

"By telephone. He mails me a list of numbers to public telephone booths, minus the exchange. His return address will have the name of the town associated with the exchange. At the appointed time, I call through the numbers. If I don't get him at one of them or if I get a busy signal, I try again at five-minute intervals until we either connect or fifteen minutes has gone by. I never try any number more than three times."

"Does he pay you?"

Rigby nodded. "He does when we meet. Not much. That's not why I do what I do. But we got together at a pub occasionally when I had hard documents to pass along."

Ritter looked at Mannheim and inhaled. "You've been doing this for some time now. Why haven't you been caught?"

Rigby shrugged. "Why hasn't Weber?"

Ritter accepted the sense of the response. Meanwhile, Mannheim stood and addressed the colonel. "Oberst, let's confer in the other room for a few minutes."

They moved off while Rigby sat in his chair looking out across the lush lawn and garden. He was surprised at how calm he had been under the grilling. But, he reminded himself, he had barely slept in nearly forty-eight hours.

In the other room, Mannheim and Ritter conversed in whispers. "Everything he's said checks out against what Weber transmitted to us," the colonel said.

"Agreed," Mannheim replied, "but we've got to dig further. The stakes are so high. Based on what he says, someone is likely to decide where to defend against an Allied invasion, and it's coming soon. We think it'll be at Calais. Rommel thinks it will be at Somme. Others think along the Mediterranean coast.

"Nimrod's appearance at just this moment seems too convenient, like perhaps an attempt by British intelligence to deceive us into reinforcing in the wrong place."

"I see your point," Ritter replied, "but think of this: according to Weber, he's known Nimrod a long time, and they've been working together for many months. Weber even paid for his studies at the University of London. He really is a commando with No. 10. We've checked that independently, down to the name of his commander. If he were feeding us false information, Weber would have spotted it."

"He's obviously not after money. Look at the way he's dressed," Mannheim said. "Maybe he's really a loyal German wanting to do the right thing for the motherland. Let's ask him directly why he's here, and find out if he's brought documents. If he did, we can vet them and find out if they're genuine."

Rigby was standing by the window enjoying the view when the two men returned. Arngross and the lieutenant had retired to seating on the opposite end of the room. They returned to stand behind Rigby again as he took his seat.

"Let's get down to details," Ritter began. "Why are you doing this? What do you hope to gain?"

Rigby grunted. "The quick answer is that I'm doing my duty for Germany. I'll admit to some personal motivation too. You probably know that I was interned in Canada because of my German background. That did not endear me to Britain. I have an engineering degree that the government found useful, so I agreed to join the Royal Pioneer Corps—that's a British Army combat engineering arm. Doing that allowed me to get back to England and have a bit of freedom. From there, I was allowed to volunteer for the commandos. I thought the training might be useful to the motherland."

"Which unit?" Mannheim pressed.

"No. 10 Commando. I joined in North Wales. Harlech, to be precise."

"And where are they now?"

"My troop is in Sussex. The others are spread all around."

"Let me ask a particular question," Ritter cut in. "It pertains to why you might have come. Are you familiar with the 58th British Infantry Division?"

"Yes, sir. It's part of the First US Army Group, under the command of the 2nd British Corps. I don't know exactly where they're stationed, but I think it's near Grantham, in Lincolnshire."

For an hour, Ritter and Mannheim quizzed Rigby on his knowledge of the unit, until at last Rigby cast a beseeching look at Ritter. "If you don't mind, sir, I need to stand a minute to stretch my legs."

"Of course," the colonel replied as Rigby took to his feet. "And bear with us. We cannot afford to make a mistake. We have to know that you are who you say you are." He stroked his chin in thought. "Before taking a break, perhaps you can answer this: did you bring us any documents?"

Rigby nodded and smiled. "My apologies. I should have given them to you at the outset. I was tired. They slipped my mind." He started taking off his jacket. "They're sewn into my sleeve. I reduced the documents to photographs using a camera that Weber provided, and brought the negatives. They show troop dispositions, orders of battle, logistical tables and plans—they're quite thorough, and they're signed by British, American, and Canadian officers of the units shown. The names can be easily checked.

"In one, a document marked top secret, you'll find a black-and-white enlargement of a movement order for the 4th Canadian Armored Division. The document is number forty-one of fifty-nine copies.

"Another deals with the Royal Electrical and Mechanical Engineers' manual for waterproofing tanks. It's stamped as the property of the 4th Canadian Armored Division and shows the modifications that must be made to exhaust systems, how to protect the ignition system, and the like.

"Yet another one is a memorandum from the Chief Medical Officer of the US 3rd Army in East Anglia. It pertains to avoiding and treating sea-sickness, which is important to an army planning an amphibious invasion over rough seas.

"Of course, there is much more. As a commando, I had immediate credibility, and I picked up what I could everywhere I went. I hope what I brought will be helpful."

"How did you get the documents you just mentioned?" Ritter asked incredulously.

"A major on a Grade II general staff visited Baker Street. He had locked his briefcase in a safe. I had another key, and those documents were inside."

Mannheim stood abruptly. "Let's get these negatives out for developing while you take a break." He started for the door, but turned back and looked piercingly through Rigby. "Why now? You've obviously been doing this for some time. Why did you feel compelled to bring this over at this particular time, and why in person."

Rigby faced Mannheim directly. "I came personally, sir, for two reasons. First, the volume of documents could not have been transmitted in time to be useful—the Allies *are* going to invade. Soon. We know that.

"Secondly, I thought bringing the intelligence in person might add emphasis to their importance. I can provide further context through your questions.

"When and where the Allies will come ashore is their most closely guarded secret. You know that. We'll need all the time and information possible to prepare."

Mannheim studied Rigby inscrutably through his thick horn-rimmed glasses. Then, without another word, he turned and left the room. Ritter followed.

Late that afternoon, Field Marshal Erwin Rommel strolled in La Roche Castle's garden with one of his newly appointed division commanders and long-time confidants, *Generalleutnant* Kurt Meier. They had taken many such walks when assigned together in the past, using the occasions to speak openly without concern about being overheard.

"It's great to have you back working with me again," Rommel said.

"It's nice to be back in your command, sir."

Until his leg was wounded, Meier had commanded a battalion under Rommel during the German invasion of France at the beginning of the war when the *Wehrmacht* seized Dunkirk. Rommel's division had been at the front of that assault, and Meier had commanded his lead battalion. Upon his recovery, Meier had re-joined Rommel, already in North Africa, and the two had fought the Allies together until Rommel's recall to Berlin. Although Meier remained faithfully aware of their difference in rank and maintained respect, the two officers formed a fast friendship in which neither held back in expressing opinions.

"What did you think of this fellow Stephen Rigby, codenamed

Nimrod?" Meier asked. They had just come from Rommel's suite of offices where Rigby had been brought for Rommel's personal assessment.

"Rigby." Rommel repeated the name pensively. "Alias Stephane Dubillier, originally named Stefan Rosenberg. Born in Germany, raised in England. Pretending to be a Brit while in England, a Frenchman while with the Resistance, and now passing himself off to us as a German. But his accent is off, and I dare say that it doesn't quite hit the mark when he speaks in either English or French.

"Nimrod is a Biblical figure. A great hunter. So the question becomes, who is he hunting for? Who is he really, and where do his loyalties lie? Does he believe the information he's giving to us, or is he a good liar?"

"I don't pretend to know, sir," Meier said, pursing his lips. "He speaks forthrightly, and his answers come naturally, not like he's trying to remember his lines. He was delivered into France by the SOE. That we know from the interrogation of another SOE agent we captured who was on the same night flight with him.

"Nimrod was picked up by the Resistance. If he really is one of our true and loyal agents, he had to fool them. One of its members took a shot at him when Arngross' patrol retrieved him. Our soldiers killed one of theirs in the fracas. So Nimrod was in danger with them from the start and is in more danger now if they can get to him. Meanwhile, he knows what can happen to him here if we don't believe him."

Rommel grunted. "Hmph. Mannheim is an *Abwehr* officer, one of Admiral Canaris' men. Ritter brought him in to be sure that German national intelligence and our *Wehrmacht's* operations section avoid a turf battle. The *Abwehr* is jealous of its prerogatives. That was smart of Ritter, but unfortunate for Nimrod. Mannheim will not hesitate to have him tortured if there is a hint that something is being withheld."

"Nimrod must know that," Meier said. "He's very intelligent, aware, confident, and properly respectful. He is forthright that his father was a Jew. I'd say he's very brave."

"Agreed," Rommel replied, "which brings us back to the question of which country he serves, Germany or Great Britain? Mannheim has already arranged to take him to Berchtesgaden to sort that out."

"That surprises me," Meier cut in. "I'd have thought they'd take him to Berlin?"

"Yes, well, Hitler is at the Berghof in a conference at the moment, and the main topic of discussion is where the Allies will invade. Mannheim thinks that having Nimrod close by in case the *führer* has questions might be wise. That makes sense. The interrogation facilities there are equal to those in Berlin."

They walked on in silence for a time. Meier struck up the conversation again. "As I understand the situation, Nimrod came to us through one of our *Abwehr* agents in England—Weber, they call him. Mannheim states that Weber has transmitted good information to us for years. I think you said that since interrogating Nimrod this morning, Mannheim has already sent inquiries to compare notes with Weber and received back messages confirming Nimrod's information."

Rommel nodded. "That's true, but the timing of Nimrod's appearance is too perfect." He stopped in the middle of the garden path. His elbows were crossed, and he moved one hand to rub his chin. "I'm not sure if you're aware that last year, six weeks before the Allies invaded Sicily, a dead British Marine officer, Major Martin, floated ashore in southern Spain with a briefcase chained to his wrist."

Meier shook his head. "I'm not aware of that."

Rommel cocked his head to one side, and his eyes narrowed. "Inside the major's briefcase were, among other miscellaneous items, a set of documents marked top secret, purporting to order the Allied invasions of Sardinia and the Balkans instead of Sicily. By the Spanish government's good graces, our agents were allowed to view and photograph the contents before Madrid returned them to London." He shook his head, and a sardonic tone entered his voice. "Spain *must* maintain its neutrality, you know."

He continued, "In any event, the *Abwehr* checked out all aspects of what was in the briefcase and on the dead major's body. On the basis that they found nothing amiss, they sent the documents to Berlin.

"The contents made their way to the *führer*, who, after much discussion, ordered the transfer of whole divisions out of Sicily to Sardinia and the

Balkans. The thing is, Major Martin appeared at just the right moment to influence that decision."

Understanding crossed Meier's face. He grasped Rommel's elbow. "Ahh," he exclaimed while striking his forehead, "and the Allies went ashore in Sicily almost without a fight. Thirty days later, they ran our troops off of that island because it was not well defended. So was Major Martin a deliberate deception or a coincidence?"

Rommel shrugged. "Exactly. No one can say for sure, and no one wants to suggest it was a deception because it was our brilliant *führer* who ordered the transfer of those divisions." He faced Meier directly. "But in retrospect, a reasonable conclusion is that the affair *was* a very elegant, deliberate ruse."

Meier grimaced. "North Africa was lost because Hitler wouldn't supply us with sufficient Tiger tanks, despite his personal promise to you," he said angrily. "The ones he sent came too late, and he had spread himself thin in the Soviet Union.

"Italy is about to topple, and now the Allies are knocking on France's doorstep. If their invasion succeeds, wherever it comes, the war is lost. They're already bombing our cities into rubble." He looked wildly about, and when he spoke again, he did so with bitterness. "How much longer will we allow that fool in Berlin to destroy our country?"

Meier glared intently into Rommel's eyes. "I'm serious. Now is the time if there ever was one."

Rommel recommenced ambling along the garden path. "I don't disagree, but my point is, what's to say that Nimrod is not a deception? The circumstances are similar to those surrounding Major Martin. The British have their agents in Germany. They must know of the conflicting opinions on how best to defend in France and what Hitler's position is. As the major did, Nimrod appears just at the time such a decision is about to be made, and he provides information that aligns exactly with what *Herr* Hitler thinks."

Rommel grunted. "As an aside, the British have anticipated our moves so often that I've wondered if they're reading our messages. I recall the conversation you and I had in North Africa about that girl, Jeannie Rousseau. You had just arrived there and the Japanese had just struck Pearl Harbor. I mentioned wondering about whether or not the Brits had cracked our code. You said that Rousseau was suspected of transmitting troop dispositions to the Resistance—"

Meier broke in. "I remember the conversation, sir. I stand by what I said then regarding the code and Rousseau, that I checked into both issues and felt assured that the code could not be broken. I also don't believe anything amiss about Mademoiselle Rousseau. I was in Paris earlier in the year, and she was then working at our headquarters there with the full faith and confidence of the high command. She had been with them for quite some time. Regardless, I understand that she's no longer there. Apparently, she went off to do something else with no adverse reports."

Rommel listened and smiled. "Isn't that exactly how a successful spy would be perceived?" he mused. He continued impatiently, "Anyway, regarding your question of what to do about our *führer*, you're not the only one who's approached me on the subject. The problem is getting to him. Generals Jodl and Keitel would never go along, nor would anyone in the SS. They run his bodyguard and swear personal oaths to him, not to Germany. Everyone knows that he can make or break anyone around him with a single utterance. None of them will take the risk. So, until we find a way in, we'll have to bide our time. Until then, we're left with doing our best to defend Germany, and right now, that means defending in France."

They climbed some stairs to a terrace with a view to the east overlooking the Seine and the verdant fields beyond. "This really is a beautiful country," Rommel said wistfully. "I have to be in Berlin tomorrow for the *führer's* conference, but my wife's birthday is on the sixth. I'll need to be back for that. She loves it here."

He stood enjoying a breeze against his face, and then returned his thoughts to the present. "The strategic dilemma we face is how best to defend the coastline all the way from Norway to southern France. You know that Hitler believes that Norway is also a prime candidate for invasion."

"Doesn't he think the Atlantic Wall sufficiently protects against an enemy invasion there? You've been in charge of fortifying all of it."

Rommel scoffed. "Another one of *Herr* Hitler's ideas. I've done my best, but the Atlantic Wall was poorly conceived in the first place, and haphazardly constructed with slave labor. Besides, walls have historically been breached. Look at the Great Wall of China and the Maginot Line. Our wall will slow the Allies down, but we need a concentrated army to stop them. We don't have it. Ours is spread too thin. Besides, they've gained overwhelming air superiority that they'll unleash against our counter-attacks. In North Africa, we saw what their air forces could do."

He grasped a handrailing at the front of the terrace. "A major enemy offensive might be brewing in the Soviet Union too. Our armies are stretched along a two-thousand-mile front there. That leaves no troops to spare to reinforce in France.

"The *führer* is convinced that the Allies will invade at Calais because the distance between there and Dover is the shortest across the Channel. If they go in anywhere else, they will need to keep soldiers on rough seas for an extended time, wearing them out before they come ashore. He also believes that they've seen air reconnaissance of the launch pads we've been building around Calais for the pilotless winged bombs. He believes the Allies would like to destroy those pads as quickly as possible."

Turning to face Meier, Rommel continued. "Hitler has a point regarding those launch pads. I agree with him on that."

His eyes narrowed as he contemplated. "If the Allies could establish a beachhead at Calais—and don't forget that it's only twenty-five miles across the Channel at that point—they'd have an easier time getting reinforcement troops across. There are plenty of roads into Dover for transporting divisions to English ports, and plenty of roads leading out of Calais to invade farther into France and threaten Germany's border. Allied bombing has been greater in northern France than in other parts of the country, which could be for softening up their targets.

"Hitler also points to the large build-up of US troops in southeast England under General George Patton. I grant that Patton is the best combat general the Allies have, but I'm not convinced that build-up is real."

"Another deception?"

Rommel laughed. "They did it to me in North Africa. They set up dummy tanks and trucks way south of my position and set up a lot of tents. They even generated a lot of radio traffic. I thought they had moved several divisions down there to flank me, so I sent a sizable force to block them. Then they attacked across the middle of my main front. It was embarrassing, to say the least. We even took a map from a dead British major with markings showing where soft and hard sand were located on the desert floor. The only thing is, the markings on the map had been reversed, and my tanks got bogged down as a result." He grunted. "So you see, I know a little about that matter.

"In any event, I found Nimrod's comments about Patton and his army around Dover to be quite intriguing."

"You'll have to tell me about them," Meier interjected, "but getting back to the dead major and his map, is that another instance of false documents being planted on dead bodies? If so, that seems a recurring theme."

"I don't have confirmation that Major Martin's documents were deliberately planted. For that matter, I have no indication that the map was planted deliberately on the other dead British major, the one in the desert. But it is true that I received such a map, that it was taken from the dead British major, that we used it with catastrophic results, and that it was very coincidental, as was the timing of the Major Martin affair. And this time, with Nimrod, the Brits might have sent us a live gambit."

Rommel took a deep breath as he gazed out over the countryside. "Getting back to the subject of where the invasion will probably take place, in terms of pure simplicity, Calais is a logical choice, and we are right to deploy strong defenses there."

"But you don't agree that Calais is the most likely landing?" Meier asked.

Rommel shook his head. "I don't. I think it's a possibility, but they know we expect the invasion there. They've been probing us since the beginning of the war. They'll look for a place where they perceive weakness."

"Then where do you think it will be?"

"Somme."

"Hmm. Somme. Why there?"

Rommel shrugged. "I believe it'll be somewhere between Dunkirk and the mouth of the Somme River. The Allies have been probing there, so that's where I've been reinforcing the most. We caught two commandos in rubber dinghies there two weeks ago. They were probing the riverbanks. Landing craft can thrust much farther inland, assault both sides of the river, and the main roads are nearby. That area offers the Allies almost the same advantages of Calais without the disadvantage of four years of defensive build-up."

"What about Normandy?"

"Our navy concluded that the sand in Normandy is too soft to support the heavy equipment that must come ashore. My response is that there are ways to overcome that issue. Granted, it's less defended than Calais, and at the western end, Cherbourg has a good port for bringing in reinforcements and supplies. But that's a long stretch of beach—eighty miles. The Allies will need more ports in between Calais and Cherbourg to support sustained operations.

"They'd still have to fight hard to take Normandy. Calais is better defended, but the defenses at Normandy are impressive. Our beach obstacles there will rip open the bottoms of landing craft, and the barbed wire will snag and drown a lot of enemy soldiers and slice open arms and legs of others. Any that survive will run through firestorms of machine guns, mortars, and artillery, and they'll have no cover. And that occurs *after* they've been shelled at sea by shore-based big guns. The Allies will factor all that in and decide that Somme is a better choice. That's what I think.

"We've lost air superiority, so regardless of where they come in, they'll pound our fortifications with naval guns and bombers with impunity before landing, and if the ground forces make it past the beach, their bombers will keep hitting our convoys and facilities from the air."

Meier pondered that, and then asked, "They'll do that at the Somme too."

"Of course, and they've been probing, as I said, but I think the reinforcements we've built there will hold them back." He sighed. "Others in the high command think they'll come in first along the Mediterranean coast." He threw his hands up in the air. "Who really knows? We do the best we can, and the *führer* has put us in the position of having to defend everywhere at once. The Allies are obliging him in that regard."

Rommel suddenly looked tired. "The cold fact is that we must beat them on the beach and prevent a bridgehead, wherever it occurs, or the war is lost."

He swung around with a disgusted shake of his head. "The inverse is probably also true. If we drive the Allies back into the sea, we'll have won in

Europe. We could then consolidate in the countries we still occupy and either concentrate forces for a surgical campaign against Moscow or negotiate peace with the Soviets.

"Our saving grace here in France could be our XII Panzer Group. It's being held in reserve to reinforce wherever the Allies land, but it's stationed up near Calais, under Hitler's personal command. It should be positioned farther south where it could be transferred to other potential invasion sites more easily. If Hitler doesn't release them in time to counterattack—and regardless of his self-indulgent perception of his own military genius, wherever the invasion occurs, without those tanks, we're in a losing position."

"What's the timeframe? When do you think they'll come in?"

"July. The weather will clear by then, and the tides will be better." Rommel gazed at the sun sinking over the horizon. "Hmph. You know the great irony? After all the planning, fighting, strategizing, developing weapons, training and equipping armies, establishing international allies... After all of that, the outcome of the war is likely to turn on information, whether false or true, provided by this obscure blond-haired, blue-eyed Jew and whether he can confirm for a half-crazed narcissist"—he spat out the last word—"that the Allies will attack where Hitler already believes they will."

The two mulled in silence for several minutes. Then Rommel started back toward the stairs. Meier walked alongside him.

"So, sir, what will you do?" Meier asked.

"Do?" Rommel chuckled. "I'll continue the only course available to me since this war began. I'll go to Berlin, state my opinions, which will be discounted, listen to the sycophants agree with the *führer's* edicts, and come back here to fight to the best of my abilities, using my own judgment, to meet the objectives placed in front of me."

"And you'll never pursue the ultimate option?"

Rommel swung in front of Meier, stopping the *generalleutnant* in his tracks. He stared into Meier's eyes, his jaw set. Then he smiled and clapped a hand on Meier's chest. "Never say never, my friend. No one who's come to me has shown me a plan. The 'how' is the challenge."

June 3, 1944
The Berghof, Berchtesgaden, Germany

Someone jostling his shoulder caused Rigby to awaken from a deep sleep, his first in many hours. He was in a room of the guesthouse of the large compound surrounding the Berghof, Hitler's vacation home. He had been flown in early that morning in a Storch from La Roche, accompanied by Mannheim and Arngross, and housed in the facility until further decisions were made about what was to be done with him.

Arngross stood by his shoulder and shook him again. "Wake up," the captain called. "You won't believe the news. The *führer* himself, *Herr* Adolf Hitler, wants to see you. I am ordered to bring you to him."

Rigby sat up, wiping his eyes.

"Did you hear me? We're going to see Adolf Hitler. I can't believe it. I've never been to the Berghof before, and now I'm going to meet the *führer* himself. This is such an honor."

Rigby shook himself fully awake and stared. "Can you imagine what this means to me? I share your pride."

He hurried to dress. He had been offered new clothes but had declined, and so he would appear in a cheap suit and shabby shoes at the chalet that was Hitler's second seat of government. He had been astonished on driving into the complex at the enormous size of the *führer's* getaway near Obersalzberg and Berchtesgaden. Situated in the scenic Bavarian Alps with its forested slopes and snow-covered peaks, this was Hitler's favorite of his twelve headquarters scattered across Germany, France, and the occupied countries. He had spent more time here than in Berlin. Only the *Wolfsschanze*, his "Wolf's Lair" headquarters in East Prussia, occupied as much of his time.

The expansive compound built behind the Berghof for its protection could intimidate enemies with less than stout hearts. The road entering the area passed by a large barracks for an *SS* contingent permanently assigned to patrol a cordoned security zone that encompassed the Berghof as well as nearby palatial chalets belonging to ministers of the Third *Reich*. A neighboring hotel, the Türken, had been converted into housing for a special section of the *SS* that patrolled the Berghof itself. In addition, across the road was another barracks for the *Führerbegleitkommando*, those soldiers brought there when Hitler was in residence, to provide personal security inside his house and wherever he went.

In addition to those facilities, as Rigby and Arngross were driven through the complex, Rigby observed anti-aircraft positions as well as large vegetable and flower gardens, motor pools with maintenance garages, an antenna-studded communications center, and other facilities required to support this second center of Nazi power. He stared out the window of the sedan at the serene green mountains across the valley, struck by the irony of such tranquility surrounding this imposing complex.

"To even get into the Berghof," Arngross whispered to Rigby as the sedan wound deeper into the compound, "a special pass must be issued on an individual basis. The highest-ranking field marshal or minister can't gain entry based on his usual government credentials. He must have a special pass. Few get them." His eyes lit up with enthusiasm. "And we have them."

The cold mountain air was clear when they stepped from the sedan, and the sun shone brightly, casting sharp shadows at a set of great granite stairs. Rigby recognized them from press photos of Neville Chamberlain's infamous visit with Hitler in an attempt to regain "peace in our time." A stone-faced lieutenant gestured toward the top of the stairs. Mannheim stood there, his expression implacable. With him were two soldiers, obviously a security escort.

Joined by Arngross, the group of five set off through the great house, drawing curious glances, some disapproving ones from puffed-up personages busily striding by and taking second glimpses at Rigby's disheveled clothes and worn shoes. As they passed through the wide halls with the varied scents of flowers, polished leather, and natural wood finishes, Rigby observed the walls, bedecked with large oil paintings of chivalric events and naked ladies, and steepled ceilings with oak rafters. His escorts' boots clicked on the stone floors as they strode rapidly through the rooms, and Rigby noticed that the sentries, smartly uniformed at every door, bore "Adolf Hitler" embroidered on their left sleeves.

The group approached a large door, and from the other side, Rigby heard the high-pitched, angry voice he had heard so many times ranting over the BBC about the actions of Germany's enemies. Coming through the thick walls, he could not understand what was said, but the fury in the *führer's* voice was undeniable.

Rigby's scalp suddenly felt cool, his nerves tingled. He quietly took deep breaths to maintain calm and stem the blood rushing from his face.

A sentry at the entrance made eye contact with Mannheim, then opened the door and allowed the group to pass through before closing it again.

Hitler's tirade ceased. The room was suddenly quiet.

At the other end of the giant hall, Rigby recognized a large picture window he had seen in photographs of the Berghof's interior. Beyond it was reportedly one of Hitler's favorite views, the grandeur of the Bavarian Alps. However, it was now cloaked with heavy drapes, the room being lit artificially.

Taking a quick glance around, Rigby saw faces he knew from newspaper reports: *Reichsfuhrer* Göring, *Luftwaffe* chief and Hitler's chosen successor; Field Marshal Wilhelm Keitel, Chief of High Command of all German Armed Forces; Colonel-General Alfred Jodl, Hitler's Chief of Operations; Field Marshal Erwin Rommel, commanding general of Army Group B; *Generalfeldmarschall* Gerd von Runstedt, Commander in Chief West; and General Kurt Zeitzler, the Army Chief of Staff. Other officers of possibly equal stature but whom Rigby did not recognize stood with legs apart, their hands behind their backs. All of them were gathered around a large map table. Grouped behind them were senior officers of lesser rank.

On the opposite side of the table, standing by the single chair in the room and flanked by Jodl and Keitel, was Adolf Hitler himself.

The *führer's* most notable and famous feature was impossible to miss, and Rigby found himself resisting the urge to stare at the small, square patch of whiskers above Hitler's upper lip. The man's intense eyes below the lock of hair that so often fell across his forehead bored into Rigby. The Nazi leader looked older in person than he had in news clips and even in recent photographs. His face was lined with creases, his hair was grayer, and he was bent slightly. Then again, Rigby reminded himself, Hitler had been leaning on the table when the group entered.

Rigby stood at attention as he had during commando training in Scotland, his thumbs aligned along the seams of his trousers. Ignoring the sense of all eyes in the room staring at him, he kept his own locked on Hitler's.

Arngross stepped forward and lifted his arm in a crisp Nazi salute. "*Hauptman* Arngross, *Mein Führer*," he announced, and indicated Rigby. "This is Nimrod, the agent sent here from our intelligence source in England, *Herr* Weber."

Hitler lifted his forearm in a perfunctory salute and shifted his eyes to Rigby. "You have pertinent information about the Allies' planned invasion? How did British intelligence allow you to leave England with it?"

"I didn't ask permission, sir. My degree is in wireless communications engineering. The French Resistance near Paris needed assistance with their radio communications, and I was qualified to help. I offered my services on the chance that they would send me and I could bring this information to you, *Mein Führer*."

"You took a grave risk. What is your name?"

"My codename is Nimrod, sir. My real name is Stefan Rosenberg."

"What information do you have for me?"

Rigby stood motionless. He started to speak but found his mouth suddenly dry. "May I have some water?" he rasped.

"Of course." Hitler turned irritably to glare at one of his senior aides, but a colonel was already rushing to get some water.

"I apologize, *Mein Führer*," Rigby managed. "This has been a long trip. I've been interviewed quite a lot already, and my voice is going."

"Take your time."

The water arrived, and Rigby drank deeply. As he did, thoughts of Hitler crossed his mind, this man standing only feet away who had influenced the lives of millions, whose armies had fought in far-off places at his command. Submarines lurked below the oceans and great warships had deployed because he had ordered them to do so.

As he drank the last drop, Rigby heard Mannheim say, "The *führer* is waiting."

He nodded. When he spoke again, his voice had gained resonance. He looked squarely into Hitler's eyes. "I came, sir, to inform you that the main Allied attack will launch from the south and east coasts of England to

Calais. I've delivered reams of evidence to your generals, advisers, and intelligence professionals to support that conclusion. In my estimation, having been there and seen it for myself, I think the conclusion is irrefutable."

Hitler stared at him. Then he straightened and gazed around at his generals with an exultant look. "You see, gentlemen, I was right."

He faced Rigby again eagerly. "Some of my colleagues consider Calais too heavily fortified for the Allies to attack. What do you say about that?"

'Mein Führer, the Allied High Command has watched the construction of fortified Calais for over four years. They believe they have air superiority, and that with an overwhelming aerial bombardment supported by heavy naval barrages, they can soften our defenses enough to allow an amphibious assault."

"Some of those walls are thirty feet thick," someone called. "Their bombs would not destroy all of our defenses, and we'd still hit their landing forces hard."

"They're also counting on the effect of the men manning the guns on this side of the Channel," Rigby replied. "Those soldiers would absorb the impact, the explosions of falling bombs and naval artillery as well as the concussion that comes with firing our own weapons. Those effects could shatter the minds and nerves of our men." He added, "They could also be blinded and disoriented.

"The Allies point to how our *Wehrmacht* sliced through the Maginot Line at the beginning of the war. They believe they could penetrate the Atlantic Wall. They also point out that Dover to Calais is the easiest supply route because it's the shortest distance. They believe the roads and railways into Brighton on the British side with ports in the southeast are sufficient for sending over war materiel and other cargo. Calais is also the nearest big French port to the German frontier. They'd have less distance to cover to get to our border. If they attack anywhere else, they'll have a long slog all across France."

"What about Cherbourg? Or Normandy? Biscay? Or the Mediterranean?"

"There could be subsidiary landings at Cherbourg, and possibly at other locations along the coast, even diversions. I don't know about the last two locations you mentioned. I've neither seen nor heard anything on them one way or the other."

Keitel broke in. "Do you know where they'll strike first?"

Rigby shook his head. "They'll execute one or more of their diversionary landings first—at least that's the information I have. They want to draw our forces away from Calais, and then strike there."

Hitler listened intently, and then stared around at his senior officers with a triumphant gleam in his eyes. "I've been listening to you, my generals, all this afternoon, telling me your opinions. I no longer have time to listen to opinion. Facts are facts, and those delivered by this young man support what I've been telling you all along. He's shown remarkable bravery in bringing them to us. Do you have questions for him?"

The room remained silent, permeating with the sense that further discussion was useless and potentially perilous. The führer's gleaming eyes and set jaw spoke volumes. His mind was made up.

Hitler turned to Rigby. "On behalf of the German people and my staff, thank you for your courage in coming to us with your information and analysis."

Rigby clicked his heels smartly. Arngross saluted. They bowed and left the room.

38

June 4, 1944
Bletchley Park, England

Claire hurried to Travis' office and knocked rapidly on his door. Hearing the commander call out to her, she entered and rushed to her regular seat. "Sir, we've received messages regarding Nimrod."

Travis looked at her in surprise. "It must be important. I've never seen you quite so urgent. You're almost breathless. Let's hear it."

"Yes, sir." Claire inhaled and leaned forward. "The German High Command is confused over whose agent Nimrod is, ours or theirs. They've had messages going back and forth between the Berghof in Berchtesgaden and several agents they have here in England. They've gone so far as to check out Nimrod's physical appearance, his military experience, his educational background, and his family history.

"So far, they are satisfied that the information he's given has been independently confirmed. However, there is some concern that his information is too pat and the timing suspicious. Rommel, in particular, is not persuaded that Nimrod is genuine. He argues for the release of the XII Panzer Group from Hitler's personal command to be positioned farther south for transfer to reinforce wherever our invasion occurs. He hasn't said so in these messages, but my sense is that he thinks Nimrod is a plant sent there to buttress what we know to be Hitler's position, that the invasion will occur at Calais.

"But here's the most intriguing part, sir. Yesterday, Nimrod was escorted inside the Berghof for an audience with Hitler."

Travis sat forward, stunned. "Are you serious? Do we know the outcome of that?"

"No, sir, we do not. A little while ago, we received a summary of the issues in a message between Rommel and a fellow general, but he was silent on the meeting itself, only stating that it had taken place."

"God help us," Travis breathed. "Do we know where Nimrod is now?"

"He flew back last night to La Roche on board Rommel's Storch. There's some talk of taking him to the Paris or Berlin *Abwehr* headquarters for further meetings."

"By 'further meetings,' I take that to mean in-depth interrogations using unsavory methods," Travis said. "Interesting, though I don't know what to make of it. Thank you, Miss Littlefield. That will be all."

Claire started to leave. Then she turned back. "May I ask a question? It's not my place I realize, sir, but just this once my curiosity is getting the best of me."

Travis smiled. "Just this once, Miss Littlefield, we can allow a bit of impertinence. But I'll anticipate and answer your question. Is Nimrod an Allied or a German agent?" He leaned back and took a deep breath. "I haven't a clue."

La Roche Guyon, France

The doorknob to Rigby's room twisted, and Arngross appeared, smiling and ebullient. "Good news," he enthused. "Your presentation to the *führer* was a smashing success. Everyone at high levels is talking about it. Paris and Berlin both want you brought for further consultation." He paused and observed Rigby appraisingly. "Anyone can see that you're exhausted. We're to allow you to rest up, and then in two or three days, we're to bring you first to Paris, and then to Berlin."

Rigby smiled. "I'm happy to have been of service, but is it possible to get out on the town for a while. I'm cooped up here under lock and key. I need fresh air and to stretch my legs. My door is always locked."

"I'll see what I can do. Your door is locked for the same reason that we have guards standing outside of it and along the passageways leading up here. You're a known entity now. Allied agents could be anywhere, and the French Resistance is searching for you. We must protect you."

Rigby sighed. "I understand that, and I'm appreciative. It's just that— well, I'm going a little bonkers. Cabin fever."

When Arngross left, locking the door behind him, Rigby closed his eyes and took a deep breath. Clearly, he was not trusted by the men, aside from Hitler, whom he had addressed.

Worse still, he was a prisoner. Paris? Berlin? He saw nothing good coming from that prospect. If the invasion did not go reasonably similar to what he had indicated, or if a successful Allied invasion materialized anywhere other than Calais, a scapegoat would be needed. He would be tortured into a confession of whatever the *Abwehr*, the *Gestapo*, and/or the German High Command needed for him to say.

He saw only one alternative. He must escape.

39

London, England

General Pierre Koenig, Commander-in-Chief of *les Forces françaises de l'intérieur*, known colloquially as the Free French, the Secret Army, or the FFI, reacted in surprise when his secretary announced that two unexpected visitors were on their way to see him. He thought perhaps they were dropping in to wish him well in his new assignment. He had only received his appointment and settled into his London headquarters on Duke Street four days earlier, and he still lacked final confirmation of his command.

He was a fit man, one who had seen the worst of battle and had remained faithful to those he commanded. Tall with a thin face, he had a high forehead and sported a mustache. He was also a bona fide French hero from the North Africa campaign, having held off, with ten thousand men, constant attacks by two of General Rommel's Afrika Korps divisions for three weeks in the desert at Bir-Hakeim. Near the point of desperation when he had only twenty-two rounds of small-arms ammunition remaining for his entire unit, he had led his beleaguered soldiers through a seam between German units at night, and brought them safely behind British lines. The feat had been heralded throughout French forces, elevating Koenig as a symbol of the French tenacity and courage that would lead to victory. He was a man whom the Free French would gladly follow into battle.

He wondered as he waited what could be so important that these two particular gentlemen would visit him together, almost unannounced. Given their stature, however, he could not refuse. They entered several minutes later, one American and one Brit, both senior officers and both well known within Anglo-American senior ranks. The secretary showed them in. "General Gubbins and Colonel Bruce are here to see you."

Koenig welcomed them and led them to a seating area near a window across the room from his desk. "This is a surprise," he said, and after niceties, he asked, "How can I help you?"

General Colin Gubbins, head of Britain's SOE, spoke first. He was a big, no-nonsense man with straight hair combed against his scalp and a well-manicured mustache. "We need to clarify some confusion over the coming invasions and supporting activities. You understand that the one planned for France's southern coast is postponed?"

"Of course. I've been briefed that Operation Overlord in the north absorbed all available resources in the European Theater and that the southern one, Operation Anvil in Provence, will follow in a few months."

"Correct," Gubbins replied. "You know too, I'm sure, that this war is being won by guile as well as by kinetic force."

Koenig frowned. "If by 'guile' you mean the deceptive methods used to fool and confuse the enemy, I'm aware of what was done in Africa." He laughed. "General Patton is doing a masterful job of commanding a ghost army around Dover while keeping the *Wehrmacht* pinned down across at Calais."

"He is," Colonel David Bruce, chief of the European branch of the US Office of Strategic Services, or OSS, interjected. Slender, clean-shaven, and with serious eyes, the colonel reflected a quiet, thoughtful personality. "The Germans know Patton as America's best field commander. As long as he's seen to build up forces that threaten northern France, they'll continue to reinforce there."

"And the plan seems to be working," Koenig said. He turned to Gubbins. "Our Resistance groups, the *Maquis*, are prepared to sabotage railroads, bridges, power stations, military facilities all across northern France.

They've already done some of that, but will do more on D-Day and there-after. Frenchmen are pleased to do our part, and your SOE agents have trained them well. When Operation Dragoon unleashes in Provence, you'll find our people there equally prepared."

He returned his attention to Bruce. "And now with American help, more of them will be trained and fighting with us."

He shifted to address both officers. "I'm particularly pleased that we'll have teams composed of members from each of our countries. That should enhance effectiveness." He added with an air of resoluteness, "When General Eisenhower gives the order to execute, he'll find us ready."

"That's good news," Gubbins said, "and we never doubted that was the case. You've personally exhibited the French fighting spirit, and most effec-tively, I might add."

Koenig accepted the compliment with a nod. "Thank you. I did my duty."

"As we all must," Gubbins replied with a sigh, "and for soldiers, that is often unpleasant. You stated that your people are prepared to support Overlord on D-Day."

"Of course," Koenig said, concerned. "But you know that. Are we lacking in some way?"

Gubbins shook his head. "No. They've prepared well. The sabotage they've carried out is remarkable, and the intelligence they've provided is invaluable."

"Then how—"

Gubbins raised his hand to interrupt. "I'll explain. I'm sure you know the concept whereby, in order to deceive the enemy fully, we must not only make him believe we are not going to do a certain thing, but we must also convince him that we plan to do the opposite of our actual intention."

Koenig nodded, looking perplexed. "Isn't that what we're doing?"

"Not to full effect," Gubbins replied, arching his brows. "So far, we seem to have convinced the Germans that our cross-Channel invasion will be in northern France."

"Agreed."

"They must continue to believe that through D-Day and beyond. Right now, they believe we'll also come along the southern shore at Provence on the same day. If we don't continue that deception after the landings begin, they'll quickly reassess and transfer divisions out of Provence to reinforce in the north."

Koenig held Gubbins' steady gaze as understanding dawned on him and his face drained of color. "You want me to activate our Resistance forces in the south too? They train around the clock, but they don't have adequate weapons. They've requested them, even heatedly and repeatedly. If they attack and the Germans strike back, they'll be cannon fodder. It'll be a massacre."

"Nevertheless, it must be done. The Germans must be led to believe that an amphibious invasion will occur on the Mediterranean coast in Provence simultaneous with the one in northern France. Our chaps there will need as much time as possible to establish a bridgehead."

Koenig folded his arms and exhaled. His eyes narrowed. "You're ordering me to deceive my people and knowingly sacrifice them. I am to lead them to believe that arms are coming when they are not and order them to activate and carry out sabotage raids to support an invasion that won't occur, in which case many will be sacrificed."

"That is correct, sir." Gubbins took a deep breath. "The order comes from the Supreme Allied Commander."

"Eisenhower?" Koenig sat in stone-cold silence for several moments. "Does he understand that the Resistance, the *Maquis*, is mainly made up of civilians, and that among them are many women?" He rubbed his temples with both hands, the strain showing on his face. "In better times, we would think of many of these fighters as boys and girls."

"I understand that, General, I assure you," Gubbins replied softly. "And I don't envy your task. You might consider the useless casualties that would occur at sea and in France should the northern invasion fail. That's small compensation, but it might help ease your mind—"

"Easing my mind has nothing to do with it," Koenig retorted, his voice sharp and clear. He sprang to his feet and paced across to the window where he stood staring out. "You, our allies, don't trust us with either the time or place of the operation, yet you come in here and order me to sacrifice my people.

"German retribution will follow whatever the Resistance does, you know that. Whether I do or don't go along with this order conjured in hell, we are talking about the lives of men, women, and children. I'm left to choose which ones to sacrifice."

Gubbins watched him with a somber look. "It's a decision that generals face often. Those on the side of evil initiate the actions; those on the side of good answer them. But answer them we must."

Koenig snorted angrily, almost derisively. "Spare me the platitudes."

Gubbins stood with a glance at Bruce, who also rose to his feet. "There is another element that I must mention." The general inhaled deeply. "A storm is blowing over the Channel, which means that our troops are likely to wade ashore in high waves, gale force winds, and heavy rain. They'll need every minute we can give them. Let us know your answer quickly. We need to know that we can count on you all across France. Overlord launches within hours." The two visitors headed toward the door. "We'll show ourselves out."

"General," Koenig called as Gubbins reached for the handle. His voice shook with emotion. "Tell General Eisenhower that it shall be done. I have a request, though. Let me know that I'll be able to withdraw the *Maquis* in the south from combat at the earliest possible moment. They'll need a chance to escape back into the mountains."

"Of course," Gubbins replied. "We need only a few days."

40

June 5, 1944
Lyon, France

Despite appearances of light conversation, a discussion between two men taking a leisurely stroll along the Rue du Plat was one with far-reaching implications for the Vercors and the fight to rid France and Europe of their Nazi oppressor. However, one of the men, Eugène Chavant, could barely contain his exhilaration.

He was a robust man, approaching six feet and just past fifty years of age, with a high forehead, thick white hair, and a chiseled face bearing a mustache. Born in Grenoble and a decorated veteran of World War I, he had joined the Resistance almost as soon as the new war began, and he had gravitated to the Vercors for its unique topographical advantages, which afforded freedom of movement. Very quickly, due to his ability to be equally at home in a business suit or the rough garb of the high plateau, he had become the undisputed civil leader among a population that held its freedom dear and was willing to fight for it.

His companion on this promenade, Colonel Descour, was the Region 1 commander of the Free French Secret Army. Walking in the streets was the colonel's preferred method of conducting clandestine meetings, as he had learned of too many "secret" conferences held in Lyon during which the *Gestapo* or the *SS* had suddenly broken through doors and arrested everyone present.

Dressed in civilian clothes, walking among crowds, and appearing intent on nothing, Descour found that he could talk about anything so long as he kept his voice to a moderate volume and appeared neither too intense nor emotional. Of course, he had to ignore the blood-red swastika-emblazoned banners posted seemingly everywhere along the thoroughfares and the armed patrols mixing among the pedestrians.

Descour was a lean man of courteous countenance and average size, and he moved through the pedestrian traffic easily, matching its ebb and flow, stopping periodically in front of store windows or taking an interest in some random object, using those moments to check for anyone appearing to follow. On this afternoon, he encountered some difficulty in containing Chavant's eagerness. "So, you've just come from Algiers? Was it a good trip?"

"It was," Chavant said, barely able to keep his voice from matching his elation. "I suppose you've heard about Rome? General Clark and his Fifth Army entered today. The city is now free of the Nazis. Maybe that's a harbinger of good things to come in France."

"That is excellent news," Descour agreed. "Tell me about your trip."

Chavant grinned. "They listened to me, Colonel. Do you believe it? Me, a restaurateur from the Vercors plateau. I didn't think they'd take me seriously."

"And why not? We're all in the same fight. You're the chosen leader of your people. You should be heard."

Chavant beamed. "Let me tell you, a patrol of four US Navy motor-launches picked me up off our southern coast at Cap Camarat near Saint-Tropez. They sent a dinghy to bring me from the beach, and then they ferried me to Bastia in Corsica, where a plane was waiting for *me*. I still can't believe it. It flew right into Maison-Blanche Airport in Algiers, and I was escorted straight away to Free French army headquarters.

"I had to pinch myself. The offices were in an ancient Arab palace overlooking the casbah." He laughed heartily and then paused, a wide smile crossing his face, his eyes bright from reliving the experience.

Descour patted his back. "That's good, but be a little calmer. Remember where you are." He gestured toward a patrol of four German soldiers strolling past them in the opposite direction.

"Of course." Chavant took a deep breath. "My first meeting was with Colonel Jean Constans, and I pointed out the Vercors' strategic position on a map. I explained our ability to be self-reliant and the way we can block the passes; how we can operate as a base to attack from the German rear. I explained to him and his staff that hundreds of *maquisards* live in more than thirty camps at the Vercors, training hard to join our French army to take back our beloved country. And I reminded them that Moulin himself had approved the project.

"I suddenly found them taking me seriously, and I was asked to repeat my briefing at more meetings. At each one, they treated me with greater and greater respect, and I saw them become enthusiastic, even calling it Operation Montagnard as opposed to just Plan Montagnard.

"I did not meet with de Gaulle. I'm not sure he was even there. But I met with Soustelle, his chief of staff, and went through everything again. He left the room for a few minutes, and when he came back, he gave me this order." He handed a document to Descour, who read it and handed it back.

"This is wonderful news," the colonel said. "And I have some for you as well. I've found a new military commander for the ex-army veterans and the *maquisards* camped at the Vercors. He knows the plateau and your surrounding mountains very well."

"What's his name?"

"Major Francis Huet."

"I think I've heard of him before, but I don't know him."

"He's combat experienced, and his personality will be good for dealing with both the veterans and the civilian *maquisards*. He'll also work well with the SOE agents, Roger and Labrador."

"Will he be Geyer's boss?" Chavant growled.

Descour chuckled. "Technically, yes—"

"What do you mean 'technically?'"

"Chavant," Descour scolded mildly. "Geyer is fighting our war, the same as you."

"But he's arrogant and insolent, and he thinks he's better than our civilians."

"And he's an effective fighter. Huet can handle him. I'm bringing him in, technically to command, but more diplomatically, to liaise between you and Geyer. We need to be sure that we're getting the best from our old soldiers and our civilians. Huet will also oversee Captain Beauregard in the northern part of the Vercors."

Chavant remained unconvinced. "I'll keep an open mind, but I don't like Geyer."

"Eugène," Descour remonstrated, "you've received an order from the Secret Army. It supports you and Operation Montagnard. Be happy. Major Huet will be there tomorrow."

"Good. I'll arrive back in the Vercors the next day. I'll see him then."

Autrans-en-Vercors, France

Major Huet climbed down from the bus that had brought him from Grenoble to this northernmost town within the Vercors Massif and looked around at the beauty he had known from vacationing there regularly with his family since childhood. Set in a wide valley rimmed with forests on rolling foothills and steep escarpments, and irrigated by the clear water of melting late-spring snow, the area was lush with green farmland speckled by wildflowers of every color and variety.

Huet took only a moment to savor the scenery and the familial memories as he set out to climb up the slope of *la Montagne de la Molière* to a shepherd's barn at Plenouse. There, he found Captain Roland Beauregard training his men on the side of the mountain with expansive views across the verdant, spacious valley.

Beauregard was a big, wide-faced man with an equally broad smile. He wore a black beret that appeared glued to his head and which he seldom removed.

Huet having arrived unexpectedly, the captain was somewhat embarrassed by the state of the men under his command; only thirty-five of them were present, and only seven had weapons. They were a gangly lot, *maquisards* all, eager to fight, but thin, unshaven, wearing unwashed civilian clothes, and with no military training aside from what Beauregard had taught them since his recent arrival. Hence, no military discipline. Nevertheless, the good captain lined them as best he could, and the seven with rifles presented arms.

Dismayed at the forces arrayed before him who were to defend the passes in the northern sector of the Vercors, Huet nevertheless passed in front of and inspected each man, inquiring about home and family; and when he had finished, he stood at attention in front of the motley formation and saluted.

"The men like and respect you," he told Beauregard later as the two strolled in the vicinity of the barn.

"I like to think so, sir," came the reply. "They're not soldiers and don't want to be. They're here because the country is under occupation, and they'll train and fight willingly. But they don't want to be paraded—"

"I understand. Quite the opposite of Geyer and his unit, I gather."

"Have you met him yet?"

"Just once. I've a vague memory of him. I'll look forward to meeting him, probably tomorrow."

"He's an interesting fellow," Beauregard continued. "Very military, a cavalryman, and very much a man of his own mind. He and Chavant don't like each other. It's the chasm between military and civilian methods that causes the friction. My entire command is civilian, and if we hope to win, we will have to employ military methods. I try to keep that in mind and keep a foot in both camps, military and civilian." He chuckled. "We *do* have a machine gun."

Below them on a flat area, the men practiced maneuver procedures developed to cover each other alternately as they proceeded into combat. "They seem to get the basics," Huet observed.

"They throw their hearts into it," the captain replied.

"Are these all the men you have?"

Beauregard shook his head. "They're all that we can support in the camp. The others have regular jobs and live with their families. They come to us on weekends, or when we have missions, like a patrol, and then go home afterward."

Huet considered the concept. "If it's working, that's fine. We must train them hard to be as efficient as possible. We owe it to them. German bullets won't consider that they're civilians." He looked across the mountains and the valley below. "Have you met this Englishman, Roger?"

"I have. He works hard to get our *Maquis* what we need. He has a deputy, Labrador, who's equally dedicated. They've been up here to teach the men where and how to place demolitions for best effect on locomotives, power junction boxes, bridge critical points, and the like. Labrador is a veteran of Saint-Nazaire, and knows what he's doing." Beauregard sighed. "I've seen both men frustrated that we haven't received the heavy guns and ammunition we've been promised, but it's not for their lack of trying."

Huet furrowed his eyebrows. "That's a concern, a major one. If the Germans attack in force, we'll be hard-pressed to keep the passes closed."

Saint-Martin-en-Vercors, France

As midnight approached, Marcel Chapuis, Chavant's man in charge of wireless communications across Vercors, sat listening closely to messages broadcast by the BBC. They seemed innocuous, but their significance was intended for disparate audiences. A phrase like "Janice has her birthday today" might order a *Maquis* group to blow up a certain bridge in Brittany. Similarly, "Peter took his dog to the vet today" might send another group to sabotage a power station in northern France, and so on.

As the hour approached midnight, the transmission became garbled, and the number of messages was long, approaching seventy. But Marcel was certain that he heard, "The chamois leaps from the mountains."

He wrote it down, barely containing his excitement, and read it again as he compared it against his notebook of messages to listen for. "The chamois leaps from the mountains," he intoned out loud as he sat alone in a shed behind his house with his illegal wireless.

He panted now, and burst through the shed door into the night looking for anyone to tell that the order to activate Operation Montagnard had been received. He found his wife half asleep in the bedroom, but when she heard the news, she pulled herself out of bed, threw on a robe, and the two danced around in the kitchen.

"I must go spread the word," Marcel told her. His face broke into a grin. "Chavant is not back yet from Algiers, but I must tell the others."

His wife threw her arms around his neck. "*Bonne chance*," she said. "I'm so proud of you. You were the first to know."

"And you were the second," he said, laughing happily while he kissed her.

41

D-Day Minus 1; H-Hour Minus 7.5
Saint-Brieuc, Brittany, France

Jean Monmousseaux, codenamed Faucon, shook Lance awake. "It's time," he whispered excitedly. "We received the BBC message."

Lance whipped the sheets off, leaped out of bed, grabbed his trousers, and pulled them on. "I'm ready."

When he was fully dressed, the two grabbed their Sten guns and equipment bags and stole out into the night. They had come to this house, the home of Faucon's cousin who was also active in the Resistance, earlier in the day. The three of them had scouted their area of interest during the day, re-visited it after dark, and now with mission execution less than an hour away, their excitement over what it portended approached uncontrollable levels.

After Lance had collapsed at Milàn and Angeline's farm near Henriville, the couple had revived and fed him, and then, with friends, they had smuggled him south to Faucon's vineyard outside of Montrichard. The trip took several days as Lance was hidden under straw on farm trucks or in tiny concealed compartments in cars and utility vehicles.

The journey, tortuous as it was, had been worthwhile. Having just escaped Colditz, Lance found that the destination provided a sense of freedom with a touch of irony resulting from Germany's continued occupation of France, particularly under heightened security measures stemming from invasion fears.

Faucon had been thrilled to see Lance again. His vineyard was the place where the Resistance had brought Lance on his last escape. Both Jeremy and Horton had also worked there with him at earlier times. The two brothers and the sergeant had formed lasting friendships with Faucon.

Son of a vineyard owner of regional repute, Faucon had taken over much of the family business by the time of the German occupation. Square-faced with rugged features and thick hair, and still in his mid-twenties, he was tall and muscular, and bore himself with quiet confidence.

Despite his young age, he was a veteran of the Phoney War preceding the evacuation at Dunkirk. On returning home, he had downplayed his military experience to the extent that his father was unaware of his Resistance activities; but Faucon had used his resources to build an organization in the Loire Valley, going so far as to take apart and reassemble whole wine barrels with a person inside each one to be smuggled through checkpoints, across borders, or wherever else the person was needed. He smuggled arms and explosives the same way.

After Lance's arrival, Faucon told him, "I'm leaving in three weeks to join an active group at a farm near Vannes."

"Why not stay to fight here around Montrichard?"

Faucon shook his head. "This is vineyard country. The Germans love to steal our wine, but the hot war will start along the coast. The farm there is a little way inland from Vannes, but it's in an area with thick vegetation that's hard to get through, so the Germans don't bother. It's located where we can shift to Normandy or the Morbihan coast, depending on where the landing takes place. A lot of my *maquisards* are going there. Around two thousand *résistants* are there already. The Allies need us to sabotage key targets just before the invasion, to block German troop movements. I'm going to be part of that. I can help you get back home—"

"I'm staying in France," Lance interrupted. He grinned. "Could you use a fighter with a talent for getting caught?"

Incredulous, Faucon stared at him, and then laughed. "And an equal talent for escape." He scratched his head. "We could have a British commando fighting with us?"

"The invasion's coming," Lance replied. "We know that much. I could spend several months trying to get home only to be killed along the way. Even if I succeed, I might get sent right back to France. I might as well stay and make myself useful."

Faucon clasped Lance's hand. "Welcome, brother."

In the subsequent weeks, Lance had rested, and Faucon had taken pains to provide food for him. Although still recovering from the depravations of Colditz, Lance looked less haggard. The two men had been welcomed at Monsieur Pondard's farm, La Mouette, in the Malestroit region. There, they helped train *maquisards* in ground tactics, shooting, hand-to-hand combat, and demolitions. Lance found himself constantly amazed at the young men's spirit and determination to learn despite inadequate supplies, and he grew to be an accepted adviser.

Early on the day that Lance and Faucon left La Mouette, the Secret Army's Major Morice, who commanded the *Maquis* group there, called the two men to a briefing at the farmhouse. Despite his small size and pencil mustache, Morice carried himself with natural military bearing. He had already brewed coffee when the pair arrived.

"I'll be brief," he began, addressing his comments to Faucon. "I can't tell you much beyond that we have two similar operations going on in opposite directions, and more coming in." He smiled. "I suspect, but don't know for sure, that our time of waiting is over. You'll receive a drop of eighteen French commandos tonight at Saint-Brieuc. Take your weapons and explosives with you. You'll take further direction from their leader." He chuckled. "I'm quite sure that you'll be hitting demolition targets by this time tomorrow."

Faucon's eyes shone bright. "It's on?" he demanded, barely able to contain his enthusiasm. "The invasion is on, and with French commandos?"

The major smiled. "I can't confirm that. I'm assigning missions as I receive them."

"But it's thrilling to think of French soldiers coming to liberate France."

"It is," Morice agreed. "Your drop will take place shortly after midnight. It should be at 00:30 hours, to be specific, but you know how that goes. Here are your coordinates." He handed Faucon a slip of paper. "I've also written down the phrase to listen for over the BBC letting you know that your mission will execute."

He turned to Lance. "Faucon needs no adviser—"

"You think I should stay here, at the farm, while this is going on?" Lance shook his head. "Respectfully no, sir, that won't happen. I'm going. I'll obey Faucon's orders."

Morice chuckled. "I thought you might, which is why I called you both in."

Cold wind blew and rain drizzled as Lance and Faucon stole into the night. They rendezvoused with twenty *maquisards* who gathered by twos and threes around a field outside Saint-Brieuc. The summer's full moon hid behind thick layers of clouds as the wind and rain continued.

Faucon had some of the best and most experienced *maquisards* in his group. Among them were veterans of raids, sabotage missions, assassinations, prisoner rescues—most importantly, they had survived and grown in skill. They needed little guidance to understand and execute their individual tasks. He had assigned them specific duties for the mission: four men to shine flashlights into the sky to identify the drop zone, its length, and breadth for the pilots; one to flash a red light to mark the end of the field for making the drop; and eight to watch for, track, and retrieve the commandos as they descended. The rest of the men would station around the drop zone to provide security and intercept any of the commandos who might have missed their reception committees and sought to leave the field.

Despite the weather, Lance could not quell his elation. After all that he had endured in the aftermath of the Dunkirk debacle, the thought of participating in this great military operation, launched to free a continent, was all but over-whelming. The odds against his being there were astounding, yet there he was, near a French coast, expecting that Allied forces would soon come ashore.

The wind died a bit, but the rain continued. Lance sensed that the Allies approached a now-or-never moment. He had no doubt that the date had been chosen partly for the phase of the moon so that pilots could iden-tify their targets, soldiers could see obstacles, and commandos could antici-pate ground contact. But the weather had not cooperated. Storms had prevailed across the Channel for several days, blocking out the moon, and they had abated only late in the day that had just ended.

The concept of assembling a fighting force of men, equipment, and the navies to transport them across that rough stretch of violent sea, setting them on shore with the initial and follow-on logistics to support an amphibious assault, and sustaining an inland invasion, all of that in the face of blistering enemy fire, boggled the mind. Lance imagined soldiers and commandos hunkered down in their landing craft, and paratroopers preparing to leap into a dark, stormy sky over enemy territory bristling with guns. He thought suddenly that nothing he had faced could compare with those terrifying propositions.

The drone of aircraft broke his reverie. Cupping his ears, he listened to the roar of a vast armada of B-17 Flying Fortress bombers approaching from the north and continuing into France's interior. Similar raids had occurred nightly for months. Obviously, too many of them flew too high to be carrying this mission's paratroopers. They were on their way to bombing missions farther inland.

The drone of aircraft faded, but before they were fully gone, another engine sounded, again from the west. Lance stood to listen, recognizing that a single plane flew low toward their field. At midpoints along the field's length, he barely made out the dim glow of shielded lights aiming toward the aircraft. At the end of the pasture, the red light blinked, indicating the point over which the commandos should jump.

The C-53 Skytrooper circled into the wind and dropped to a low altitude.

As Lance searched the heavens following the engines' noise, he made out a dark blot against the inky sky. It traversed the field, and when it reached the end where the red light was, it began to climb.

Lance continued his search of the dark clouds above the field and picked out multiple small, dark blotches falling to earth. They plunged rapidly, and then suddenly slowed in their descent. He listened, and heard the quiet *whoosh* of parachutes opening and muffled impacts against the ground. Then he saw shadowy figures running about the field collapsing canopies and collecting gear, and he heard low recognition whistles just before commandos met up with guides.

Several minutes later, at the rally point, he greeted the commander of the first of the French commando teams, Lieutenant Charles Deschamps, escorted by one of the *maquisards*. Faucon soon joined them with Lieutenant André Botella, and shortly after that two *maquisards* brought in the commando teams' senior sergeants, Henri Stéphan and Alfred Litzler. The latter two reported to their officers that all men and equipment had landed safely and were accounted for.

"Greetings," Faucon enthused in a low voice. "We're thrilled to see you." He indicated the townspeople, gathered with his cousin at the edge of the field with their farm and utility trucks and vans. "They will take us to a safe place to coordinate."

A celebration in a barn well away from the drop zone was cut short by Lieutenant Botella. The villagers remained in their trucks outside the barn, but their excitement too was palpable. They sensed that an enormous event was about to unfold.

"Thank you for the warm welcome," Botella told the gathered *maquisards* while the commandos stood behind him. "We have immediate work to do." He held up a cautionary hand. "Keep your celebration quiet. We don't need German patrols hearing us and getting curious. But—" He smiled broadly and looked at his watch. "The invasion starts in five hours."

The civilians stared at him, Lance and Faucon with them, their eyes wide with disbelief. Then the *maquisards* turned to one another with huge grins, jumping up and down in pure joy and slapping one another on the back.

Botella called out to them, "Please, we have a lot of work to do and not much time."

The *maquisards* quieted down. "Where is the landing?" someone called.

"We don't know, and it doesn't matter for our missions. It could be Calais, Normandy, along the Morbihan coast, or at the beaches of the Mediterranean. We'll know in five hours, wherever it is. Our first job was to contact you. That's done.

"For the Germans to fight back effectively, they'll need to communicate and move troops. Our second mission is to disrupt those movements and communications—that means blowing up trains, power stations, and communications centers."

The *maquisards* paid full attention now, nudging each other eagerly. A few could not resist the urge to whoop in celebration, elbowed to silence by their compatriots.

"Our third task," Botella continued when they quieted, "is to establish a base to receive British Special Air Service paratroopers. By this time tomorrow, a battalion of them will drop in, prepared to conduct combat operations against the *Wehrmacht*."

The *maquisards* started to revel again, but Botella quelled them. "We don't have time for that. We've brought explosives, and you have some of your own. We have designated targets, and you have the people who know where they are and the trucks to get us there. We'll match our commandos with yours, forming small teams. One general caution: you must complete your missions. If you're found out, blow the target. It's better to detonate early than not at all.

"Just before we make the assignments, let me tell you that similar actions are taking place all over France, particularly along the coasts. From now until the *Wehrmacht* is defeated, our job is to disrupt their operations wherever we can. Over the next few days, we'll take any and all actions to hinder their convoys moving toward the coastal invasion, wherever it is, and we'll do that with bombs and bullets."

Lance glanced around at the happy faces. The men flexed their fingers, shaking themselves loose under the constraint of keeping their merriment quiet. Intermittently, one would close his eyes and thrust a weapon in the air, joined by others; and some jumped up and down in excitement or stomped their feet.

"I'm nearly finished," Botella said. He gestured toward Lance. "I'm informed that we have a British commando among us who's trained a lot of you. We appreciate that he came to fight for France the same as the SAS battalion that arrives tomorrow. That said"—he bowed slightly to Lance and addressed him directly—"Friend, you should feel free to join in our missions that start in a few minutes." He held up a finger. "But know that these are French operations, conducted by the Free French army and our *Maquis* volunteers, one of the first such patriotic units to fight on French soil in this war."

Lance caught Botella's eye and raised a thumb in approval. "I'm honored to fight alongside you, and await your orders."

Botella studied Lance for a second. "We're honored to have you," he said. "Today, you and I will work side by side." He faced the group again. "So now, we'll assign the missions. We move out in fifteen minutes." He looked at his watch again. "We'll meet back here in four hours. That's long enough before daylight."

Lance was both amazed and proud of the *maquisards* he had helped train. They demonstrated their proficiency with weapons and demolitions to the satisfaction of the French commandos they would accompany. They had learned the subtleties of effective sabotage—that placing a small bomb on the connecting bar that joined the wheels of a locomotive would disable it; that destroying a junction box on a factory would put the plant out of action; that planting explosives at key points on a bridge would bring it down. Those actions, taken much more swiftly than attempting to destroy an entire factory, avoided the need for much larger explosive loads that could also kill friends and loved ones and would remove valuable economic assets.

Lance was happy to join Botella, who was headed for Saint-Brieuc's railroad station. The lieutenant was wiry and full of energy, evinced by his manner as he moved from team to team and listened to their interactions as commandos and *maquisards* briefed each other. The French lieutenant interjected suggestions where they made sense, gave advice when needed, and issued orders as imperative.

Lance shadowed him. Fifteen minutes later, the two rode on the back of a small farm truck heading toward the train station. "We'll need this station and most of the railway intact to move Allied troops," he told Lance. "Right now, we'll disable as many locomotives as we can."

"You'll be surprised at how fast that will happen," Lance said. "We have an alert system and a train engineer designated for each engine. One of our group will call ahead to tell the chief engineer at the station what time you want the charges to detonate. He'll take care of it."

Botella regarded him dubiously. "Seriously?"

Lance nodded with pursed lips. "Faucon and I have been in the area for a few months. We identified and trained *résistants* who had access to targets. The locomotives will be disabled on schedule, the bridges on the main highways will be knocked out, railroad switches will be thrown. The *Wehrmacht* will wake up to chaos while they try to contend with an invasion."

"The *Maquis* have done a remarkable job," Botella replied. "I had heard that most are untrained, undisciplined, and have no idea what to do. We thought their motivation was that they didn't want to be taken to Germany to be slaves."

Lance shrugged. "No one wants to be a slave. If they had wanted to be military men, they would have joined the army. Most are patriots who'll do anything to save your country, but as you say, many are not trained. Things are different from place to place. The unit at the La Mouette farm had veterans to teach them some things."

Botella brought the tips of his fingers to his forehead in a small salute. "It shows."

The little truck wound through the dark back streets, without lights, to the train depot, always on the lookout for German patrols. Saint-Brieuc's station was larger than most for a town of its size because of its position at a crossroad for north/southbound and east/westbound rail traffic, providing the junction with an outsized role.

The driver parked a few blocks away and then led Botella's small group on foot through the night. Reaching a street that ended across from the station, they slowed their pace and approached warily. The depot was also cloaked in darkness for fear of Allied bombs, but the guide, an old, grizzled man and longtime resident of Saint-Brieuc, knew the way into the railyard.

They entered through a back gate that was unguarded and unlocked. The clouds thinned out and the moon gave just enough light to glint off the railroad tracks and the station's slate roof. Lance noticed the slight increased illumination and urged the group into deeper shadows.

The saboteurs paralleled the rails for a few hundred yards. Ahead of them, sheltered under an awning, the monstrous black shape of a locomotive appeared. Botella called a halt and left Lance and one *maquisard* to pull security while he and the others went forward. When they returned, Botella whispered to Lance, "You were right. The bomb was already placed where it should be, and armed correctly. Move on to the next one."

Only three engines were in the station, each of them now with a disabling bomb placed against its main wheel. When they had been checked, the guide led them back to the truck and drove through the dark to the barn.

They had been gone two hours, and other teams had already returned, having completed their missions at closer or easier targets. For the next two hours, other teams arrived, and the men conversed in a low murmur, thrilled to be taking part in the first large-scale operation to cripple the Third *Reich* in Europe. Botella and Deschamps had drilled their commandos that, upon returning from their sabotage missions, they should begin instructing their teams on actions required to establish the base to receive the British paratroop battalion. Those actions were underway.

An explosion in the distance brought the assembled fighters to silence. All heads turned.

42

June 6, 1944
D-Day
Dragon's Farm, near Saint-Laurent-sur-Mer, Normandy, France

Chantal's sleep was interrupted by high-pitched whistling ripping through the sky, and seconds later, before she could contemplate the possible cause, the earth shook, and loud concussions rent the air. Almost as suddenly, an acrid smell permeated, and billows of smoke filled the basement room where she had slept.

Her pulse leaped, and she ran for the door, coughing in the dark. She flipped a switch on the wall, but the light failed. Fearing suffocation, she turned the knob and threw the door open. Dragon was there, outlined by flashes of light accompanied by thunderous explosions. He grabbed Chantal's wrist. "Follow me. Hurry."

Grateful for his reassuring presence, Chantal shouted, "Is this—"

"The invasion? I think so."

Thrill coursed through Chantal. "This house is on Douin's map," Dragon called above the din. "It's in a no-fire zone. The nearest German gun positions are at least a mile away. We shouldn't be hit, but we're going to feel the tremors and hear the explosions. And we're still subject to error.

We'll go to the wine cellar farther underground with better ventilation. We should be safe there."

They hurried down some stairs, and the air grew cooler and cleaner as they went. Reaching the bottom, they hurried through an open door. Soon, other farmworkers and members of Dragon's Resistance group arrived. They huddled together with anxious faces between the large vats lining the walls.

Despite the whistling and thunder of artillery shells, the mood was exultant. "It's finally here," someone murmured in awe. "Our day of liberation has arrived."

"If we live through it," another called. "If we take a direct hit, we'll have tons of stone masonry on top of us."

"But France will be free of *les boches*," another person said, "and our families will have lives again. Pétain can take his motto to hell with him. We'll take back *liberté, égalité, fraternité*."

A series of bombs fell close by, drowning out all chatter. Everyone instinctively crouched and covered their ears, and when the reverberations had cleared, they stared around as if expecting to find the others dead, their expressions morphing into relieved half-smiles on finding no one injured.

More shells fell farther away and continued for hours.

Then, the heavy guns ceased.

Chantal joined Dragon and a few other brave souls to creep up the stone stairs and stare out across the expanse of the Channel that they could see from a mile back. Dawn had broken not more than thirty minutes earlier, and the sun rose, obscured by thick, roiling clouds and heavy rain.

Despite the distance, Chantal and the group were astonished to find the waters dotted as far as they could see to the west, and from the northern to the southern horizons, with sea-going vessels of every size and shape. They seemed so small from this vantage, appearing as an army of ants crossing a field, approaching inexorably. She wondered how any of them could have hurled the huge steel projectiles this far with the explosive force she had felt and heard.

As she continued to watch, tiny specks appeared among the frothing waves, departing from the larger vessels and streaming toward the beach. She sucked in her breath, thrilled. Allied landing craft were coming ashore.

Turning to Dragon, she said, "We have work to do."

He nodded with a wry smile. "You might be a bit too eager, *Papillon*."

"Hah," she retorted. "It's time to give back to the Germans. You must have received our activation code from the BBC?"

"I have. I've already sent messages out. Our *Maquis* will gather at our headquarters in the woods in ninety minutes."

"I'm ready." Chantal flew downstairs to her room and returned minutes later with a Sten gun, a full ammo pouch, and four grenades attached to her equipment belt.

By the time she was back upstairs, Dragon was pulling his sedan from its hidden position. He beckoned to her from the driver's side. "You're not coming."

She looked at him askance, ran to the passenger side, and jerked the door open. "Let's go."

"You're too youn—"

"Drive."

Dragon half-smiled but did not move.

"We don't have time for this, Dragon. We've been all through it. I'm trained by the British. I'm older than my sister was when the war started, and she was constantly put in dangerous situations. And I'm older than a lot of soldiers on both sides of the war.

"We've got to hit that *Feldgendarmerie* at Bayeux. Our *maquisards* will be waiting for your leadership." When he did not move, Chantal blurted, "I've been at all the rehearsals. You'll need me."

Dragon sat regarding her stubborn face. "Chantal, listen to me. We're going into real battle this time. We'll be shooting at the German civil police. They will shoot back."

"Not if we achieve surprise and execute swiftly. I won't be the only teenaged girl shooting at Germans today, I assure you. Besides, our compatriots' skins are as soft as mine. They bleed just as easily. I'm going, and you're wasting time."

With a reluctant half-laugh, Dragon put the car in gear and stepped on the accelerator.

Sword Beach, Normandy, France

Paul Littlefield stared into the darkness over the top of his landing craft. The hiss and boom of incessant Allied naval barrages and aerial bombing sweeps had receded to background noise as the China-doll image of Ryan Northbridge floated before his eyes. She had been the only woman he had dared approach romantically, the only one he had loved, and now she was gone, a casualty of the aerial battle over Britain.

She had been a ferry pilot on a delivery run, flying a bomber to a forward base in England. A German fighter on a cross-Channel foray had attacked and downed her.

Stifling his grief, Paul watched the French commandos as they scanned the dark outline of their country that rose from over the horizon in the pre-dawn half-light. Through mist and rain, they beheld it quietly, reverentially, some with tears in their eyes from bitter memories of four years earlier, when they had been rescued in a flotilla of British ships and boats ahead of the *Wehrmacht blitzkrieg* at Dunkirk. For some, that was the last time they had seen their homeland. Others had raided targets on the French coast, but this time, they would go ashore intending to stay and, ultimately, drive out their conquerors.

Two commando troops comprising one hundred and seventy-seven Frenchmen rode in two assault landing craft. All of them volunteers, none had accepted their commander's offer to be exempt from this mission without shame or consequence. That was after telling them their survival odds: one in ten.

The commander, *Capitaine* Philippe Kieffer, had joined the Free French in the aftermath of the French defeat in 1940. Then, inspired by the successes of the British commandos on the Norwegian coast in 1941, Kieffer had petitioned to organize a unit of *Fusiliers-Marins*, patterned after the Royal Marine commandos. Granted permission, he had recruited volunteers and trained with them in the Scottish Highlands. He then led them on raids along the Dutch and French coasts, including at Dieppe, the first Allied raid against the *Wehrmacht* on French shores two years ago.

The unit, No. 4 Commando, organized under the 1st Special Service Brigade, was commanded by Brigadier Simon Christopher Joseph Fraser.

He was the 15th Lord Fraser of Lovat, descended from the 11th Lord Fraser of Lovat, the last person to be beheaded in the UK. Inheriting his ancestor's roguish spirit tempered by military discipline and a call to duty, the latter Lovat had been awarded a Distinguished Service Cross for his actions at Dieppe.

Lovat had been responsible for bringing Paul into the unit. Bent on ensuring smooth communications and coordination between the British and French components of his command, he had cast about for an available combat-experienced officer who was fluent in both languages. He had found Paul by accident as the two had waited for separate flights at the airfield in Gibraltar back in April.

Lovat had recognized Paul. "I say, aren't you the young captain I saw at the Dieppe out-brief with Prime Minister Churchill two years ago?" He had glanced at Paul's rank insignia. "Now you're a lieutenant colonel. That was a fast rise."

Paul, having just arrived and en route to be reassigned after his battalion had been demolished in Italy, was exhausted to the bone. He studied Lovat's face. "I remember you, sir. And now you're a brigadier. You've risen further than I have."

Lovat grunted in response. "I've been promoted once to your twice."

Paul let the jest ride and thought back, remembering. "You were angry because you felt that your men had not been adequately supported. I found your concern and tenacity in pressing your disgust quite admirable. I believe you requested the meeting with the PM, and you told him in strong terms of your dissatisfaction."

"I might have been a bit forward, Colonel." Lovat frowned. "I took note of you because I wondered why a captain was in that room at all."

Paul chuckled. "I wondered the same thing. But alas, if I remembered why and told you, I'd have to kill you. Respectfully, sir. Or, I'd have to take a cyanide pill."

"Ah, one of those." The two laughed together. "Where are you off to now?"

"I just came out of Italy. I was in that early effort to cross the Rapido. It didn't come off well for my battalion. We got across all right, but in follow-on fighting, we took a lot of casualties."

"All the units took huge casualties," Lovat interjected. "I can't imagine the horror."

Paul agreed. "When the corps reorganized, my superiors decided that I had done my bit for the time being, and sent me for rest and reassignment."

The two continued chatting about various subjects, including home, units in which they had served, and battles they had fought in. On learning that Paul was from Sark, Lovat's ears perked up. He peered closely at Paul. "Do you speak French?"

"We all do on that island. To us, it's as natural as English."

Lovat studied him closely. "Any preferences for what you do next?"

Paul shook his head. "Wherever I can best serve."

The two men spoke for hours, and when they were finished, Lovat offered to pull strings to bring Paul to his commando unit. "I've had similar training, but strictly speaking, I'm not a commando," Paul said.

"We'll have you ready in time. I need a combat commander who speaks French fluently."

"Will the commandos accept me as their commander?"

"Leave that to me. You were trained at Camp X in Canada. That's equivalent. Let's get you home and rested up, and then you should prepare to come to Scotland."

At the time, Paul had no idea what the mission was. Now, as the landing craft sped to shore, he wondered if he had accepted Lovat's invitation too blindly. The truth was, however, that he had attended the mission briefings with Lovat, Kieffer, and the other commanders of the British I Corps, and he knew the risks.

Paul liked Kieffer and found the man to be unquestionably competent and respected by his men. The French officer had been so eager for his unit to fight in the first operation to take back France that he agreed to subordinate himself under Paul in No. 4 Commando.

Their first objective was in Ouistreham, a village at the eastern extremity of the landing area that was joined by a bridge to Caen. The bridge, codenamed "Pegasus," was a strategic target and was to be seized before H-Hour by a British unit landing by glider. However, being that the unit would be lightly armed, it would require reinforcement. Providing such buttressing was Paul's mission, and so the beach in front of the village was necessarily the place where Allied boots would first strike land for the amphibious landing.

Recognizing the longing of the French unit to free their homeland, their tenacity, and their skill, Paul kept Kieffer in command of the French unit; and he further afforded the captain the honor of being the first to lead Allied troops onto French soil.

All night, the Allied fleet, numbering nearly seven thousand ships, had crossed the English Channel under blackout and radio silence. Arriving on station they then circled or held steady short of launch position. Protected by Hawker Typhoons, a vast armada of bombers British Lancasters and B-17 Flying Fortresses had droned overhead to drop thousands of tons of munitions along the coast to soften up German defenses.

For two hours before launching ground troops, the combined Allied navies lobbed massive bombardments from two hundred warships, with shells arcing to shore. Even from over the horizon, the sky flickered with ghastly light only partially obscured by black smoke and rain; and like the peal of thunder, the rumble of thousands of simultaneous explosions rolled out to sea.

Dawn broke with dark, gloomy clouds. Paul looked across the waters at the vast array of ships spread out as far as he could see behind him to the west and to his north and south. The fleet was even larger than what he had witnessed at Sicily.

The naval bombardment ceased. The last of the bombers disappeared into the eastern sky. Momentary quiet fell over the fleet.

It broke, suddenly and furiously, by the sound of revving motors and incoming artillery fire. The landing craft lurched forward and gained speed. As they plowed through the water across a fifty-mile front and closed on land, enemy fire increased in volume. Shells whistled through the air and splashed, generating huge geysers. As the vessels drew closer to shore, deep-throated, rhythmic machine gun fire joined the amphibious invasion's terrible cacophony. The landing craft slowed to a crawl as they maneuvered around the mass of General Rommel's obstacles, put there to rip out hulls and snag soldiers on barbed wire stretched below the surface.

Looking across the front of the boat, Paul observed Kieffer, stolid, prepared, checking his commandos' weapons for the umpteenth time. Rifle rounds struck the vessel, and holes marked its front and sides. Wounded already cried out for help. To the left and right, more landing craft pushed into the shallows, inviting a hail of mortar fire.

An odd sound mixing with battle clamor caught Paul's ear. He recognized the eerie, high-pitched, musical tones of Scottish bagpipes. Then he remembered. Lovat had commanded, against orders, that his troops would be piped ashore to raise spirits.

The vessel churned to a halt. The ramp dropped.

Kieffer sprinted down it into ankle-deep water, rushed out of the surf, and charged up the beach, urging his men to follow. Only the weight of his equipment slowed him.

Paul remained by the landing craft under fire only long enough to see that the rest of his command had come ashore, and then he followed, headed toward Pegasus.

Gold Beach, Normandy, France

Sergeant Horton swallowed hard as his landing craft cruised toward shore at a village called Arromanches. Once again, he was about to assault a beach with soldiers he barely knew, and this time, as opposed to when he had landed at Anzio, the enemy was already shooting back, with devastating effect.

Despite early successes at Anzio, the unopposed landing, Lieutenant Hargreaves' unbelievable patrol into Rome, and the capture of one hundred and eleven prisoners at Aprilia, subsequent fighting had all but destroyed the 5th Grenadier Guards' Carrier Platoon of the 24th Guards Brigade. Casualties had been so high that three months ago, it existed in name only, its few remaining members dispersed to other units. Horton had been shipped back to England and assigned to the Sherwood Rangers Yeomanry to train for the expected invasion of France.

As opposed to being a replacement among raw recruits going into battle, as had happened when he had re-joined the 24th Guards ahead of the Anzio landing, Horton found himself among seasoned, battle-hardened veterans, having served at the siege of Tobruk and on Crete. They had retrained on tanks to fight Rommel's panzers at the Germans' last attempt to break the Alamein Line at Alam Halfa two years ago.

Succeeding there despite limited practice with tactics and technology that was new to them, they had fought on to further victory at Tunisia with the Eighth Army a year later. Then, recognized as a skilled, highly experienced unit, the Sherwood Rangers were sent back to England to train for the invasion of France as part of the 50th Division's independent 8th Armored Brigade. Unknown to the rangers, they had already been designated for a specific target: Gold Beach, the westernmost of the three British and Canadian assault landings. And they would be equipped with Sherman tanks.

The losses Horton had seen at Anzio had taken their toll on his naturally good humor. Although he was still a willing team player and pleasant when spoken to, his normal demeanor had become grim and guarded. The men in his new unit had fought together in the sands of North Africa for over two years. They had celebrated victory and grieved over lost comrades. They had an affinity for each other that Horton saw little hope of sharing.

His own combat experience was respected to the extent that he had been assigned as a platoon sergeant, a role that did not thrill him. He would rather be a squad leader, in charge of men at the ground level, taking combat objectives. Nevertheless, recognizing that soldiers at the front needed to be fed, resupplied, and cared for if wounded, he accepted his role without complaint.

Now, as the landing craft sped toward the beach, Horton was almost glad not to have found his way into the fellowship of his new unit, and that he was one rank removed from the close-knit camaraderie of a squad. He looked around at the wide-eyed, anxious faces and wondered how many and which ones would be among the missing and fallen by day's end.

The landing craft slowed to maneuver around Rommel's obstacles.

Ahead of them, the 1st Battalion Hampshire Regiment were supposed to land at Jig Green sector of Gold Beach. The battalion would face the first barrage of gunfire against open landing craft and men running down ramps. By the time Horton's platoon disembarked, he expected that the beach would be strewn with many of Hampshires' dead.

He pushed aside the grim image. However, as his craft churned through the shallows, he saw that the reality was worse than he had imagined.

Several of the Hampshires' landing craft had hit offshore reefs. Believing, incorrectly, that their vessels had beached, the coxswains lowered the ramps. The soldiers at the front, weighted down with their equipment, jumped into deep water and drowned. The ones who managed to remain on the boats as they continued to the shore found that they had drifted west, out of their target area.

Ahead of them, the Royal Engineer breaching parties had landed in the proper sector and were clearing lanes. To reach them, the Hampshires moved along the beach to the east into the worst path of German gunfire from fixed guns at Le Hamel.

Horton had seen British Hawker Typhoons drop one-thousand-pound bombs on Le Hamel before the Hampshires' final drive to shore, but with little effect. Now it was the Sherwood Rangers' turn. To make things worse, the Sherwood Rangers were to have supported, with their tanks, the Hampshires' drive to quell Le Hamel's gun positions. Several of those tanks had been lost in the Channel crossing.

The tide had reached its high point. Ahead of Horton's landing craft and only yards beyond a thick seawall, he saw stately beachfront homes belonging to Arromanches residents. The houses had obviously been requisitioned by the enemy, as machine gun fire spewed from ground-level positions built into their lower levels.

Far to the right of Gold, the beach lay flat and narrow from the tide. Then the inland ground rose sharply over high cliffs. There, on flat ground set back from the cliffs, at a place on the map called Longues-sur-Mer, four heavy shore guns, each protected by massive concrete casements, rained down artillery rounds onto landing craft coming ashore at Gold, and at the adjoining Omaha Beach.

The 50th Division's main objective was to link up with a Canadian division to the left of Gold at Juno. Together with American divisions coming ashore to the right at Omaha, they would push inland to secure the roads intersecting at Bayeux and leading to Caen. Their intent was to block the *Wehrmacht* from reinforcing coastal defenses.

The ramp dropped. Horton ran down into waist-deep water. Guns blazed red and yellow flame from the fortified positions at the beachfront houses. Rounds hissed by.

Horton stopped to one side of the vessel, urging his men forward even as the first soldiers fell. A few yards behind, he heard his lieutenant urging the troops on at the ramp of the second Sherwood Rangers' landing craft.

On the beach, soldiers zigzagged across the sand, rushing for the shelter of the seawall and firing at the guns inside the fortified homes as they went. All around, men called for medics.

With the Hampshires far down the beach to the west, the Sherwoods' Shermans had not arrived. The Rangers who had not been hit as they ran to the seawall hunkered down below it. The plan for the Gold Jig Green sector was in total disarray.

Empty of soldiers, the landing craft backed into deeper water to go after the next load. Horton crouched over and ran for the seawall, dodging bullets all the way. Catching his breath at its base, he looked out to sea to watch the vast armada of ships loitering offshore with men and supplies and the tiny landing craft streaming in both directions. The tide had begun to recede, exposing tall wooden spikes fixed vertically in the sand, their obvious intended use being to shred the thin wooden hulls of Allied landing craft coming in at high tide.

In that glimpse, Horton found hard to fathom what had been briefed before he boarded the transport ship in England less than twenty-four hours earlier: that within days, this stretch of beach at Arromanches, with no infrastructure aside from the small village itself, would be turned into a vast harbor for large ships. Their cargoes, weighing in the hundreds of thousands of tons, would transfer to long convoys of trucks, which would drive them to shore atop things called "Mulberries." The concept eluded Horton, but he understood that for the invasion to succeed and progress inland, bringing massive re-supply ashore was imperative.

He took in a long breath and glanced down the beach. The first of the remaining Sherwoods' tanks were coming ashore. They were late and out of position, but they had arrived. All he had to do now was lead his men back across the sand through the deadly fusillades they had just escaped and retrieve the war machines.

Omaha Beach, Normandy, France

Sergeant Ray Lambert shielded his face with his hand from the rain and the spray of seawater and vomit as his landing craft thrust through frothing high waves. The sun had risen an hour ago, but it was invisible behind a gray curtain of clouds. He had bade his brother farewell aboard the same ship where he had launched. He had also watched individual members of his medic team as they joined their assigned companies. Then, he climbed over the rails onto the wet rope-ladder to descend into a Higgins boat. It would carry him and the men he supported to the blistering wall of bullets and artillery shells that would meet them before they reached shore. If they reached the beach alive, laden with rifles and ninety pounds of equipment each, they would struggle through sand while the merciless rain of bullets and shrapnel continued.

Amphibious operations were not new to Lambert. He had been on landings in North Africa and Sicily, and while he had seen experience increase the effectiveness of Allied landings, he had also noticed a commensurate escalation of German defenses. Beyond the reality of Hitler's famed Atlantic Wall were the obstacles that these thirty soldiers riding with him would face along with the thousands of other landing craft.

Sketches he had seen of Normandy's beaches had been terrifying. Near the center of the length of the entire landing zone was a small town near the coast, Saint-Laurent-sur-Mer, just above his unit's section of coastline. He had been amazed at the detail of the sketches, and wondered how such minute geographical intelligence could have been gained. Thinking it might have come from aerial photography, he sent a quiet word of thanks to those pilots who had so risked their lives.

The drawings showed barbed wire along the ground and more at waist

and shoulder height, stretched between all manner of obstacles with nick-
names like hedgehogs, Belgian Gates, and tetrahedrons. The drawings
showed the beaches as they would appear at low tide, and behind them, an
array of fortified emplacements for heavy artillery, machine guns, access
routes, ammunition dumps, supply depots, and all other direct and support
munitions to be deployed against the soft tissues of American, British,
French, and Canadian troops intent on establishing a beachhead on the
western part of France's northeastern coast. They even showed no-fire
zones.

Sergeant Lambert had been perfectly suited to be an infantryman. Born
and raised on a farm in Alabama, he had been physically active for his
entire twenty-three years of life, and he was often out hunting with his
father and brother. His farm-grown training and work ethic had prepared
him such that he adapted well to the army.

Assigned to be a medic, he was glad to be able to help the wounded
rather than cause harm. His guiding principle under fire was to "make sure
the infantrymen know I'm there," and already, he had earned a bronze and
a silver star in the North African and Sicilian landings for courage under
fire while saving soldiers' lives.

He knew the torment that combatants experienced, especially those on
their first landing, as the boxy wooden Higgins boats plowed the waters to
the coast. With bullets striking the vessels' thin skin, and mortars and
artillery rounds raining in, many men sat with their heads down, their arms
held close to their bodies, seeking solace in the notion that being alive and
unharmed this moment might mean they would continue to be safe from
harm in the next.

They knew the lie contained in that hope. Some saw a vessel to the left
take a direct mortar hit and then the passengers screaming in panic and
agony, and struggling in their flaming combat attire to leap into the water
that then drowned them.

With every landing, a thought struck Lambert unbidden: *Which of these
men will I bandage? Which ones won't make it?*

He recalled his first time. The sense of being frozen, incapable of movement, understanding that when the ramp dropped, someone from another
country, another culture would be intent on killing him. As a matter of fact,

that enemy would kill many of his buddies and perhaps Lambert himself, within seconds.

When the ramp came down on that first occasion, Lambert had prodded himself to move forward with his comrades. Then he found, to his own surprise, that he was already shuffling forward in the water. He had suddenly vomited when, amid thick swirls of blood, he saw bodies pushed along by the surf, weighted down by their heavy equipment.

"I'll see ya later," Lambert's brother Bill had called to him earlier, just before the two siblings clambered over the edge to make their way to their respective landing crafts. They had joined the army together, trained together, and now found themselves to be medics in the 16th Infantry Regiment of the 1st Infantry Division. Nicknamed the Big Red One, the division was one of the US Army's most experienced fighting units.

As Lambert understood the overall plan, the landing would span Normandy's coast, from Merville on the eastern limit to Sainte-Mère-Église on the west. It was split into five codenamed sections. The British would seize the most northeastern one, Sword Beach, landing its 3rd Infantry Division there. Adjacent and to the west of the Brits, the Canadians would take their 3rd Division ashore at Juno. The British would also land their 7th Armored and 50th Infantry Divisions in the next section to the west at Gold.

The US First Army would strike the final two beaches, with the 29th Infantry and the 1st Infantry Divisions seizing Omaha, and the 4th Infantry Division taking Utah east of the western boundary along the Cotentin Peninsula. Altogether, the full Allied amphibious force would strike the beach with one hundred and fifty-six thousand men.

Once the Brits secured their beachhead at Sword, the plan called for them to protect the eastern flank of the invasion against a German armored counter-attack. The Canadians, at Juno, were to move inland and seize the towns of Courseulles, Bernières, and Saint-Aubin. The British at Gold were to occupy and control an area between Asnelles-sur-Mer and La Rivière while keeping Arromanches intact between them and the Canadians. That was the town where the artificial harbor would be built.

At Omaha, the Americans were to secure a beachhead five miles deep between Port-en-Bessin and the Vire River. The British at Gold would link up with them, and together push inland to Isigny. Meanwhile the units at

Utah would secure the western limit on the Cotentin Peninsula, seize the Cherbourg port facilities, and join with the British and US forces at Isigny.

The throaty roar of Lambert's landing craft cut suddenly. His heart missed a beat and his throat formed a knot. His already wet hands suddenly became clammy. He heard the purr of waves dragging the Higgins a few more feet to shore and then breaking on the beach. And above the moaning wind he heard the menacing staccato of machine gun fire and the screams of wounded soldiers.

The ramp dropped.

"Go, go, go," the platoon leader and the platoon sergeant yelled.

"Let's go," the squad leaders shouted, and soldiers ran down the ramp into the surf, Sergeant Lambert among them.

As soon as he stepped two feet down the ramp, he was in water—the front of the craft had hit sand sooner and farther from shore than expected. At the bottom of the incline, a soldier floated, face up, eyes staring, arms stretched out, beyond help. Lambert ran past, as did all those coming behind him. His focus had to be on helping the wounded.

At that moment, searing heat pierced Lambert's left elbow. He had been hit, his bone crushed. While engaged in combat, medics were constantly exposed to gunfire. They did not allow being wounded to relieve them of duty.

Lambert continued wading forward, keeping underwater as much as possible, and when he surfaced, he scanned for troops who had already been wounded. All the while, the merciless onshore gunfire assaulted soft flesh, and waves hurled dead bodies ashore.

The beach offered no shelter. It sloped slightly upward and was sprawled with hidden mines intended to maim and kill and with obstacles designed, spaced, and placed to deny cover while inhibiting advance. As Lambert scanned the beach and beyond, he saw that clouds and rain had obscured pre-planned targets. The Allies' hours-long naval barrages and bomber runs had barely dented enemy shore defenses.

He caught sight of a large wedge-shaped rock, or perhaps it was a concrete section of a destroyed pillbox from the last war. It was embedded in the sand partway up the beach. Roughly eight feet long and four feet high, its sloped side faced the enemy and away from the roiling, blood-tinged surf. It could provide life-saving cover.

Cries of the anguished floated on the stiff breeze above the beat of rain and gunfire. Lambert hunched down and ran to the nearest wounded soldier, who was clinging to an obstacle in shallow water where waves broke against him. Under the weight of a soaked uniform and boots and medic bags, Lambert struggled to reach the man. "Don't you know this is no cover?" he yelled, then realized that the man could not hear him.

He grabbed the soldier's uniform and tugged, to no avail. The man was caught in barbed wire under the surf. Lambert plunged, found where an equipment strap was snagged, and freed it. Resurfacing, he found the man being dragged under by a heavy backpack. He grabbed the troop's uniform and sat him up.

Hot steel whizzed by.

Ignoring his own wound, and under relentless rain and gunfire, Lambert pulled the soldier through the surf and past the long mishmash of bodies floating at the water's edge. Slowed by the sand, bearing up under ear-splitting barrages, with men falling all around, Lambert dragged the barely conscious soldier to the relative safety behind the wedge-shaped rock and out of the line of fire.

Lambert checked him for wounds. Finding none more than superficial, he yelled, "Stay behind this rock." The man did not hear him.

Lambert looked around for the next of the wounded to rescue, and spotted one he might be able to save struggling in the surf. Running back to the water's edge while scanning myriad prone figures for any that might be alive, he noted the size of the holes left by German machine gun bullets plowing through bone and sinew.

He reached the soldier he had seen struggling in the water. The man had turned over, face down in the surf. Lambert grappled to right the man, but when he had succeeded, the man stared through vacant eyes.

Barely noticing his own wounded arm, Lambert cast about again, and saw another man thrashing at the water's edge. He and another soldier helped the troop to his feet and got him closer to shore. He had lost his rifle. "There are plenty lying around," Lambert yelled. "Grab one and get to your unit."

Another round burned into Lambert's right leg, exposing several inches of the bone. He reeled with the pain and dropped in the sand where he was. Shaking, in agonizing pain, he groped for his medic bag.

Bullets whizzed by. Mines exploded. Men cried out for help.

Lambert applied a tourniquet to his own leg and injected it with morphine. Then, lying flat on his back to avoid being a target, he waited long enough for the drug to take effect. When the pain had receded, he struggled to his feet to rescue more soldiers, dragging behind his rock those he found still alive but unable to function.

Making another trip to the surf and finding yet another soldier needing rescue from a snag in submerged barbed wire, Lambert dove down and freed the soldier.

He surfaced.

The coxswain of an arriving landing craft, not seeing him, dropped its ramp on him.

Hours later, Lambert awoke on a hospital ship. He had been saved by another soldier who had witnessed the accident.

Lambert's back was broken in three places. He lay with images of the horror he had lived through plaguing his dim consciousness: the sights of bodies roiling in the surf amid reddish goo; the sounds of wind, rain, gunfire, and explosions; the mixed smells of salt, fish, excrement, and smoke; the burn of bullets rending his muscles; and the excruciating pain he had been compelled to ignore.

They seemed surreal now, a conjured horror that could never have occurred.

But he could not move, and despite anesthesia, pain jabbed his wounded arm, his leg, his back. Worse still was the acute sense that, along Normandy's beach, his comrades, some whom he had treated in earlier battles, still fought in that hell, and most assuredly, more of them would not return.

Unable to move, staring at the ceiling, Lambert sensed that he might not have a future and questioned whether he wanted one. He found life in the thrall of evil unappealing, the stark cruelty that men inflicted on one another to be incomprehensible. Hell could not be worse.

Then a voice whispered to him. "Ray," he heard his brother say, "it's me. Bill. I'm in the bed next to yours."

Isle of Sark, Guernsey Bailiwick, Channel Islands

The poodles barking at her front door alerted Marian to close down her wireless. She was in a storage room at the back of the house where she had just listened, thrilled, to President Roosevelt's address concerning the invasion at Normandy. "It's actually happening," she breathed. "Rome is already taken, and the Germans will be routed from France. Sark will soon be free."

Hurriedly, she put the radio into its designated suitcase and then pushed it under a stack of luggage left in her care by residents who had departed during the occupation, most having been deported to internment camps in France for various infractions. She often wondered if she would ever see them again.

When she walked through the hall toward the front of the house, her servant told her that Joseph Wakley was waiting for her in the sitting room and looked distraught.

"Charles Machon's seventy-four-year-old mother tried to bring a tin of his special food to his cell in the jail," Wakley said when she met with him. "It's for his ulcer. She was refused."

Wakley related that the interrogators threatened to do bad things to the elderly woman if Machon did not reveal the accomplices who helped publish his newsletter. Machon had finally caved, and gave up the names of Cecil Duquemin, a baker; Ernest Legg, a carpenter; John Gillingham, a brewery stoker and Legg's brother-in-law; and Frank Falla, a reporter at the *Guernsey Star*. "They've all been arrested," he said.

"I'm so sorry to hear that," Marian said, taking a deep breath. "When did it happen?"

"A few weeks ago. They've further limited travel between the islands. This is the first chance I've had to come over to Sark. I knew you'd want to know."

Later that evening, after Wakley had left, Marian sat at her desk and penned a letter to her husband, still interned in Ilag VII at Tittmoning Castle, Laufen, Bavaria:

"Dearest Stephen, I hope you are getting along well. The challenges continue here on Sark much as they were when you left, no better, no worse. I apologize that all I could send by way of making your life better were some old, dried onions. I'll try to do better next time. Hopefully, you've heard about the doings on Normandy's beach. I find ironic that I can send a letter to you in that camp more openly than I can to Claire in London, but for the moment, *c'est la vie!* The good news is that I have no worse news. We're keeping our spirits up here, as I'm sure you are as well, and we all look to your safe return and that of our friends and loved ones. All my love, Marian."

Dragon's Farm, near Saint-Laurent-sur-Mer, Normandy, France

Late that night, Dragon and Chantal arrived back at the farm. Their operation had been a success. They had attacked the *Feldgendarmerie*, the German civil police at Bayeux, and the operation had been a complete surprise. It had been planned to seize the weapons and ammunition, which necessarily meant guns and shooting, and probably killing Germans, and that had happened.

After the fact, Chantal had taken no joy in the deaths. She could not even say for sure that any of her bullets had struck anyone. At the outset of the assault, the first officers they had encountered put up no resistance. Only two of them had been there initially, and they were obviously astonished at being confronted by citizens with guns coming to seize their armory. Their attack added to the shock of the invasion taking place only a few miles away.

The surprised entry of a third officer had upset the applecart, and suddenly, the German police officers had a fighting chance, which they exercised. It had been futile and their attempt cost them their lives.

Dragon had been angry, seeing no excuse for the third officer to have entered unopposed, and he made a mental note to better train his *maquis-*

ards on rear security. The remaining officers, ten in all, had made their way to the station, in haste, out of concern stemming from the invasion. Each was waylaid, disarmed, and shut away inside their own cells pending turning them over to whatever Allied force moved forward to liberate Bayeux, a few miles south of Arromanches. Meanwhile the weapons in the armory were taken away for use by Dragon's *maquisards*. They had little fear of reprisal, confident that Allied forces would soon control the area.

Chantal had noticed that Dragon had become quiet in the early afternoon after a messenger whispered to him. He did not volunteer the nature of the message, and she did not ask. As they drove back to his farm that night, the changes wrought by the day's fighting were already manifest in the absence of German soldiers in the sector and by the number of civilians now on the roads celebrating deliverance, even as they heard bombs exploding in the distance.

Chantal had glanced at Dragon, but he maintained a grim, silent countenance. She sat back in her seat, thinking about the day. Inevitably her thoughts meandered to Horton. She wondered whether he was part of the invasion, and if so, where. Fear seized her as she imagined him lying face down in the low surf off the beach.

When they arrived at the farm and had parked the sedan inside the garage, they walked together into the house. Chantal started downstairs to her room, and unusually, Dragon followed her.

"Let's go on down to the wine cellar," he said. "I need to talk to you."

His manner struck Chantal's heart. "What is it?" she asked.

"I'll tell you when we get below," Dragon replied.

With a lump in her throat, Chantal climbed down the two remaining flights of stairs and entered the wine cellar, flipping a switch by the door to turn on a dim light. "What is it, Dragon? You're scaring me," she said.

"Please have a seat," he said, and Chantal noticed that his face was as grave as she had ever seen it. She pulled a chair away from a small table against a wall.

"Tell me. What's happened?" The vision of Horton in the water that had plagued her earlier played in her imagination in vivid detail now. "Is it Horton?"

"Who?" Dragon faced her with a sad smile. "Ah, your British sergeant." He shook his head with a gentle smile. "No, I have no news of him."

His face contorted as he fought strong emotion. "It's Douin."

Tightness gripped Chantal's chest. "What is it? Was he captured?"

Dragon nodded. "Several days ago. He was executed today. I'm sorry, I know you had become close. He was my friend too."

Chantal stared in disbelief. "Douin? Dead?" Tears flowed from her eyes. "No, please tell me it's a lie. Someone got it wrong." She leaned over, her arms crossed, gripping her abdomen, sobbing uncontrollably. "Oh please tell me this couldn't happen. He had become a second father. And Rémy like a brother."

Her face jerked up, her eyes wide with concern. "What about Rémy? Where is he?"

"We don't know, *Papillon*. We know that Douin was always concerned for his son and would have made escape plans for him. He's probably in hiding."

Dragon moved over and leaned down to comfort Chantal. She leaned into his chest, her body shaking with grief.

"I'm so sorry to be the one to tell you, and on such a day."

He stood for some time, his arms encircling Chantal while her grief ran its course. The sobbing abated, her breathing became more normal, and at last, she stood up.

"Thank you," she said, kissing Dragon's cheek. She started for the door and then turned back to him. "We need to find out about Rémy," she said. Then she gritted her teeth. "And we need to make sure that Douin's sketches were not done in vain."

43

Saint-Martin-en-Vercors, France

Loud honking awakened Jeremy. He dressed hurriedly and ran into the street where crowds had already gathered. Despite the early hour, they were jubilant, and instinctively he knew the reason.

"The invasion!" a man shouted. "It's begun. I heard it on the radio. In Normandy. Allied soldiers are already onshore. The Vercors has been activated."

A strange sensation overtook Jeremy, one of simultaneous exultation and dread. Exultation that the long wait was over and the war was being brought to the Germans in France. Dread from seeing clearly that Roger had been right about the critical need for weapons, both heavy and light, with ammunition—but they had not materialized.

Despite fields being prepared for a paratrooper drop at Vassieux and La Chapelle, no coordination with them had been accomplished, begging the question of whether any supplies or other support would arrive. At this late date, that was doubtful.

Still, on the fervent faces of residents and *maquisards* alike, he saw reflections of hope, joy, relief, deliverance, triumph, and every emotion that could be associated with having the shackles of tyranny thrown aside. Written on every face was the message, "We are liberated."

He headed to Hôtel Breyton. Roger was away at Guilliestre, a town a hundred and twenty miles to the southeast in the high Alps. He had gone there to train *maquisards* of another Jockey group, expecting to return within a few days. As they had anticipated might happen, Jeremy was now the main SOE operator in the Vercors.

Autrans-en-Vercors, France

Huet stirred from deep sleep, awakened by an excited messenger who shook him vigorously. "Sir, the Allies are in France. In Normandy. They've invaded."

The major shook himself awake as he lunged from the cot inside the barn, threw his clothes on, and went to meet with Beauregard. The captain had also just been informed, and he wiped sleep from his eyes at the front of the barn under a lantern.

The two men set out immediately on foot to Saint-Martin. As they went, villagers, *maquisards*, children, and women rushed into the roadways to hug Beauregard, thanking him over and over again for being there. Some had heard from families on the plains outside of the Vercors via telephone. They told of *Maquis* groups already engaging German units in fierce combat.

"Get to the camp," Beauregard called to the *maquisards*. "Spread the word to others. We need to be at full force. I'll come as soon as I know the situation."

Halfway down the mountain, an auto met them. Villagers they had passed along the way had called ahead and exhorted friends to provide faster transportation. They stressed that "*our* Captain Beauregard" was needed in Saint-Martin, more than ten miles away, and that Major Huet should be there too.

Bedlam reigned when Jeremy entered the Hôtel Breyton in Saint-Martin. Chavant had not yet arrived back in the Vercors. The other leaders were there: Dr. Samuel, second in authority behind Chavant; Malossane and Tessier, who administered the north and south sectors respectively; and Huillier, who handled supply.

Jeremy had met them previously only peripherally. He guessed that Dr. Samuel was in charge for the moment, but the man seemed overwhelmed with the turn of events, and bewildered by it.

People crowded into the café, some with functions Chavant had established, others without authority who nevertheless shouted loudly into the cacophony, whether or not anyone listened. Villagers pushed through with urgent reports of fierce fighting between the *Maquis* and German forces on the plains outside the Vercors; and already, they said, a column of tanks pressured defenders at Crest, a village straddling one of the key passes outside the southwestern rim. The loud babble grew in volume, repeatedly quoting the BBC message regarding leaping chamois.

Jeremy left the hotel and hurried to his signaler. "Get this message out to London immediately," he said, and wrote out, "Urgent. Confirm order to activate the Vercors heard on BBC tonight, per 'The chamois leaps from the mountain.'"

When the message had been sent, he instructed, "Bring me the response as soon as it comes in. I'll be at the café."

Major Huet walked calmly up the stairs of the Breyton and into the mayhem at the hotel's café, accompanied by Captain Beauregard. Together, they pushed against those in the rear who, recognizing Beauregard and the authority of the uniforms of both officers, moved aside to allow passage. Those ahead, sensing quiet behind them, turned, and then, seeing the uniformed soldiers, they too fell away. The two officers pressed to the center of the room where Dr. Samuel and the other leaders sat in obvious frustration. The cacophony continued unabated.

Huet nudged Beauregard and whispered in his ear, whereupon the captain stepped onto a chair, and then onto a tabletop, bellowing, "Silence!"

The villagers began to quiet, and as the captain shouted again, more people followed suit.

When finally the tumult had subsided sufficiently, Beauregard announced, "Your attention, please. I present to you Major François Huet, the new military commander of the Free French army at the Vercors." He waited until everyone in the room had fallen silent, and then gestured to Huet. "Sir, the floor is yours." He laughed. "Or the table, if you prefer."

Huet waved away the comment with a smile while stepping onto a chair. Then his face turned serious. "We have no time for niceties," he began in a loud voice. "No time to waste, my fellow citizens. As you've heard, the Allied invasion has begun. The Americans and British are on our beaches, and we pray that they continue onshore and make it all the way here.

"Reports from citizens are coming in of landings all along the northern beaches of Normandy, French commandos among them."

An approving murmur rose from the crowd. Huet held up a hand for quiet.

"We're hearing that American and British paratroopers jumped into Saint-Mère-Église and all along the coast behind the beach."

"I heard they also dropped dummy paratroopers," someone yelled. "They had recordings to sound like they were shooting and throwing grenades. They made it look like the paratroop force was much larger."

"That's true," Huet said. "The invasion is here, it's real, and we have our own duties to perform."

"Who are you?" someone yelled. "How do we know you have any authority."

"I recognize him as my commander," Beauregard called out.

Huet raised his hand and acknowledged Beauregard with a nod. "It's a fair question and deserves a fair answer. But now is the time for action. Many of you know me. I've been among you since childhood. Doubt me if you will, but stay out of my way or face consequences by military tribunal at first opportunity."

A murmur rose among the crowd but quickly subsided when Huet raised his hand again. "Your civilian leader, Monsieur Chavant, is not here at present. I need to confer with your other leaders so we can make sense of the situation and decide on next steps. So clear the room, everyone, except for the designated authorities."

The crowd started to move, but some people objected and hesitated to budge.

Huet's eyes narrowed. "Now!" he snapped, and turned to Beauregard. "See to it."

Amidst much grumbling, the Vercors residents filed out to wait in the streets for what would happen next. The celebratory mood, dampened though it was, continued as more rumors flowed in.

After the room had emptied, Huet took a seat and addressed the men at the table. "Let's get to business. Tell me briefly who you are and your role."

Dr. Samuel introduced himself first. When he had finished, he added, "We received an order to activate."

"We'll get to that," Huet replied, and listened while the others presented themselves. "I grasp how you're organized," he said in summary. "Dr. Samuel is essentially Chavant's deputy. Captain Beauregard commands the military component of the northern sector of the Vercors in cooperation with Monsieur Malossane, who commands the civilian *maquisards*. Is that correct?"

On receiving nods and affirmations, he continued, "And Captain Geyer does the same for the military units in the south in cooperation with Tessier, who commands the civilians there?"

Again, agreement. "And Monsieur Huillier is your logistician. He's supposed to keep us all fed and supplied with bullets, the most important job of all." He smiled, and tension broke.

Huet looked around. "Does anyone know where Captain Geyer is?"

"He'll be along," Samuel broke in. "I have no doubt of that."

Huet noted a tone of underlying antipathy. "Is there a problem?"

"There is," the doctor said. "He brought his unit here uninvited. If he fights for us, he's welcome. But he's assumed an air of being our better and feels no hesitation about ordering us about, and we're not going to trade one tyrant for another. And we don't need him provoking German retribution with his raids."

Huet grimaced while simultaneously displaying a half-smile. "I see. Well, I'll try to pull things into line. I've met the man only once, but I hear he's a fighter.

"Now, changing the subject, what do you see as our first order of business? On the way in, I heard a lot about activating the area."

Samuel nodded solemnly. "We received that word overnight via the BBC." He explained the coded message about chamois. "In addition, the very last message was '...*Blessant mon Coeur d'une longueur monotone.*' That's the last line of a Verlaine poem, and its mention constitutes General de Gaulle's orders for the entire Resistance, nationwide, to rise up and fight."

Huet listened carefully, and when Samuel had finished, he remained in silent thought. Finally, he said, "The Vercors is a special place, militarily speaking. Operation Montagnard has been accepted, which means that the Vercors will serve as a base from which to attack the Germans from their rear in every direction.

"But Colonel Descour gave me no order to mobilize the Vercors. If we do that too soon, the consequences could be disastrous." He inhaled sharply. "So, the Vercors will not mobilize until we've heard that paratroopers are on their way from Algiers."

The other men stared at him, stunned. "Our *maquisards* want to fight," Malossane growled. "The men and women who've come from other places want to win this war and return to their homes and families, their lives."

Huett shook his head. "If they go against regular German soldiers now," he said calmly, "they will be mowed down. No one doubts their courage, but we don't have heavy, long-range weapons, and those are crucial. Without them, we're dead."

Huet sat quietly while his words sank in. "This is what we're going to do," he continued. "The *maquisards* will stay in their camps and prepare to reinforce at their designated passes on a moment's notice. Everyone else will go about their business but be ready to join their companies on command."

"But, sir, the BBC message—"

"I have information on that," Jeremy called from the doorway where he had been listening.

As he entered, Beauregard told Huet, "This is Labrador, one of our SOE operatives. I told you about him yesterday."

Huet called to Jeremy, "I know about you. Join us. What do you have?"

Jeremy held out a slip of paper. "I just received this in answer to a query I made."

Huet scanned the paper and read it aloud. "BBC states that it did not broadcast the subject message regarding leaping chamois."

"That comes from SOE headquarters," Jeremy added.

Huet looked at the crushed faces, now with downcast eyes. "Gentlemen," he said softly. "I believe in Operation Montagnard. So does my boss, Colonel Descour, and it has been approved at the highest level. But it is not ready to launch, and I know you don't want our young people's blood spilled needlessly."

He turned to Jeremy. "You've communicated to London and back since the invasion began?" When Jeremy nodded, the major growled, "Then send another message telling them that we need the heavy weapons and ammunition. Now."

"I've done that, but I will again, sir, stating that the message comes from you."

While Jeremy hurried away, silence hung in the café. Then the rhythm of galloping hooves sounded and ended abruptly in front of the hotel. Shortly after, *Capitaine* Narcisse Geyer appeared in the doorway followed by several other officers. His boots echoed sharply as he strode across the wooden café floor, and on standing in front of Huet, he saluted. "We meet again, Major."

"We do. Have a seat, Captain. We were discussing next steps."

Huet noticed his own dislike of the captain, although he had to admit that Geyer was a good-looking officer, clean-shaven with a firm jaw and steady eyes. Obviously full of spirit and himself, he reminded Huet of the cavaliers of General Lafayette's day in the late 1700s. Geyer was fully confident in himself, his horse, and his sword, but perhaps did not internalize that the technology of war had moved on.

A messenger appeared at the door and hurried to deliver it to Huet.

While the major read it, Geyer lit a cigarette and regarded the others with a grin. "Now we are going to have some sport."

"The Vercors is not activating now," Huet cut in sternly. "We are supposed to be receiving a regiment of French paratroopers from Algiers. I just issued orders that we will not activate until receiving word that the paratroopers have left there. I'll fill you in." He held up the message he had just received. "Meanwhile, this is from General Koenig, our new army chief of staff in London. He says, 'The battle for liberation has begun. Now all Frenchmen must put aside political differences and cooperate totally in the fight to drive our enemy from France.'"

"That seems to say that we should activate," Geyer said.

"I disagree," Huet countered. "It says to put aside differences and *cooperate* in this war. As I stated earlier, the Vercors is a special place that can be a base from which to attack the enemy from his rear along the south, the west, and the north. But it can't do that if we're overrun, and we lack the heavy weapons to fight effectively.

"As we sit here, we know of no further support coming from Algiers. Until we do, our role is to do nothing to provoke a move against the Vercors, and meanwhile—if the Germans attack—to defend the passes until support arrives. That's the only way we'll be prepared to host the paratroopers and the support they'll bring."

Geyer eyed Huet without expression. Then he said, "I agree that it is too early to activate. Until we have support, we should continue with guerrilla strikes, which my unit has proven to be quite adept at doing."

Huet shook his head. "The Germans are preoccupied now with defending in Normandy and preparing for an expected landing in Provence, so they'll leave us alone for the time being. This command is not equipped to defend against a strike in force by the Germans. Until the promised support arrives, we will do nothing to provoke them." He shot a stern look at Geyer. "And that includes your guerrilla strikes."

The faces on the assembled group fell, as did those of listeners at the doors and windows, their fervor of the morning checked by Huet's reasoning. Dr. Samuel scraped his chair back and rose. "I must go." He regarded Huet with angry eyes. "You'll keep us informed?"

"Of course."

Others took their leave, and outside, the crowds dispersed. Geyer too stood as if to depart, his jaw set.

"We need to talk," Huet said.

The captain sat back down reluctantly, and Huet told him, "I'm here to supervise the military liaison between the Drôme and Isère departments."

Geyer held Huet's steady gaze. "Major, that is precisely what I had to do when your predecessor departed. Are you replacing me as commander of the Vercors?"

Huet studied Geyer. To the major's mind the captain was an able and dedicated officer, but despite being ten years younger than Huet, Geyer was stranded in the glamor of cavalry legend. Huet recalled that France had entered WWI under the romantic motto "Esprit de Corps," believing that superior fighting spirit alone would win France's battles. History had demonstrated otherwise.

"You are the commander of the Vercors south, Captain. My job is to liaise between the military and the civilian commanders for greatest coordination and cooperation. But understand that I hold the highest local military authority. I'll expect you to comply."

Geyer stared at the major. Then, visibly angry, he stood to attention. "Sir, I think perhaps I should remove my unit to the plains beyond the Vercors. Maybe I can do some good down there."

"I hope you don't do that, Captain," Huet said evenly. "You're a fighter, and a great one. Yours is the only command here with trained veterans. We've both recognized that the Vercors is poorly equipped to defend itself. We can't know when or if the *Wehrmacht* will turn its attention on us, but when they do, the people of the Vercors need you here." He left unstated the disciplinary measures that could ensue should Geyer pursue his own ends.

Geyer glared silently. Then he swallowed hard and saluted. "Sir, I will do my duty." With that, he turned and strode from the café.

Seconds later, Huet sat alone listening to the sound of receding hooves.

44

Bletchley Park, London

"Heavens," Travis said, glancing at his watch when Claire entered his office. "It's nearly midnight. You're still here."

"As are you and most of the staff. It's been an incredible day. I hope a good one, at least on balance. I suppose history will tell."

"We do have challenges ahead of us. The war is far from won, but we've made successful forays inland. I heard that one of our British units in the 6th Airborne Division was tasked with capturing a bridge between Ouistreham and Caen. Pegasus, they're calling it. I believe the commander was Major John Howard."

Travis warmed to the story as he related it, his eyes glowing with enthusiasm. "His gliders went in before midnight last night. They landed within thirty meters of Pegasus and completely surprised the Germans. They had a short firefight, but within ten minutes, they controlled the bridge."

Claire started to say something, but Travis went on. "There was a house next to Pegasus. The Germans abandoned it, so Howard and his lot became the first Allied invading troops to set foot in France, the bridge was the first objective seized, and the house was the first to be liberated. It was owned by the Gondrée family who had provided information to the Allies through the Resistance. Major Howard used it as an aid station."

"That's marvelous, sir," Claire exclaimed.

"Here's the best part," Travis continued excitedly. "They were reinforced by No. 4 Commando, a French unit under *Capitaine* Philippe Kieffer. He led the first French soldiers onto the beach at Sword, and they were the first to come ashore in the entire Overlord operation. As they made their way through Ouistreham, Howard was alerted to Kieffer's approach by the sound of Lord Lovat's bagpipes. Captured Germans said they had not shot the man playing the pipes because he also wore a kilt and they thought he was crazy and thus harmless."

"Truly remarkable," Claire interjected, caught up in Travis' enthusiasm. She wondered fleetingly where her brothers might be in any part of the day's actions. "Bully for the French. They deserve a victory." Then she added, "I'm afraid I missed all the public pronouncement by the PM and the American president."

Travis waved away the comment. "They said the things you'd expect them to say. Nothing new that you didn't already know." A querying look crossed his face. "Do you have something for me?"

"Yes, sir, I do. How should I put this?" She took a moment to gather her thoughts. "Whether Nimrod was for us or against us, or whether he affected an outcome at all, messages are flying around German High Command regarding the XII Panzer Group. Rommel wants it at Somme; von Runstedt wants it too, farther south—"

"And Hitler?"

"He won't let it go. He believes that Normandy is a diversion, and that the main invasion will still come at Calais." Claire sat up straight and inhaled deeply. "Sir, I would say that our invasion was a complete surprise. And it seems that somehow, Hitler has still got it in his head that Normandy is merely a diversion."

Travis could not suppress a smile. "Ah, bless be. Do you think so?" He sat back, exulting in the moment. "And what of Nimrod? What's become of him."

"It's funny that you ask, sir. For nearly two days, his codename was all over German wires. With a few exceptions, most notably Rommel, Nimrod was praised for his courage and insights. Recall that the *Abwehr* wanted to bring him to Berlin for more consultations." She lifted her eyebrows. "I don't know if they intended those interviews to be friendly, but if the *Abwehr* or *Gestapo* in Berlin get their hands on him now, I can assure you that his torture will be horrendous."

A puzzled look crossed Travis' face. "If they get their hands on him?"

Claire nodded. "He seems to have escaped. At least they're looking for him high and low, and they've put out an order for his arrest. He apparently took out a high-ranking *Abwehr* officer, a man called Mannheim. A chop to the neck. The officer's body was found floating in the Seine."

"Well then, Nimrod seems to have been one of ours. If so, let's wish him Godspeed on his way home."

"Agreed, sir."

Stony Stratford, England

Claire dragged herself up her garden path into her house. Strangely, a lamp still gleamed at the edge of the blackout curtains. Large-scale German bombing had ended months ago, but the public had been warned that they still could happen, and not to drop their guard.

Having anticipated a long night, Claire had called ahead to ask the nanny, Elsie, to stay overnight. She had done so in times past, and Elsie had been in bed asleep when Claire came home. That the nanny was still up was a surprise, but a comfortable one. She had been an invaluable aid in raising Timmy and keeping life sorted out as the war raged and Claire managed her secret life at Bletchley.

A woman's voice greeted her from the sitting room as she entered, and Claire, recognizing it, was immediately delighted. "Sherry? You're here? How wonderful."

Claire rushed into the sitting room and threw her arms around her cousin. "What a surprise. I couldn't be happier." She rolled her eyes and added, "Under the circumstances."

"I had a few days of leave," Sherry said when they took their seats. "I've been recalled, so I'll be leaving in the morning. Of course I was taken by surprise like everyone by the invasion of Normandy. I'm glad to have a few hours to see you."

"For so little time?" Claire said in dismay. "But the day's events have been thrilling, in the abstract."

Somberness clouded their expressions. "I just hope our brothers are okay," Sherry said. "Do you hear from them?"

"Paul was here for a short while a few weeks ago. He had just come out of the maelstrom at Rapido and was on his way to command a unit under a Lord Lovat—I think that was the man's name. I'm sure it has something to do with Normandy, but I have no idea what. What about your brothers?"

"I hear from them occasionally. Josh was in those operations at Truk Lagoon. That's all I know about him. And Zack is still in Italy. He must have been close to where Paul was because he mentioned Rapido, but that's the sum total of my information on him too." She sighed. "It's so frustrating not knowing if they're all right."

"I know. Let me get you a drink."

"What about Lance and Jeremy," Sherry called while Claire poured out two brandies.

"Lance has escaped again," Claire called back, "but he's not made it home to England, so I don't know where he is. And Jeremy is also in France, although exactly where and what he's doing, I don't know." She handed one crystal goblet to Sherry and clinked it with her own in a toast. "Tell me about your work?"

"It's sad, and difficult to talk about. All I see are badly wounded men. And they look at us with such adoration, hoping against hope that we will be able to save them." She fought back emotion. "And it's not just their lives they hope for. It's to have meaning restored. They look to us, their flight nurses, for that."

She tossed the brandy down her throat and held the goblet back out to Claire. "I could use another one of those. With this invasion, we're going to see a lot more horribly wounded men." She set her glass down and dropped her face into her hands.

Claire went to sit close to Sherry on the sofa and put an arm around her back. "You really are angels," she said. "I am so proud of you." She took Sherry's glass and went to pour another brandy.

Sherry took a deep breath. "What are you going to do when the war's over? I mean after today, it's inevitable."

Claire tossed her head. "I don't know. I haven't thought that far ahead. I'll probably go back to Sark. We used to call it our little piece of paradise. I could use its normal tranquility for a while."

Sherry smirked. "Do you mind if I come? I could use some of that serenity."

"You're always welcome, and I mean that. In fact, I'll plan on it. Jeremy and Amélie are to be married there. You must be there for that."

Sherry leaned back. "Ahh, optimism. That's the best news I've heard recently. I'll certainly plan to be there." She leaned back into the sofa and gazed around. "The nanny let me in. I hope you don't mind. Timmy was already asleep. May I look in on him?"

"Of course," Claire said. "I always like to see him just before I turn in."

They went to Timmy's room. The child lay fast asleep, his mouth slightly open.

"I needed to see him," Sherry said when they came back into the sitting room. "He reminds me why we do what we do." She glanced sharply at Claire. "I'm sorry. I didn't mean to slight you. The work of the people on the home front, taking care of our countries' futures, are every bit as important as those on the front lines."

"Thank you for saying that," Claire said quietly while averting her eyes to her drink. "We all do what we can."

45

June 7, 1944
Saint-Martin-en-Vercors, France

Having just arrived from Lyon via an ancient, rambling bus spewing black smoke, and amid jubilant cheers, a triumphant Chavant strode across the floor of the Hôtel Breyton to the center of the room and mounted a chair. He held his fists over his head and joined in cheering. Then he gestured with his hands to quiet the crowd.

"Did you hear our hero, General Charles de Gaulle, on the radio last night?" he shouted. "Did you hear him?" He paused for effect. "He has that rich, dramatic voice, and he proclaimed, 'The supreme battle is being fought. For the sons of France, wherever they are, whoever they are, the simple and sacred duty is to fight the enemy by every means at their disposal.'"

His audience erupted into wild cheers again. Chavant waited for it to subside. "I've just come from speaking with Jacques Soustelle in Algiers," he told the hushed crowd. "He is charged by de Gaulle with countering Pétain's diplomacy and with providing support to Resistance groups. The Free French army in Algiers now stands at four-hundred-thousand men, and we have ships and planes. I have seen them with my own eyes."

Amid approving murmurs, he took a folded sheet of paper from his jacket pocket and held it while he continued. "I also met with Colonel Descour in Lyon two days ago. He has appointed a new military commander for the Vercors, Major Huet." He waved the document in the air. "This piece of paper," he shouted, "orders the execution of Operation Montagnard, the plan that Jean Moulin himself approved before that butcher of Lyon, Klaus Barbie, murdered him." He paused for effect. "The Vercors Massif will gain its place in the glorious history of France."

Once again, the crowd erupted in cheers.

"Wait!" Chavant called over the roar. "Listen. I'll read it to you."

His audience quieted again. Chavant lowered the document to his front, found the pertinent part, and read, "'The directives issued in February 1943 by General Vidal for the organization of the Vercors continue to be valid. Their execution will be pursued by the regional military delegate in liaison partly with the *Maquis* mission sent from London, and partly with head-quarters in Algiers.'"

Chavant looked up from the paper and pointed out Jeremy. "Of course the sentence about London refers to our good friends, Roger and Labrador. And Algiers refers to Major Huet, whom I will meet later today, and the paratroopers who will parachute into the Vercors."

The gathering was quiet now, except for low murmuring. Then someone called out, "Chavant, what does that document mean?"

Chavant beamed. "It is signed for General Charles de Gaulle," he proclaimed proudly. "It means"—he paused and looked over the crowd—"the Vercors will be pivotal to ridding France of the Nazis."

The crowd went wild, now in full celebration. "Wait, wait," Chavant called, once again waving the paper in the air as the hubbub subsided frac-tionally. "That starts with a big part in the coming battle. As I mentioned, we will host and support airborne troops, four thousand of them. They will drop into Vassieux and La Chapelle to conduct operations against the *Wehrmacht* toward Marseille and Nice—" He stretched and pointed dramatically southward. Then he continued, pointing west. "And toward Bordeaux."

As the crowd cheered, he held up his hand and pressed an index finger to his lips, calling for silence. When he spoke again, his voice rose to a crescendo, and again he pointed. "And northwest past Lyon and on to Vichy. And then we will liberate Paris!"

The tumult rose to an uncontrollable pitch with people dancing on tables, hugging each other, and kissing. Then a few men rushed Chavant, pulled him from the table onto their shoulders, and paraded him around the café and out into the streets where word had spread and the towns-people celebrated at full throttle.

Jeremy had watched the merriment from a corner of the café and now moved to one side of the street as the festivities continued. "I'll be damned," he remarked quietly, "Chavant seems to have pulled it off." Even as he said it, he was sobered by Huet's concern that no word of any support being on the way had been received.

Later, when the festivities had attenuated to excited conversations, Jeremy settled into a chair at a table in the hotel with Chavant and the other Vercors leaders. Jeremy had met Chavant shortly after first arriving in the Vercors. He had found the man to be indisputably charismatic, dedi-cated to the Vercors and the liberation of France, and a mover of events who refused to accept subservience.

"Congratulations. You've done a marvelous job," Jeremy said. "Tell us about your trip."

Chavant glowed and related the things he had told Colonel Descour two days earlier in Lyon, about the escalating meetings that culminated in a personal audience with Soustelle. "I told them that if they play the Vercors card—Operation Montagnard—it should be a surprise to the enemy. The *Wehrmacht* will be unsure and confused after the landing. We should add to their confusion. Of course, I didn't know then that the invasion would happen yesterday."

"Chavant," Dr. Samuel broke in, his eyes betraying his anxiety. "Only Normandy was invaded. Operation Montagnard required an invasion along our Mediterranean coast. Will that happen? You mentioned in your speech that de Gaulle had called on every man to enter the fight."

Chavant smiled confidently and met the gaze of each man around the table. "I explained the plan in detail at every meeting in Algiers, including your point, Dr. Samuel, about the invasion from the south. I said that, rather than seeing the Vercors as a place to hold, it should be treated as a vast base from which to attack and exploit German disruptions. I made sure they understood that for Montagnard to work, the invasion from the south was imperative." He let go a deep belly laugh. "Do you believe it? I'm telling these things to our highest generals, and they're listening to me."

He enjoyed the merriment as the others laughed with him. Then he continued, "When Soustelle brought that order to me, which he personally signed for General de Gaulle, I had to pinch myself. But here it is." He displayed the document again, and then returned his gaze to Dr. Samuel. "So, to answer your question, my friend, the Vercors is to be that special place, and we will receive orders to activate when the second landing occurs on our southern shore in Provence, which will happen very soon."

With a contented smile, Dr. Samuel stood and clapped Chavant on the back. "When this war is over," he said, "your name will be celebrated among your countrymen as a hero of France. We're proud of you."

"Ah," Chavant replied, glancing at Jeremy, "the fighting spirit of the Vercors along with Roger's and Labrador's presence here, and the support which Colonel Descour expressed, makes this a reality."

He grunted, opened a satchel at his feet, and displayed its contents. "Look what else I brought—2.5 million francs and current code books." He looked around the table. "Friends, prepare to do battle."

Tension was obvious at the introduction of Chavant to Major Huet later that afternoon at a private home in Saint-Agnan, a few miles south of Saint-Martin. Understanding Chavant's antipathy to military personnel, Colonel Descour had orchestrated the rendezvous by prevailing upon Father Vincent, the parish priest, to host the initial meeting. The gregarious priest had been highly influential in establishing the Vercors as a refuge for maquisards.

Regardless of the preparations toward conviviality, and to Vincent's dismay, Chavant, flush with confidence from the success of his Algiers mission, refused to shake Huet's hand. He stood back, feet apart, studying Huet. "You and I won't see eye to eye. I'm a socialist. I oppose the Catholic Church. And I don't like the army."

Taken aback, Huet scrutinized Chavant. At last he replied, "I stay away from politics, *Monsieur*. I'm a devout Catholic and a professional soldier."

Watching from the sidelines, Jeremy held his breath. Then Chavant broke into a grin, guffawed, and clapped Huet on the back. "You have strong convictions. I like that. We can work well together." He laughed again. "I'll take you up this evening to Rencurel to meet the chiefs of each camp. They're gathering up there now to review plans."

"I shall be pleased to meet them," Huet replied.

Later, after the short meeting, Jeremy and Huet spent time becoming acquainted. Huet confided, "I saw the order that Chavant brought back. It made me uneasy. It was signed *for* de Gaulle, and not *by* de Gaulle. Chavant says the Free French army plans to station four thousand troops here. Where is the schedule with points of contact to coordinate that? What's the communications plan? We can't put all that together magically overnight.

"The codes he mentioned are useless without the wireless telegraphs, and the money he brought back won't go far. It sounds like a lot, but it can't be more than a few tens of thousands of US dollars. That's supposed to handle our part of an operation as big as Montagnard?"

He grabbed Jeremy's arm and swung in front of him. "Labrador, even if de Gaulle plans to parachute the promised forces in, he's late. The drop zones are cleared, but we only have light weapons, not enough of them, and not enough ammo. We need mortars, field artillery, and tank destroyers with full loads. If we don't get them, and the Germans attack in force, we're done for."

He sighed. "I'm sorry, Labrador, and I hope I'm wrong, but I just don't see things happening as Chavant was led to believe."

Jeremy listened closely. "I'm confused. Why would the Free French mislead him."

Huet sighed. "I'm sure their intentions are good, and maybe Algiers isn't yet sufficiently staffed to think this through thoroughly, which would mean that our forces are not yet developed into a true fighting force. And we're relying on them."

"I see your points. What more can we do?"

Huet shoved his open hands out in front of him in a gesture of exasperation. "You've already begged London. They've promised but not delivered.

The only thing we can do now is repeat the requests, state the urgency, and exercise the *maquisards* even more to be able to defend the passes when the time comes."

Later, to the major's surprise, he found that Chavant agreed with his position regarding mobilization. Chavant said that, without such support, a massacre was inevitable.

"That's one person I don't have to convince," Huet told Jeremy. "That's a relief."

June 8, 1944
Saint-Martin-en-Vercors, France

Colonel Descour hid his agitation when he arrived at the Hôtel Breyton, greeting Huet cordially. "I've set up Region 1 headquarters in a house five miles south of town. Are you set up here?"

"Yes, sir. I've taken over the third floor of this hotel. I'll show you." Huet turned and escorted the colonel through the foyer to a set of stairs. "My staff is still arriving."

"That's good. You've met Chavant?"

"Yesterday, and we got along well. As long as we keep our focus on liberating France, we'll work together very well."

"I'm glad to hear it." As they walked through the lobby, Descour informed Huet of a message he had sent to the headquarters in Algiers the previous day. "I wrote that the need was urgent, and that they should drop light weapons for two thousand *maquisards*, heavy weapons, and at least one regiment of paratroops immediately—the drop zones are ready."

"Have you heard back?" the major asked, keeping his tone intentionally bland.

"Not yet." Descour's voice changed tenor and became stern. "I told them that the Vercors had been activated."

Huet's head snapped toward the colonel.

Descour continued as if not noticing Huet's reaction. "I said that if the Vercors were attacked in force, we had insufficient arms here even to stop much less repel the enemy, and therefore we required immediate rein-forcement."

The two officers reached the bottom of the stairs. Descour nudged Huet's elbow and turned in front of him abruptly. "Why haven't you acti-vated the Vercors?"

Huet was at first at a loss for words. "I've received no order to activate," he replied at last. "Operation Montagnard depends on an invasion in the south. So far, we've heard no word of that happening—only that the Allies invaded at Normandy. I've had a full discussion with Chavant, and we agree on steps to mobilize rapidly when we've received such an order."

Descour's eyes glinted. "But the whole country was called to action via that line from Verlaine's poem over the BBC. And de Gaulle himself called on every man to fight with whatever they have." The colonel gazed around the hotel foyer at villagers wandering in and out with curious glances at the two officers. From this vantage, he saw inside the café where, even now, Chavant held court with his fellow citizens. He turned back to Huet. "I confirm your orders, Major Huet, here and now. Activate Operation Montagnard immediately."

Chagrinned and in shock, Huet locked his heels and saluted. "It shall be done."

That evening, as Huet prepared the mobilization orders, and in spite of his earlier stance, elation seeped in at the notion of striking at *les boches*. Nevertheless, he could not rid himself of an undertone of dread. On balance, viewed objectively, he believed his initial posture had been correct.

Across town, having adopted Roger's habit of moving frequently to a new location without informing anyone of where that might be, Jeremy settled for the night at a farmhouse where he had been welcomed and fed by a grateful family. He lay in bed that night thinking through the events of the last two days and weighing Huet's caution, ignorant of the fact that Operation Montagnard had been activated. He sighed deeply. Dark days loomed.

June 9, 1944

Jeremy entered Saint-Martin wondering at the flurry of activity. Realization dawned that activation had commenced. Speaking with people in the streets, he learned that Huet's orders had gone out during the night, and the people of the Vercors and those in the areas around it responded with alacrity.

In effect, the activation order created a Free French territory, governed by Frenchmen, the first since the German invasion four years ago. Streams of *maquisards*, many of them women, had crossed through the mountain passes overnight. Some had gone straight to their assigned fighting positions. Others waited on the streets and fields around the village for further instructions.

When Jeremy entered Hôtel Breyton's café, Chavant was meeting with various leading citizens to appoint a police chief, a postmaster, and other critical positions required of a national government, including someone to handle diplomatic relations.

Jeremy observed for a few minutes, then passed by the logistician, Huillier, who haggled with farmers and truckers over plans to bring in sufficient supplies to feed the newcomers, including those out guarding the passes.

Jeremy climbed the stairs to Huet's headquarters on the third floor. The staff had moved in rapidly, evidenced by a murmur of voices as he reached the landing at the top. On either side of a long hall to his front, typewriters clacked, phones rang, and as Jeremy passed by various rooms with open doors, he saw that maps lined the walls. Officers conversed in insistent tones.

Huet stepped out of a room, spotted Jeremy, and beckoned to him. When the two were alone and the door was closed, he said tersely, "I couldn't reach you. I met with my companies' liaison officers at 06:00 hours this morning. I wanted you there."

Jeremy locked his eyes on the major's but made no reply.

Huet held his gaze. "Sorry," he said grimly. Obviously, he had been up all night. "You couldn't have known. Last evening, Descour ordered activation." He rubbed his eyes. "This is not going well. It's happening too early and too fast."

He told Jeremy about Descour's message to Algiers requesting para-troops and weapons.

"Has he heard back?"

Huet shook his head. "My subordinate commanders are executing plans they've had in place a long time. The organization is working as it should. The plans are complex, detailed, and the *maquisards* are motivated and performing well. The passes are closed and reinforced to the best of our abilities."

He looked pained. "The trouble is that once things have been set in motion, we can't reverse them. The Germans are alerted to our activities, and to stop now is to invite retribution."

Huet took a deep breath. "The success of what we do here hinges on the promised support from Algiers and the amphibious landing on the southern coast. Without those two things, a lot of people are going to die for no reason." Anxiety crept into his voice. "Would you go through your channels in London? See if you can at least get a parachute drop of ammunition."

"Yes, of course." Jeremy glanced through a window at *maquisards* waiting under leafy trees lining a courtyard in front of the church across the street. Beyond them, he took in the grand view of green mountain slopes rising to the base of sheer stone cliffs reaching into the sky. He sucked in his breath. "This really is a special place, isn't it? I think I've fallen in love with the Vercors."

"It's a place worth saving, Jeremy. So please, get that message sent."

"Sorry," Jeremy replied, "I'll do it at once."

"I've requisitioned a motorcycle to tour all the passes to make sure we're making best use of our defenses. I'm going out tomorrow. I'd like you to go with me. You might spot something I've missed."

Jeremy laughed. "You want me to go on the back of your motorcycle?"

Huet chuckled. "I'll requisition another one."

46

June 10, 1944
London, England

An exhausted Rigby sat in an SOE office on Baker Street. He wore a new set of clothes and was nursing his left arm where he had been shot. Ahead of him were more hours of interviews similar to what he had endured in La Roche.

When Arngross had left him in his room high in the tower at La Roche after flying back from Berchtesgaden, Rigby had lain flat on his back in the trundle bed. It was the same room where he had slept on first being brought there. He found that he was locked in, and a single window overlooked a high vertical drop. Further silent exploration had revealed two bugs, one he was intended to find, and one more subtly hidden behind canvas painted to look like wood on a bedstand next to his cot.

In the true sense of the word, irrespective of the regard with which he had been treated, he was a prisoner in La Roche. Whether or not Mannheim, Ritter, Rommel, Hitler, Arngross, or anyone else who had interviewed him believed what he had told them or the documents he had produced, they were taking no chances. He would remain captive until his information proved itself to be true or otherwise.

Heavy with fatigue, he had nevertheless been amazed at the events that had occurred during the five short days that had elapsed since he had flown into the field south of Paris. Thankfully, Arngross had not come to shake him awake this morning. The sun was high, and apparently no one needed him for the moment. He wondered if he had succeeded in his mission.

An orderly brought breakfast on a tray. It was full and sufficient, with eggs, cold cuts, orange juice, and real coffee, but when the orderly left, he again locked the door.

The release of nervous tension after departing the great hall at the Berghof the day before had left Rigby trembling with nausea. He had leaned against a marble balustrade on the famous balcony at the front of the chalet and let the mountain air refresh him, barely cognizant of the magnificent mountain view to his front.

Arngross had been understanding and solicitous. When Rigby's knees seemed about to give out, the captain had placed an arm behind Rigby's back to hold him up. An unsuppressed smile accompanied by light shining from Arngross' eyes indicated that the officer considered the meeting to have been a resounding success and just might forward his career.

Rigby had nibbled at his breakfast, and then lay flat on his cot, letting his mind drift back to when he had joined the commandos. Having enlisted in the Royal Pioneer Corps in order to be allowed to return to the UK after being deported because of his German ancestry, Rigby had responded to a government call for young, fit men to join a special unit "for dangerous assignment" in the war effort. He had been previously rejected from British military service because of his German ancestry, but he had wanted to be part of fighting the Nazis.

At the back of his mind constantly were images of a November night in Vienna, six years earlier. His father had owned a jewelry store there. Already by then, German law required Jewish owners of businesses to mark their establishments with a prominent Star of David. On that night, all across Germany, Austria, and the Sudetenland, the Nazi Party's *Sturmabteilung* paramilitary and *Schutzstaffel* paramilitary, along with Hitler Youth and German civilians, had broken into Jewish shops, offices, manufacturing facilities, and other enterprises, and trashed them.

The rioters had broken windows, thrown merchandise into the

streets, hauled the owners and their wives and families out, beaten them, and publicly humiliated them. Rigby had watched as his own family's store had been destroyed, his father dragged into the night before a jeering crowd, stripped naked, and forced to sweep up garbage. Shortly thereafter, the family sold the business for a pittance and moved to England.

The posting to which Rigby had responded was for a special commando unit. It was composed of young men of Jewish ancestry who wished to strike at the German war machine. Given the political sensibilities, it had been designated as No. X Commando.

The major in charge of Rigby's mission had been fastidious in selecting him. The criteria had been that the chosen candidate must be fluent in English, German, and French. He must be blond-haired and blue-eyed, able to meet the standards of the commandos, and pass their training.

"Yours is a deception mission," the major had explained. "For such a mission to succeed, we give our enemies a hard fact that can be verified. We give them two more that sound true. If they believe those three pieces of information, they'll probably believe the fourth with only cursory checking, and so on."

Behind the information provided, the major had explained, was a whole apparatus of British disinformation that had operated since the early days of the war on myriad other missions. "You see," he explained, "we've captured every German operative sent into our country, and we've turned them. They work for us. They don't do so necessarily willingly, but the alternative is a long life in prison, or worse.

"We teach these turned operatives to recruit large numbers of spies to do their bidding. The spies are mostly fictitious personalities who nevertheless draw compensation from the German treasury, have family problems like any normal person, run into difficulties with landlords, regular jobs, etcetera. The operatives do run a few real spies—under our supervision, of course—but the advantage of a fictitious spy is that they do our bidding without any fuss or objection.

"These German operatives and their recruited spies interact via wireless with their supposed German masters on a regular basis. They answer any query coming from the *Abwehr* with whatever information we provide, and we have coders who are experts in their language to ensure that what they send is what we intend."

Rigby had been astounded to learn that Weber was a man whom he had known after moving to England from Vienna. The man's name had then been Werner, and he *had* taught Rigby piano. He had also been a German operative before the war, and had been caught and turned after conflict began. Part of the reason that Rigby had been selected was for his prior acquaintance with Weber.

He was astonished to learn that Weber, before his capture and as Werner, had intended to recruit Rigby himself as a spy. Weber had since become a principle conduit of passing intelligence to the *Abwehr* that the British desired it to have. Of course, it was all designed to misinform.

On the last night before Rigby's Lysander flight to northern France and under the major's watchful eye, Weber had told Rigby sadly, "I wish us both luck." The German operative knew that his own best outcome now was for Germany to lose the war, and that he be afforded the opportunity to remain in Britain under a new identification.

The major told Rigby, "Here's the situation, Nimrod—that's your code-name, which will be known to German intelligence. They will know your true name and background, aside from what happened to your family at *Kristallnacht*. We'll move the time of your emigration from Austria to pre-date that night, and your motive for your loyalty to Germany will be your deportation to Canada. With some checking, they could find out the truth, but we'll overwhelm them with other verifiable information about you so that there is no need to check deeply.

"Hitler et al. expect an invasion. Among the German High Command, there is a difference of opinion about where it will take place. We know that Hitler himself believes it will be at Pas de Calais. That's good. Some think it will be at Somme, others in Normandy, and still others along the Mediterranean.

"You can easily see that, for an amphibious operation to succeed, it needs every available minute to establish a beachhead, consolidate its position, and invade farther inland. If we are pushed off the beach back into the sea, we'll lose the war."

"I see that, sir," Rigby had interjected. "Where do I come in?"

The major had taken his time to reply. "The German intelligence apparatus and command structure now operates in fear. No one dares to be wrong or to cross the *führer*, and that includes the vaunted Desert Fox of North Africa, Field Marshal Rommel.

"It's important for you to understand that your task is not to change minds in any way. You're not the load for the camel to carry; you're the straw to break its back. In plain terms, you are to provide *the verifiable information* that Hitler needs to solidify what he firmly believes, that the invasion will come at Calais. If you succeed, he will force his view and the indicated action on his lackeys.

"Here's the desired effect. The *führer* personally controls XII Panzer Group, held in reserve. It can move nowhere except by his order. We need for it to stay put as long as possible. You don't need to know where the invasion will take place, but Hitler must be shown strong reason to hold steadfastly to his own belief that Calais is the main target.

"Further, he should be left with reason to believe that any other landings are feints, designed to cause him to commit his reserve away from Calais. If we gain only a matter of hours because he holds the XII Panzers back from reinforcing elsewhere, we increase, by magnitudes, the probability of success for the actual invasion."

"Sir," Rigby had inquired, "you've given me a new name, Stephen Rigby. The Germans will know my real name, Stefan Rosenberg, and my Jewish ancestry?"

"That's because they will easily find out both of those things—"

"I get that, and that the negative connotation is mitigated by my Catholic mother and my blond hair and blue eyes. But you've also given me another name, Stephane Dubillier, with forged papers to use with the French Resistance. And you've given me a codename, Nimrod. In addition are all these facts I'm supposed to regurgitate and documents I'm supposed to discuss knowledgeably." He had grimaced at the thought. "That's a lot to remember, and we have only a few days before I depart."

"Yes," the major had replied, "and you'll spend the remainder of your time until then with a professional hypnotist going through everything repeatedly until it becomes natural. One thing to know is that the *Abwehr* has been aware of Nimrod for many months. We've been preparing this gambit a long time. Nimrod has sent reports that have been confirmed, and he is already a reliable source of information for German intelligence, and he was ostensibly recruited by Weber. We had to find the right man to bring Nimrod to life. That is you."

As Rigby lay on his cot in the tower at La Roche, he had reflected in amazement at how well the hypnotism had worked. He had responded to questions put to him by reflex, as simply as he might have given his date of birth. He had resolved seemingly contradictory facts with ease, and he had presented and discussed difficult concepts with confidence, not the least of which was the case for an invasion at Calais. And he had done it surrounded by men he hated, wished dead, and could do him the most unimaginable harm should he be found out.

However, the effects of hypnotism were wearing off. He could feel it. Facts that had been at the front of his mind had now receded and could be called forward only with effort. Added to that was his certainty that the invasion must be only days away. That had been evident from his initial instruction: "Within forty-eight hours of arrival in France, you must demand to be presented to corps intelligence or higher."

"Tell me how you did it, Stefan? How did you escape?" the SOE major said.

Rigby, now reverting to his real name, Stefan Rosenberg, smiled distantly. "With the help of two obliging ladies of the night who kept the good Captain Arngross busy for several hours. I was to be transferred to Berlin the next day, and since he regarded me as a friend who had put a feather in his career cap, and we would be parting the next day, I offered to pay for the entertainment at a nearby brothel as a token of comradeship. I then feigned a stomach illness and escaped through a lavatory window."

"How did you get wounded?"

"Quite by accident. I had chosen a point on the Seine where I had observed a river barge going by daily at specific times. My plan was to swim out to the barge and ride it downriver until it came to a town with a railway station, and then I planned to stow away on freight cars.

"When I went to the river, that dreadful *Abwehr* Nazi, Mannheim, was taking a walk right at the place where I had to enter to have a chance of reaching the barge. I had no choice but to deal with him. If I'd missed the barge, I'd have been stuck at La Roche under even tighter security."

"Not to mention deeper suspicion," the major interjected, and then added strangely, "Perhaps."

Stefan took note of the comment and continued. "I chopped him across the throat just as I'd practiced so many times in commando school. Then I rolled his body into the river."

The major took a deep breath. "It's a shame about Mannheim, though."

Startled, Stefan looked sharply at the officer. "Sir? Was he one of ours?"

The major shook his head. "Not officially and not that we can say definitely, but his sentiments seem to have leaned our way. He was one of Admiral Canaris' close subordinates."

"Canaris? Isn't he Hitler's head of intelligence, the *Abwehr*?" Stefan asked skeptically.

"Yes, but increased evidence indicates that Canaris undermined the *führer* from the beginning. What is certain is that the admiral caused Spain to stay out of the war. Hitler sent him there to convince the dictator, Franco, to enter it on the Nazi side. The exact opposite took place. That's only one of many tidbits evidencing Canaris' true sentiments and actions. Reports coming through our intelligence sources indicate that he's falling under suspicion. In any event, we have little doubt that, without Mannheim, your audience with Hitler would not have taken place. He orchestrated your move to Berchtesgaden and he attended the conference at the Berghof during which someone suggested that you be brought in for Hitler's direct questioning."

Dumbfounded, Stefan could only stare.

"Go on," the major said. "How did you get out of Germany?"

Stefan exhaled. "The rest of the plan worked out as I'd hoped, with a few setbacks here and there," he said slowly. "I didn't so much infiltrate through friendly lines as let the front roll past me. The Germans were on the run, and the Brits and Americans were in hot pursuit. Dirty as I was, they hardly noticed me.

"My arm became infected along the way—"

"You were shot while escaping from German guards on a train?"

"Yes, sir, but I made it to Arromanches in one piece, and after hearing my story, an intelligence sergeant there was kind enough to get my arm treated and put me on a barge coming back to England. I have to say that I am truly amazed at the size of the port facilities that've been built there in such a short time. Whole convoys laden with supplies roll off big ships over docks that seemed to have come from nowhere."

"That's good to hear," the major remarked.

Stefan took a deep breath. "What happens with me now?"

The officer grimaced. "Our advice is that you take on yet another new identity—and undergo plastic surgery. We've had to do that with other No. X Commandos. We'll resettle you anywhere within the British Empire that you desire. You'll be starting afresh, with a completely new background, and you won't be hunted. Right now, the Third *Reich* has your likeness, and its agents are looking for you everywhere they still occupy."

"Hmm. I suppose they would do that. Having met *Herr* Hitler personally, I'd rather not be the object of his wrath." Stefan sat as though transfixed. "I can tell you that, much as I'd like to forget standing in front of all those men whom I hated with every fiber of my being, it is an experience, a feeling, that I shall never shed."

He snapped out of his reverie. "All right, let's get started."

47

Same Day
Saint-Martin-en-Vercors, France

The *maquisards* living near Saint-Martin had moved swiftly to tackle tasks required to activate the Vercors. Messengers rode bicycles, hopped rides, and hiked the slopes into the *Maquis* camps. They crossed over passes into towns surrounding Vercors, including Grenoble itself, to deliver orders. Hence the stream of people who had met Jeremy on his way in the day before.

By 09:00 hours yesterday, telephone lines had been cut to Grenoble and towns known to host German garrisons. The railroad tracks were switched at Saint-Nizier. Trucks were deployed to the town of Romans by a wealthy family of freight haulers, the Huilliers, to bring three hundred *maquisards* into the Vercors. The men beamed as they arrived in Saint-Martin and clambered to the ground.

"The roads in the plains are packed with *maquisards* coming to the Vercors," one of them chortled. "We displayed our contempt and our weapons openly to the *Wehrmacht* soldiers and the *Milice*. They didn't dare detain us. They're too worried about Normandy and what's going to happen in the south."

On mid-morning of the fourth day after D-Day, Huet and Jeremy set out to inspect the passes. Despite the circumstances, Jeremy thoroughly enjoyed the sense of freedom from riding a motorcycle along the tree-lined lane crossing the gorgeous plateau. The wind whipped through his hair, and the forest-cloaked mountains rose on either side into a deep blue sky. Most thrilling were the hordes of *maquisards* along the way, each of them going to pre-designated places in the Vercors. They came from Voiron, Lyon, Train, Crest, Bourg-de-Péage, Die, Grenoble itself, and countless villages in between. They came by bicycle, bus, trucks, horse and cart, tractors—by any means available; and they cheered, their arms raised in pure joy as Huet and Jeremy roared past.

"By tonight," Huet told Jeremy, "we'll have four thousand within our fortress."

They headed to Col de la Chau, a pass at the southwestern end of the plateau, traveling through Vassieux on the way. The burned-out houses and the remembered screams of terrified and dying children sobered Jeremy to his task.

When the two sped up narrow roads winding into the foothills and the high ridges beyond, the memory dampened the enjoyment they would have derived from the tugs of gravity and centrifugal forces while careening around curves and the throaty sound of their engines as they accelerated out of them.

Jeremy allowed himself a moment to think of Amélie, imagining her honey-colored eyes and the scent of her auburn hair. Too much time had passed since he had last seen her. He could only hope that she was still with Fourcade. Then he redirected his thoughts to the task ahead.

The first stop was at the pass leading into the town near the bottom of the outside slope, Crest. Spirits were high among the defenders who cheered on their arrival. Fighters who had rifles thrust them over their heads to celebrate. The company commander took Huet and Jeremy around to the various firing positions, proud to display his readiness. This unit's target area was steep and narrow, and was effectively sealed for all but those whom the *Maquis* allowed through, and at present, large crowds still sought passage.

The major and Jeremy moved on to the pass straddling the steep incline above Die, with a similar reception from the fighters there. "They're in high spirits," Jeremy remarked.

"Because they believe support is coming," Huet replied. He shook his head and looked skyward. "I hope it does."

They visited two more passes that afternoon. Then, with the day wearing long and the motorcycles' vibrations bringing on fatigue, they spent the night at Col de la Rousette, the crossing below the outside, eastern rim of the massif overlooking Chamalac. Arising early the next morning, they continued their inspection, finishing that evening near Engins.

The joys of riding the mountain curves had worn thin, challenging their muscles, and they were pleased to be greeted by the enthusiastic company of *maquisards* guarding the northeast pass. The unit defended a long, wide swath of open pasture, bounded on one side by a deep gorge and on the other by steep hillsides. The slope descended to the plains northwest of Grenoble and was fairly gentle, providing good approaches for tracked vehicles. Without major roads, wheeled vehicles and dismounted troops would find uphill progress to be tough, slow, and exposed.

June 11, 1944
Saint-Nizier-du-Moucherotte, Vercors, France

Early in the morning, satisfied that the command near Engins had deployed its defenses as well as could be expected, Jeremy and Huet wound around the mountain roads to the last of the passes. There they would meet with Captain Beauregard. His unenviable mission was to defend the pass at Saint-Nizier.

The village sat atop the northernmost and most difficult to defend of the eight passes, for being situated on a wide break in the mountains' walls. Overlooking Grenoble, site of the regional *Wehrmacht* headquarters, and with more maneuverable terrain than any other part of the Vercors, and good roads that led to Saint-Nizier without overhanging bluffs, it straddled the most likely approach for an assault in force.

It had been a popular ski resort before the war, which accounted for the quality of the roads. Its slopes were gentle in some areas, steep in others, and the route an armed force would take was circuitous, with many hairpin turns; but against light weapons, a well-armed unit taking its time could grind up to the village with minimal casualties.

As if melding minds, Colonel Descour, Major Huet, Captain Beauregard, Captain Geyer, and Jeremy converged on the town. Geyer, impatient with inactivity, had driven to Descour's headquarters to learn of any news regarding the progress of Allied forces in Normandy and the disposition of *Wehrmacht* forces closer to the Vercors. He had arrived just as Descour left for Saint-Nizier. Geyer followed him.

Surprised to find Descour and Geyer there when they arrived, Jeremy and Huet joined them and Beauregard at a traffic circle in the center of town. The normally composed Descour shook with anger. Without even a greeting, he thrust a scrap of paper into Huet's hand, a telegraph from General Koenig in London.

The major scanned it. Then, visibly enraged, he handed it to Jeremy.

As Jeremy absorbed Koenig's one-sentence message, he felt the blood drain from his face. It read, "Send the men home. They mobilized prematurely."

At that moment, from down the mountainside to the northeast, the crackling pops of a firefight arose. Huet and Jeremy cast questioning glances at Beauregard.

"That's been going on for three hours. So far, nothing serious," he said.

"A probe?" Jeremy asked.

"Probably."

"*C'est impossible!*" Huet exclaimed, taking the note back from Jeremy and shaking it in the air. He directed his comment to Descour, his eyes narrowing in simmering anger. "If we demobilize now, the Germans will be unmerciful. Retribution will be—" He exhaled and his voice fell an octave. "There are no words."

"Agreed," Descour said.

"Is there no support coming at all?" Jeremy asked.

Descour shook his head. "And no sign of a second landing in the south either." He inhaled deeply and let his breath out. "I sent a second message to Algiers and London the day before yesterday appealing to their moral responsibility. I reminded them that of the four thousand *maquisards* here at the Vercors, two thousand need weapons. I stated that we urgently need the paratroops along with fuel, food, and ammunition—all of it already promised." He glanced at a group of fighters squatting nearby and watching them anxiously. "I said that initial high spirits were ebbing as our men realize that we cannot mount an effective defense with only the equipment we have."

The colonel was quiet a moment, his eyes fixed on Huet. "You were right from the beginning, Major." Then he took a deep breath. "I told them that defeat here would result in merciless retribution and would be disastrous for this entire region."

"Did you get a reply?" Huet asked.

Descour nodded. "This morning. Finally. Algiers sent word that bad weather had prevented a response and delivery of support. They reiterated that it would come, conditioned on weather and transport availability."

"Do you believe them?"

Descour shrugged.

Jeremy watched Huet.

The major's jaw tightened, his eyes piercing. He turned to Geyer. "Get back to your unit. Things are likely to get hot very soon." When Geyer hesitated and looked to Descour, Huet growled, "That's an order, Captain."

As Geyer departed, containing his anger, the remaining group stood in silence. Jeremy turned to stare at the dramatic panorama spread down the mountainside to Grenoble. The view was unobstructed.

Suddenly, they heard men singing the French national anthem, their voices partially drowned by the sound of an engine. Moments later, a bus swung into view. The volume of male voices and the stirring lyrics and melody of "La Marseillaise" increased. As the bus rolled into view, maquisards emerged from their positions, raised their fists over their heads, and cheered.

In spite of the grim circumstances, Jeremy felt his own spirits lift, and slight, querying smiles formed on the mouths of the other officers. The bus continued around the traffic circle and came to a halt a few yards from them. A non-com hopped out of the front door. He approached the group, scanned their rank insignias, presented himself at attention to Descour, and saluted.

"Chief Sergeant Abel Chabal reports, sir."

The colonel returned the salute and peered at him. "What unit are you with? What are you doing here?"

"I command the 6th BCA commando unit, sir. We're here to reinforce."

Jeremy's ears perked up on hearing the word "commando."

"How many men do you have?" Descour demanded.

"Thirty, sir, including myself."

Before Descour could respond, Beauregard stepped forward. "I know these men, sir. They're the best trained, and they're worth a regiment to me now. That firefight down the mountain keeps going on. I welcome their reinforcement."

On impulse, Jeremy blurted, "I'll join you."

Abel regarded him dubiously.

"He's a British commando," Beauregard said roughly. "He was at Saint-Nazaire."

Doubtful looks turned to respectful admiration. "Your people trained us," Abel said. "Let's go. What's your rank?"

"Doesn't matter. You're in command."

Abel turned to Beauregard. "What are your orders, sir?"

As the three started off, Abel waved his hand over his head in a circular motion. The bus door squeaked open, and the French commandos came rumbling out, pulling their equipment with them. They lined up in three rows, and a non-com took a position centered on the platoon's front.

Abel called to him, "Sergeant, dispatch the detail for that special mission we discussed. Move the others under those trees over there"—he pointed—"and be prepared to move on my order. We're going into combat." As his men cheered, he turned to Jeremy. "You stay close to me."

The trio started off to coordinate. Then Beauregard halted, turned, and walked back to stand at attention before Descour. "This is all with your permission, sir."

Startled, the colonel stifled a chuckle. "Of course. Carry on."

As the three headed off, Huet turned to Descour. "Sir, I intend to send my own response to London and Algiers, with your permission."

The colonel rubbed his chin and regarded Huet solemnly. After a moment, he said, "How can I refuse? I should have had your judgment—we wouldn't be in this mess if I had. My radio and operator are inside Beauregard's headquarters. Use them."

Ten minutes later, Huet waited while the operator tapped out his encrypted message in Morse code:

THERE IS NO QUESTION OF SENDING THE MEN HOME AFTER HAVING COMPROMISED THE ENTIRE POPULATION BY MOBILIZING AND NOT RECEIVING A SINGLE SHRED OF SUPPORT WHATSOEVER TO RESIST!

"There's a machine gun nest near a critical turn in the road," Beauregard told Abel and Jeremy. "It's above a train embankment running along the side of the mountain. If the Germans seize that turn, they'll have a clear path onto the plateau where they'll command all the low ground. So far, we've been able to keep them at bay, but we haven't been able to knock out that gun position. We're burning up ammunition for nothing more than a stalemate."

"Where is it?"

"On Charvet Hill, about three miles northeast of here. The mountain drops off steeply on the east side, and the road at the top follows the crest. If they get there, they'll easily take Saint-Nizier."

Watching Abel, Jeremy recognized an immediate affinity. Several years older than he, the chief sergeant exuded confidence and a no-nonsense manner respected by his men, although Jeremy noticed that they felt no reservation about tossing good-natured barbs their leader's way. When Abel spoke sharply to bring them back to seriousness, they were just as quick to return to a strictly-business attitude.

"How's the terrain on either side of the road on the route up here?" Abel asked.

"Steep slopes on the downhill side, then thick conifers on the uphill side," Beauregard replied. "The enemy doesn't have much room to maneuver. They're channeled to the roads, but if they make it to the top, they'll spread out."

"All right," Abel said. "First priority is to take out that machine gun, and if possible secure the railbed below. Is that right?"

When Beauregard nodded, Abel said, "Good. Send a runner ahead to Charvet Hill to let your men know we're coming. I don't want them shooting at us. We'll figure out from there how to handle the machine gun nest."

Fifteen minutes later, Jeremy found himself double-timing at a good clip alongside Abel. They chose a route where the ground was reasonably flat and below the crest.

"You were at Saint-Nazaire?" Abel huffed between breaths as they ran. "And you're still alive and not a prisoner?" He laughed. "That's why I want you close to me."

"Just tell me what you want me to do."

"I will, when we get to Charvet Hill."

They slowed to a stealthy pace and spread out within tree lines as they neared the objective. A *maquisard* met them and guided them to a position overlooking the gun emplacement. "They've built up heavy cover around it," the man said.

He pointed it out, roughly a thousand meters down a road that climbed up to the plateau. "It's in as good a position as they can get, but they're having to shoot uphill," Jeremy said.

Abel agreed. "We'll have to get behind the gun and take out the riflemen on its flanks." He grimaced. "Like everyone else on the Vercors, we have no ammo to spare."

He and Jeremy maneuvered closer for a better look, crawling on their bellies to a ridgeline and peering around a rock. Then Abel rolled away and onto his back. "It's a gamble," he said, "but we can do this."

They crawled back to the relative safety of their line. Abel beckoned his senior subordinate. "English and I—" He gestured at Jeremy. "What was your name again?"

"Labrador is fine," Jeremy replied, giving his codename.

Abel shot him a dour glance. "Labrador and I are going to cross that open wheat field south of here on the downhill slope. The enemy shouldn't be expecting us, so when you get the signal, lay down covering fire on both sides of that gun position, heavier on the right side, but conserve ammunition."

The sergeant broke a wry smile. "Covering fire with conserved ammo." He made no attempt to hide his sarcasm.

Abel nodded. "Spread the men out on a line. When the shooting starts, everyone fires at once. After that, have them shoot intermittently with a count of three between rounds. Keep it slow and steady like that until we're across the field."

"So now I'm to conduct an orchestra."

Abel grinned. "Figure it out, Sergeant. I have faith in you."

"Will I be able to see you when you start into the open?"

"No, not at first. You'll have to set up a relay of signals. We won't go until we hear your barrage. We'll come into your view before we reach the other side. Stop firing when we're in the trees." Abel chuckled. "I don't want you to be the one who shoots me." He became serious again. "While we're in the woods, shift some men to provide covering fire on that field. We'll be coming out the same way. Don't fail me."

The sergeant smirked. "I'll try."

Abel turned to Jeremy. "Are you up for this? I have good men who've fought next to me. I'm taking you so I don't have to expend one of them." He grinned.

Jeremy deadpanned, "You'd better hope I'm still competent."

Abel's face snapped to a serious expression. He eyed four No. 36M Mk I grenades on Jeremy's equipment harness. "Do you know how to use those?"

"Oh, these Mills bombs?" Jeremy chuckled and patted them. "Let's hope so."

"Get ready." He turned to the sergeant. "Bring the squad leaders in so I can brief them. Then set them in position."

After forty more minutes, Abel and Jeremy stood in a stand of trees at the edge of the field. It was flat relative to the surrounding ground, with a slight downhill grade, and it appeared to be two hundred meters wide. "I'll go first," Abel said. "You know what to do." He turned and waved at one of his men just visible through the trees behind them. He, in turn, relayed to another comrade farther uphill.

Seconds later, the commandos and Beauregard's *maquisards* opened up with a fusillade. They were answered by much heavier return fire, including the heavy rat-tat-tat of the German MG 131 machine gun. Then the firing from the friendly side decreased in volume and continued at a steady but slow rate.

Jeremy turned to find that Abel had already sprinted into the wheat field and now ran full bore, his legs churning, his arms pumping, and after every few steps he changed direction slightly. Within seconds, he was into the trees on the other side, and no one seemed to have fired in his direction.

Jeremy waited. Moments later, Abel appeared at the edge of the woods. He waved, waited to see Jeremy's return signal, and ducked into shadows.

They had no time to spare. The sun had begun a slow descent, but with the high walls of the mountains to the west, daylight would be lost much sooner than on flat ground.

Friendly fire continued. With his heart beating, his breath coming in short gasps, Jeremy took off over the field. It had been plowed earlier in the year, and the furrows made the going rough, complicated by the crop of wheat and needing to change directions every few yards as Abel had done. He tripped twice but caught his balance, and then he was in the relative safety of the trees and their shadows.

The friendly firing stopped. Shortly thereafter, the German shooting stopped too.

Abel appeared next to Jeremy. "They haven't seen us," he whispered. "I've fixed their position. We'll take out the machine gunner first by lobbing in two grenades each.

That should disable the gun. The men on the flanks will take a few seconds to turn around. You take out the ones immediately to the left. I'll get the ones on the right."

They crept downhill through the underbrush, reached the floor of a gully, and started uphill. Then the ground leveled out and they were within sight of the gun position, approaching from its rear. They dropped to their bellies and slithered forward.

Jeremy inched ahead, his eyes on the target, now twenty-five meters to his front and facing uphill toward Charvet Hill. The machine gun nest, a field expedient position, was built with logs on three sides, a firing port cut into the front, and open to the rear. Jeremy scanned to the left and spotted four riflemen. Glancing at Abel, he saw the French commando checking the right flank.

Abel turned toward Jeremy, made eye contact, and pointed a finger forward. Jeremy nodded and eased toward the target.

Soon, he heard the low clink and clatter of soldiers going about their business, drinking water, opening rations, relieving themselves. Cigarette smoke wafted his way. Obviously the soldiers, thinking the firefight over for the time being, lapsed into relaxation mode, although with wary eyes toward Charvet Hill. The gunner and loader in the gun position had stretched on their backs on the ground and covered their faces with their helmets, apparently intent on napping.

Jeremy and Abel continued edging forward, checking with each other continually. When they were within forty feet, Abel signaled a halt. Then they each pulled two grenades from their belts and laid them on the ground. After taking a few moments to spot their subsequent targets, they again made eye contact.

Abel nodded.

Jeremy grasped a grenade in his right hand and rose to his knees.

Abel did the same.

With firm pressure on their release levers, they held the deadly pineapple-looking explosives chest-high, grasped the safety rings with their left index fingers, and pulled. Then they cocked their right arms back, and let fly.

They hit the ground, peering from under their helmets to see the result.

The levers, springing from the lobbed grenades, made a slight ringing noise as they arced into the air. Jeremy's went long, landing in front of the gun. Abel's landed in the middle of the position, between the two napping soldiers. It rolled to the front with a barely audible thump against the front logs.

The grenades exploded with flashes of flame and thunderous claps. Jagged, razor-sharp shrapnel flew. Smoke spewed. Men cried out in agony, and then died.

The rain of shrapnel ceased. Soldiers on either side of the position yelled to each other, looking frantically about to find the direction of attack. Two ran into the gun position to check on their comrades.

Lying prone on the ground, hidden by bushes, Abel signaled to Jeremy. Again they rose to their knees, pulled the rings, lobbed the grenades, and hit the ground. Both grenades landed within the log enclosure this time, finishing off the two soldiers who had just entered and demolishing the gun.

A soldier to the right spotted the two commandos. He yelled a warning to his comrades, and fired.

Jeremy grabbed his rifle, took swift, careful aim at a figure to his left running through the smoke, and fired. The man dropped. To his right, Abel fired, and the soldier who had spotted them went down.

Seeing no one else through the smoke, but hearing far-off voices, Jeremy looked to Abel.

"Let's go," Abel called.

They leaped to their feet and ran full-out the way they had come, zigzagging through the trees. Branches slapped their faces. Loud reports from rifle fire followed them, and all around, bullets struck the trees.

Abel tripped over a root and sprawled across the ground.

Jeremy heard footfalls behind him. He darted behind a thick tree.

A German soldier rushed by. He spotted Abel picking himself up, and raised his rifle at point-blank range.

Jeremy lunged, knocking the soldier sideways and the weapon from his grip.

The man fought for balance.

Jeremy lunged again. This time, he grabbed his commando knife from its scabbard on his leg, and thrust it up through the soldier's abdomen and into the heart.

The solder dropped without a sound and lay twitching.

Jeremy retrieved his own rifle and that of the dead German, as well as the soldier's ammunition. When he looked up again, Abel stared at him.

"You are my new best friend," Abel rasped. "Let's go."

As soon as they headed across the field, the fusillade of friendly fire started up and continued until the pair reached the safety of the woods on the other side. Then, they made their way back to Charvet Hill.

The sergeant met them as they staggered in. "We lost one."

"Who?" Abel asked.

"Louis."

Abel nodded grimly. "He died for France. Now for the railway embankment. Pull the squad leaders in."

When they were gathered, he laid out his plan, a downhill frontal assault. The German machine gun would have been a threat on their right flank, but with it now out of commission, Abel held one squad in reserve and ordered the other two to attack from the right and left.

With Jeremy accompanying him, he led to the right while his sergeant took the other element to the opposite flank. The Germans, however, had shifted position and reinforced. Under blistering fire, Abel lost two men and one was wounded. He pressed the attack, but with the sun waning, and concerned about ammunition, he ordered a withdrawal.

"Back to Charvet," he told Jeremy. "To defend."

However, the enemy did not pursue, and firing ceased. Puzzled, he and Jeremy went forward to the crest and peered over. Far below, the Germans retreated on the road down toward the plain.

Abel turned and beckoned to his men. They came forward cautiously, and when they saw the Germans filing away, they let loose a wild cheer.

Abel turned to Jeremy. "I'm not sure how, but we seem to have won that one."

While Jeremy watched, Abel joined in the cheers.

When the celebration had subsided, Jeremy gazed around to take in the vista of jagged rocks and mountain peaks in every direction. To the west, the sun was about to set above a gently sloping rise.

Abel came and stood beside him. "This is a beautiful place," he said.

"Worth fighting for," Jeremy rejoined.

"It is," Abel said, "but we fight for freedom. Without freedom, we would be removed from here. With it, no one can take it."

Jeremy thought over Abel's comment. "Fighting for home or fighting for freedom," he said thoughtfully. "That's a subtle distinction, but a crucial one."

They remained silent a few more moments. Abel looked somberly at the ground. "And now, I must honor our dead." He started to walk away.

Jeremy called after him, "Wait. I meant to ask earlier. Right after you arrived in town, I heard you order your sergeant to send out a detail on a special mission. What was that about?"

Abel smiled and pointed to the southeast. Jeremy turned to re-direct his view to where Abel indicated, a bare spot near a mountaintop. "That's Moucherotte. From Grenoble, that crest is clearly visible, and from all the towns around it."

Jeremy peered through squinted eyes. "I see your French flag flying. It's enormous."

Abel smiled again. "My commandos put it there. Look closely. It's been modified."

Jeremy strained to see. The wind had caught the blue, white, and red banner, and it flew full out, but its wave motion made picking out details difficult, particularly in the waning light.

"There's something on the white section, maybe a symbol? It's black, and it looks like an arrow pointing down with two horizontal lines crossing the shaft."

"You have good eyes, my friend. The arrow looks black from this distance, but it's blue, and that"—he thrust a finger toward the banner— "is the flag of the Free French Republic of the Vercors. When people in the plain look up there, they'll see it. Word will spread that, at least for a moment in this part of France, in the Massif Vercors, Frenchmen breathe free."

EPILOGUE

Saint-Nizier-du-Moucherotte, France

Descour and Huet walked onto the porch of the villa where Beauregard had set up his headquarters. The firefight at Charvet Hill, audible from the town for its duration, had ceased. No Germans were reported heading their way.

"Our fighters did a magnificent job this afternoon," Descour said.

Huet agreed skeptically. "They did, but I'm sure that was only a probe. The Germans will be back in force. It's good that we moved the townspeople away. This will be a main avenue of attack. The residents who remain will pay a heavy price."

"They will at that," Descour agreed, "but a victory is a victory, and small ones often lead to bigger ones." Noticing Huet's grimace, the colonel added, "I know. Sometimes they don't. But keep in mind what's going on in Normandy. The Allies have made it off the beach."

"In some places, but they're bogged down in others. The troops near Sainte-Mère-Église are in full pitched battle, and it's been going on for days. Caen is no easy fight either."

"No one expected a walk in the park, my friend. But Allied troops are pouring in. I'm hearing reliable reports that a full-scale port is rearing up almost out of thin air at Arromanches."

Huet shook his head and exhaled. "I know. I'm confident that we will win this war, but I fear for the residents of the Vercors. I see no sign of support on the way. Promises were made, and these people acted on them. A bloodbath is coming. I feel it."

Descour sighed. "I fear you might be right."

The two of them gazed across the traffic circle toward a lookout point. Beyond it was a grand view of Grenoble and its neighboring villages nestled in the wide valley. The sun had descended, its last rays still lighting up the western sky.

The two officers' attention was drawn to a cluster of resolute Saint-Nizier villagers, those who had refused to leave their homes. They gathered at the lookout, joined by several *maquisards*. The group looked up to their right, cheering.

"I wonder what that's about," Descour said. The pair ambled over.

The *maquisards* came to attention and rendered awkward, unpracticed salutes. Respecting their intent and appreciating their attempts at military decorum, both Descour and Huet returned their salutes.

"What's the hubbub?" Descour asked one of them.

"Up there, sir," came the reply. He pointed. "On the mountaintop."

There, flying proudly in the wind, was Abel Chabal's Free French flag.

Huet whirled on the *maquisard*. "How long has that been there?" he demanded angrily. "Who put it there?"

Startled and reluctant to respond, the young man shrugged. "The commandos, sir. Several hours ago. Right after they arrived."

Huet turned to Descour. "I'll order Beauregard to take it down immediately."

Descour shook his head gravely. He steered Huet by the elbow to where they could speak without being overheard. "Don't be hasty, Major—"

"But sir," Huet interrupted, "that's a red cloth in front of a bull. The Germans will see it. They won't let it pass. If the Vercors is allowed to declare itself free of Germany, then so will other parts of Fran—"

"I share your concern, but the flag's been flying up there for several hours. I assure you the Germans have seen it. The damage is done." Descour paused and rubbed his chin. "Look at the reaction of this group,

Major. Now they're smiling, ready to take up the fight. This morning, they were in despair. Our friends in the valley live with that dejection every day."

He glanced up at the flag again. "It's not just the Germans who'll see that flag. Our fellow citizens down there will see it too, well over a hundred thousand of them. Their spines will stiffen. We've put a chink in the *Wehrmacht's* armor. Word will spread about what's happened up here."

"But sir—"

"Major, if I had known that Chabal was having that done, I would have stopped him. But as you've stated more than once, we can't reverse. To take that flag down now would be to announce to our same countrymen that we've capitulated. The Germans will see it that way too. The effect will be worse than if it had never gone up at all.

"Right now, the *Wehrmacht* knows we've gathered thousands of *maquis-ards* and some organized veterans here. They don't know how many, how well we're armed, or how well we're supplied. They'll be cautious, and that could gain us time for our support to arrive and for the Mediterranean landing."

Huet remained silent for a time, mulling. "You are correct, sir," he muttered at last. Then he pivoted to gaze up at the banner billowing in the wind. "Let fly the Free French flag of the Republic of Vercors."

INTO THE CAULDRON
Book #7 in the After Dunkirk series

In the vast theater of World War II, the fate of one family weaves into the larger tapestry of the fight—even if victory asks for the ultimate sacrifice.

Normandy. Sark Island. London. The Pacific. The Littlefield siblings, separated by the grim tide of war, fight on all fronts.

The Dame of Sark, the Littlefield matriarch, faces starvation on Sark Island, while Lance grapples with the Wehrmacht on French soil. With every step shadowed by death, his sole goal is to liberate Paris and prepare for the final assault on Germany.

In London, Claire deciphers enemy communications, her work pivotal in shaping the battlefield. Meanwhile, Jeremy leads a band of refugees through the treacherous Vercor Mountains, nursing the hope of rejoining the battle against the Germans. Across the globe, Josh prepares for a decisive amphibious assault as momentous as the one at Normandy.

With World War II raging, the Littlefield's stories intertwine with old and new friends alike. As narratives converge, the tension escalates, culminating in the decisive Battle of the Bulge in the dense Ardennes forest—with the family ready to pay the ultimate price to tilt the scales of war.

Get your copy today at
severnriverbooks.com

AUTHOR'S NOTE

Some readers have noted that I often review pieces of information and events from previous books. I try not to do that too often or in too great detail. My aim is to write each book such that any reader who has not read the previous books will possess the full story represented in the one he or she is currently reading. Along that same vein, I avoid cliffhangers at the end of the books that would thus require a reader to purchase the next book to get the full story.

That latter consideration was not possible with Driving The Tide. Originally, Book 6 was intended to tell the story about the events of 1944 through the eyes of (mainly) the Littlefield siblings and cousins. However, the story was too big for a single volume, and so I split it into two books, leaving a very obvious cliffhanger at the end of this book. Hopefully, that will resolve in the next one, Into The Cauldron.

Also, a quick note about the medic included in the story about the landing at Normandy, Sergeant Ray Lambert. The story, as written, is true. He and his brother, Bill, enlisted, trained, and were assigned together. They both deployed onto Normandy, took care of the wounded, ad ended up on adjacent beds aboard a hospital ship. They both arrived safely, home, recovered from their war wounds, and lived out their natural lives among their families and friends.

ACKNOWLEDGMENTS

Once again, the list of people to whom I am indebted for their kind contributions and for the success of my previous books has swelled. That includes my readers. I have taken pains to thank those who made particular contributions, and doing so is always inadequate but heartfelt.

For the above reasons and for fear of leaving anyone out were I to list them here, instead, please know that I know that without such help and support, I would not have enjoyed the success that is attributable to all of those who fill in the gaps left by my abilities and knowledge. Thank you.

ABOUT THE AUTHOR

Lee Jackson is the Wall Street Journal bestselling author of The Reluctant Assassin series and the After Dunkirk series. He graduated from West Point and is a former Infantry Officer of the US Army. Lee deployed to Iraq and Afghanistan, splitting 38 months between them as a senior intelligence supervisor for the Department of the Army. Lee lives and works with his wife in Texas, and his novels are enjoyed by readers around the world.

Sign up for Lee Jackson's newsletter at
severnriverbooks.com
LeeJackson@SevernRiverBooks.com